Pacific Odyssey

The Curious Journey of Lew 2.0

A Novel

Chet Nairene

AUTHOR'S NOTE:

This is a work of fiction. The story's characters and names, businesses, events and incidents are wholly the product of the author's imagination. The Kingdom of Amazia does not exist. Any resemblance to actual persons, living or dead, or places is purely coincidental. .

www.bananaleafbooks.org

Copyright © 2024 Chet Nairene
Copyright © 2024 Banana Leaf Books
All rights reserved.

For Fay, always.

PART ONE:

Entrepreneurial Spirit

CHAPTER ONE
Superhero Condoms and The Lizard

At 5:55 a.m., a sleek white Mercedes eased up the curving drive at Mega Brands Tower, an imposing glass spire in Midtown Manhattan. Lew Clarke lounged in back, sipping a latte and pondering the day's incredible promise. Sure, it looked like a typical, miserable mid-December morning, but he knew better. With any luck, this day could redefine his life.

And it had already started well. The ride in from Central Park West went off like clockwork, thanks to city crews working all night to clear the streets of snow and slush.

"Please go get some breakfast, Jakob, and then pick up my laundry," he told the driver, a handsome young Israeli man in a dark suit, expensive leather cap and tan driving gloves. "Then stand by at the parking garage. Emily will phone if I need you." The chauffeur nodded back with a respectful smile.

The twenty-four seven hire car was a helluva perk, all paid by Mega. The mother ship had awarded Lew the S-Class service two years ago, upon his last promotion.

It made him chuckle to recall his earlier years at the conglomerate, fresh out of Harvard B-school, how he used to bicycle to Midtown from a seedy shared flat in SoHo. It was fast, fun, and combined fitness with youthful flair. Not lost on him, too, was how displays of executive vigor played well with The Twenty Old Men, the geriatrics running Mega.

Once Lew's career blasted off, his financial trajectory soared and his days of bohemian transport of course ended. By now, in his mid-thirties, he was not just another hot young executive on the come, but a genuine rock star in the tech world, wielding control over the corporate behemoth's staggering power and resources.

Mega loved him and no doubt would soon upgrade him to a full-blown, primo limousine. A Bentley or a Rolls? He asked Emily to research options and—with her usual efficiency—she flooded his desk with brochures from luxury car vendors.

Just before 6:00 a.m. the sterile marble lobby was still empty. Lew marched in and paused at the corner news kiosk where a wiry Indian man, Vijay Patel, yawned inside the newsstand, picking lint off his hand-knitted green sweater.

"Morning, Veej." They exchanged nods. The two had been friendly for a decade, ever since Lew first arrived at Mega.

Lew scanned the rack of papers and skimmed the usual scare headlines. *The Post* bannered something about an impending *next* pandemic. Lew smiled. He wasn't complaining. Ever since the world went pandemic-crazy with COVID, associated fears had underpinned some of his biggest product hits.

"This morning, Sir is perhaps forgetting?"

Lew looked up from the magazine. "Sorry, what was that, Veej?"

The man bobbled his head and handed Lew a pack of extra-strong mints. "For the breath! Sir is meeting Mr. Harry this morning. Isn't it?"

"You're right."

"And is special meeting, yes?"

"Mmm." Lew grinned. So Vijay already knew. Well of course he did—there was no slipping anything past him. The wizened kiosk operator's connections spanned all of Mega, forged over years of smiles and morning chit-chats, so he knew virtually everything important transpiring in the tower. It was no surprise he was aware of Lew's morning meeting Harry Oberhauser, his enormously powerful boss.

By longstanding tradition, yearly performance review meetings were when *everything* good, career-wise, happened at Mega—when promotions were awarded, nosebleed comp packages handed out or career-making deals struck. And today, Lew was due for a monster bump-up in class. So, be minty fresh for Harry? Good idea.

"Thanks for the save, Veej."

"No problem. And Sir is also please not forgetting—"

Lew chuckled as their longstanding private joke resumed. "No, Vijay, believe me, I can never forget, mainly because you won't let me. So yes, in our *next* lives—"

"Yes, sir! In next life, I am owning you." The news agent smiled sweetly.

Hmm, now there was a new twist. *Owning*? More than a little odd, too.

"Well, I'm sure you might hope for something like that, Veej, and more power to you! Go for it. But as for the *Next Life*, well, that's just a fiction as far as I'm concerned. There's no spiritual world, no astral plane. None of that. *This* is all there is, the here and now.

The kiosk operator grinned, surprisingly bouncy for 6 a.m., a gold incisor sparkling within his smile. "Yes, I understand, indeed. Sir is doubting. But still, hedging of bets is always wise, no?"

Lew shrugged. "Meaning what?"

"Well, meaning my *tipsy* . . . whatnot? I am hoping Sir is not forgetting."

Oops, right. His tip. Lew handed him a ten-dollar bill. "Well played, Veej. Just keep the change." Ten dollar breath mints! "But a decade of your *tipsy* has by now cost me thousands."

Vijay jiggled his head in a vague subcontinental bobble. "Perhaps, but is wise investment, Sir. Hedging of bets—and very good value! In next life, when I am your master, surely I am remembering."

"My *master*?" Funny guy. "Come on, Veej, you're not satisfied to just be my boss? Now you're planning to own me or something, as some kind of slave?"

"A slave? Oh no, Sir. My goodness, not at all!" Vijay cackled. "Rather, I am speculating in next life, Sir is perhaps being Vijay's *pet*. Or whatnot." Another head wobble. "Returning as, I don't know, dog or cat, perhaps?" He rubbed his chin in thought. "But if Sir has luck and is somehow returning as human, then I am assuredly being most providential boss. Not to worry!"

"Well that's a relief. Thanks a lot." Vijay, clearly not impressed by Lew's glorious achievements, always made him chuckle.

Lew spotted a vacation magazine, *Amazing Tropical Splendor,* its glossy cover overflowing with green palm trees, brilliant blue water and bikini-clad maidens. Tropical splendor? Those two words were not in his vocabulary. He couldn't remember his last vacation.

"Maybe in my next life," he grumbled as he headed for the farthest elevator bank—Floors 68-90—and entered the last car.

Lew's mind wandered as the lift whooshed him upward. He met almost daily with Harry, but today's session—the annual performance appraisal— had been blocked out for months.

Harold Oberhauser was an utter titan at Mega, preeminent among The Twenty Old Men and presiding over a massive portfolio of companies operating worldwide.

Despite so critical an impending meeting, Lew remained at ease. Over the years, despite different jobs and bosses, his evaluations always played out the same. They started with pleasantries to create intimacy, the room overflowing with good vibes, followed by praise for his targets all being over-achieved (sales, profits, new product launches). Then a cheery discussion ensued about his bloated new compensation package, with details revealed about his annual cash bonus and stock option awards. It was indeed a love fest, and usually wrapped-up with an exploration of preferred future positions, with promises to keep Lew in mind when one opened up.

His bosses generally just seemed grateful to have this totally reliable, hard-working superstar achieve his magic for their teams. After all, he was making them look brilliant, too.

Lew's record was genuinely phenomenal, a steady drumbeat of

tech breakthroughs under his lead—modern miracles now taken for granted like bio implant chips and robotic surgery systems, artificial intelligence and augmented senior care systems. Video doorbell systems were an early Clarke hit, along with speech recognition software and security systems.

He exited the elevator at eighty-eight, sauntered down the darkened hallway, and flipped a switch just inside his office door. Rows of fluorescent lights flickered to life. At 6:05 a.m., he was first man on deck, as always. A few other ambitious go-getters would soon start to drift in.

Just before seven, the squeak from Emily's clunky pink galoshes alerted him of her arrival. She wore them for the winter walk up from Port Authority and changed into sleek high-heels at the office.

He made it clear from the very start she didn't need to arrive before 7:30. But Emily was ambitious, too. Bright and efficient, she locked onto tasks like a bulldog. Slim and ginger with hazel eyes, she was the most attractive woman on the floor, maybe in all of Mega, and early on Lew realized their pairing was serendipitous—in a stodgy corporate world where appearances mattered, having a talented and stunning secretary only helped to enhance the his image, another glistening aspect to the Clarke career perfection.

He browsed through email while the office world woke up around him. The smell of fresh-brewed coffee drifted into his office and glass rooms on all sides began to light up at random, blinking on like sudden lightning strikes.

Despite the breathtaking tech portfolio he'd delivered for Mega, working in the Manhattan global headquarters always felt like time travel—once inside the beast, one was transported back to the 1970s. Mega Tower was a world where private secretaries still guarded spacious, fern-decorated executive offices with substantial walnut desks. Three-martini lunches remained a fixture and upstairs, many of the ruling elite upstairs, The Twenty Old Men, clung steadfastly to their old-time rotary dial phones and squawk boxes.

In an age of electronic communication, office boys still pushed overflowing document carts around Mega's headquarters twice a day, a direct reminder of the current chairman's fabled rise from the mail room. Grads from top-tier MBA programs leapt at those entry-level opportunities, knowing six months of cart-wheeling and upper-floor schmoozing was often enough to insinuate the best of them into lucrative, fast-track management positions.

Thanks to a corporate cash flow that dwarfed most medium-sized nations, Mega was able to fend off internal change. Its crusty culture was deep-rooted and unshakable, barricaded behind walls of money inside a fortress built upon a century of selling soap, perfume, cookies, and artificially processed potato chips.

Despite Mega's archaic culture, Lew's new-tech adventurism catapulted the business monster into dominant positions in a wide array of stylish fields, creating a deceptive external image of modernity and breakaway profit growth that Wall Street adored.

While laboring behind Mega's obscuring corporate veil, he became an internal star, famous within the commercial starship yet all but invisible to the outside world. This odd cloaking was integral to something called *The Mega Code*, a covenant all executive elite were forced to embrace. It rendered them anonymous to headhunters (who never called) but that did not matter because, in all the business world, there was no greater opportunity than to soar within the commercial galaxy known as Mega Brands.

To rise and dominate there was akin to scaling a commercial Everest or landing solo on Mars. Executives typically worked there for entire careers, amid internal glory and external anonymity, eventually retiring in absolute splendor.

Lew picked up a sparkling crystal paperweight from his desk. The block of cut glass was shaped like an oversized bar of soap, Mega's iconic first product, with the base engraved:

LEWIS NATHANIEL CLARKE—WELCOME TO MEGA.

The knickknack summoned a decade-old memory of wisdom

imparted under the guise of humor. On his first day at Mega, HR paired him with a seasoned young executive as something of a big brother or temporary mentor, and Adrian Miller seemed delighted to take the rookie exec out for an expense account lunch at Four Seasons.

There, to the newbie's surprise, they knocked back martinis—Lew's first, ever. Welcome to Mega, kid.

"Half of you new hires will be gone in a year." Miller softly poked Lew in the sternum. "And every year after that, the survivor pool shrinks again by half. Might as well face it, the odds are totally stacked against you."

Lew tried to look casual and dabbed at his face with a brilliant white napkin, but involuntarily gulped.

Crap. Did Miller notice? Stay calm.

"Lucky for you, Lew, I'm gonna share the Four Golden Rules for Executive Survival at Mega. May not guarantee survival but it's definitely fatal to ignore them. Now pay attention and commit all this to memory." Miller winked.

"Yes sir." Sounded important, but what was with that wink? Lew forced a smile, hoping to look relaxed.

"First, absolutely no extraneous facial hair. Not a single whisker! No beards, mustaches or long hair. No stray ear hair follicles and not even a single curling nose hair that just happens to appear one morning. All are instantly fireable!" Miller scowled at Lew. "Got it?"

"Check!" Good. Miller was just being scary-funny, right? But was any of this serious? Lew took another sip from his second martini and felt a warm buzz.

"Second. Only tailored wool business suits. No polyesters and nothing off the rack. Vested is always good, dark blue or grey with pinstripes. Plain, sober rep ties. And never, *ever*, wear brown—not unless you are planning to quit later that day to go sell used cars in Parsippany. As for shoes, always go with black wingtips. Again, *never* brown and never slip-ons. You're not in kindergarten, right?"

"Copy all that, sir." Lew smiled but wondered about this anti-brown thing. Was Miller being serious at all?

"Third. Unless you're going on a camping trip straight from work, or returning to junior high school, never *ever* be seen toting a backpack! It looks juvenile at best, but more like you're some kind of fucking idiot. So use a briefcase, like an adult." Miller smiled. "Course, you already know all this. But I'm reviewing, just in case Harvard didn't cover corporate etiquette"

Miller drained another martini and nodded at Lew, who hesitated. This *was* his first day, after all. And he was already feeling those first couple drinks, tripping up his diction and clouding judgment. Maybe Miller could just close his office door and take a nap, later, but Lew had to be able to function back at work.

He ignored the drink in front of him and looked the man straight in the eye.

Miller smiled. "Afraid of that third martini? Atta boy. Smart!"

"Roger all that, Adrian. Any other magic tips?"

"Sure. This last one may sound strange, so believe it or not. But in an environment as dangerous as Mega—and believe me, people die there every day, at least their careers do—perception is far more important than reality."

Hmm. "And what, exactly, does that mean?"

"You'll eventually understand. Just be guarded and always remain aware of *how* you are being seen. Naturally, you must *always* deliver the goods. That goes without saying—over-achieving targets is the bare price of admission. But superstars also project constant calm and make their brilliance appear easy and unforced, the only possible outcome for such superior beings."

"Like the cool kids back at school?" The second martini at work.

"Sort of. So Rule Four is *Always be cool*. Make your output look effortless, like part of the natural order. It suggests you were born to a higher rank and *deserve* promotion."

Lew placed the crystal paperweight back on his desk. Funny how he remembered all that, on this special day. Though just martini lunch humor, some of Miller's advice stuck with him. Lew always wore bespoke pin-striped suits, zero facial hair and kept his hair short.

But after a decade of pulling new-tech rabbits from his hat, most rules no longer applied for Lew anyway. He'd been more productive than a hen on egg-multiplying steroids. And despite normal human anxiety and failings, he always managed to make his staggering output look almost too easy.

Emily handed him a pour-over coffee with an espresso shot, just the way he liked it.

"Morning," she said, passing him a sheaf of memos.

Paper! Another oddity, how Mega still largely operated on the stuff. It started with The Twenty Old Men and trickled on down through the rest of the organization.

She gently placed a stack of correspondence (envelopes already slit open and documents smoothed flat) into his old-fashioned wooden in-basket and deftly squared the trade journals littering his desk. She tucked the *Wall Street Journal* and *NY Times* atop his coffee table, beside the leather couch.

"An easy morning, Lew. Just your nine-thirty with Mr. Oberhauser."

He smiled. Cute, her playing coy like that. Emily knew full well how momentous today's morning meeting would be.

"Oh, right, my nine-thirty with Harry. Almost forgot. Thanks for reminding me." Two could play that game. He yawned and kept his face neutral while watching hers. But she didn't react.

In reality, Emily had assisted him for weeks in the meticulous process of gathering files and assembling the master dossier for his performance review. Lew liked to march in armed with graphs and charts, a barrage of unshakable evidence of the battles he'd won during the past year for dear old Mega. Sure, he could have loaded it all onto a tablet, but Harry loved paper, like his fellow dinosaur elites, foraging upstairs.

The morning coffee coursed through him so he ambled over

toward the men's room, along the way nodding at allies, friends, or whatever (not always easy to tell). The grapevine was no doubt abuzz. This very day, the next phase in Lew's storied career was due for liftoff and many probably hoped to hitch a ride aboard the Clarke Express. But some (people being people) just rooted for a cock-up, a slip to prove he was only human, after all.

Lew stood over the porcelain urinal, bored and trying some target practice, alternating his stream between the deodorant cake and drain holes. A shadow intruded—someone moved in at the urinal just to his right, ignoring the half dozen other vacant positions.

"Hey, *Trailblazer*, you seeing the old man soon? Entire floor is excited for you!" Austin Lazardi's too-loud laughter echoed off the tiled walls of the empty bathroom. "No worries. I'm sure your turn in the barrel will go smoothly. Haha."

Oh, great, *The Lizard.* Last thing Lew needed was a dose of this guy's shtick. Lew finished up quickly to make a getaway, rather than let Lazardi spoil this morning of mornings.

"Hello, Austin," he said, careful to not smile. Don't encourage him. "But please, stop already with the *Trailblazer* stuff. Not cool. Asked you a hundred times."

The nickname stopped being funny years ago. Lew's parents never explained why they named him as they did, but the result was an irresistible hanging curve ball for elementary school comedians. Lewis Nathaniel Clarke became Lewis N. Clarke. Just a short trip to Lewis & Clark, explorers of the Pacific Northwest. *Trailblazers.*

Lazardi probably thought tossing around Lew's childhood nickname would draw them closer. But after two years, Lew still couldn't trust the guy. All that fake familiarity! By now nearly everything about Lazardi irritated him, even the calculated hipster look—his unshaven stubble, the thick black-framed glasses, outrageous bow ties and odd wardrobe combinations like cardigans with suspenders. Clearly, the Lizard never heard about the Four Rules (though that was the least of his problems).

Lately, the mere sight of Lazardi always reminded Lew of his only career smudge, the Adult Intimacy Products (AIP) division, a failing low-tech business the board saddled on Lew, eighteen months earlier.

"Come on, Harry, sex toys?" Lew had howled. "They want me to fix the *Screwing Aids Division*?" But the old dragon just smiled and let him vent. "I'm about life-changing tech, boss, not this sleazy crap. For me, Adult Intimacy is the wrong kind of AI. Not what I do."

The assignment felt suspiciously like a test or sick joke, a silly hobby he found neither interesting nor fulfilling. Was this the chairman's doing, Godzilla playing around with him? *Okay, superstar, let's see you do something high-tech and amazing with THIS.*

His protests were ignored so Lew, knowing bugger-all about sexual aids and not caring to learn, fobbed it off on the Lizard and kept both at arm's length. Surely the board didn't expect him to waste energy and focus by giving dildos and artificial vaginas the full Clarke Treatment.

So by now, Lazardi's fingerprints were all over AIP. Not that it mattered—just a flyspeck of a business, so tiny as to be nearly invisible. By comparison, Lew's futuristic new products had raked in hundreds of millions, just the past year, another bravura performance rendering him nearly bulletproof and a minor ascendant god at Mega.

Lew zipped up, washed, and left Lazardi still midstream at the urinal.

"Hey, Lew, good luck today and—"

The pneumatic door closed, truncating the Lizard's speech.

As Lew shuffled back toward his office, a hulking figure fell in line behind him, following in his wake. He sat back at his desk and just seconds later, Salvatore Weissman trailed into Lew's office, barging in and not waiting to be acknowledged.

No knock, no greeting, no formalities.

The man was massive and hairy and had to stoop a bit coming through the door. But Sal was also handsome in a fine tailored blue suit with a diamond stud sparkling from one ear.

The two fist-bumped, close friends ever since Harvard B-school more than a decade ago and then landing at the same New York employer. Both started out at the bottom but Lew found his groove right from day one and lifted off like a Saturn rocket. Sal's measured success was more like a Nike missile.

Sal dropped into the armchair facing Lew's desk and an enormous grin lit his swarthy face. "Hey, bro! Big day, huh? Breakfast with *der Oberfuhrer.* Nervous?*"*

Lew smiled—loved the guy, no question. The two were tighter than brothers, as close as white on rice.

"Jitters, me? Come on, Sally, you know me better. Last time I was *really* nervous was what? Seven, eight years ago? Remember, when you brought those Colombian hookers back to our shitty little flat? Both way tougher than either of us . . . and one was even bigger than you."

"Maybe, but you liked her chunky friend, no? Remember that cute little mustache?" Sal chuckled. "Am I right or am I right?"

Lew shook his head and grinned. "But seriously, regarding the meeting today with Harry? With my track record I'm just about untouchable. Pelts cover the wall from all last year's home runs. A couple stomach butterflies, sure, but that's normal."

"Nervous, but in a good way." Sal winked.

"Exactly."

"Well, Lewis *Effing* Clarke is way overdue for his ginormous reward—high time you got your own Mega subsidiary or continental division."

Lew smiled modestly.

"Heck, Mega's tech breakthroughs are always your doing. They start with your intuition or a clever idea, get developed by teams you set up and drive and—"

"Okay, stop already! My head's gonna explode. To be totally honest, Mega's massive resources backing me *really* helps . . ."

"Nobody's denying that. But you're the brain. If was easy, others would be doing it, too."

With no false modesty, Lew knew all that was true. And his reward was but an hour away. The best assignments at the global giant were running operating companies, a galaxy of which were sprinkled around the globe. To head one or a cluster was like becoming the potentate ruling over a business kingdom, instantly a huge friggin' deal at some foreign locale, with a big house and servants, meals with kings or primed ministers, ten thousand staff.

Of course, *much* later in his career he would join The Twenty Old Men and run the entire musty conglomerate, buried in that penthouse crypt upstairs. But that was for old age.

"You know, Sal, I could *really* dig the President-Europe slot. Dream gig with a score of companies under me." He suddenly frowned. "Though ever since the divorce, guess I just wish there was somebody to share all this with."

Sal's face softened with empathy before again brightening. "Yeah, I know, amigo. But if you wanna share, well, what about me? Or doncha love me no more?" Sal's laughter boomed off the office walls. Lew balled up a piece of paper and tossed it at him.

Sal downshifted, his tone going softer. "But the divorce is ancient history, bro. Ship sailed long ago, so stop it already with the self-pity bullshit. Besides, that split was MJ's fault, not you—she was the one who got fouled up in an affair and fell in love. Right?"

Lew sighed. "Yeah, but no, it's not that simple." The failed marriage was a dagger that cut fresh slices from Lew's heart, any time he allowed it.

He'd met Mia Jeanne at a Manhattan cocktail party. They became engaged within a year, married six months later, and divorced in another eighteen months. MJ was a fast-riser at Bridgerton Shields, a premier hedge fund, and both got too caught up in the dizzying fizz of their own all-consuming, high-pressure careers. Little time was left for either to foster a newborn marriage. Lew fully understood MJ's affair with one of the Bridgerton's partners was ultimately an effect, hardly a cause.

"Just lonely sometimes, Sal. No one to share my victories."

Lew chewed off a stray cuticle. How, he wondered, had his doofus buddy managed to successfully juggle career and marriage? They had both wed around the same time, a few years after arriving in Manhattan, and joked how both had moved out from the SoHo flat for roommate upgrades. Lew once naively pictured their future selves as graying couples, taking Viking River Cruises together in Europe. Old friends sharing Golden Years.

The buzzer on Lew's desk broke his reverie.

"Sir," Emily called in over the speaker, "I have a few more files for the meeting with Mr. Oberhauser. Bring them in?"

Lew looked at Sal and jerked his head toward the door. "Close it behind you."

Sal rose but stopped halfway to the door and turned back. "Seriously, babe, good luck with the old man. And if you do get Europe, bring me along. Don't go forgetting your friends."

Lew sniffed. "Friends? What friends?"

Sal shot an airy laugh and pantomimed a pistol that he fired at Lew. "Totally serious now, chief. We're a team, right?"

"Sure, like Penn and Teller. I do the magic, Sal, and you do the jokes."

"Whatever. But even if you only need a combo bodyguard and bottle washer."

"I know. That'll be you!"

But Sal didn't have to ask. Lew already counted on him, wherever and whenever.

Sal would forever be his wing man.

CHAPTER TWO
Empire of The Twenty Old Men

Lew inserted his platinum key card and the gleaming doors of the private elevator slid open. He pushed the single button on the polished chromium inside wall and was whisked up to the ninety-seventh floor, the inner sanctum of The Twenty Old Men—Mega's hallowed demigods.

There, surrounded by priceless art and magnificent tapestries, his feet sank deep into thick, cinnamon plush carpeting, with only the sound being that of water gurgling in the fountain at the center of this grand circular floor. There rose a marble statue of Atlas, his muscles rippling as he bore the world upon his shoulders. And implanted in that globe were 138 color-coded LED dots, each highlighting a country where Mega operated. The company joke went that whenever a new market was penetrated by Mega, so was Atlas. Lew had personally caused Atlas to be drilled for new LEDs thirty-three times.

Twenty offices circled the bubbling centerpiece, one for each of the conglomerate's overlords. Ten of the chieftains divided the earth on the basis of business or product lines. The other ten divided the same planet again, but purely on the basis of geography. This intentional overlap guaranteed heartburn and friction, trying to please two Mega bosses with conflicting goals and interests. Business theory posited the structure optimized results.

The superficially peaceful atmosphere up on ninety-seven didn't fool Lew, who knew a mirage when he saw one. The luxurious setting was a battleground in disguise, where constant internecine warfare led to more bloodshed than in most slaughterhouses.

Of course, while being crushed under relentless pressure, The Twenty Old Men were obscenely compensated—delightfully swamped in stock option wealth and nosebleed salaries. They were a score of rat-gods locked inside a celestial cage, intent upon consuming one another.

Many didn't live long enough to enjoy all that wonderful wealth. Lew wondered how long Harry would hold up, especially with his recent medical incidents. His heart, the ulcer, hypertension. But Harry was his guy, his mentor—bastard *better* hold up!

A platinum blonde secretary behind an IBM Selectric typewriter, straight out of a museum, guarded the door to Harry's posh office.

"Hey, Ida, good weekend?"

"Morning, Lew—sharp suit. New? Haven't seen it before."

"Heh, thanks. Hope you and your daughter enjoyed the Rockettes. Great Christmas show, no?"

"Absolutely wonderful, Lew, and thanks again for the tickets—really *too* nice of you. Please let me pay . . . what do I owe you?"

"Ida, I already told you—those tickets were free. Honest! Radio City comped me, so I comped you."

She shot him a disbelieving look.

"No lie. They just love Mega (and therefore, me) ever since installing our new control systems for sound, ticketing, camera and lighting."

"More Lew specials?"

"The truth? Well, yeah—and they bought the works."

Ida Martin was the ultimate senior executive secretary. Mid-thirties like Lew and also divorced, she'd been on ninety-seven at least ten years, mainly working for Harry. She joined Mega straight from high school and worked her way up. Lew genuinely liked Ida but also worked hard to enhance their relationship, as she was a primo source for the inside buzz.

He peered over her shoulder, through the door. "Harry gone? Thought I'd booked him for nine-thirty."

"You did, but he was called upstairs just a minute ago. Something urgent."

Upstairs meant to the penthouse floor to see Frank Cushing. The Chairman, aka *Godzilla.*

Strange. Cushing never urgently summoned *anyone* as nothing was ever impromptu for that man. Godzilla's every moment was prebooked months out. The company joke went that Cushing's secretary even scheduled his daily visit to the enormous penthouse lavatory for his midmorning constitutional.

"Geez that's weird, a sudden call up to Godzilla's lair. What couldn't wait?"

Ida shook her head. "No idea. But when Doris buzzed she sounded flustered. Said the chairman wanted Mr. Oberhauser up there *immediately*." She motioned toward Harry's sumptuous office. "Why don't you just go in and make yourself comfortable, Lew? I'll get you some coffee."

Lew gazed back at the grand staircase rising and curving around the Atlas fountain, the only route up to the penthouse floor on ninety-eight, the elegant private domain of the chairman and CEO—multiple offices, a boardroom and private dining room.

With no sign of Harry trotting down, Lew thrust his hands into his pockets and trudged into his boss's office. He sank into the butter-soft brown leather sofa and began leafing through a trade journal. The cover story featured Mega and, of course, detailed one of Lew's triumphs. No surprise, his name wasn't mentioned. Mega Code.

Over the tradition-bound company's 150-year history, which started with soap bars peddled via itinerant donkey carts, a strict ethos developed to ensure all customer praise fortified and inflated the corporate brand, not individual egos. Under what became dubbed the *Mega Code*, all personal glory was obscured from the outside world.

As it grew, this business Goliath developed a culture that intentionally rendered its executives anonymous, all while dumping truckloads of cash upon them and providing ultra-powerful positions, rich in job satisfaction. Rising to power in so enormous a commercial empire was more than enough reward, and well worth keeping one's head down.

And inside Mega, all ruling powers not only *knew* Lew and his sizzling contributions, they adored him as their fastest rising star, a young luminary on a near-vertical ascent. This spectacular lift-off had transformed him into something of a *Business Jesus* at the conglomerate. In comparison, Sal's lesser stardom rendered him only a minor apostle, say, a *Business Thaddeus*.

"It's unfair," Sal once complained, "that outside Mega nobody knows you were godfather to all those tech miracles."

"Maybe so, but coming in, we already both understood the Mega Code. The mandatory anonymity. And we've both done fine."

"True dat," Sal chuckled, "but being only half as brilliant, I've only been screwed half as bad as you."

But Lew's time was arriving. Maybe that very day he would be catapulted skyward into the Mega stratosphere, with a launch propulsion so harsh that the G-force stripped away some of that external cloaking.

Lew glanced through the office glass again, back toward Atlas, but still no sign of Harry descending the circular stairway.

"Hey, Ida," he called out, "if it's no trouble, I'll take that coffee, after all."

Harry was a genuine bull elephant in that animal kingdom that rampaged across ninety-seven. His opulent office suite was adorned by carvings, museum-quality antiques and fine paintings from around the world. A stunning antique Persian carpet covered an entire wall, splendidly detailed and worth a year's salary for most executives. His massive mahogany desk backed against a glass wall revealing Manhattan in all its glory.

In a far corner beside a mirrored bar and private bathroom stood an executive trophy case stuffed with mementos of past victories. Many of them—heck, nearly all—were Lew's. He'd been awfully good for the old guy, and vice versa. Harry provided Lew unlimited resources and corporate political air cover.

A world map filled a wall, studded by colored pins denoting Harry's many operating subsidiaries. His venerable portfolio was the largest in Mega and included the hallowed Consumer Products Division that dated back 150 years to the company's original product, the thick yellow bars of laundry soap sold by founder Archibald Harper from his patent medicine cart.

Lew scanned the map, shopping for his next position. Yes, President-Europe, resident in London and overlooking the entire continent, that called his name.

Hmm . . . but what about Asia? Supposedly, this *was* their century, though he didn't know dick about the Eastern hemisphere. Still, President-Far East might be a superb position, with half the world's population residing in his domain. And as a bonus, the job was resident in Singapore or Tokyo, at his option.

Ida glided in to interrupt his musing, setting a tray on the glass table at Lew's knees. Coffee and a cheese Danish. He sipped quietly as Harry's massive grandfather clock ticked the morning away.

He began to bristle, a little. After all, his time *was* valuable. And despite the Godzilla Factor (always uncontrollable), this was so unlike Harry to blow off an important, long-scheduled meeting. Lew was his top performer, so his annual job reviews mattered a lot, special events that—

Blam!

The office door slammed behind him and Lew turned to see his distinguished mentor, head down and face grim, wordlessly scramble toward his imperial desk.

Strange. The august tycoon toted a brown paper sack, like a sandwich lunch with its top folded closed. He roughly flung it onto his desk, exhaled loudly and sank into his sumptuous recliner, absently massaging his temples with his thumbs. Then he fumbled for an extended time with his thick black fountain pen, a Montblanc Meisterstück.

"Lew," he said in an odd, quiet tone, when he finally looked up, "why not come closer and sit down here?" He gestured at the chair beside his desk. Harry's usually placid face was flushed, with pinked skin setting off the silver of his mustache and hair.

Something was very wrong. Why was Harry sweating like that? All of this was way more than just a little weird.

Harry reminded Lew of a John le Carré character—elegant, patrician and mid-sixties, with silver hair, a mustache and the slightest trace of a German accent. Proper, Teutonic and always decked out in impeccable, dark bespoke suits. He was an indefatigable pipe smoker and so uniquely treasured at Mega that they installed a hermetic, high-capacity filtration system for his office, allowing him to privately indulge whenever the tobacco urge struck.

Harold Oberhauser was *that* important.

But just now he looked shaken, his hands trembling inexplicably. Was it nerves or anger? Whatever, clearly upset, he seemed unable to look Lew in the eye.

Lew glanced at Ida through the office glass, hoping for a hint, but she just shot back a bewildered look.

After a silent, uncomfortable eternity, Lew opted to just bluster through. Always worked before—after all, Harry *loved* him.

"So, sire, back I understand from an emergency summons to see Godzilla, eh? And still alive. No blood. All good!" Lew grinned. "But just to be safe, I'll arrange for immolations to be offered, thanking all the gods for your safe return! We'd sacrifice a virgin, if only we could find one in this part of Manhattan." *Ba-dum-bump!* Lew winked.

But Harry ignored the lame jokes and just kept stuffing cherry blend into his pipe, over-concentrating for so simple a task.

Lew dropped his tone, seeking intimacy. "So what's up, sir? Cushing on the warpath?"

Harry remained mute, just studying his desk blotter.

"Well never mind, chief! Whatever it is, we'll fix it—*I'll* fix it." Lew snorted a quiet laugh. "Anyway on to cheerier matters, right?

The annual Clarke Performance Appraisal is always a mood brightener. Time we bear joint witness, uh . . ."

But the office remained silent as a morgue and the levity sounded way too forced. Was Harry even listening? Lew noticed how strange his own voice sounded.

"Uh, remember, Har . . . our nine-thirty?" Lew tried to decode his boss's ashen face. "Anyway, here's the 30,000-foot summary." Lew nudged a file across the massive desk. "But why bore you? We both already know it's been a simply outstanding year—another!—so if you want, we can just skip ahead and chat about my new comp package and future prospects."

In a blur, the elegant executive suddenly slammed his pipe on the desk, sending tobacco crumbs and ash flying everywhere. "Lewis!" he barked. "Would you please, just for once, shut the fuck up?"

Fuck? Harry never used profanity. Lew fell back into his chair, as stunned and dizzy as if he'd just been slapped. The senior executive inhaled deeply and then continued in a lower voice. "Sorry, son, but please give me a moment to think. Okay?"

What the hell was going on? Lew's reviews were always celebratory events, even affectionate. What's more, he was coming off a particularly fantastic year. He—and Harry by transitive association—had really scorched the earth. Time for champagne and balloons.

Lew noticed a small arterial squiggle pulsing on Harry's bright red forehead. He'd seen that only once or twice before, like the time a pompous SEC agent served Mega papers initiating proceedings that ultimately set the corp back $1.5 billion in fines. All hinged on a poor decision Harry clearly owned, the sole smudge on a shining career. But the impact was monumental and derailed him in his race for chairmanship, catapulting Cushing past him, never to be caught.

No, that tiny throbbing worm was a terrible omen. Lew froze, as requested, and waited in silence. Harry sat deep in thought, rubbing his chin, as if meditating or mentally rehearsing something. His breathing seemed labored.

Then he folded his hands and drew in another steadying breath. "All right, Lewis," he said, exhaling a sad little puff of air. "No easy way to do this. So let's just rip off the plaster."

Good old Harry with all those Euro expressions littering his speech. *Plasters* instead of bandages, *the loo* or *WC* instead of toilet. Lew himself even picked up a few from his role model.

"Okay, boss, let her rip." Lew smiled.

"Well here it is, my boy. You, with immediate effect, are being DFAed." The old man appeared instantly relieved to unload that burden. "So there it is! Simple as that. DFAed."

Simple? There was never anything simple about anyone being DFAed! Lew's cocky smile evaporated. "Whaaaaa . . .?" was all he could choke out.

Harry's message was so profound and sudden, totally unexpected, that it left Lew woozy. His palms went slick and the room threatened to spin. Surely he misheard. "Sorry Harry . . . b-b-but *what* did you just say? I don't—"

Harry grumbled in a voice sour as rotten lemons. "You heard me just fine. Don't make me say it again. It disgusts me, too."

But how could Lew Clarke, the tech wonder boy of Mega, *ever* be designated? It seemed like the worst of bad jokes, impossible and certainly not funny.

DFA was short for Designated for Assignment, company code that signaled career death, the business execution of a high-level executive. When one was DFAed, he was exiled into a meaningless, temporary position from which to then exit the company. It amounted to a slow-motion firing.

"But me, designated? That makes no sense, Harry. Don't kid around . . ."

Lew felt the blood draining from his head and an angry tingle starting to crawl down his neck and radiate out his arms and legs. The light started to pixelate. But no matter how shocked or stunned he was, this was no time to faint, so he manned up and forced in a deep breath.

Maybe he just imagining all this, some kind of weird hallucination or bad dream. Yes? But once his initial flood of confused, protesting thoughts began to subside, Lew realized Harry had continued talking, all along, and was concluding some kind of explanatory speech.

". . . and so you see, Lewis, it may really not be all *that* bad. The location selected for your temporary assignment is Mega's customer call center at Weehawken. You know, New Jersey. Just the other side of the tunnel. Not too inconvenient a commute."

What? They were sending him to Wee-*fucking*-hawken? And Harry had the stones to portray that as *not that bad*? This was all moving too fast.

Litigation-obsessed, and with teams of lawyers up the wazoo, Mega never outright sacked top executives. High-level targets for termination were instead moved into theoretical holding tanks, to await imaginary next positions. But of course, there never was a *next* position for the DFAed and everybody understood that cold reality.

The victims were basically pushed aside and left to rot. The temporary exile to a remote outpost signaled the abrupt, fatal tumble off one's career track—stripped of all power and access and quarantined into oblivion. The only logical alternative for a DFAed executive was to negotiate favorable resignation terms and move on. The sooner the better.

Mega borrowed the term from Major League Baseball, where veteran players on the verge of being cut were first DFAed while the ball club sought ways to trade or otherwise dispose of the athlete. But Mega's version was far colder.

Every high-level Mega exec understood this aspect of the Mega Code. Resignation was one's only option and a moral duty. Go quietly, make no trouble, don't litigate, and negotiate a fat severance package. Use the desk in temporary exile to network for a landing spot. But pack up and just leave, soon as possible.

Harry and Lew themselves had DFAed dozens of high-flying

executives, down through the years, so both fully understood the drill ... which made it especially rankle to hear the old man peddling that line of bull, how it wouldn't be so bad.

How could his business godfather do such a thing to him?

Lew's blood pressure jacked up and his mouth went dry, anger replacing his initial confusion. He tossed a thick manila file across the polished hardwood desktop, slewing papers everywhere, some falling into Harry's lap and others fluttering to the floor.

"Know why that file is so thick, Harry?" Lew loudly tapped a finger on the desktop. "They detail my work, just this past year. New projects banking hundreds of millions for Mega while covering *you* in glory, too. You had no trouble taking credit when I successfully licensed new tech to Apple, Google, Cisco and Amazon, did you? Well, none of that just happened—it was *all* my hard work! Developing ideas, driving teams, acquiring start-ups."

Harry nodded back, now looking pale. Lew paced as he vented, his hands curled into fists.

"I've spilled my blood for Mega, Harry. A decade now, so this just feels like treachery. And especially coming from *you*."

The elegant businessman wiped sweat from his mustache, slightly bowed his head and then began to quietly weep. His shoulders juddered in shame.

Holy Christ, Harry Oberhauser crying! In a morning filled with upsets, that was the one that really floored Lew. The old man never showed emotion. Ever.

By reflex, Lew reached out and patted Harry's shoulder. "Hey, wow, ease up there, Har." Lew's gentle imploring tone was barely audible over the airy whine of the office filtration system. "But honestly, chief, it's time to come clean and tell me, what's *really* going on here? Please! Why's my head rolling?"

The old man looked up, sniffling a sad smile. Then he shrugged. "Lewis, dear boy, this of course is none of my doing. It's Cushing who wants you out. The order for your firing came directly from the chairman."

What, Godzilla *himself* wanted Lew gone? For God's sake, why?

Harry took Lew's hand. "My boy, I was just up there, and he personally ordered you DFAed this very day, immediately and with no possible appeal, no second chance, nothing!" The old man dabbed at wet eyes with a crisp white silk handkerchief.

"Believe me, this is absolutely killing me. I'm deeply, incredibly sorry. But the fight is already lost. You've been like a son . . ." His voice broke. "But this very hour, you must clear out your office. And tomorrow, head over to that call center in Weehawken. And there isn't a single thing any soul on earth can do to change that."

Cold reality walloped Lew. The chairman—*God Himself* at Mega— had ordered him vaporized. The heavens had spoken and there was no way of undoing that.

Lew stared into his mentor's steel blue eyes and took a shot.

"Listen, Harry, we've always played straight with each other. No bull."

The old man sighed.

"Please, just hear me out. It's been an extraordinary year. The whole world is lining up to license our technologies. Artificial intelligence, robotics, voice recognition—"

"Damn it, Lewis," thundered the old man, "just stop already! Don't you get it? None of that matters." He stuffed more tobacco into his pipe with an awkward violence. "For Chairman Cushing, this is *personal*."

Personal? How? Lew only saw the chairman every few weeks, if that, and usually felt respected, if not beloved. How could he have *personally* offended the old bastard?

Harry fired up his pipe with a gold blowtorch lighter. "AIP. That was your fatal problem. A total disaster."

The hell? AIP was too insignificant to matter; certainly not enough to move the firing needle. With its microscopic bottom line, it shouldn't even register on Godzilla's radar. "Come on, Har. AIP is almost nothing. Minor league all the way, less than a rounding error, in the greater scheme." Lew kept his tone soft, selling.

"Damn it, Lewis! Try telling that to Cushing!" Harry grabbed the brown paper sack and tossed it at Lew. It sat unopened on the desktop, while Harry railed on, his eyes wide. "This morning, Cushing tore off strips of my flesh! He yelled that we—meaning you *and me*—brought shame to Mega. Never seen him so upset. He hurled this bag at my feet, cursing, when I entered his office, and hollered that Mrs. Cushing—"

Oh, Christ . . . *Mrs. Godzilla* was involved in this disaster? That couldn't be good.

"—was shocked and mortified Mega even sold such 'sinful' products." Harry trembled recalling the scene. "I was totally humiliated. Lewis, whatever were you thinking?"

Lew shrugged. But right about now, he was thinking he should've kept a much closer eye on that fuck-wit, Lazardi.

Harry grabbed the bag and reached in. He pulled out a small blue cardboard box labeled *The Bam Cam,* decorated with lurid, nearly X-rated cartoon graphics. Apparently, it was a micro camera to mount near one's privates parts. Harry threw the thing against the wall. "Who on God's green earth would want to record *that*?"

Incredible. He was in trouble for the *Bam Cam*? Such stupid stuff. Lew just shook his head. A glimmer of hope arose. Perhaps, once tempers subsided, the damage could be undone.

"Completely agree, boss. Totally gross. But betcha, worldwide, we didn't sell more than half a dozen of those idiotic things. So for all practical purposes, it hardly exists out in the marketplace. So we immediately cancel the line, pull back all inventory and it basically disappears. Tell that to Cushing for me?"

The old man pursed his lips. "Wouldn't help, Lewis. That fool camera is nothing. Other products were your fatal missteps." Harry rummaged in the sack, fussing with colorful boxes.

Damn it! How had Lazardi managed to screw up so much?

"Like this." Harry held a box under Lew's nose, his liver-spotted hand mildly shaking. "Really my boy. *Superhero Condoms*?"

Lew felt anger warming his face. Why had Mega forced this non-tech crap onto him, anyway? It seemed unfair, considering his vast body of stellar work, that anything as picayune as AIP could matter. But he definitely should have kept a closer eye on Lazardi; in that, he *was* culpable. "Lizard, you diseased son of a whore ..." he muttered under his breath.

"Hmm?"

"Nothing, chief."

One more try. "Sir, I fully and humbly agree: this is all in dreadful taste. I'm not even sure how any of this got past the mock-up stage. In fact, perhaps some of these may only be prototypes, eh?" Lew tried to look contrite. "Anyway, I apologize and will immediately fix everything, shut it all down. This very hour! I mean, that's a pretty disgusting idea, having Spider-Man or Superman's head on the cap of your penis, a cape running down the shaft—"

Harry held up a wavering hand for silence.

"Goddamn it, Lewis, for such a self-proclaimed genius, you don't seem to understand much. See, the problem is that these products screwed with Cushing's *family*." The old man slammed down a fist and flushed crimson. "For heaven's sake," he roared, "Cushing's own goddamn grandchildren! The Chairman's wife found the third-graders playing around with these prophylactics like fucking balloons."

Whoa, a second *fucking?* Harry was absolutely livid.

The patriarch rubbed a palm against his forehead. "Picture this, will you? The chairman's wife found them studying the obscene boxes and blowing up the condoms. Lord knows what else they were doing—highly graphic instructions on the boxes, you know. She stormed into Cushing's home office and all hell broke loose."

"Oh boy . . ."

"It gets worse. One of the little sneaks hid a box away and took it to their private school the next day. Naturally, he got caught showing it to friends. The chairman and his wife were personally summoned to the Barnstokes Elementary Academy along with the parents, hats in hand, totally ashamed and humiliated. Can you picture Cushing, being scolded by some mere low-status principal and having to silently take it? And only because he apologized so profusely and deeply, all but prostrating himself, the children weren't expelled."

Lew inhaled. "Geez . . ."

"Back home, during the postmortem, Cushing's wife exploded anew upon learning those were *Mega* products—elevating the crimes—and that Cushing himself brought them into the house. He'd planned to browse through a large box of promo items over the weekend, totally unaware what was inside. But the kids sure found 'em, fast."

Lew gulped, his throat dry and sticking.

"So just imagine the weekend of unremitting hell Cushing underwent. By Sunday night, he finally retreated to the company suite at the Carlyle, just to get some sleep. So now you understand. *Somebody* had to pay. A head on a pike. A sacrifice, first thing Monday morning. *You.*"

Lew shook his head. "Okay, Harry, totally I get it. An utter fuck-up." Lew offered an embarrassed smile. "No surprise, this is Lazardi's handiwork, the personal master of this disaster. I shoulda kept a closer eye but, believe me, he's already good as gone." Lew reached for Harry's hand. "But *please,* sir, can't you help me with Cushing? Personally now, a favor. I'm begging you, Harry."

The old man stared at his desktop, giving his head a barely perceptible shake.

"This is *me,* Harry, your business godson! After all we've achieved the past decade . . . done it all for you."

Harry looked up, eyes glistening. Thin, twisting red capillaries streaked the whites. He spoke in a barely audible voice.

"Listen, Lewis, I know you don't have kids, so perhaps you can't understand." Harry sighed. "But you buggered with the chairman's family. Deadly serious stuff. Now, were it only up to Cushing, perhaps you *might* survive, but even he's under the gun. Zero leeway if he ever again wants a peaceful home life. An execution is required." Harry shrugged. "So there it is. No choice. I'm under direct orders to DFA you."

After a decade together, Lew knew the old man's voice inside out, when his boss was being truthful. Right now, he was registering one hundred percent.

The old man scanned the glass case on the wall, stuffed with victory mementos achieved with Lew. "Here's how serious it is. Cushing gave me an ultimatum. Either you go . . . or we *both* do! Can you believe that? After forty-five years here, Fucking Godzilla threatened to sack me, also?" He slammed a fist on the desk, roaring. "Me!"

Lew sat straight up, startled.

Fucking Godzilla? That completed an unprecedented trifecta of Oberhauser profanity. And, for the first time ever, the always-respectful Harry had used Cushing's movie nickname.

The office went silent a full minute. The elder man stared out his wall of windows, intently studying ant-like pedestrians milling about, a thousand feet below. When Lew's boss finally spoke, it was with a new tone, saccharine and even optimistic.

"Obviously, Lew, at this stage in my career, so close to retirement, I can't possibly take that kind of fall. But you? Hell, you're still just a kid!" Harry smiled. "It's not going to be a big problem. You'll bounce right back, somewhere or other."

But *not* at Mega. That was loud and clear.

So Harry's predicament was a matter of self-preservation over honor, fire or be fired. Studying him, Lew saw a wounded beast. Desperate and dangerous, his usual impeccable bearing gone.

"Okay, Harry. I surrender." Lew laughed sourly. "No need to say more, other than to ask your advice for a former protégé. Guidance from Harry Oberhauser as my friend, rather than my executioner?"

The old man slid open a desk drawer and clicked a hidden switch. The filtration system kicked back on and impermeable seals locked into place. A muted, ambient hiss filled the room and Harry again began to fill his pipe. "Advice? Of course. You know I'd do anything for you, Lewis. You're family."

Lew prepared for sparkling nuggets of wisdom distilled from a lifetime in the business jungle. Litigate against Mega for wrongful dismissal? March across the street and seek employment at Mega's biggest competitor? Advice like that.

Harry swept up stray tobacco crumbs from his desktop and then gathered the AIP promo items back into the brown paper sack. He carefully rolled up the top and handed it over to Lew.

"Now, what I suggest is this." He drew on his pipe and sent puffy clouds of smoke to gather at the ceiling before being sucked into vents at the office corners. "It's time, son, to wake up and think straight."

Oh boy.

"Considering all the legal papers you've signed over the years—heh, Lewis, we *all* sign them—Mega is beyond bulletproof. Absolutely invulnerable, protected by ironclad legal armament."

"Meaning?"

"Meaning don't waste any time thinking about suing. Not unless you want to burn up your life savings for nothing. Make this easy for Mega and you'll walk out of here with a fat severance package. So just quietly pack up your personal things, right now, and go home. Don't speak to anyone." Harry bounced a shoulder. "Then tomorrow, have a hearty breakfast and head over to the DFA post at Weehawken. Things will look better after a night's sleep. There you can figure out your next move."

This was beyond surreal.

"Hmm, okay. Thanks, Harry. Naturally, I'll be counting on you for a glowing ref —"

"Sorry," the old man interjected, shaking his head. "No reference letters. Forbidden, remember? The Mega Code."

Lew stumbled out of Mega Tower an emotional jumble, benumbed and his thoughts a mess. Forgetting about Jakob and the hire car, he just walked off into Manhattan and killed the remainder of the day wandering around the Met. He found surprising solace in the brilliance of his favorite Impressionists, their genius a reminder, somehow, of a bigger picture.

Maybe this problem would just be transitory, a minuscule blip in his own grander scheme. After all, he *was* Lew Friggin' Clarke and sure to find his way. Always did, right?

CHAPTER THREE
Weehawken Exile

Lew left his apartment before 6 a.m., per usual, but found a ten-year-old Volvo idling at the curb, instead of the usual Mercedes S Class. Same driver, though frowning and rubbing his stubble and no uniform. Lew stuck his head in the passenger door.

"Jakob? What gives?"

"Sir, the Benz and my contract to drive you were both abruptly canceled last night. No explanation. Strange, huh?"

"You're telling me."

Jakob shrugged. "The agency says I'll receive a new assignment later today, but I swung by in my own car, just in case you still needed a ride."

"Good man. Thanks, Jake."

Lew pushed aside a mound of juvenile debris atop the back seat: puzzle pieces, loose Lego bits and a transforming action figure. He handed the driver a scrap of paper with the New Jersey address.

Not far outside the tunnel on the Jersey side, they pulled up at an aging gray building, an anonymous sprawl of interconnected corrugated iron warehouses. Entering through the creaky front door, Lew confirmed in just one Weehawken minute that he'd landed in seedy, white collar hell.

The call center was vast and surprised him. All interior walls had been knocked out to create a single monstrous room, cavernous as an aircraft terminal. It dwarfed and made him feel insignificant. A honeycomb of countless work stations spilled out across faded green linoleum as far as the eye could see.

A vague ambient noise enveloped the place, the mix of ringing phones, a thousand voices, and the HVAC's ominous low hum. Despite the early hour, the place was, of course, busy as high noon. Mega's global call centers were places without time, operating around the clock.

Layers of grime coated everything, along with a stale musty odor—the product of a moldy ventilation system, body odor, and ethnic fast foods gone bad.

Hovering above an army of phone workers was an endless nest of rusty ductwork and trussed pipes that snaked across the ceiling. Lines of conduit fed racks of fluorescent lights lined up like piano keys. Strays flickered here and there in a dizzying strobe effect.

Lew shuddered to imagine the colonies of rats and other critters that probably thrived there, living off worker refuse and wandering duct passages like a private superhighway system.

He knew better than to expect any kind of welcome or even recognition. The entire DFA process floated along in secret at Mega's highest levels, kept invisible to the likes of the Weehawken call center management. They would be unaware of him even being posted there.

He spotted an empty work station not far from the front door, good as any, and just moved in. He dropped his coat and gloves on the cubicle's gray metal side table and plopped down onto the wobbly chair. The computer was a decades-old Compaq with a blinking green cursor, an absolute antique probably still running on MS-DOS. The phone was also a collectible, originally issued in the 1960s by Ma Bell in white but faded to a yellow-gray and dotted with dark fingerprints. He picked up the smudged receiver. The line was dead.

Perfect.

The entire place was a pure disaster, as if designed to fail, and he fully understood.

Despite the trendy modern image Mega gained via Lew's tech innovations, at heart the company remained a stodgy 1950s-style anachronism, a doddering business monster. With seven hundred companies and subsidiaries worldwide, Mega marketed twenty thousand products and services per year, millions of units, and each came with a toll-free phone number for customer service. To handle all those inquiries, a half dozen gigantic networked call centers were scattered across the globe, from Mumbai to Sao Paolo. Including Weehawken.

Reflecting Mega's old-school business culture, the primary customer service goal was to just make the problems go away, as fast and cheaply as possible. The result was an army of poorly-trained agents who parked or derailed complaints, rather than addressing them, allowing calls to wither and die while wandering the branches of endless telephone trees.

Mega call centers were notoriously depressing places to work, filled with rude and unhappy people. And now he'd joined them.

Welcome to your new home, Lew Clarke!

He snorted a disbelieving laugh. Yup, he was white collar walking dead, a corporate zombie, after an execution as certain as a bullet to the cranium. His Mega career was over and the past ten years up in smoke. He was back to zero and soon to depart Mega forever.

A middle-aged woman with black hair and a vaguely Eastern European look strode into his cubicle and stood there, frumpy and imperious. Her glasses swung from a lanyard and her crimson sweater (with a sad Christmas motif) fuzzed with pookies.

"Hey, fella, whatcha think you're doin'?" She hovered over him way too close and her sweater, just inches away, gave off the odor of last night's dinner. Lew pictured stuffed cabbage and sausage and gave her a bemused look.

"Around here," she grumbled, "you don't just grab any workspace you like. There's rules. A system." Perfect: this was his *Welcome to Weehawken* moment. "I suppose you didn't report in to Mr. Valdez when you arrived."

Valdez? Okay, now *there* was a familiar name. Before exiting Mega Tower, Lew had Ida print out the call center file, mainly for info like the address. It indicated all twenty sections and twelve hundred employees reported up through a single manager, Tomas Valdez. A big job, for sure, but that was all relative. Valdez was at least fifteen salary grades down from Lew . . . or rather, from yesterday's pre-DFA version.

Lew was typically adroit at handling people, but this particular morning he didn't feel much like schmoozing the managerial *babushka* lady. "Thanks for the information, ma'am, but I'm pretty busy right now." He stood up and leaned forward and she backed away. "Don't worry, I'll chat with Valdez soon."

"Goodness!" she blustered, raising a hand to her forehead in a theatrical move. Lew pressed slowly forward until he maneuvered her out of the cubicle.

"Young man, I don't know *who* you think you are—"

Lew just sighed. "Yeah, me too, ma'am. Sometimes I wonder. Sorry, but life can be a real bitch. Believe me, I know."

She huffed. "You miserable punk. You'll be sorry!" Balling her fists, she marched away.

As he turned to sit back down, he noticed hundreds of heads bobbing above cubicle walls across the enormous room, watching. Many smiled or buzzed at the spectacle of a bossy supervisor being taken down a notch. Lew tossed his hands overhead like a triumphant gladiator, the Maximus victory move from that Russell Crowe movie. A wave of laughter swept the mammoth enclosure but soon died out. And then all the heads disappeared.

Funny, he was actually smiling. Maybe he was already getting over the initial shock. Buck up, he told himself. He wouldn't stay there long.

Within the hour, a second visitor arrived at Lew's cubicle. The thin man entered with his head bowed modestly and moved with great care, as if in fear of slipping or falling through rotting floorboards. His white name badge identified him:

Tomas Valdez, Manager - Mega Service Center (Weehawken).

Appearing no older than Lew but prematurely balding, Valdez wore proper Mega managerial attire plus a little ad-libbing for flair. Stylish and dignified in a dark blue suit, gold cuff links and a sparkling tie pin, he added nerdy spectacles and hot pink shirt that said professional, but also cool and open-minded. Ironic.

"Um, excuse me, sir?" Speaking in a gentle, solicitous tone, Valdez folded his hands as if in prayer, his shoulders hunched forward. "By any chance might you be Mr. Lewis Clarke?" Valdez stretched out a business card.

"Guilty," Lew said with a smile.

They shook hands.

"Yes, thought I recognized you, sir, from your photo and bio on the Mega intranet. This is quite an honor."

"And you," Lew said without studying the business card, "must be Tomas Valdez, boss of this whole operation. Delighted to meet you."

Valdez beamed as he shot his pink cuffs. "Weird, sir, but I missed any notification about your visit. Completely unaware."

"Well that was by design, Tomas. No need, really, to bother you. This visit is classified, so there's nothing you need to know about."

Relief washed over Lew. The sole merciful aspect of the DFA process was confidentiality, and that held up. Typically the receiving location hadn't a clue what was transpiring, allowing the victim to arrive, catch his breath, balm his broken spirits and make a plan. And then depart soon into the outside world, with no one any the wiser.

Valdez appeared nervous and wary, almost hesitant to make eye contact, like he'd been locked in with a wild animal. Lew felt empathy and smiled. He touched the man's shoulder.

"Anyway, please relax. I'm not here to spy on your operation, my friend, or assess you in any way. This visit has nothing to do with you. Your rep is rock solid at HQ." A charitable white lie. "My visit is temporary but top secret, maybe just a few weeks. Sorry I can't say more."

Valdez perked up and looked relieved, nodding understanding.

"So just ignore me, best as you can. I'll try and stay out of your way. But one thing—"

"Anything, sir!"

"It would be great if I could get a better work area. This cubicle, well . . ." Lew picked up the greasy phone receiver between two fingers and made a sour face. "And that machine —" he nodded at the Model T computer "— not much better."

Valdez grinned. "Why, of course. Right away, sir!" He pondered a moment, wringing his hands. "Oh and sorry if Ms. Kaminski was out of line in any way, just now. Just doing her job. She had no idea. I only have five supervisors running a thousand staff here and turnover is constant. We're constantly on-boarding newbies. Awful lot of babysitting."

"Completely understood." Lew nodded. "And please tell Mrs. Kaminski she's got zero problems with me. Tough job. She must be a star."

Valdez scurried off and within the hour ushered Lew into a double-sized cubicle fitted out with new equipment. Far higher status and as good as it got in Weehawken, where not a single private office existed on the immense call center floor. Not even for Valdez himself.

Then, as requested, Lew was left alone.

Lew maintained his usual schedule those first few weeks at Weehawken, for a sense of normalcy. He left his apartment each morning before six and hailed a yellow cab for the run across the Hudson. After years luxuriating in a chauffeured car, the taxi was a grating daily reminder of his downfall. He stopped a few times for breakfast at one of Jersey's bustling diners. His favorite channeled an oversized silver railroad car plopped onto a cement foundation.

The four Mega survival rules didn't apply to walking dead, so he soon dropped the tailored business suits and started dressing for comfort, favoring jeans, a colorful sport shirt and a cashmere sweater. And in an attempt to lighten his mood, he began to wear cowboy boots, a favorite pair of beauties hand-tooled from lizard skin, purchased (along with a magnificent oversized Stetson) during his glory days on a deal-seeking trip down to Austin.

At first, he mainly just killed time at the call center, nursing his wounded ego and doing whatever was needed to stop his mind from replaying that horrific DFA scene with Harry. It was a firing, no question, and had savaged his pride. He was destabilized and felt his former sky-high confidence shaken.

The same tiring question nagged at him. Why had this *really* happened? In a heartbeat, he'd gone from rock star to black hole resident, from a top VIP to a bottom-feeding FIP—Formerly Important Person. He endlessly pondered what he should have done differently. Top of the list was his mismanagement of Lazardi. And for that, yeah, he was totally to blame.

He wondered if his ex-wife would even recognize the sudden failure he'd become. MJ had only known Lew as flashy and confident, an overachiever, but he no longer felt like that. Sure, she'd be sympathetic, but her pity would burn even worse.

He found himself aimlessly sitting there, staring at the cubicle's antique phone and illogically waiting for it to ring, delivering vindication. His favored fantasy had Harry on the line. "*Godzilla finally came to his senses! Manned-up and got his wife under control. Get back here soon as possible, Lew. We can't survive without you!*"

But the days rolled by and the phone never rang.

After a period of full-on wallowing, he became disgusted with his own behavior. Enough already! It was time to phone Sal, first contact with anyone inside Mega since the DFAing. He dunked a cinnamon donut into his macchiato and thumbed Sal's icon on his cell.

"Lewis!" boomed Sal's familiar voice.

"Hey, pal, sorry I've been out of touch."

"Nah, amigo, completely understandable. Didn't want to bother you, so I was waiting for you to call first. Anyway, you good?"

"I guess as good as possible, under the circumstances." Geez, it was great to hear Sal's voice. "See, I've been DFAed."

"Heard that. Unbelievable."

"And I'm in Weehawken."

"Jeez," groaned Sal. "So how's the new digs? Y'all settling in okay?"

"Heh. Bite me." Lew sniffed a small chuckle. That guy! Sure didn't take long for the familiar teasing to resume. "Actually, amazing luxury, Sal. State of the art, circa 1980. Drop by any time to see it for yourself. I'll buy you coffee from a rusty machine." Lew paused and then tried to sound casual. "So anyway, what's the buzz back at the tower? What're people saying?"

"About what, bro? The Jets' new QB?" A pregnant pause. "Oh wait, you mean about *you*?"

Too funny. "No, about the papal elections. Just how *do* they do that white smoke, black smoke trick?" Lew growled a laugh. "Of *course* I mean about me, you dipshit."

They both chuckled. Yeah, it felt good to reconnect.

"Well, so far the mother ship has officially gone radio silent on the fate of one Lewis Nathaniel Clarke. No press release, no HR announcement, nothing. So, naturally, a shitload of rumors rushed in to fill the void."

Oh boy.

"Some insist you're dead, bro. A bloody suicide! Hey wait, am I talking to a ghost? What do phone calls from Hell cost, anyway? Is your receiver hot?"

"Me, a suicide? Heh, not yet . . . but check back later." Lew immediately regretted that one, not so funny. Sal didn't laugh, either.

"But a really good one goes that you had a bad accident in some sex club dungeon, Lew. Imagine . . . the mind simply boggles!"

"Hey, if fucking Lazardi is spreading that crap—"

"Relax. Word has it the Lizard's head will imminently be hoisted on a pike. Though after he's beheaded, it might grow back. Reptiles, you know?"

Good. "But if they DFA him, make sure he doesn't get sent here."

"I'll put in the word. Not that anyone around here listens to me." Sal yukked it up. "Hey, another rumor puts you in a Mexican jail. Juarez . . . or was it Tijuana? But my goofiest favorite is that you suddenly gave up the material world to become a Buddhist monk. Dropped everything and levitated up to some mountaintop ashram in Bhutan."

"Not a bad plan. Maybe later, if I tire of this thrilling new call center gig." Lew sipped his coffee. "But what's the more educated buzz?"

"Naturally, every office on eighty-eight immediately knew something was up, the very first morning when you didn't materialize at 4 a.m. or whenever it is you usually turn on the lights. King of Office Go-Getters! Quite a few suspect—or perhaps truly wish—that you were nabbed for something seriously illegal, a high crime, and are in custody. Others fear you were romanced away for a top job at an evil competitor, like the hated Imperial Brothers."

Lew snorted a chuckle. "And Emily, how's she holding up?"

"Busy for a couple days packing your business trophies and whatnot into boxes. Those are now stacked up in the corner of your old office, the lights switched off."

"Completely unimportant career detritus," Lew said.

"So now she just sits in front of your darkened office, worrying."

"Poor kid. But she'll be okay. Those twenty dinosaurs upstairs all know how good she is. Mega is sure to slot her into something great." Lew drew a breath, realizing Emily's reassignment would also serve as unimpeachable public confirmation he was truly history.

"And what about Harry?"

"Curious! *Der Oberfuhrer* went on extended leave." Sal's voice dropped. "No pressure for now, buddy, but whenever you need or are ready to privately share anything, I'm here for you."

Good man. "Nothing to discuss in detail yet, but later? Sure."

That kicked off a run of daily chats, for weeks, like a pair of garrulous old washer women. Sal alternated between sounding board, rabbi, and inside informant, providing his friend pep talks and advice.

But one gray, snowy morning, he shifted gears.

"Look, dude, I know you've been through a torrential shit storm, but ain't it time to stop acting like such a pussy? I mean, the Lew Clarke I knew was a steel-spined guy who willed tech miracles into existence. He'd never just curl up in defeat."

Whoa, was that what Sal really thought? That hit like a bucket of ice water. Lew caught his breath until the momentary shock faded. "Okay, go on. You've got my attention."

"Good. So, time to stop all the moping already, right? I mean it's kinda disgusting, man, your acting like a whiny little girl." Sal was gaining momentum. "It's time for you to act. Find a better company than Mega. Or maybe start up your own shop and quit working for geriatric assholes, altogether."

Sal was dead-on the mark. Unfair or not, the DFAing was history. Lew even embraced accountability for the Lazardi mess. His lack of oversight allowed it to happen. He owned it.

"You're absolutely right," sniffed Lew. "Time to get back to what I do. Find a company or concoct a new one. Either way, younger and healthier. Modern values and a superior culture."

"Fuckin-A, babe. There you go." Sal chuckled. "*That's* the badass we all know and love."

Lew vowed to turn his recent pain into a blessing. Fueled by a new optimism and renewed energy, he dove head-first into a networking drive.

First he worked his circle of friendly professional contacts but began repeatedly hitting a roadblock, being told he was *too* good for the existing vacancies. A real Catch-22. He branched out and also tried working friendly enemies, peers at former competitors like The

Imperial Brothers. It really felt strange to reach out like that, hat in hand, to former business foes . . . and yes, in some of those voices he detected a tinge of delight at his misery.

After a month of frustration, he shifted to his fallback plan and began to cold-call headhunters and Fortune 100 companies. To a man, all were familiar with his groundbreaking innovations but none were aware of Lew's role in stewarding those triumphs. Many, in fact, sounded doubtful. The Mega Code was royally screwing him.

In a few promising instances, his interviews climbed high in company hierarchies before stalling out. Cushing, it was rumored, had circulated a no-hire order along the CEO grapevine. And if Chairman Godzilla wanted him out on the street, then that's where he belonged. Nobody screwed with Mega. It all felt cruel and wore on Lew, unaccustomed to failure.

One afternoon, after a particularly disappointing call, he hurled his yellow legal pad across the cubicle and knocked over a coffee mug, which shattered noisily on the floor. Heads popped up at surrounding cubicles, call center ghosts who just stared at him, people with whom he never interacted. Word had spread, early on, that Lew was heat from the head office and potentially dangerous. Someone to avoid.

Feeling untethered and fast losing direction, Lew fell into a deeper emotional nosedive.

CHAPTER FOUR
Magnificent Little Palaces

The way the DFA drill worked, Weehawken was just supposed to be a way station. Few weeks, maybe a month. So by week seven, Lew's departure was overdue.

His days fell into a depressive, unproductive pattern. He pitched up around ten most mornings but no longer phoned around for leads. Why bother? He came to expect rejections. Embittered and embarrassed, he even ghosted Sal rather than be forced to share details of his continuing failure. He mainly just surfed the web, killed time, and left by lunchtime to aimlessly wander Manhattan, parking by midafternoon in some random, darkened bar along his path.

Totally demoralized, he stopped shaving and lost most appetite. His well-fed businessman's frame withered by twenty pounds and a full beard came in, dramatically altering his appearance. He wore the same stale clothes and changed his socks and underwear when he thought of it. His new uniform was a sweatshirt and jeans, cowboy boots and his oversized Stetson.

His luxury penthouse off Central Park West transformed into a disaster zone. Early on, he suspended the cleaning service after a maid disturbed his post-DFA pouting. Big mistake. So now, two months later, the place was flooded with empty beer cans, liquor bottles, and pizza boxes. Dirty socks and underwear piled up and the place stank, though he didn't notice.

Meanwhile, he installed an app at the call center to open his own private portal through Mega's firewall and control software, granting him privacy and unimpeded web access, a level of surfing privilege enjoyed by nobody else. But with nearly all motivation gone, he could barely summon the energy to browse sports, porn, or gambling websites.

He lost thousands playing Texas hold 'em yet felt nothing. He was certain the poker website out of the Caymans wasn't on the level but didn't care, being so psychologically maimed. He stopped consuming all social media and isolated himself, having lost all interest in former friends, associates or scuttlebutt from back at Mega.

He even stopped picking up Sal's frequent phone calls, so those petered out, replaced by occasional short emails that Lew didn't bother opening.

He felt tired all the time and immobilized by a dark mood, stranded between sad and numb. Life felt like a constant burden and everything wore on him. Things couldn't go on like this, he understood, but there seemed no escape. After all his past success, how could he accept anything less for the future? His former stardom created an insurmountable barrier to his future happiness. He was his own toughest competitor.

About the only good news was that his severance would be generous. Mega floated a bloated, first-cut exit package and he knew they would go higher. So at least money would never be a problem. But what about the rest of his life? Who *was* he, even? This sudden flop, washed-up at thirty-six?

One Thursday morning he trudged in at ten, already weary, and glanced at his online stock portfolio. It was massive and doing great, but he felt nothing. He checked last night's Knicks score—failed to cover again, so another ten K gone. He didn't care.

But something picayune *did* bother him, the meaty garlic aroma that invaded the call center. What the hell, gyros at 10 a.m.? "Christ," he grumbled, leaning back before beginning to randomly click around the web.

A small ad at the bottom corner of a financial website caught his eye. Inside a box with thick purple borders was a bright pink cartoon elephant, strutting and smiling, decked out in jewels and golden ornaments. The creature looked regal as it danced atop a world globe, standing on the map outline of an unidentified country in Asia. Its message blared:

Act Now!
Don't Miss Out!
Life-Changing Opportunity!
Join Us Today!

Life-changing? Ha. Could certainly use some of *that*. Awful lot of exclamation points, though. Whoever these elephant folks were, they were awfully juiced up. But it intrigued him into another click, and with that, the entire screen went black.

"Oops," he mumbled, "jackpot." A computer worm was probably already downloading, a virus to infect the entire Mega system. He certainly didn't care. Royally screw up The Twenty Old Men? Great . . . fine with him.

An intricate golden filigree began to hypnotically weave itself around the edges of the screen. Then a proposition in bold white script flashed at the center.

Dear Global Friend!
Welcome to Amazia!
We Are Lotus Creations!
Today Your Karma is Excellent!
Your Lucky Day!

Luck? Right.

He shook his head with a sour laugh. But Lotus Creations, he liked that—sounded exotic and intriguing. The screen blinked to reveal more.

Our Business Offer Will Change Your Life . . . Forever!
The Opportunity We Offer is Serious.
But Please Hurry!
Do Not Miss This Chance!

Lew, a hardened and pragmatic tech warrior, could sniff out garden variety internet fraud like a bloodhound. Every day, amateurish con jobs flooded his spam bucket, Nigerian princes and oil ministers anxious to send him riches. Questionable sites dangled wild commercial schemes or sexual fulfillment. Virtually all were scams masquerading as opportunity.

But there was something different about this quirky elephant pitch—the innocent exuberance? He was bored and, what the hell, this might be fun. The clincher was just a small thing, the silly yet endearing greeting. *"Welcome to Amazia!"* It made him chuckle.

Amazia? Never heard of it. Probably some obscure backwater. So Lew—unemployed, disrespected and depressed, but idly curious and with nothing to lose—clicked one more time. And something astounding happened.

The screen drenched itself in sumptuous royal purple and at the center appeared the image of a magnificent white marble palace topped by a soaring golden roof, all supported by golden pillars. The exotic, dramatic edifice gleamed like a work of art, where even mundane fixtures like window frames appeared covered in precious metal.

What was this? Lew stared, open- mouthed but then grinned for the first time in a month, teased by this cool, welcome mystery that had emerged from nowhere. A message crawled across the bottom of the screen and repeated in thick red font:

Exclusively Yours . . . Meticulous Asian Craftsmanship . . .

That, for some reason, really tickled him, and he snorted out a rich laugh. Right, just what he needed, an ultra-luxurious golden palace somewhere. Exclusively, too.

But he'd had enough by now and moused over to the corner 'X' to shut the window when a final message began to flash. Massive golden letters filled the screen, over a scarlet background. The effect that was near-blinding and, for a moment, he feared it might trigger a migraine.

Seeking International Partners!
Awarding Exclusive National Territories!
Yes, Only One per Country!
Act Now! Do Not Delay!

Ah, now finally came the hard-sell, and quite the proposition it was: territorial exclusivity for the entire US market! Well worth deeper investigation. Almost regardless of product, any such monopoly might potentially be a money machine.

His gut ordered him to slow down, be more thoughtful. He pulled his chair closer, sipped his double latte, and kept reading. His entrepreneurial pistons began to fire for the first time since who-knew-when and it felt good. After guiding Mega through so many past deals, acquiring tech start-ups and the like, this kind of initial review came second nature. Sure, the weirdness quotient here ran awful high, but skinny threads of legitimacy seemed evident.

He pored over the Lotus website for several hours, clicking on every link and studying every picture and file. The more he saw, the more he felt compelled to continue. After all, there was no harm in exploring, even if just for entertainment value. (The idea did amuse him, of a former tech overlord falling for an online con job, but he knew he wouldn't.)

He ran down the obvious angles. He verified that Amazia, the host country, was real, though just a quirky little Asian kingdom with only a microscopic footprint on the internet.

The more he nosed around, the stronger grew the aroma of genuine opportunity. Bizarre and off-the-wall, no question, but it was a possible the curtain was rising on the next act in his professional life. He tingled with a sweet, familiar anxiety—the good kind—from chasing a deal. A sudden realization shook him.

If this offer was genuine and not a con (as was indeed growing more likely), others might already be ready to pounce and steal this opportunity, while he was just half-assing around. With only a single winner for the entire American market, just one aggressive competitor could destroy his chances.

There was no way to tell how long the proposition had already been floating around the web, too. He might already be too late. New urgency gripped him. He'd never forgive himself if he allowed a genuine, diamond-class opportunity slip away because he'd been too slow to react.

Fully adrenalized, he sprang into action and spent the next hours elbow-deep in research, just like pre-DFA Lew. By 4 p.m. he'd seen enough and fired off a text to Sal.

Meet me at PJ's at 6. Absolutely top urgent.

Lew staked out their usual booth along the back wall and cleared away soggy racing forms. PJ's was a sloppy pub in SoHo that reeked of spilt beer, stale tobacco smoke and popcorn, their go-to bar for years. Most evenings the place was jammed and the juke box blaring, but not at six p.m., nor this early in the week.

The front door flew open and banged against the wall. A temporary flood of light washed through the darkened room, partially blocked by Sal's mountainous figure. He spotted Lew and stomped over, kicking snow off his black rubber boots. The throwback galoshes were Sal's way of saying, style-wise, he didn't really give a shit.

"Hey, Mary," he bellowed. "Couple sausage sandwiches, vinegar fries, and two icy drafts. Foaming." He did a double-take. "And better check with Lew, too, in case he's hungry."

"Your usual, Sal," the woman chirped. "All that just for you. Still got that healthy appetite."

"Growing boy, dear."

The brutish man dropped onto the seat beside Lew and raked fingers through his curly black hair. He pinched his nose with a frown. "Jeez, bro, *pee-yoo!* You really kinda stink, heaps. And look at that beard and raggedy-ass clothes." He touched the shiny material of Lew's jeans.

"Sorry, I know," Lew said. "Believe me, I really do. But just try to ignore these remnants of the old *DFAed Lew*. He finally left, a few hours ago, and the real me is making a comeback."

Sal smiled. "Great! But why'd you drag me here? Marissa had other plans tonight, so you just bought me a ticket on *The Shitville Express*. This better be *reeeal* good. Still trying to stay married, you know?"

"Ouch." Lew bit his bottom lip.

"Oops," said Sal, his face softening. "Sorry, wasn't thinking."

"No sweat. But thanks for coming. Wouldn't push so hard if it wasn't super important."

Sal gulped his lager and wiped foam from his chin. "So, my long-lost buddy is reemerging? Great. Wouldn't want to miss the unveiling of *Lew Clarke 2.0*."

Lew smiled. "Found something potentially extraordinary today, but need your take . . . just in case I've wandered off the deep end."

"Always here to protect and serve, Hoss."

Lew pushed a large brown envelope across the table and Sal slid out a large color print. He studied the photo with a sour, questioning face. "So here's some emperor's palace or castle. Big frickin' deal. Good for the lucky dipshit who owns it but otherwise, who cares? Not me." Sal bit off a mouthful of sausage. Meat bits and juice squirted down his shirt. "You not eating?"

"Too excited," Lew said, pulling out his phone. "Now check this out." A video streamed, showing a jungle workshop. Tropical birds sang and insects droned while petite, latte-skinned people in sarongs patiently sawed, sanded and hammered with the relaxed demeanor of artists rather than laborers.

"Where's this?"

"Amazia."

"I'll bet." Sal laughed. "The fuck?"

"It's a teensy tropical kingdom in Asia."

"Never heard of it."

"You and about eight billion other humans, Sal. Kinda the ass-end of nowhere."

Sal frowned. "Okay, and we care because …?" He raised his eyebrows.

"Sit back, my boy, and listen. Because herein lies the magic." Lew rolled up his sleeves. "Amazia has virtually zero internet presence, just a couple old travel sites. No Wikipedia page. Smaller than Iowa and a population less than Wyoming. Mainly cut off from the rest of the world. Its culture, though, borrows from its many neighbors, like Laos, Burma, Vietnam or Thailand. All kinds of religions, too—Buddhists, Muslims. Hindus. And many Animists."

Sal sighed, starting to look frustrated. "What-a-mists?"

"*Animists*. From the Latin, *anima*, meaning *life* or *soul*. Animists believe deities inhabit nature. In rocks, flowers, mountains and forests."

"Spirits, huh? Sounds kinda dumb. And that name, Amazia? Way too goofy." Sal chewed on a fry.

"No at all. It derives from the main ethnic group, the Amaza. Around for centuries. Nothing amazing."

"Okay, so welcome to freakin' Amazia," Sal grumbled good-naturedly, "but who gives a rat's ass?" Sal picked random bits of sausage from his teeth.

"Sal, picture a real hole-in-the-wall little kingdom, hidden away with no money or resources. Never colonized. No tourism." Lew smiled. "That's Amazia."

Sal clinked down his empty stein. "So I'll send 'em a charitable donation in the morning. But what's the point, Lew? You show me a castle photo and a jungle factory video and tell stories of an impoverished lost kingdom. I don't care. And you better talk fast because I gotta run, bro—already in deep *kimchi* with the missus for coming. And, frankly, already regretting it."

Lew gave Sal's shoulder a squeeze. "Patience! That was just atmospheric backdrop. Let's zoom in on our glorious future."

"Our?" Sal looked worried and glanced again at his watch. "Better be *really* good." He loosened his tie. "But lucky for you I'm awful hungry tonight. Thirsty, too." He waved at the barmaid. "Two more of everything, darling."

Lew dramatically slapped down a second glossy photo and Sal leaned in. Another castle.

"Screen shot from the Lotus website. But this one is taken farther back and makes clear *this is no castle*. See how it's perched on a pole? It's actually a lawn ornament of some kind, like a birdhouse or something, but just as majestic as a sultan's palace."

Sal stopped in mid-gulp and put his beer down. A concerned look clouded his face. "Dude, you're bananas! Oh geez, please don't tell me you left Mega just to wind up as a birdhouse salesman for some company in Outer Bum-fuck, Asia."

Lew laughed. "Ah, Sally boy, relax. You should know me better by now. Humor me just a bit longer, okay?"

"Humor? Ain't nothin' funny about this, dawg." Sal shook his head and mumbled, "My poor little buddy."

Lew pulled out a yellow notepad and scribbled numbers. "For different sizes—say, some like washing machines but others big as pickup trucks—what kind of prices could we charge?"

"For lawn decorations at retail?"

"Yeah, at the Home Depot in an elite zip code. What would some rich snob pay for such extraordinary quality? Assume *really* motivated buyers."

Sal stared at the ceiling, thinking hard. "Of course, I know zip about birdhouses and landscaping. But still, this workmanship *is* quite astounding. So, say, four hundred bucks for the washing machine size. And eight for the Ford F-150 size, okay?"

Lew shrugged. "Nah, my gut says that's too low. And I called around to check the market. Remember, these are like fabulous works of art. Open your mind!"

"Dude, you're going Morpheus on me?"

Lew smiled. "Yeah, Neo! These could trigger a new wave in pricey landscaping for the super-wealthy. The Next Big Thing in mansion decoration. And product extension opportunities are endless. We start out selling them as birdhouses but quickly expand. Take a big one, install some piping and *presto*, it's a fountain. Bury somebody underneath one and it's a shrine. Add seats and swings and you've got a backyard gazebo."

Sal put down the fork. "Shit, Lew, you really think super-rich folks will buy these for their hedge-fund neighborhoods?"

"They will absolutely kill for them. I am certain." A powerful trend had taken hold after COVID, as a flood of money roared through elite neighborhoods for home environment upgrades. "Hell, the *Wall Street Journal* has an entire weekly 'Mansions' section. Our market."

Lew was gathering steam. "Remember, for moneyed folk, being first is everything. Imagine installing one of these in your gated community, to cap off an already grand property?

"Well they *are* magnificent and totally unique." Sal's signaled to the barmaid. Two ice-cold mugs arrived in a flash, foam dripping down the sides. "So yeah, could probably sell a lot of them. I know, never bet against the Clarke instincts on new trends. But for tech stuff, not royal birdhouses. Like Mega's new bio health chip. Hell, not even I could resist getting one implanted last week. Right ass cheek."

Lew chuckled. "Business is business, Sal, just as long as the money's green. But I've not yet told you the best part."

A huge smile parted Sal's late-day stubble. "Ah, thank God, so you *were* holding out on me!" He dabbed perspiration from his forehead with a beer-soaked napkin. "Kinda was hoping that, for *your* sake."

Lew moved in for the kill. "Assume we can sell small ones for five hundred each and large ones, a thousand." Sal started to object but Lew cut him off. "Don't quibble—just ball-parking. Those prices aren't outrageous for such quality, for status-seeking show-offs in Martha's Vineyard or Sausalito."

Sal conceded that.

"Now listen," Lew said, his voice dramatic. "In a land of paupers like Amazia, everything is cheap, including jungle wages." Lew wriggled his fingers at Sal. "So *this* is our cost."

"We pay in fingers?"

"Ha, funny. No, that was a *ten*. We'll buy these hand-made artistic miracles for a lousy ten bucks! Twenty each for the big ones."

Sal's jaw dropped. "But then we turn around and sell 'em for a thousand? Holy cannoli, you sure? Whoa, near-infinite profit margins!" He thumped the table and splattered beer everywhere. Other customers turned and laughed.

Lew grinned. "Not only that, here's the cherry on top. Our supply deal would be *exclusive*. A national monopoly for America."

"Get outta here!"

"I mean it. Every single unit *must* be purchased through us."

"Lew! Well butter my butt and call me a biscuit!" Sal chortled, shaking his head.

"And we'll sell 'em everywhere, Sal. Direct to luxury home builders and high-end landscapers. At every big box home improvement store in the land. And direct to state and municipal governments, to adorn public parks."

Sal whistled low. "Well I'll be a monkey's bare-assed uncle." He stood and brushed crumbs from his shirt. "Okay, you win. I shoulda known better. Yup, it's a killer concept." He crumpled his napkin and tossed it onto the table.

Lew chugged the last of his beer, bursting with delight. His most reliable sounding board had roundly approved. "Naturally, Sal, this is just early research. But so far, it looks promising. So if this goes forward, would you be in?"

Sal smiled wide. "Does the Pope shit in the woods?"

Lew grinned. Some things never changed and this habitual joking exchange of theirs always tickled him. "Dunno. But is the bear a Catholic?"

Sal snugged up his galoshes. "Just to be clear, Hoss, that was me saying *yes*. I'm in. But as for now, big guy, I'm outta here. Really gotta move."

"Great," Lew said, "but be advised, this could go super-fast. With a single winner for the whole US market, we're at risk of being pushed aside, any moment. Soon as I confirm enough, I gotta move."

"Roger that," Sal said. "And I'll let you pick up the check tonight, amigo. It's clear once this little maneuver takes off, you'll be printing your own money.*"*

CHAPTER FIVE
Lotus Creations

Lew delighted in the familiar buzz—adrenaline or endorphins, whatever—from chasing down a deal. And this time, the transaction was entirely *his*, not Mega, further amping up the sweet tingle. What he now needed most was impeccable information for potentially the biggest risk of his life.

He scratched down endless questions onto a yellow legal pad—about storage, distribution, sales channels, staffing, licensing. But the incredible profit margin dwarfed all other considerations. Imagine, selling ten dollar items for a thousand each, and on a monopoly basis? How could any other concern really matter? Still, this was no time to get sloppy. He summoned focus and plowed ahead.

Information on Lotus and the flyspeck kingdom of Amazia was sketchy, impossibly so. He eventually tracked down a decaying website from a French religious order that web-published field journal entries from its far-flung missions, including one penned by a frustrated young minister after a fruitless year in what he called *Inner Amazia*. Father Pierre failed to win any converts but attested to the high moral standards and universal integrity of the Amaza. Sweet, virtuous folk.

Lew smiled. Wow, imagine having innately honest partners—like teaming up with monks. What could be better?

He returned to the Lotus website to repeatedly hunt for missed information. The company background section detailed a tiny, unremarkable family enterprise that sold temple paraphernalia: candles and joss sticks, vermilion religious robes, brilliant orange parasols and simple stands for Buddha statues. But in a recent major strategic shift, they ramped up to manufacture and export palatial lawn ornaments (birdhouses). Talk about a shift in vision!

Lew whistled low.

All signs indicated it was still early and that he was there at The Creation. A ground floor opportunity. And he thanked the heavens for this thrilling turn in his luck and reminded himself remain calm and cautious, calm and to concentrate. To not allow optimism to blow out his rationality circuits.

He searched hard for fatal flaws, any evidence debunking the offer, but found none. The opportunity refused to yield and lacked the telltale stink of common internet scams. No rogue third world finance ministers or exiled archdukes lurked in the background.

Buried deep within the Lotus website, he found a previously unnoticed link. When clicked, it summoned forth customer testimonials—videos, photos and glowing blurbs from early Lotus partners, like one in Germany. The web file properties indicated the data was fresh, too. Good: he could contact them to compare notes. Bad: he was far from being the global first-mover. That meant the offer had been floating out there a while so the US deal might vanish at any time . . . gobbled up by a competitor.

He needed to move fast to lodge his proverbial foot in the door. There was no harm in immediately contacting Lotus as he didn't commit to anything. As more details emerged, if anything felt wrong, he could always pull out. But it was critical he nail down a place in line and avoid being prematurely aced out.

Skilled in the old-fashioned hard sell, he drafted an attention-grabbing proposal, strong as King Kong, designed to kick the Lotus door wide open. He pitched himself as a perfect US partner, and detailed his unprecedented succession of new products brought to market in North America. Alluding to stellar business connections and substantial financial resources already in hand, he closed by emphasizing his ability and intention to move forward quickly.

Lew's heart jumped upon checking his email the next morning.

A reply from Lotus sat atop his queue—they had risen to the bait and struck hard:

> *Dear Mr. Clarke:*
>
> *We were delighted to receive your email. Your credentials are highly impressive and you appear a perfect fit for our USA market initiative (including Canada and Mexico).*
>
> *To answer your question, no, the exclusive agency for North America has not yet been awarded. But discussions are already advanced, with several strong candidates.*
>
> *However considering your credentials, if you moved quickly, you might surpass our other candidates. And for the right partner, we can progress a decision expeditiously.*
>
> *If you are still keen to proceed, please join us for a video conference tomorrow at 9 a.m., Amazia time.*
>
> *Sincerely,*
> *The Management Team, Lotus Creations Co.*

Holy shit, the US monopoly supply position just expanded to include *all* of North America? Lew laughed. Wonderful! Surely Mexican drug cartel lords and Canadian oil tycoons also needed to decorate grandiose estates, right?

His heart beat faster. Lew checked the time difference and determined that tomorrow morning in Amazia, on the opposite side of the planet, would be just later that evening, in New York. Crap! He had less than a half day to prepare for the most important business meeting of his life.

With precious little time left, too much was still unknown. He tapped his foot with anxiety before catching himself. Relax! This was to be just an exploratory meeting.

Going retro usually helped him to hyper-focus, so he grabbed a yellow legal pad and a handful of colorful felt-tip pens. He inserted earbuds to stream some Thelonious Monk; jazz nicely stimulated him, keeping him relaxed but focused. Soon his pad bloomed with a rainbow garden of intricate, multi-colored diagrams with data and names of lawyers, bankers and associates. His personal hieroglyphics squiggled with boxes, lines, and arrows highlighting information needs, decision points and key dependencies.

He confirmed the North American market was indeed virgin for this unique product. No competition. Such estate decorations simply did not yet exist here. He could lock it all up.

He worked nonstop, only taking minutes for a tuna sandwich and Coke at the call center machine room. Then he raced back for a series of afternoon calls, already growing confident he'd be fully primed for first contact, that evening with Lotus.

He rang his personal financial manager at Morgan Stanley.

"Good afternoon, Mr. Clarke," chirped Joel Platt, sounding a little nervous. "Been a while, hope all is well. Heard maybe some, uh, developments over at Mega?"

Rats! Was bad buzz already trickling out from Mega? "Everything's great, Joel. No time for details right now, but I'm launching a thrilling new venture. Huge, and my *own* bottom line."

"Why that's terrific, sir." Platt sounded genuinely relieved. "How can I assist?"

"I need you to free up cash for me, Joel, and fast. Get me liquid right now—my entire portfolio, actually." Did he just hear his finance guy gulp?

Though a long shot, Lew needed to be ready for *any* eventuality, just in case Lotus surprised him with a prompt money demand. Not that things *ever* moved that fast. But he wanted to ensure maximum optionality and be ready for anything. His personal motto was *Semper paratus*, always be prepared . . . like a mid-thirties, high-tech, uber-aggressive businessman Boy Scout.

His next call went out to his team of personal lawyers. He peppered the three men with sundry legal questions about doing business with a foreign supplier. None knew anything about Amazia, but their general answers based on US law allayed his concerns. He instructed them to immediately set up a new limited company, "Avian Luxury, Inc."

Lew felt stoked as he continued to cruise down his checklist. The prospect of a major win always adrenalized him. His energy level soared. By mid-afternoon, with a half-dozen pages of tightly scribbled notes, he was drinking in knowledge like a sponge and learning fast, confident he would soon understand the opportunity, inside-out.

Next, he phoned associates from his Mega years—useful, friendly contacts perched at high levels in business and government. This was tricky, carefully probing for information while hiding his intentions, never showing his hand. He confirmed numerous sales channels already existed to provide his imports broad access to the nation's retail and commercial markets. He felt giddy. If things broke right, the fabulous things might almost sell themselves!

He tried to phone that Lotus partner in Germany but got fouled up by time zone problems.

So he next rang Horace Michener, a former college fraternity brother now riding an Asia desk at the State Department. After initial pleasantries, Lew got down to business—surely State had a treasure trove of reassuring info about Amazia and doing business there.

"Amazia?" Michener giggled over the line. "Whew, eons since anybody's even mentioned that place. Hermit kingdom, you know."

Not good. "Well, somebody there at State must have current Amazia responsibility, right? I'm mulling a huge investment and need to raise my comfort level. To whom do I speak?"

The man sighed. "Sorry. Nobody. Just too insignificant a backwater for *any* deployment of our assets. Nobody even visits. But with a lot of luck, many years from now, Amazia might attain the importance of, say, Haiti or a Paraguay."

Lew whistled. "That bad?"

"Worse! But lemme check something." A keyboard clacked over the phone line. "Got it. If we ever need help, supposedly the Vietnamese will cover for us. Just in theory."

"So, nothing you can do?"

"Even less, old man. Sorry."

His tax dollars at work! Lew momentarily felt let down but rebounded, knowing he was already fully prepared. And the video call would only be an introductory conversation, short but hopefully sweet enough to lodge his foot in the door. Prevent the deal from landing elsewhere.

He sent a text to invite Sal to his flat, to join the call. Then he gathered his cubicle belongings and waved goodbye to the now-friendly Ms. Kaminski. She smiled back as he headed home for a shower, shave, and a bite to eat, the video conference just hours away.

CHAPTER SIX
Decision at the Dog Pound

Lew toweled off, feeling a little jazzed up with pleasant, deal-triggered butterflies. The video conference was less than an hour away, hopefully launching his comeback as Lew 2.0, as Sal liked to joke. His mouth was a little dry and chest felt tight.

He shaved, dressed, and pulled on his lucky sweater. It was a silly superstition, but he loved his elegant cinnamon brown vicuna sweater, dappled with artistic color blotches. Plenty of empowering memories. Purchased at a chic Manhattan boutique his first year at Mega, when he couldn't afford such extravagance, it set him back a heart-stopping grand. Back then, for him, that was *real* money. But always making a strong statement, it paid for itself, many times over.

He studied himself in the mirror. With his DFA beard freshly shaved and the recent weight loss, he looked more much younger.

His mind raced—tonight would be all about showing empathy, business knowledge and good taste. He'd treat Lotus to a world-class partner, one they can't afford to let get away.

His eyes wandered across the apartment and he flinched, only now seeing the chaotic, disgusting squalor previously rendered invisible by his depression. The accumulated wreckage from months of wallowing and self-pity had swamped his luxurious flat in a sea of greasy old pizza cartons, leaking Chinese take-out boxes, and empty beer cans.

The worst possible backdrop for the video call.

He hurriedly began pushing debris around but could hardly dent the clutter and soon realized that all such efforts were doomed. Even after clearing enough to tidy a video backdrop, he himself would still be immersed in trash. Hardly optimal setting to perform at one's best.

To avoid distraction, he decided to use the *Dog Pound*—the elite teleconferencing center he'd relied upon, his entire Mega career. Anyway, it made sense to go full-tilt professional for this initial Lotus meeting. Too critical to just casually dial-in. But now he really had to hurry, only forty minutes to zero hour.

He texted the venue change to Sal and headed for the lobby. Lew stood outside at the curb beside the doorman, hailing a cab, when Sal texted back.

FU. But k, see u there.

Lew grinned.

A yellow rust bucket taxi rattled up and Lew slid into the back seat. The vehicle smelled of sweat and assorted spices. The turbaned driver looked ambiguously Central Asian and wore an earpiece as he chatted nonstop online—not to Lew—in a phlegmy foreign language.

"Hotel Grand Metropole," Lew called out loudly. Really on the clock now, no time for mistaken directions.

The driver nodded and accelerated into traffic amid a chorus of tooting horns and bellmen's whistles. The route swung down below Central Park and then up a few blocks, where the taxi lurched to a curbside halt. Hotel doormen and valets descended upon the cab.

Recognizing Lew, they all saluted. No surprise. As Mega's point man, Lew for years had built those relationships upon a mountain of little folded-up squares of cash, pressed into palms.

Since its opening first shook the city, the Hotel Grand Metropole had shouldered aside glitzy rivals to win over clients like Mega's corps of executives. Built on the laundered cash of Russian oligarchs, the Grand Metropole became New York's premiere venue for classy business dinners, offsite presentations, cocktail receptions, and video conferences.

As Lew cruised through the lobby, greetings echoed after him. "Good evening, Mr. Clarke!" The fawning respect felt bittersweet, aimed as it was at his former self, Lew 1.0, the recently career-assassinated Mega Man.

He hustled into a private express elevator at the lobby rear and asked for the business center. The operator wore an elegant burgundy uniform and pressed an illuminated button. The doors whooshed closed and torque from the silent, high-speed levitation felt good. The shining metal doors parted to reveal an elegant business center. All marble, chrome and ferns behind a glass wall.

Mega execs once constantly used The Dog Pound, affectionately comparing it to a high-class SPCA facility, the video rooms like luxurious kennel cages. Recent advances in personal conferencing technology eliminated most of that but Lew still enjoyed the ambience and kept his relationships there alive. The Dog Pound had been part of his winning routine, a calming ritual and way to summon confidence and focus.

"My goodness, Mr. Clarke!" The attendant beamed and jumped to stiff attention, clearly surprised by the sudden return of an elite customer. "Wonderful to see you, sir. Been a while."

Lew peered deep into the man's eyes for awareness of his career descent. Nothing. Good. Mega brutally kicked him to the curb but hadn't dragged his good name through the muck. "Yes, Charles. Been rather busy."

"Sir, we didn't know you were coming." A few beads of sweat glistened on the attendant's forehead as he frantically ran a finger down the reservation list. "Hmm, no Mega reservation. But, of course, it's no prob—"

"Sorry for the short notice, Charles. All my fault. But something urgent came up, an important overseas conference in just a few minutes. Is a private room free?"

"For you sir? Why, always, of course! How many from Mega are joining? If your group is large, we can access your usual ultra-premium room, The Empire Suite."

Lew understood the man was talking in code—if the grandest room was desired, management would last-minute cancel some other unfortunate party's reservation.

"No need, but thanks." Lew smiled warmly. "Just me and one associate. Anything private and comfy will be great."

"Absolutely." The clerk picked up his clipboard. "I presume this goes on the usual company account?"

Lew snorted a chuckle at the very notion of Mega eating this bill. Would be poetic justice. But he shook his head *no*. "Actually, all charges tonight are mine, for my personal account. I'll settle directly." The last thing he needed was for word on the Amazia opportunity to leak out before he got it totally locked down. Nope, he'd leave no trail for Mega's bloodhounds.

A little paranoid? Sure, but it felt healthy—the deal was potentially *that* epic and needed to be kept totally under wraps.

The attendant ushered him into posh quarters the size of a hotel grand suite, resplendent with purple velvet curtains, a large brown leather sofa against one wall and a coffee table. Off to one side was a massive walnut desk with chairs, all facing a gigantic flat-panel TV. The room was miked-up for conference calls routed through the immense TV screen and notepad computers. Interactive whiteboards, scanners and other electronic gear were also tastefully positioned around the room.

Lew glanced at the digital clock ticking below the TV and exhaled with relief. Five minutes to spare. Would Sal ake it on time? He dropped into the plush sofa and got comfortable before hearing a knock at the door, three quick raps.

"Yes? Come in, please."

A blonde entered to deliver a tray of snacks, coffee, and carbonated beverages. With high cheekbones and big eyes, she was stunning despite her dark, austere business suit and pinned-back hair. She smiled and placed the tray on the coffee table. Lew motioned for her to pull the office drapes closed. Didn't need the distraction of the Manhattan night skyline.

Charles, the shift manager, returned. "We'll now be leaving you alone, sir. You don't need the usual briefing—heh, you probably know our systems better than most staff here. But just buzz if you want anything." Lew nodded politely.

A moment later came a loud banging on the door and a large form entered.

"Hey, chief, you bargaining with Lotus yet?" Sal made a show of stomping his feet and hugging himself to warm up. "Brrr, chilly out there tonight." He gazed around the suite. "Good idea, returning to the Dog Pound. Surely an upgrade from your bombed-out apartment." He walked over to the wall with four manifolded sixty-inch TVs. "Good double feature tonight? Got a hankering for maybe a Western and then some zombie apocalypse stuff."

Lew just shook his head, smiling. "Ah, Sally, me boy."

Once the pneumatic door eased shut, Lew rose and turned the deadbolt lock and motioned Sal toward the corner sofa. "Make yourself comfortable over there, buddy." Lew sat at the desk and typed in the meeting's connection information on a wireless keyboard.

"Any special instructions, Hoss?"

"Yes. Drink it all in and digest. Stay quiet and provide *silent* backup. My second set of eyes and ears. And take good notes on *everything*. Taking the lead, I'll be too busy for that."

Sal mimed zipping his lips and the two laughed. Then using the slim black remote, Lew fired up the video wall. At exactly 9 p.m., it blinked to life in a blinding orange-yellow flash.

At center screen, a gem-studded crown floated above the words:

LOTUS CREATIONS CO.
THE ROYAL KINGDOM OF AMAZIA.

Beside the crown, a smaller video window popped open, showing a smiling, bespectacled man in a vermilion robe, his bald head glistening. A birthmark scarred his right cheek, a glaring purplish blotch the size of a golf ball. His title appeared under the window:

KHUN KHON
ASIATIC MEDIA AGENCY.

Gazing out, the man brought his hands together as in prayer and bowed his head. Lew had seen that gesture before, though not in person. Called a *wai* in Thailand or *namaste* in India, it was a mark of respect. Lew liked it—a nice way to honor others—and without even thinking, automatically returned the gesture, or at least an approximation.

"Hello, Mr. Clarke!" the man called out. "And good evening to you in New York. Though it's already tomorrow morning here in Amazia." He smiled. His speech featured a slightly clipped accent, odd but somehow familiar, a bit like colonial British.

But who was this Khun Khon? And what was the Asiatic Media Agency? He had expected the Lotus management team. And wow, that unfortunate birthmark was a helluva distraction. The big purple blob that looked like a pigmentation map of Texas or India.

But it was the way he said Amazia that most caught Lew off guard: *ah-MAH-zee-ah*. Even Michener at State had mispronounced it—the place was *that* picayune and unknown.

Lew felt blindsided. How had he missed that? Easy, everything was moving too fast, that's how. It was understandable if things got a little sloppy, but still no excuse. The pronunciation made eminent sense—after all, the Kingdom took its name from the *Amaza* people. Nothing to do with the English word *amazing*.

Lew made eye contact with Sal in the corner, who hit the mute button.

"Steeee-rike one, eh, Lew? Well I say *to-MAY-to, to-MAH-to*. One in a million English speakers would pronounce that right, first time. Don't we all say 'Paris' rather than *Pah-REE*? As screw-ups go, that's small beer, so don't sweat it. And as for me, it'll always be *Amazia as in amazing.*" Sal winked and unmuted.

Lew could allow no more rookie errors. He resumed smiling into the camera and tried to project a friendly tone. "Hope it's a beautiful morning there in Amazia." He really stressed that middle syllable, intoning it like a nice long *ahhh* for the doctor. Lew spoke slowly and carefully, over-enunciating words, a brand of English he often deployed for foreign ears. "Hopefully this begins a beautiful relationship between our companies, Mr. Khun Khon."

The bespectacled man flinched and looked a little perplexed. Now what?

"Mr. Clarke, a small matter, if I may? You called me 'Mr. Khun Khon'. But to clarify, in our language, the word *khun* already means 'sir' or 'mister.' So you might call me *Mr.* Khon or *Khun* Khon, but never *Mr. Khun* Khon. That's redundant, like *Mister* Mr. Clarke."

Crap. Lew was really on his back foot now, off to a doubly bad start and on the defensive. "Oops, sorry, *Mr. Khon*." He smiled into the camera. "But see, I've already got it."

A benevolent smile spread across Khon's face, wrinkling the map of India. "Mr. Clarke, if we can just wait a minute longer . . ."

As abrupt as a kernel of popcorn bursting, a second small video box popped open on the other side of the crown. But instead of a second live video feed, it contained only a generic head-and-shoulders participant icon. Below the box appeared the names:

KHUN APIWAT ETERNITY
& KHUN BOBO ETERNITY.
LOTUS CREATIONS CO.

Good, so the actual Lotus had arrived. But those names, the Eternity Brothers? Kinda sounded like an Asian comedy team.

Khon appeared relieved. "Good. There they are. The Eternity Brothers are joining us from Biti, far upcountry. High mountains surround their rural town in a peaceful green valley. Biti has no internet, naturally, so they are linking in via basic phone patch. No video."

Naturally no internet?

Khon's tone dropped an octave as he began to chatter in the local dialect. Two other voices responded over a crackling phone line that regularly broke up.

*"*They apologize for their humble situation and beg your indulgence, Khun Lew. Oh, may we address you that way? *Khun* Lew feels much friendlier than *Mr. Clarke*."

"Of course." Nice people.

"But regardless of their circumstances, the brothers promise to ensure their humble company meets all your needs."

"Their company?"

"Indeed, sir! The brothers completely own Lotus, with head office and facilities in Biti."

Hmm. Lew mulled that over. An international export company, head office and factory, all buried deep in the sticks of rural Asia? How could that even work? He rubbed his forehead and made an unintended sour face. "Guess I don't quite get your whole setup over there."

Khon babbled something in their exotic language and it triggered a gale of responding laughter, booming across the Pacific. Lew muted the teleconference, looked over at Sal and covered his mouth. "Like, what the actual fuck, Sal, you know? And all the private chit-chat and asides in their language. Seems rude, no?"

"I know, Lew. Dunno." Sal shrugged and Lew unmuted.

"Mr. Clarke, the brothers are far up-country, in Inner Amazia, and speak no English. Hence, the job of Asiatic Media, here in the capital, is liaison. To provide their face to the world."

"So they are in Biti and you are in Ruangbang, the capital."

"Correct. You really must visit here. RB now has several modern hotels, one even with satellite TV! But still virtually no internet anywhere in Amazia. Since that's a must for a public relations company, Asiatic has our own private arrangement by satellite." Khon smiled. "Did you like the website and videos we created for Lotus?"

"Yes, a great sales pitch. Impressive." Lew and Sal again made quick eye contact, off camera, communicating mutual surprise. This whole teleconference with its unexpected twists was starting to have a *Twilight Zone* feel. Lew wouldn't have blinked if Rod Serling popped up in a third video box, smoking a Chesterfield.

"But I am surprised, Mr. Khon, that a company with global export ambitions, like Lotus, isn't also located in the capital."

Khon's translation spurred a fresh round of soft chuckles. Well, they certainly sounded like agreeable partners, almost jolly. The Kingdom's language seemed a flood of short syllables interspersed with tongue clicks and glottal stops popping like bubbles.

Khon translated. "Biti is indeed a small rural place, a little backward, but the brothers cannot bear to leave their home. So Lotus must be there. But they guarantee when you visit, you'll have a wonderful time. You'll love it there. Like paradise."

Lew played along. "I also look forward to that. Are domestic air connections good, from the capital up to Biti?"

Khon nodded and smiled, as if agreeing, so his next words surprised Lew. "Actually there is *no* internal air service in Amazia. The best way to Biti is by overnight mail train."

No, thanks. And why was Khon nodding *yes* when saying *no*? Though oddly charming, these Amazia folk were definitely unusual. The yawning cultural gap was throwing Lew off balance, so far. Working together might prove a challenge.

"Well," Lew replied, noncommittal, "they say there's nothing like a good train ride."

"And the overnight mail express is fast," Khon continued. "Only twelve hours!"

But in so flea-sized a place, how could it take twelve hours to get *anywhere*? But enough already with the ice-breaking idle chit-chat; Lew steered the conversation back to business.

"Mr. Khon, tell them I am delighted the Lotus owners are on the call, as I always prefer to deal with principals. And advise them, in the strongest possible terms, how enthusiastic I am to become their sole partner for North America. I am completely ready to go, right away, and money is no problem. All funding is already in hand."

As Khon translated, the brothers interjected *oh's, ah's* and soft tongue-clicking noises.

Lew pushed ahead. "They've already seen my initial proposal, documenting my rock-solid business credentials, so I won't waste time with any false humility. Unhelpful. My record clearly shows that, as Mega's top product innovator, I'd be their ideal partner for America."

Khon translated and the brothers burbled a response. "They are curious, Khun Lew, why the globally famous Mega Industries is interested in their humble products."

Lew was ready for that one. Careful. "Please be very clear, friends, I do *not* represent Mega today. I am speaking on my own behalf. After launching so many successes for Mega, it was time to strike off on my own. And this opportunity with Lotus is perfect. I predict an unbeatable partnership. Once, of course, both sides complete the usual due diligence."

Khon looked puzzled. "Do *what*, Mr. Clarke?"

Lew chuckled. "Due diligence. That just means both sides are allowed to verify the other's claims. Nothing difficult. Lotus would assist me to check them out further, and vice versa. I need to confirm your products are as superb as they *appear* online. And that supply will be reliable. As prospective partners, we must each also prove financial reliability and provide appropriate guarantees. Plus all the things that normally go into a basic contract. You know, like international arbitration, things like that. Nothing unusual, just normal business practice."

"Hmm," Khon said. "I see."

He cleared his throat and began a lengthy sidebar with the Eternity Brothers. Their exotic language filled the air with soft clicks and pops, sounding a bit like an antique film projector. Then one of the brothers lowered his tone and launched into a monologue.

Giggling preliminaries were clearly over and Lew read the vibe. This was the serious stuff. So he opened a bottle of water and waited patiently, giving Lotus room, letting the whole thing breathe a little.

He looked over at Sal, who just rolled his eyes. Both had already been here, done this, so many times before.

The Lotus sidebar discussion ebbed at last and Khon cleared his throat. "Mr. Clarke, thank you for your patience. This, the brothers say, is the sign of a good partner."

"Happy to oblige. This first meeting has been excellent—very helpful! Shall we discuss next steps?"

"Well, actually, sir—"

"Please." Lew smiled and held a hand up to the camera. "I suggest that as soon as possible, we should meet in person. Perhaps bring our legal teams together. I trust you are as serious as I am, about speeding this along. Maybe a week from now at a mutually convenient central location, say, Tokyo? Singapore or Hong Kong are also fine. You decide—whichever has the best flights from Amazia."

"Yes, Mr. Clarke, but—"

Lew smiled and barreled ahead. Having done so many prior deals, he knew what was now needed and wanted to direct this part of the program.

"And in the meantime, perhaps Lotus can forward its boilerplate partnership contract to me—the one for exclusive national agencies? My lawyers can quickly vet it. Naturally, also feel free to request any documents or information the brothers need from me."

"Yes, sir, and thank you. I shall advise the brothers." Khon started translating but seemed to finish far too quickly. Something felt wrong. How could that brief summary have possibly captured all of Lew's comments, or even the general flavor? Listening carefully, he hadn't heard anything remotely sounding like a mention of Tokyo, Singapore, or Hong Kong.

A long silence hung in the air, broken only when Apiwat and Bobo spat out a couple monosyllables at Khon, who coughed and fiddled with the neckline on his vermillion gown. He scratched at the Texas blotch and wiped perspiration from his top lip.

"Mr. Clarke, the brothers thank you sincerely for making this call. And also for your valuable ideas. They were very much appreciated."

That sounded strange. It was a tone Lew didn't often hear and at first couldn't decode. But then in a heartbeat he recognized it as possibly the sound of impending rejection.

Shit! They were softening him up for the bad news.

Where did he go wrong? Did they detect his desperation? Or perhaps had they actually wanted a deal with Mega, not him? He pasted a grin on his face and bravely tried to ignore the odor of approaching doom.

"Well, friends, equally, my thanks to all of you."

A smile crinkled Khon's face. Lew had read that a smile in Southeast Asia might mean anything. They could be angry, sad or placating smiles. Even fake-happy smiles, used during disasters. All required educated interpretation.

"Having digested your suggestions, Khun Lew, the brothers now wish to share *their* thoughts. For your kind consideration."

"Fine." Lew nodded back, nothing really to lose anymore. But man, these guys were really making a nine-course meal out of saying *no*.

The usually soft-voiced brothers began to bark out a torrent of comments. The tone confused Lew. Were they angry, excited, or what? Couldn't tell. Maybe they were pounding Khon with instructions: *Don't forget this. Be sure to tell him that.*

Khon for the first time appeared knocked a bit off balance, even unnerved. He quietly reached for a glass of water and took several slow slips. Stalling, but why? Then he coughed into his handkerchief and folded it up neatly.

Finally, he looked ready and Lew braced for the bad news.

"Mr. Clarke," Khon said in a wobbly voice, "the Eternity Brothers have ordered me to advise you that today was our *final* meeting."

So there it was. Rejection! Lew felt absolutely numb, dumbstruck, while Sal gasped in disbelief. Lew inhaled deeply, calming himself, and found his voice.

"Khun Khon, I . . . I really don't quite understand! Honestly. Up until just now, I thought it all was going splendidly. How can Lotus just abruptly reject me?" He opened a bottle of water to take a swig but just spilled it on his shirt. Everything was going wrong.

This venture that had promised him possible resurrection, a glorious new way forward, was suddenly dead.

Once Khon translated Lew's protests to the brothers, all three Amaza burst out laughing. Khon's grinning face filled his video box.

In the corner, Sal slammed the leather couch with his palm. "Wow, chief, these bastards are cold." He didn't even bother to mute.

"The coldest," Lew agreed. "They are quite *enjoying* this, crushing my hopes." Why had they even bothered inviting him to phone? Lew stood up, embarrassment and rage coloring his face pink. It was time to end this humiliation. He reached out to click off the video call.

"Wait, Mr. Clarke. Stop!" Khon called out. "What are you doing, sir? Please relax, dear friend, and hear us out." The man patted palms downward in a universal calming gesture. "Kindly sit back down . . . please?"

But Lew had already heard enough. Why wait? He really didn't care what the explanation might be. Sal interceded from the corner. "Might as well hear them out, Hoss. Costs nothing and we're already here, anyway."

He was right. "Okay, Khon," Lew said, wearing a pissed-off-as-hell smile. "I'm listening."

Khon grinned wide, looking unperturbed. "To summarize, Khun Lew. The brothers were delighted with today's meeting and feel, like you, it went extremely well."

None of that made even a mouse turd of sense. "Great. So why are they ending our chances at a partnership?"

"What?" Khon raised his chin and frowned. He paused and stared across the Pacific into Lew's eyes, sighing. Confusion clouded his face until his mouth fell open in undisguised surprise. "Oh, my goodness. I see!" His expression morphed into a happy smile. "Khun Lew, please forgive me! I'm so sorry but only now do I realize there's been serious miscommunication, from a language or culture gap."

Khon broke off and narrated a quick play-by-play in the Amaza tongue to the brothers, who tittered appreciatively.

"It appears you have totally misunderstood us! Today is the *final* meeting, sir, only because the brothers have already made their decision. They will award you the North American monopoly supply contract. With immediate effect."

"What?" Lew dropped his notepad. "Uh, you mean I win?"

"Precisely."

Down was suddenly up again. "Right away?"

"Quite. From this very moment, should you accept."

Confusion and pleasure collided as a tidal wave of endorphins flooded Lew's system. His fate had just pivoted on a pinhead, whipsawing his emotions. The overwhelming anger and shock of just seconds ago transformed into a buzz of pure joy.

Sal, too, exploded in brief raucous laughter before quickly stifling it.

Lew slowly shook his head and smiled. "I completely missed that they were picking me. But now that you've clarified, Khun Khon, of course I am thrilled. Overjoyed! Please tell the brothers my lawyers—"

"Sorry," Khon cut him off, "and excuse me, but no lawyers will be involved."

What? Words failed Lew. He stood there mute with his mouth open.

Reading his concern, Khon launched into a backgrounder. "We have no such entities in the Kingdom, sir. No lawyers or courts. That is simply not our way. There are no contracts or written laws. Please do not take this as a rejection of your Western ways. Those concepts simply do not exist here and make no sense to us, like a language we cannot speak."

Lew rubbed his face. "Then how does anything work?"

Khon chuckled. "Surprisingly well. People naturally DO agree on things, all the time, and honor what is agreed. Disputes are so rare as to virtually be nonexistent."

That sounded like crazy talk. A hermit kingdom with no lawyers? For a split second, Lew wondered if he actually dreaming or hallucinating. Amazia seemed to follow common law on steroids, with a population so ethical that courts were unnecessary to enforce anything.

Okaaaay?

"Honestly, Khon, I don't like lawyers much, either. So maybe Amazia's got a good idea there. But in America they are still a necessary evil. So how—?"

"Oh, Khun Lew, it works surprisingly well. We have a saying here, and perhaps it will help you. We say: *Don't think so much.*"

Right, there's the answer, all right. Just stop thinking, go with the flow and get carved up in this deal. No, Lew was having none of that.

"But for your comfort," Khon continued, "we could always write up a document of sorts, just to make you happy. It would describe our mutual understanding, like a memorandum from our meeting. But remember: it is not, nor can ever be, an enforceable contract. Not in any way. Because—"

"I know. Contracts do not exist in Amazia."

Khon smiled.

Lew thought for a moment. "Fine. So what about police?"

"Now, those we actually have. A few. But nobody ever gets arrested here, like in American movies. Our police are more like social helpers."

Lew digested the fast-arriving information and Khon just barreled ahead. "But back to that possible memorandum, Khun Lew? Both sides are free to sign, or not. Though it really makes no difference —"

"I know: because there are *no laws* and the memo is *not a contract.*"

"Perfect, you completely understand. We are grateful our new partner respects and understands our ways."

Lew nodded with a noncommittal smile and fought off a small, rising fear. Could this all be an elaborate practical joke? He skimmed a quick mental list of candidate pranksters (both friends and former business foes) but none had the capacity to pull off something quite so brilliant and quirky. Pure fantasyland stuff that felt real.

"You see, we Amaza value integrity higher than any other virtue. A foundational belief is that once we commit to another (like in a business arrangement), our souls become inextricably joined. Bound together in a way far more powerful or important than mere words on paper."

Nope, this was no hoax, it was real, all right. Real crazy. Sal let out a huge stage sigh and Lew gestured him to shush.

"Mr. Khon, though I don't yet entirely follow, what does *Lotus* think are our next steps?" This all felt surreal, like Lew was listening to somebody else speak with his own voice.

"The next step comes now, Khun Lew. Time for your final decision and commitment. The brothers already totally commit to you and pray you are also equally ready."

A little dazed, Lew shook his head in disbelief, chuckling quietly. "So from this moment on, both sides would be bound and I would be the exclusive North America distributor for those astonishing Lotus products? Just like that?"

"Yes, sir. Just like that."

Khon abruptly motioned Lew, almost comically, closer to the camera. He dropped his tone and spoke quietly, almost like a conspirator. "I have temporarily muted the brothers for this next part. They don't know I am telling you this, but it only seems fair you clearly understand."

Oh good. A final juicy twist. "And what might that be, Khun Khon?"

"Just that if you are cannot commit right now, a second video conference is scheduled for the North America partnership in thirty minutes. What you Americans call, I think, a *fallback position.* So this really is your decision deadline, sir."

Lew gulped. Wow, for such sweet-sounding guys they sure played hardball.

Then Khon unmuted and picked up a thick felt-tip pen, and wrote something on a sheet of paper that he held up to the camera. "And this, sir, is the amount you must immediately wire transfer, on an irrevocable basis, to the Royal Bank of Amazia, Ruangbang branch, paid to the account of Lotus Creations Co."

The enormity of the abrupt demand—an eight-figure sum in US dollars!—floored Lew and made his mouth go dry. Just short of his total personal net worth, built over a decade of ultra-generous compensation at Mega. Stock options, huge salary, all of that. He coughed. "B-but I, I—"

"And that payment, sir, must be received here within the next twelve hours."

That meant at opening of business early next morning, New York time.

"Yes, but—"

"It is a large sum, we understand, but that amount fully prepays your first five years of supply at the mandatory annual minimum number of units." As Khon stared out from the screen, it felt as if his eyes were probing Lew's very soul. "So, we need your decision, please. Now, Khun Lew. Do you agree to be our new partner?"

The room fell silent, other than the sound of the air conditioning and a soft mumbling between the brothers, from ten thousand miles away. Lew looked over at Sal on the sofa, hoping for something helpful—anything!—but his friend just leaned back and softly groaned, an arm covering his eyes.

Throughout his business career Lew had always been prudent and disciplined, never rushing into decisions, with a well-deserved reputation as a careful and stubborn negotiator. Dispassionate and methodical, deeply patient, he typically explored hundreds of opportunities to locate a single winner.

It was just his nature to resist being stampeded into anything—especially a deal as personally important as this one.

But this night, something weird happened and Lew ignored his principles and virtually everything he believed in. He just went with his gut. Surely he could find a workaround, later, for his significant legal concerns.

"Okay, gents," he grinned, "I'm in. You've got yourselves a deal!"

CHAPTER SEVEN
Avian Luxury Lift-off

Though the hour was late, Lew and Sal sat at the hotel lobby bar doing a postmortem, rerunning every detail from the video call. Sal smiled brightly but kept shaking his head. "Dude, you *do* realize what just happened up there, right?"

"Affirmative, Little Grasshopper." Deep inside, Lew fully understood. It was so unlike him to accept such harsh terms, and on the spot, almost by sheer impulse. Those humiliating months on DFA must have really rocked his confidence and eroded his standards. But other than Amazia, he had no options. The quiver was empty.

"I kinda folded, huh?"

"Totally—like the cheap bamboo parasol in a lady drink."

"You think I was bamboozled." Lew loved that word.

"Ha! Dunno, but you were like Lotus' little bitch in there tonight, dawg." Sal smirked. "Appropriate venue, the Dog Pound."

They clinked beers. "Thanks, Sal. You were never one to spare my feelings."

Sal shrugged. "But to be honest, my spider sense is tingling a little. Maybe you got reeeal lucky. Either that, or it's a total disaster."

"No middle ground?"

"None whatsoever." Sal made an 'O' with his thumb and forefinger.

Lew raised his eyes, pantomimed a prayer, and then glanced back at Sal. "So what about you, still in?"

Sal gulped his draft. "Sorry, Hoss," he said, his voice weakening, "but I gotta pass."

That came as a slap. "But Sal, you're my wingman! Can't leave you behind." Couldn't he see the incredible upside? If this was another Sal joke, it wasn't funny.

"It's not me, man, it's the wife. Can't pour our life savings into a cockamamie Asian business scheme. She would hang me by the *huevos*."

Lew leaned in. "Hey, this is no *scheme*, you know that. Totally new product, big unmet market, North American monopoly, huge profit on every sale. What are you missing?"

Sal tapped a cigarette and flicked his lighter, his face blank.

Lew pushed on. "Honestly, when has my intuition missed?"

Sal shrugged. "I know. But all our cash is tied up. We just signed for a flashy new apartment." He grandly waved a hand through the air. "Park Avenue."

That came as little surprise. Ever since Sal married, things for him had drifted in the understandable direction of security and stability, and kudos to him for succeeding in staying happily married . . . something Lew couldn't claim.

"Congrats, but don't miss out on the biggest opportunity of your life."

Sal shook his head. "Besides, I can't even *begin* to think about quitting Mega. Annual option awards just around the corner. And my girl really digs being married to a high-powered exec. Mucho corporate status and all."

Lew smiled. "So what you're really saying is that, after all this time, Marissa still hasn't figured out what a total bozo she married?"

"Absolutely no clue." Sal giggled with obvious relief. "You got it, chief. Knew you'd understand." They hoisted mugs and their laughter broke the thin icy coating that had started to form over their conversation.

"Well relax, because this doesn't require *any* of your money, Sal, at least not for now. I'm taking the entire financial plunge on my own. Not only that, I don't want you quitting Mega, either. Not yet. Just quietly join me on the side. Part-time gig, no risk at all."

Sal thumped the table. "Well hot damn, amigo, why didn't you say that before?"

"Look, you knucklehead, I really need you with me and the train's leaving the station. Don't make me beg."

Sal began to visibly bounce from glee or nervous energy. "Well, under such terms, how can I *not* get on board? So I still show up at Mega—"

"Correct, every day."

"—but on the side, actually work at your baby company, *Bird Mansions R Us?*"

"*Our* baby company."

"Hmm?"

"And once sales start to roll and the business stabilizes, you can quit Mega then and join me full-time. And later still, if things break right, you'll get your own slice of equity."

They shook hands.

"So think up a nice title for yourself, partner. Something impressive like President? COO? Doesn't matter, whatever gets you hard, Sal. You're gonna be my right hand."

Lew phoned Joel Platt at Morgan Stanley early the next morning to open an irrevocable letter of credit to pay Lotus. The massive sum wiped out his stock portfolio and cash accounts. But what else could he do? For Lew, forward motion was as necessary as oxygen. Without Lotus, he only saw a stone-cold dead man in the mirror.

So he flipped the switch and was back in business, but this time on his own behalf, tethered to a mysterious supplier hidden away in some Asian jungle. The incredible promise and equally frightening risk took his breath away, but it felt utterly liberating to just dive in like that, head first.

The registration papers for the new private limited company, AVIAN LUXURY INC., described bright hopes:

"Avian Luxury Inc. exclusively supplies ultra-high end lawn decorations across North America, created in artisan workshops in

Southeast Asia. These spectacular works of art, designed to thrill, are manufactured to the highest standards. In serving America's wealthiest households, Avian defines and dominates an entirely new market. Like fine sculpture, our products are works of art to highlight sumptuous estates as birdhouses, gazebos, fountains and shrines. Distribution is via home builders, home improvement retailers, landscapers and direct sales."

Not surprisingly, those first days the fledgling business struggled to get off the ground. Communication with the overseas supplier was spotty and Lotus only replied after long delays, with emails that were terse and confusing. Lew blamed the language gap and hoped for the best. Phone communication was nonexistent. The number used for the Lotus video conference suddenly dropped out of service and no substitute was provided.

Against that backdrop, Lew's anxiety notched higher by the day. In his desperation, had he fallen victim to an elaborate scam? He prayed not. Perhaps business in Amazia just ground along at a slower pace, governed by different rules.

Sleep again eluded him. During the wee hours, he paced the hardwood floors of his deluxe flat, his mind ablaze with questions and concerns. If he *had* been conned—and that suspicion gained traction by the day—his life was essentially over. But if all went according to plan, the first import shipment would arrive from Amazia in ninety days.

Khon may have recommended he not overthink things, but Lew found it beneficial to keep his mind crowded with work, staying immersed in the foundling enterprise's daily struggles.

Thank heavens he insisted Sal hang onto his job at Mega. No matter what, at least his friend would survive.

The two scoured northern New Jersey like a pair of wandering gypsies and finally spotted a perfect location for the warehouse headquarters. Roomy but austere, the corrugated steel building bore a pronounced 1950s industrial look but was affordable, instantly available, and large enough for even their most ambitious plans.

They modified the building on the fly—no time for grand architectural drawings—and hived out areas on the ground floor for uncrating, inspection, and temporary storage of the imports, plus another section to prep parcels for onward shipment.

A creaky iron stairwell led to the second floor where simple glass and plasterboard offices ran the length of the back wall, hovering halfway out over the warehouse and providing a bird's-eye view of the action below.

Lew scrambled to fund the building and found the solution with Mega, negotiating a final severance package at thirty-six months of his massive former salary. Mega's lawyers were happy to see the last of him but, in a parting shot, forced him to sign papers covering every imaginable contingency. In the future, he'd need approval just to fart in the general direction of Mega Tower. But he signed, anyway.

Sal proved to be a godsend. Generous in his support and companionship, the gentle giant kept Lew emotionally afloat during these perilous times. Each day he cadged an increasing number of hours from Mega to work late into the night, alongside Lew, in their second-floor office. The two chipped away at a mountain of tasks to raise the wobbly new business.

They erected a world wall map to track the transit of their import containers across the Pacific, and marked it with colored pins.

One morning a short, exhilarating email from Lotus advised the first container had loaded onto a vessel and was already on the water. Thus began a glacially slow transit from Southeast Asia across the Pacific, through the Panama Canal, and up the East Coast. Sal was jones-ing like a crack addict and constantly phoned the shipping company or checked online for updates. Then he would make a show of advancing the colored pins to their real-time spots.

The dots inched across the map so slowly that Lew feared something was amiss. Had Lotus relegated their precious cargo to unreliable, bargain freighters?

But after weeks of slow but relentless eastbound progress, word arrived one afternoon that the first container was just days away from Port of Newark.

Sal moved the pins, did a fist pump and whooped it up. "Here we go, babe! First cargo soon and after that, a parade, one unloading every few days." The trail of pins on the map proved that point. Sal fixed Lew with an intent stare. "So it must be time."

"For?"

"You know what for, Hoss. Come on! Time for me to jettison Mega and tell those geriatric dinosaurs to get bent."

"Whoa, slow your roll, Sal. Not just yet. And when the time *does* come, leave that Mega bridge unburnt, okay? May need it later."

Sal grimaced like Lew was crazy. Then he grinned and raised his arms high in the air, looking like Moses coming down the mountain to address the Israelites. "Amigo, we're about to hit the big time, right now. I'm a true believer, Lew."

Lew smiled. Couldn't help but love his friend. "Great, but still, please promise you won't quit Mega until after our rocket blasts off and safely exits the stratosphere."

Sal scowled. "Why you doin' me like that?"

"It's not for you, Sal, as much as the nice lady you live with, and her expensive new apartment. So maintain that Mega umbilical, at least for now. If the worst thing happens, only one of us goes down."

"Boss, ain't nobody *going down*. What are we, couple of Thai hookers?"

"No. You'd starve. Ugliest street walker ever!" Lew smirked. "But promise me you'll stay tethered to the mother ship just a little longer. You can always hire me back, if things goes sour here."

"Sorry, amigo, but no can do. Our standards at Mega are too high."

Lew wadded up a scrap of paper and hit Sal square.

"Ow!" He rubbed his forehead. "Listen, it's about T-minus sixty seconds before launch. I'll wait till after we jettison the booster rockets, but no longer. Then I quit Mega—"

"In the *nicest* possible way."

"Sweet as a Hershey's Kiss."

Lew nodded.

"And then climb fully aboard the Good Spaceship Avian." Sal paused for drama. "And at that point, I obtain my *very own* little slice of ownership. That work?"

They sealed their agreement with a two-fisted handshake.

Early one morning, Lew hunched at the desk in their stark office, all glass and white fiberboard under bright fluorescent light racks, and drank deli coffee from a blue paper cup. Dark rings under his eyes attested to months of anxiety and lost sleep.

He glanced out the window and spotted his partner arriving.

Even Sal showed the wear from unremitting stress, looking noticeably slimmer after working night and day to juggle two demanding jobs. The upstairs office shook with every step as he trudged up the metal staircase.

He entered and with a loud sigh collapsed into the chair at the desk beside Lew's.

Then, as if right on cue, his phone rang.

"Hey, yeah, good morning. Avian Luxury! Salvatore Weissman speaking." He sleepily smiled at Lew and raked a meaty hand through his hair. His eyes widened. "What, that for sure? Great! What time again?" He shook his head a little, giggling. "Oh, and the directions, please?" He reached into the dustbin and uncrumpled the white paper bag from Lew's coffee and Danish. "Yup, got it," he said, scribbling on it with a broken pencil stub. "See you later. On our way! And thanks again."

He hung up and shot Lew a crocodile grin.

"What?" growled Lew. Seven a.m. was way too early for the hyper-Sal show.

His huge friend quietly rose to sit on the corner of Lew's desk and placed a meaty paw on his shoulder. He squeezed. "Podner, that was the port. Today's our day."

Lew sat straight up. "You mean—?"

"Yup. The freakin' Amazia eagle has landed! The *SS Forever Golden* offloads this afternoon at Newark with our first container on board. Probably pop open our first crate by tonight."

Such news! Lew felt his heart might explode.

The two men bubbled like teenagers, laughing and joking as they flew around the office collecting documents for the port. Both wanted to personally witness the historic first cargo. In the future, professionals could handle things.

They barreled down the metal stairs, all noise and excitement, and instructed warehouse staff to stand by. Finally *real* work later that day, after months of make-work. The two bolted out to the parking lot to Sal's flaming yellow vintage roadster.

His beloved toy was a 1960 Triumph TR-3, fully restored to gem mint condition. It never failed to amuse Lew, watching his sizable friend slowly squeeze himself behind the tiny sports car's steering wheel. Getting out, Sal always had a groove pressed into his shirt and gut.

The sexy mechanical growl of the car's four-cylinder power plant filled the cabin under a black vinyl convertible roof. Swerving from lane to lane, the compact little vehicle seemed to find every bump and pothole in New Jersey.

All the way to the port, Lew's heart rode high in his chest, threatening to choke him. Today would finally reveal if he had a chance to save himself, or if he had forever buggered up his life. He'd know as soon as he laid hands on the goods.

The two rank amateurs navigated their way around the container terminal. Everything was new to them, the customs procedures and protocols, and their printouts from the web were woefully inadequate guidance. But after ninety minutes of crawling through the bureaucratic maze, they at last stood beside a uniformed customs agent who pointed at the top box in a half-unloaded stack. "That one up there is yours."

The large brown metal container was caked in rust. A winch

lifted the oblong box from the vessel and sent it sailing through the air. Sal aimed his chin at the purple, orange and green insignia at one corner. "Either that's the Amazia flag or the container is full of Mardi Gras party decorations. And see that king's crown logo on the flag? Means our birdhouses are royal, man."

Lew buzzed with nervous energy as Sal, too, danced from foot to foot like a first-grader needing to pee.

The shipping container touched down with a dull metallic *thunk*. A customs agent opened an end panel, revealing myriad wooden shipping cartons stacked inside—some were cubes, others rectangles, each unique in size and hue and stacked close as Jenga blocks. The boxes fit together tightly, like a giant 3D jigsaw puzzle.

Lew's pulse raced like a nine-year-old on his first roller coaster ride. This was actually happening! His next act—Lew 2.0—was indeed underway. He shook his head.

"Unbelievable, Sal, but even the shipping crates are amazing. Beyond gorgeous."

They followed the agent back to an office where they initialed and signed documents until their hands ached. At the same time, their container was being fastened atop a hauler's trailer for the trip back to Avian's warehouse.

The port process was fairly painless. The inspectors didn't even pry open any of the individual wooden shipping cartons, to examine the actual goods being imported. A friendly port employee advised that, for future cargoes, occasional spot checks would suffice.

Was Lew supposed to tip this guy or what? "Here," he said, palming a Benjamin. "Lunch on us." It was already afternoon and the port worker gave him a funny smile. Lew winked. "Or maybe beers for the boys, after work?"

They waited for the truck back at the warehouse while workers just milled around. Finally a horn blared, jarring them all. A red light started to flash on the far wall as the massive segmented garage-style door began to roll up, squeaking.

Their first shipment! Lew and Sal clanged down the metal

staircase to join the action while the truck slowly backed into the warehouse, pinging a loud reverse gear warning. Once the tires touched yellow paint markers, a worker yelled "ho!" and air brakes were set with a loud gasp.

Odd but the container looked so much larger now than back at the port. The foreman hopped onto the truck's pneumatic lift and rode to deck level, where he swung the container door open, screeching on rusty hinges.

The wooden crates visible in the open container door were an amazing visual mosaic of beautiful tropical hardwood boxes of all sizes and shapes, carefully interlaced with such precision that not even a knife's edge could be inserted between any two. They precisely filled the truck compartment, right up against the walls.

"Whoa, Sal, you seein' this?"

It was again striking how the shipping boxes themselves were so lovely they could have been the treasure, not their contents.

"Fuckin' A, dawg. Amazing." Sal's eyes shone bright.

A yellow forklift carefully slid its prongs under a pallet to extract the first group of crates, including a cube the size of a jumbo refrigerator with extraordinary red-brown wood grain swirls like modern art. Nervous laughter electrified the place.

Once the fork-lift set the crate down on the cement, workers descended like piranhas attacking a wounded cow. They ran their hands over the smooth surfaces and appraised its beauty up close.

"Mind-blowing." Lew breathed in deep while gliding a hand over the shining surface. He had to remind himself this was just a shipping crate, something that usually got thrown away, but its finish was superior to fine furniture.

"I can't even find the nails sealing the crate," Sal said. "All hidden away and polished. Even these shipping boxes look *muy* valuable."

The moment of truth arrived. Lew signaled to a young, mustachioed warehouse worker to unseal the first crate. The man trudged over, brandishing a rusty crowbar, looking all business and in a hurry to please.

Lew trotted over and grabbed the crowbar. "Hey, buddy, do me a favor and go *real* easy. Don't use this thing." He patted the shocked worker's shoulder. "Pretend you're not just pulling nails. More like tweezing splinters from the paw of your girlfriend's kitty cat. Real gentle, okay?" Lew addressed the group. "Everybody, please, take your time. Marks left on these cabinets will be fireable offenses."

Duly chastened, the fellow resumed his work with an obvious tenderness. He tickled hidden nails from their seats, avoiding even a hint of nicks or scratches. Then he carefully slid the side panel upward within its precise channels, like a window, and lifted it free. He turned, smiled at his bosses, and stepped aside.

An involuntary gasp rose in a chorus. The unexpected perfection of this, the first of the Amazia imports, hit like a trans-Pacific thunderbolt, jolting them all. It felt like witnessing a genuine miracle, no less than the parting the Red Sea or the invention of fire.

Lew drank in the astonishing sight, his synapses firing like Roman candles. The sleek, perfect structure perhaps reminded him of a miniature Taj Mahal. Or was it like the exquisite palace of an ancient Babylonian emperor? Whatever. But to call it a mere lawn decoration or birdhouse seemed almost profane. This magnificent *artifact* boasted the eye-popping wonder of a mini Versailles.

"All good, boss man?" Sal rocked back and forth, chuckling.

"Way beyond good. Holy crap, Sal! What in God's vast creation do we have here?"

"Know what you mean," Sal said. "It's like if the richest ruler on earth, back in ancient days, had his most skilled artists build his princess the grandest dollhouse in the world. No holds barred. Sky's the limit." Lew liked that analogy.

They approached gingerly, carefully shuffling forward as if fearing the floor might suddenly open to swallow them. Absorbing it all, their eyes were big, black, and dilated.

The grand cubic ornament resembled a marble temple densely packed with extravagant spires, stupas and arches, under a central peaked roof. The intricacy challenged the imagination.

Lew's business sense intruded upon his artistic wonderment. What would it cost to duplicate this perfection at a US factory? He estimated and revised but finally quit, unable to get below $3500 apiece. He made a mental note to rethink their planned retail prices. Way too low!

They carefully opened more crates and found—amazingly—each was custom-built and unique, a miniature architectural gem. It was as if artisans in Amazia were free to follow their own creative muses, unencumbered by blueprints or designs.

"Each is spectacular," Sal commented. "And one of a kind."

Lew nodded. "But how? I can't explain it."

Sal shrugged. "Remember that video, how isolated the jungle factory looked? Maybe, tucked away in that hermit kingdom, they have developed their own technologies. What if their manufacturing methods are so unique as to be almost magical?"

Lew ran a finger across a rooftop. "Whatever, the quality is friggin' unbelievable!"

"Boss, customers are gonna go wild for these." Lew just smiled.

Avian products exploded onto the market, driven by word of mouth that triggered a stampede by desperate, luxury estate owners.

One morning, the two entrepreneurs leaned against their glass office wall watching the bustling warehouse below. Lew gave off a happy sigh. "And to think, Sal, I feared good fortune might never shine on me again."

"Not me, dawg. Never doubted."

"At first, with the imports arriving and initial stock just piling up in the warehouse, I felt a touch of panic. But once word got out, the retailers began to line up and our product began to fly out the door. That's when I knew we were in for a rocket ride."

"And now," Sal said, grinning, "sales are moving faster than we can process the orders and bank the money! With nothing else like these, anywhere, we'll have no competition for years."

Lew playfully knuckled Sal's ribs. "Thanks for your faith, for climbing on board like you did. Never coulda got here without you."

"And now I'm *totally* committed, too, after quitting Mega last week." Sal flashed a fake grimace but then smiled. "I can tell you this now—back when we first got going, Marissa sure didn't like it. Even threatened to divorce me, one sleepless night."

"Really?"

"But she never meant it. Everything's cool now."

"Good." Lew handed him an envelope. "Perhaps this will help."

"What's that? You paying me in lottery tickets now, or maybe French postcards?" Sal stuck a thumb under the envelope flap.

"In there is your own personal goldmine, pal. Our lawyers are still finalizing the paperwork, but this offers you a ten percent equity share in Avian Luxury. Assuming you still want to buy in . . ." Sal's price was substantial but still an utter gift, based on an early valuation that ignored Avian's now-evident, massive growth just ahead.

"Woo-hoo!" Sal yelped as he hugged Lew, pounding his back. He fanned himself with the envelope. "You'll never regret it, bro. I'll make sure of that."

Avian Luxury was primed to spew out money for its owners—more than anyone ever dared imagine. And it was all theirs.

CHAPTER EIGHT
Mean-Spirited

Before long, with demand soaring beyond expectations, Avian operated 24/7. Lew and Sal virtually lived in the office and rode a fizzy adrenaline high, existing on burgers, Chinese takeout and delivered pizza. As fast as containers could arrive from overseas, they were assembled into lots and shipped across the country

Every day delivered fresh problems and new thrills, so they winged a lot of creative solutions and never looked back. Their infant company had a voracious appetite for ever more equipment, back office systems, delivery capability and staff. And everything needed to be done *yesterday*. So whenever possible, they called in favors.

To recruit sales staff, they leaned on an old friend from Harvard Business School. Upon graduating, when Lew and Sal headed off to Mega, Joe Bonzarilla surprised everyone by joining a seamy financial boiler room operation in Jersey City.

Lew challenged it at the time. "Bonzy, you sure? Maybe a big mistake."

"True," his friend replied with a toothy grin. "But on the other hand, if things break right, I'll already bank millions while you and Sal are still shivering on the bottom rungs of Mega's ladder, receiving piss showers from the big dogs."

Laden with incentive clauses, Bonzy's comp package was indeed compelling and he rode the Jersey City opportunity for six years until an SEC bust. Heavy fines were levied but no one did prison time except the owners, a pair of Armenian brothers from

Yerevan.

A year after closure, most of the boiler room sales staff were still on the street and Bonzy was delighted to name names. Avian snapped up some stars and formed a sales team as ruthless as Navy SEALs. They camped in a large office above the warehouse, smoking cigars and swigging icy beers in a frat party atmosphere, as they sat around a massive table and worked phones, feeding off each other's energy. In a room buzzing with telephonic cacophony, with walls covered by maps and whiteboards displaying lists and extravagant diagrams (some obscene), the youthful team worked nonstop, racking up gaudy commissions.

Bonzy also supplied a handful of talented young supply chain managers to oversee fulfillment into key markets—big box home improvement retailers, luxury builders and landscapers. And a trio of tech-savvy grads fresh from B-school formed a unit to do direct marketing. In no time, they were spamming the uber-wealthy in every elite zip code, both online and by physical mail, using customer lists from investment houses and insurance companies.

Lew tracked down a hungry ad agency start-up with in-house video capability and commissioned them to make a spate of bare-bones TV commercials. Before long, viewers of stock market channels or conservative news networks became familiar with Avian's pitch.

A flattering story on the front page of the *Wall Street Journal* "Mansions" section unleashed a fresh wave of buying mania.

As demand boomed, big box retailers engaged in bloodthirsty competition for Avian's limited supply, bidding up prices. The winner finally agreed to purchase product by the full container load, directly from the terminal, using their own trucks and rail cars.

At that point, Avian officially entered capitalist nirvana, a rare sector in business heaven where massive sales required no actual effort. "Our biggest problem when selling by the full container, ex-Newark, is writer's cramp," Lew half-joked. "Endorsing all those fat checks."

Whenever media came nosing around for background, Lew loved the publicity but remained tight-lipped about the manufacturing source, nervous about his monopoly supply. Why jinx things? "Our products are produced in our own artisanal workshops in Asia," was all he would say.

The day Emily quit Mega and joined them felt like a new personal high. Right from day one, she got neck-deep in work, never needing instructions. After years working with Lew, she always knew what needed doing, as if she could read his mind. They awarded her a bodacious title—Chief Operating Officer—and wildly compensated her.

But her arrival also significantly raised the stakes for Lew, since she now personally depended on his company. Feeling that obligation, he catapulted into full-on, crazed entrepreneur mode and began often staying overnight in his bare office, sleeping on a cheap black vinyl couch to save time wasted commuting back and forth to Manhattan.

He woke at four one morning and noticed the light already streaming in from Emily's office next door. He rubbed his eyes and wandered over. "Morning, Em. Here already—don't you sleep?"

"More'n you, I bet." She laughed.

"Touché." He smiled and yawned, scratching at his stubble. "Hey, any idea where a guy can get some coffee around here?"

She pursed her lips and stared a lightning bolt at him. "So, boss, is *that* what I look like to you, Mrs. Coffee? Thought I was COO of this cockamamie joint." She smiled. "Just kidding. I need a mug myself. But while I go get us some, take a look at what I found." She slid her tablet computer across the desk. "This'll knock your socks off."

He grinned, anticipating another bush baby video. Emily's latest online infatuation featured impossibly cute sub-Saharan primates with huge eyes and remarkable leaping ability. But instead, a social media group page filled the screen: *Castles for Cardinals.*

Lew swiped through dozens of exuberant posts by Avian customers with photos of their mini-palace birdhouses or temple gazebos. "Holy shit," he mumbled, "a fan club." He tingled with pleasure to see his products as focal points for sumptuous estates across the country, from New England to Washington State and beyond, to private offshore islands.

Short picture captions gushed about the impeccable workmanship. They sounded grateful just for the privilege of buying such exclusive items. Most were deployed according to the original concept, as homes for wild birds, but some of the larger units were put to other uses. Removed from their pedestals and set on the ground, they served as gazebos, fountain bases or luxury abodes for dogs, cats and other pets. Several were perched high atop trees soaring over British Columbia and colonized by golden eagles. Others were used purely for ornamentation, as temple-like centerpieces within spectacular gardens.

Emily returned with Lew's steaming black coffee. He took a gulp and shook his head in disbelief. "Holy crap, Em. Thanks. Absolutely wonderful!"

"This coal tar? Nah, just Folgers."

"No, ha, you know I meant *this*." He handed back the tablet. "Looks like maybe we got some groupies, huh?"

She smiled back with admiration. "No surprise, Lew. And that's why I came here, your impeccable business sense. Imagine poor Mega, letting a star like you get away."

"Aw gosh, ma'am," he said, grinning and pawing the ground like a bashful cowboy.

"Stop it. Really, I mean it, this venture is brilliant. It'll make millions."

"You're almost right, Em. Try adding a *b*."

As often happened, Lew crawled out of bed at 2 a.m. one of those rare nights spent at his flat, unable to sleep. He brewed some coffee, touched his computer screen and the tablet burst to life, drenching the room in color.

The device was remarkable, a monogrammed one-of-a-kind prototype given to him by the chairman of Apple Computer, back when Lew was Mega's tech rainmaker. The Mega/Apple joint venture found the tablet too costly to sell at a profit, with a cost build-up like a European sports car, so Lew wound up with the only one in existence. "Spare parts may be a bitch," joked the Apple CEO.

Lew sipped his coffee and then flashed a few hand gestures that controlled the machine, like sign language for the deaf. Further hand gestures opened the browser and he scanned through a bundle of Avian social media fan groups.

No matter the hour, this was always a pleasant way to start his day—drenched in praise for his company and products. After his career near-death at Mega, this validation was a special joy, reaffirming his self-worth.

The screen showed vivid, high definition photos in intense color, depicting Avian's mock castles, temples and shrines, shimmering at grandiose estates. Humming happily, he sipped and surfed from one site to the next.

But then a single, strangely sour comment stopped him cold, seeming in stark contrast to the usual hoopla and celebration by satisfied owners. Even the title was downbeat: "Lousy Luck in Louisiana."

The writer was the owner of several chains of New Orleans restaurants and bars, using the forum ID of Marty Graw. Marty seemed quite legitimate, the founder of this particular Avian fan forum. Among his photos Lew recognized an early Avian unit he could vaguely recall shipping to Louisiana.

"Sorry to advise, friends, but a run of horrendous luck will keep me away from our forum chats for a while. Just too danged busy addressing some awful problems here. Would you believe all our landscaping suddenly died here at *Swannanoa*, our home estate in

Louisiana? Everything, almost overnight! Now we live in a soggy, smelly, turd-brown world of dead vegetation! And if that's not enough, just yesterday the roof to our main building caved in, forcing us to move out and into our pool house. Nobody deserves such doubly bad luck! But at least *Mockingbird Mansion,* our wonderful little palace for feathered friends, survived."

The poor guy! Lew skimmed through sympathetic responses.

Another forum participant, Lester of the Lakes, replied: "Hey, Marty, misery loves company so maybe this will make you feel better. Sudden horrendous problems have also struck here. Ours is a massive insect infestation at our North Woods estate. Never seen anything like it. Almost overnight, all our buildings and structures were swamped by termites and stink bugs. The place is crawling with them! The exterminators are using so much poison we have to move out for a month. Maybe some of Marty's Louisiana Bad Luck has migrated up here to Minnesota? Haha, just kidding. But at least our Avian mini-palace is still doing just fine. No bugs yet."

Lew sighed. And that, folks, is why one lives in *civilization*, like this luxurious apartment in Manhattan. But still, what an odd coincidence, two customers like that. Yet, with hundreds of active members on that forum, odds were strong a few might experience simultaneous, coincidental bad luck.

But after that, Lew couldn't help lurking around those Avian forums, patrolling for other bad luck stories. Sure enough, he found them. Other freakish incidents. Even though only a tiny sliver from his total customer base was involved, they still bothered him.

The complaints were shocking and colorful. Strange, frightening noises filled homes, day and night. Toilets backed up and pipes burst, creating awful stenches impossible to eliminate. Basements flooded with black muck. Home computer systems permanently crashed and jumbo flat screen televisions suddenly leapt from walls, to shatter in thousands of pieces. Chimneys collapsed and filled elegant living rooms with rubble. Fresh food in refrigerators spoiled in just hours.

Some of the more recent cases were even more troubling, like a monster sinkhole swallowing an entire garage.

Idle speculation began to seize upon the glaring common factor of Avian decorations at the accident sites. "Maybe these birdhouses are dangerous," the initial poster wrote.

A second was quick to chime in. "Their factory is in some Third World place. I read some companies out there grind human bones to make a special, powerful glue. Is that our problem?"

"No, dude," another reacted, "forget that—it's way worse. It's black magic. I worked overseas and know Asian voodoo when I see it. Plenty of those places still have witch doctors."

Lew slammed the table with a fist. "What bullshit!" he grumbled under his breath. Why not blame the myriad *other* common factors at those unlucky places? Didn't all have high exterior walls, lush trees, cedar shingle roofing, private swimming pools, guard houses, electricity, and more? Nobody was blaming any of *those* things. So why pick on us?

Lew became almost addicted to the forums, driven by a morbid curiosity mixed with business prudence. He browsed for untold hours but resisted the urge to jump in with his own comments. Nothing to gain via hostile exchanges with lunatic fringe cases . . . who also happened to be his customers! Rich as hell and otherwise great, but increasingly untethered from reality.

Sal and Emily were equally perturbed and all agreed the worst case would be if this goofy rumor spread beyond the closed-off world of internet forums. If mainstream media were to pick up the story, it could go viral and demand for his products might be destroyed. The entire business could crash.

It reminded Lew of a foolish rumor that spread during pre-internet days, when he was a boy. It alleged that a national hamburger chain was adding ground-up worms to their beef for extra juicy protein. It was utterly outlandish, but the rumor created a huge headache for the business giant. A massive, expensive PR effort eventually quashed the story. Maybe corporate giants had near-unlimited resources for such battles. Lew's little start-up did not.

They tamped down anxiety by reminding themselves this involved only a handful of crackpots. The majority of Avian's customers reported no such problems and were in fact happy to chime-in online and lecture the nut cases to wise up and pipe down.

Lew trawled the websites and monitored the hysteria's slow but relentless growth. A few bizarre new stories popped up by the week, as regular as the sunrise, but so far only property damage was involved. No human injuries.

One morning he arrived at the office and found Sal already at his desk, resting his head atop folded hands and looking morose.

"Hung over, Sal?"

The big guy raised his head with a sour look. "I wish. It's more of that *no bueno* internet bullshit, Lew, and today's load is especially *crapioso*."

"Think I'll give up reading that stuff for Lent, Sal. Obsessing is only getting me down." Lew half-smiled and fired up his computer. "But if you insist, I'll take a look."

He went to the Facebook page Avian started for customer interface and sales. Each day it gathered abundant posts, usually customer praise and thank-you's. But the lead entry that morning, already with a hundred replies, linked over to a forum called *Palaces for Parakeets (P4P),* an affinity group devoted to the clever indoor use of Avian's smallest birdhouses.

Lew clicked the P4P link and forever changed his world.

"Greetings and *sabai dee*," wrote a poster. "My name is Dr. Ueamduean Narathiwat, a professor and citizen of Amazia, a tiny kingdom in Southeast Asia."

Amazia! Goosebumps studded Lew's arms and his heart rate sped up. This was too close to home—he'd worked hard to conceal his manufacturing source, so this had his full attention.

"I am world famous as a top researcher in Asian animism, with a Ph.D. in religious studies and anthropology. Tenured at the

University of Singapore and just back from sabbatical at UC Berkeley. I present my credentials not to boast, but to reassure you I am not just some *crackpot*, as Western people charmingly call eccentrics."

Okay, so Lew was impressed.

"I apologize for coming forward so belatedly, but I only recently learned about the problems experienced by owners of Avian Luxury products. And I am deeply concerned."

Lew's heart jolted. No way was this going to be good.

"Today, on all forums for Avian customers, I am issuing a warning of grave danger, perhaps even mortal, for all owners of these products!"

Sweat beaded on Lew's brow. Sal stood behind him, growling and shaking his head.

"So far, your many incidents of 'bad luck' have only involved property damage, not human life. But don't be lulled into false security. In my professional opinion, this can change at any time and *will*, if left unchecked."

Lew groaned. Great, a nut case with an advanced degree wasn't happy just stirring the shit, he was whipping it to a froth.

The professor shared numerous images that resembled Lew's birdhouses, but looked simpler. "Here are photos from my field research in Myanmar, Cambodia, Laos, Thailand, Amazia, and so forth. Notice how these items resemble your yard decorations?"

Lew gulped, wondering where this was going.

"It is critical for you to understand that these photos are absolutely *not* birdhouses. Oh, no! They are *spirit houses,* dwellings for powerful and potentially dangerous terrestrial beings."

Spirit houses? Lew swallowed but his mouth was powder dry and his stomach clenching with anxiety.

"Across much of Asia, residents believe that powerful beings—wandering spirits—exist nearly everywhere. Lords and guardians of the land where we humans only coexist."

Nonsense! Maybe that was *their* reality-distortion field, but . . .

"In much of Asia, people erect structures like in these photographs, resembling miniature temples or palatial dollhouses, to appease their powerful, invisible co-inhabitants. These spirit houses are respectful invitations to their ethereal neighbors who, I might add, usually *do* move into the dwellings. Often bringing good luck to their human patrons."

The hairs stood straight up on Lew's neck.

"Every day the human host honors the guardian spirits by humbly placing modest offerings at these little shrines—perhaps a small woven basket with a garland of marigolds. A candle, maybe some sweet oil and an incense stick. Symbols of deference, respect and friendliness."

Narathiwat continued. "Generally, both sides understand their roles and life goes on, smoothly. But when powerful beings are crossed, their fury can trigger grievous misfortune."

This felt like a lecture and Lew bristled. If millions in Asia wanted to subscribe to such fantasies, fine, but leave his business out of it.

"Dear friends," wrote Narathiwat, "here is the key point. Such spirits reside *everywhere* around the globe, not just in Asia. Why would they not? And judging from all your reports, clearly they also live in North America and many of you have (quite unintentionally) insulted and been disrespectful to them."

Lew pounded the desktop. "Damn!"

Narathiwat went on. "Please consider. You erected beautiful, inviting dwellings (purchased from Avian) on your land, thereby issuing unspoken invitations for spirits to move in. But then you dishonored and disrespected your invited guests! Did you leave offerings? No. It probably came across like a calculated insult, placing blobs of gooey suet atop their homes or sprinkling sunflower seeds on them, to attract birds. Worse yet, those birds (as your agents) moved in and defecated on the spirits' dwellings! Perhaps you are noticing bird carcasses (more than normal) near your structures?"

Lew sighed and shook his head.

"So all your reported misfortunes? They are not bad luck, no, they are retribution! You have infuriated your local spirits, out of sheer ignorance, not ill will, and picked fights you can never win."

A photo showed an Asian village buried under a tidal wave of mud.

"This is a rural Cambodian town, Tbeng Veng, where all homes were wiped out by a massive mudslide in the 1950s. Up until today, Tbeng Veng was academia's sole documented case of angry, vengeful spirits. This disaster transpired after the town council voted to ban spirit houses (for reasons unknown), forcing villagers to take theirs down. Local spirits, previously honored, were seriously insulted. In the aftermath, half the town perished."

Lew drew in a slow, deep breath.

"So far, none of you have been injured or killed. Thank goodness. But do not therefore assume you will remain safe! Terrestrial spirits generally are peaceful so perhaps your North American spirits are patiently hoping you get the message. But that can change in an instant."

Forum members flooded Dr. Narathiwat with their responses.

Blackbird Bart in Alabama wrote, "So how do we get on their good side, fast? Start putting out candles and oil and flowers? We can do that!"

"Bart," Narathiwat replied, "you all must *immediately* begin to do that, each day, at the very least! And it may still be too late. Other factors may also come in play. For instance, when choosing the spirit house setting, did you select your estate's the most honored location? I suspect not. I doubt most of you would even be able to determine where that is. Did you anoint the spot and seek spiritual permission to build there? Are you ready to stand constant guard and chase birds away from the spirit house, not allowing them to alight? So many other considerations, too. Each case is unique."

The researcher wrapped up. "But whatever you do, friends, please *do not remove* the structures! Never forget the horrible tragedy of Tbeng Veng."

CHAPTER NINE
Wit and Wisdom of Uzzi

Once Dr. Narathiwat arrived on the scene, railing from his ivory tower and throbbing with authority, everything escalated. The specialist apportioned full blame upon Lew's company. "As if our products could trigger bad luck," mumbled Sal.

Complaints grew from Avian customers, some angrier than poked bears. "Time to sue them Avian Luxury sons-a-bitches," yowled a Montana dude ranch operator. "They shouldn't be selling those things! Way too dangerous."

An Everglades resort owner erupted in the same threatening tone. "Seems like fraud, pure and simple, to sell little Asian temples as yard decorations and expose customers to enormous risk! Lord almighty, we've been cold-cocked by evil spirits. Violates our rights as Americans."

Lew was torn over how to proceed. The issue greatly disturbed him, dominating his full attention, but the claims were clearly nonsensical, not even remotely possible. And he was shrewd enough a businessman to know such delusional charges would never survive in court. "Angry spirits wrecked somebody's house, and it's *our* fault?" he muttered. "My ass."

He tried to directly challenge Narathiwat online and anonymously raise doubts about his theories. "Why," Lew typed, "would Asian spirits stow away in shipping containers and make a long voyage across the Pacific to America? They were doing fine back home in Asia."

Narathiwat easily slapped that away. "Sir, please reread my

earlier comments. These spirits are *not* stowaways from Asia, they are *native* to America. Already living there, peacefully, prior to being disturbed."

Lew fired another salvo. "But the number of spirit cases seems incredibly small, almost insignificant, compared to the no-doubt huge number of birdhouses sold by Avian. Why?"

"Good observation," Narathiwat replied. "Perhaps outside Asia, in places traditionally with no human interaction, the spirits' expectations are low. Maybe they perceive non-Asians as less sophisticated in these matters. But once spirit houses were erected in America and used to demean the guardian spirits, that all changed. Their outrage is quite understandable."

Lew was getting nowhere. One more try. "Even assuming terrestrial spirits DO live in North America (most Americans would probably disagree), how do US native spirits even know what those houses are, in order to then get insulted? Up till now, there's never been anything remotely like that here." Typing that, Lew grinned. Got you now, mofo.

But Narathiwat dismissed that with ease. "Why, of course they *know*—why would they not? Don't *you* know, sir, what homes look like in Europe? Or what cars are like in Japan? Or the weather in Africa? Of course, you do. Do not be spirit-phobic, assuming them less intelligent or adept at sharing information than humans. The reverse is probably true." Then Narathiwat's message went dark. "With respect, sir, your arguments seem not completely sincere. So I again warn all other readers, please do not be misled! Do not underestimate the danger you are all in."

Early one morning, Lew was pouring coffee at his luxury apartment when the phone chimed and Sal's picture popped onto the screen.

"Not even five yet," Lew said, groggy after fitful sleep. "Can't this wait?"

"Sorry, boss, but no."

Lew recognized concern in his partner's voice. He set down his porcelain mug. "Okay, Sally Boy, hit me with it."

"Well, I just picked up the PO box mail on my way in to the office."

Fetching the mail at 4:45 a.m.? Good boy, Sal. "And . . .?"

"The usual solicitations and requests for brochures. But also three fat brown envelopes."

Lew's stomach sank. He could guess. "With return addresses from vulture law firms?"

"Yeah. I've browsed them and can summarize the three lawsuits. First one is from a shyster lawyer named Sturgess Gilford. An ambulance chaser."

"Creepy name."

"Yeah. Claims to be a hyper-successful injury litigator in upper New York State. Also says he sent us multiple letters before filing this lawsuit, but that all were ignored."

"That true?"

"Maybe." In these early days of rapid-fire growth, keeping up with Avian's communications was a losing battle and unhinged customer complaints got little priority.

"So what is the problem for Sturgess's client?"

"Oh, the usual. Green goo oozing up from sewer pipes, filling the house."

"And somehow, these plumbing problems are our fault?" Lew slammed a palm down against the kitchen counter and winced.

"Mm-hmm. Dr. Narathiwat's fingerprints (his arguments, actually) are all over these lawsuits. The usual stuff about disrespected spirits and our wanton disregard in not warning customers."

Lew grimaced. "And we never replied to any of these clowns before?"

"Doubtful. Just been filing complaints under 'Crazy Customers.' Remember, Hoss, that was your guidance. Don't give any oxygen to far-fetched claims. Don't even engage. Right?"

"Roger that." Lew sipped his coffee and shook his head. Was this really happening?

"Next lawsuit is from Drew, Drew & Balfour. They represent a woman in La Jolla named Lana Latour—"

"Stop, already. Sounds like either a dirty limerick or a character in a Superman comic. You making this up?"

"No, boss. Sadly, Lana's mansion slid down a cliff into the ocean. Ornery spirits."

Lew snorted a derisive laugh. "You promised a trifecta—"

"Yes, and the third is one helluva story. A potential Netflix miniseries. The firm of Bates, Bean & Perry represents one Mr. Rip Clinton, a Texas rancher with several thousand head of cattle. They suddenly came down with a strange pox diagnosed to be like a strain from Asia, never before seen in America. The animals didn't die but that would have been cheaper. Quarantine and medical treatment is costing Clinton his rear end. And even if the cattle recover, by law the meat can't be sold in the US. And Rip's insurers are declaring *force majeure*."

"So naturally, the bastard wants Avian to pay."

"Yes, please! Untold hundreds of millions should take care of it."

Damages for just those three lawsuits could bankrupt the fledgling company, especially if amplified by punitive penalties. With more cases likely on the way. Lew needed powerful legal help and fast. The best in the business.

"Sal, I'll be late coming in."

"Going on a bender? Good idea."

"No. It's time to wander over to the lawyers to start erecting our defense against this b.s."

A smile warmed Sal's voice. "Hey, we going with Steiner?"

"Yeah. Uzzi's the man. The biggest of big guns." Lew rubbed his hands. They would fire a heat-seeking nuclear missile back at this mess.

***

Uzzi Steiner chewed on an unlit cigar and paced back and forth across his paper-strewn office. His vest was unbuttoned, shirttail out and suspenders pulling his pants too high. A rumpled suit jacket lay across the back of his brown leather chair. It was just past noon but the grizzled lawyer already sported a generous five o'clock shadow, whiskers stubbling his face like poppy seeds on a loaf of rye bread.

Lew couldn't help but love the old barrister. They'd grown close working commercial cases for Mega and got along like an eccentric uncle and his favorite, wise guy nephew.

Without hesitation and beyond question, Lew trusted Steiner's legal acumen. Despite the rough edges, nobody in the western hemisphere mustered a winning court strategy like Steiner. Goliaths of business, media and politics all relied upon the idiosyncratic lawyer. Having Steiner in one's legal corner was like deploying the Death Star itself.

Lew sat on a butter-soft tan leather sofa in Steiner's office, hands folded. He tried to look in control, projecting calm. "So it's just crazy stuff, Uzzi. Absolutely no way anyone can ever prove such ridiculous claims."

Steiner glanced back over his shoulder and pulled the soggy, unlit cigar stub from his mouth. He stared at it as if examining a rare gem and shrugged.

Lew continued, pounding a fist into his palm, feeling his argument. "Damn it, I'm serious! Truth will be our best defense against anybody foolish enough to sue. Right?"

The old lawyer smiled and stared back at Lew like he was crazy. "Oh, for God's sake," he muttered, "just listen to this young *meshugana*! Innocent as a puppy." He shook his head. "I remember back when you were some kinda business whiz at Mega. But now I'm wondering, who's this *putz* on my sofa, preaching Golden Rule nonsense?"

Lew's eyes flashed. "Uzzi, this so-called *putz* is the chairman and

CEO of a company foolish enough to want to pay your juicy retainer." The two locked eyes.

Then Steiner grinned and waved his arms, like he was dispelling a gas cloud in the air. "Okay, kid, don't be so sensitive. Sorry, but save the do-gooder pep talks for the Cub Scouts. Because the sentiment you just expressed is misplaced."

"Oh, so I'm naïve? Contending that truth should easily win our cases?" Lew snorted a rush of air. "Well, in truth, evil spirits simply don't exist. Full stop. So that should be one helluva powerful defense! And even if there *were* such things—no one could ever prove Avian was connected, not in a million years."

Steiner's grin faded and his face began to glow pink, like a volcanic crater coming alive. He picked up a thick law book off the end table and faked throwing it at Lew. Then he burst into a smile so warm and generous it would melt an iceberg. He took off his glasses, breathed on the lenses to fog them and wiped them clean on his shirt sleeve.

"Ah, my young Lewis . . . you kids!" He shook his head wistfully. "How about you keep inventing that slick tech shit, but leave the lawyering to me?"

Steiner placed a meaty paw on Lew's shoulder. "Did I mention? The family's having Mega's new Alzheimer chip implanted into my mother, next week. Great for the old girl—she's ninety five. Like a bar code for old folks, all their info, live and online. She falls down? *Boom!* The medics show up. She gets lost? *Boom!* The cops instantly track her via GPS. She gets sick, the doc instantly has critical data. Some of your best work."

"One of my last big wins at Mega," Lew said. "Before I left to start my own business."

Steiner shot Lew a sad, ironic grimace.

Lew shrugged. "No, really, I'll be fine. My company is already soaring. But as for the lawsuits, truth must surely matter. Come on, we all know there are no terrestrial spirits attacking Avian customer estates."

The old lawyer snapped a suspender belt and sighed again, looking imploringly at the ceiling. He raised both hands as in surrender. "Why," he mumbled, "do You send me such a *schlemiel* for a client?" He looked back at Lew, his face stern. "You get an 'A' for creativity but an 'F' for your amateur legal musings. Now please sit back and listen. Have another bagel. Some coffee? Enjoy."

Lew nodded.

"First, let's be clear. In civil litigation, in a court of law—especially with a jury—truth hardly matters as much as a really good story."

"Well—"

"Well, nothing. What matters is only what the jury, or judge, *decides* is true. Or what they think *should be* true. You follow?" He raised his eyebrows and Lew nodded back.

"If some fancy Asian spirit researcher can convince a jury that angry spirits are out there, then for all legal purposes, as sure as your grandmother's mustache, they *are*. So Avian may be in for a shitload of trouble. All those estates with awful damage—the dead cows, the landslides and black goo? Mother of Moses! Every property had one of your birdhouse things—"

"Uzzi, come on!"

"Your company is skating on very thin ice. All you need is to lose the first case and everything could go nuclear. Breed ten, twenty more cases . . . a hundred? And you'd lose all those, too. Remember, juries just *love* punishing bad guys and their evil companies."

Bad guy? "Hey, wait a minute—"

Steiner's face went dark and he held up a palm to silence Lew. The room temperature seemed to suddenly drop twenty degrees.

"If I were litigating against you, here's what I'd do." A wicked smile lit Steiner's face. "I'd paint a picture of a slick, rich, arrogant young businessman. A real sharp guy. I mean, just look at his amazing inventions! Why, the man's a freakin' genius! But driven purely by greed, to further his monopoly ambitions, he knowingly disrespects religious forces he doesn't understand and causes innocent customers to insult powerful spiritual deities. Imagine the nerve! He imports Asian religious artifacts on the super-cheap and sells them for improper and unintended uses, racking up huge profits. So dangerous! And *of course* he knew better! Remember, this is a real brainiac. But seduced by money, he endangers his customers."

Geez, that didn't sound good at all. Horrible, actually.

"Okay, Uzzi, I get the picture. I could be portrayed as a real villain. So what do we do?"

"Well, Lew, it's like this, unfortunately. I'm still under retainer to Mega. So, since you've already left, I can't represent you."

That landed like a gut-punch.

"What? But Uzzi, we've got history! A relationship. Didn't you say I was one of your favorite clients? "

"Yeah, like a son." Steiner pointed his damp cigar stub at Lew. "But that was then. This is now." He shrugged. "Don't worry, I've got names for you. Good trial lawyers."

What a mess! Lew momentarily put his head into his hands, but refused to surrender. "Listen, Uzzi, keep those names in your pocket for now. Did you personally sign anything with Mega already, *specifically* cutting me out?"

"Not specifically, not yet, but—"

"Then I'm pleading. Begging for your help! Please, do me this favor."

The gruff lawyer rubbed his bald head and chuckled. "'Always liked your grit, Lew, and your guts. You're right. So far, Mega hasn't pushed but once they hear we are together, they will. Count on it. Until then, as a personal favor, I'll quietly stay on with you. But when push comes to shove—"

"Yeah, I know. Just wheel me off the end of the dock. But then, not now." Lew grinned and rubbed his hands. "Okay, Obi-wan. What kind of Jedi legal tricks you got for me?"

Steiner gave his head a wistful shake and sat down on the sofa beside Lew, bumping the younger man's knee.

"Okay, son, let's do this. Send me all the paperwork from your angry customers—court filings, documents, everything. I'll take a good look and start to fashion a stout defense."

"Super!"

"But in the meantime," Steiner grumbled, "you need to personally work hard to save your *own* skin."

Lew squinted. "Hmm?"

"Listen, if I were facing your problems—or my son, the stock broker—here's what I'd do." Steiner handed Lew a legal pad and a pen, plus a patronizing look. "Write all this down."

Lew nodded, his breast swelling with hope. What a character! Uzzi was like having a crazy great-uncle who was also an unmatched legal assassin.

"Okay. *Numero Uno.*" Steiner motioned with an invisible pen, prompting Lew to write. "Never let any of this get even *close* to trial. Not even in the same hemisphere. We delay, delay, delay! And every day that passes with no new case filed is a victory. And whenever opportunities arise to settle, we jump. Quickly and quietly, securing ironclad nondisclosure agreements to ensure silence."

"Sounds like this may not go away very soon—"

Steiner scowled. "Heh! Not for a long, *looong* time! Son, you're still like Baby Moses in the bulrushes. Light years must pass before you lead the Israelites out of Egypt."

That was less than thrilling. Hopefully Uzzi's better stuff was yet to come. "Okay, got it. What else, sir?"

"Number two. Your key assignment. You must personally take action! Jump on your foreign supplier like they're some fancy French whore. Yesterday, if not sooner! Last week would have been even better. What's that name again?"

"Lotus Creations Co."

"Right. Apply maximum pressure to Lotus. Be like one of those weird little anal African fish I saw on a National Geo documentary. Just slither in and swim right up that Lotus backside. Start applying maximum pressure."

Lew chuckled at the disgusting image—typical Steiner color.

"Don't laugh. Thanks to those little fish, I'll never swim in the Zambezi again." Steiner smirked.

Lew shook his head. "Yeah, but the problem, Uzzi, is that the customers are suing *my* company, right here and right now, in the US. They don't know anything about Lotus, hidden half a world away."

The lawyer scratched his chin. "And that's precisely what you need to change. Marry up the litigants with Lotus, so you can sidestep it all. A very difficult job. Still writing?"

"Affirmative." Lew waggled his pen at Steiner

The lawyer raised a finger, displaying a brown, tobacco-stained nail. "So totally beat up on Lotus. They must issue you a full refund on every single unit you imported. Recover your huge advance payment." The lawyer shot Lew a sad smile. "Your life savings. Remember?"

Lew nodded, scribbling. "Easier said than done, Uzzi."

"Think so? Well there's more, the absolute life-or-death part of your assignment. You must also obtain from them, in writing, total *indemnification*. Want me to spell that?"

"No need. But maybe spell out what you mean?"

"Get an ironclad legal document whereby Lotus accepts *all* liability for *all* their products. Lotus must hold you harmless in all lawsuits, past and future, triggered by any products they sold you under false pretenses."

An enormous ask and huge problems delivering that one. But Lew held his tongue and let the lawyer go on.

"They must take you and your company off the hook. Your goal, Lew, is to become just a relay man, handing off lawsuits to Lotus, just as soon as they come in. As the manufacturer, they must accept ultimate responsibility. All grief must channel back to that cockamamie Kingdom."

Lew drew in a deep breath and blew it out in a narrow stream. "Solid plan, Uzzi, but it's blocked by a whopper of a problem."

"Oh, a big problem? Good. I love problems. They make me rich. Tell me." Steiner sat down and listened, smiling as he masticated his cigar, carefully dribbling brown saliva down into the narrow opening of a diet cola can.

"Well, first of all," Lew smiled, "the way I hear it, courts and contracts don't even exist in Amazia."

Steiner's eyes widened with amused disbelief. "No courts? No contracts? You don't say! Why, that's impossible."

"So naturally, there are also no laws or lawyers there, either."

Now Steiner genuinely looked taken aback. "Sounds a perfectly hellish place. Straight from the Stone Age." He rose and reached out, as if to shake Lew's hand, but instead pulled him up off the couch and began to guide the younger man toward the door.

"You know, son, I'm going to miss these little chats of ours, but it sounds like you really need to get cracking. Right away. No time to waste."

Action was already starting? Lew felt heartened.

"Start flooding that Kingdom with nasty legal communications. Today! Emails, letters, facsimiles, telegrams. Hell, use jungle drums if you like. Wire intimidating threats detailing our demands. If possible, nag them over the phone —"

"Seems none."

"— and just harass the living hell outta them. Start softening them up."

"Sure," Lew replied, "I can do that. And—"

"So that's today. But tomorrow—yes, *tomorrow!*—you get yourself onto an *aero plane*." Steiner delivered that in an awful, fake British accent and grinned like it was the funniest joke ever. "Ha, yes! Get that skinny little Clarke *tuchus* over to Amazia. Immediately."

"What, Uzzi, me? *Go* there? Really?"

"I'm absolutely serious now, like a heart attack. Who else can do this, Lew? No one. You can't delegate the most important business mission of your life. Remember, Lotus *may* be able to ignore letters and emails. And they may not answer the phone. But when a tall, strapping, angry young American businessman knocks at their front door, up close and personal, well, that kind of pain in the ass is impossible to ignore."

"But I, uh, how do I even—"

Steiner tossed his hands in the air with a devilish little smile and laughed.

"Oh, how I envy you, my boy. Such fun! This will be a peak lifetime experience. The rest of your life, you'll tell stories about this trip."

Lew listened, his face blank. Was Steiner serious?

"Yep, this mess of yours, Lew, it's a real beauty. Fighting a strange company hidden away in some place with no laws? Goodness. I recommend when you go there, you adopt the Mike Tyson strategy."

"Iron Mike?"

"Brooklyn's own." Steiner leaned closer. "Lotus will try to ignore you, Lew. Guaranteed. Leave you out in the cold, make *you* the patsy taking hits for *their* flawed product."

"So you recommend I bite off one of their ears?"

"Funny," Steiner said. "But no. Just remember Iron Mike's observation: Everybody has a plan . . . that is, until they get punched in the mouth."

Lew chuckled. Loved his grizzled old counselor.

"Just a metaphor. But go there, son, and immediately punch 'em a good one, right in the choppers. Shock 'em. Make yourself impossible to ignore. And get that indemnification."

Steiner steered Lew toward the office door and gently pushed him out.

"Anyway, it's probably delightful there, this time of year. So good luck. And send me a postcard."

"Steiner? Yeah, Uzzi is great!" Back at the warehouse, Sal was pumped. "Even his first name, like a machine gun. His parents must've known something."

"Our very own legal velociraptor," Lew said. "Cold-blooded and deadly effective, ready to strike. Things will get better now."

Reviewing his notes from the Steiner meeting, Lew's eyes flew straight to the words in thick ink (he'd pressed extra hard and underscored): *Go to Amazia!* Yes, he'd do that. But first to fire off that barrage of messages Steiner also ordered.

He launched legal ICBMs, pounding Lotus by email. The communications forwarded details of the initial lawsuits and screen shots of Dr. Narathiwat's commentaries plus customer complaints. The messages were businesslike and polite, but clearly held Lotus accountable and demanded it refund Avian's lump payment and provide total future indemnification.

It felt great to push SEND. But twenty-four hours later, there was no response. Lew followed-up in a harsher tone but all his messages immediately began to bounce, marked *undeliverable*. His blood pressure spiked to witness Lotus pulling the old *Amazia Quick-Step*, disappearing from the internet and pretending to no longer exist.

Phone escalation was also impossible. He had no listing for Lotus, upcountry, only the Asiatic Media number in the capital, from the video conference. And that went dead months ago. An internet search for active listings in the Kingdom—anything!—only turned up a number for the Vietnam Embassy in Ruangbang. Lew tried several times but the line kept dropping out.

Hours later, he sat frustrated in his office, bouncing a yellow tennis ball off the glass wall. Was all that optimism after the Steiner meeting just a sugar high? He resisted a feeling of doom trying to creep up on him. And then, in a moment of total clarity, he suddenly saw everything. His choices were clear-cut and binary. Either he could descend again into self-pity or else just go on the attack and fix his problem.

As always, Steiner was right. Everything *was* still in Lew's hands and he needed—right away—to stop wasting time and just haul his ass to the far side of the planet. Go to Amazia, confront his supplier and fix this mess. There was no other way.

If he could marshal the same kind of focus and intensity that drove his past business successes, he could solve anything. But if he dallied, the fiasco could fester and he would deserve every bit of the horrific outcome.

That night back at his flat, buoyed by a new resolve, Lew packed for travel. But what did one take for just a few days jaunt to tropical Asia? He recalled a recent business trip to blistering Houston and used that as his model, laying out business shirts, ties and suit jackets on the bed. The hotel laundry would keep all that fresh. He also gathered gym gear for workouts and his favorite Air Jordans. He added a Yankees baseball cap and two pairs of stylish jeans. Finally, on impulse, remembering that scorching Texas sun, he grabbed his favorite cowboy hat—hot and bright in Asia too, right? Then on a lark, he also tossed his favorite cowboy boots into the bag.

He carefully arranged all that inside a large, expensive brown leather suitcase and secured the safety straps. Exuding pure class, the bag was a birthday gift from MJ back before their marriage tanked. Wonderful if a bit impractical, the elite bag was a throwback to the golden era of posh train travel. MJ knew he loved that stuff. By now, it also bulged with painful memories.

Last, he zipped up his simple, green khaki travel briefcase—another signature quirk.

Early next morning down at the lobby, he palmed a Benjamin folded into a tiny square and shook hands with Nick the doorman, who smoothly fielded the transfer.

"Gone a few days, Nick. One week, tops. Keep an eye on the penthouse?"

"No worries, Mr. C."

Before heading to JFK, he stopped by the warehouse office to alert Sal, whom he found hunched at the keyboard, dozing. Lew dropped his bag on the floor with a thud. Sal startled upright.

"Sleeping in the office, Sal? That's *my* thing, not yours."

Sal ignored that, got up and poured two cups of sludgy black coffee from a glass pot. The sound of forklifts moving crates around the warehouse penetrated the office. Despite recent developments, containers were still arriving at random. So the bustling warehouse contradicted the looming, worst-case possibility of a shutdown.

"Looks like you need your very own *Sal Special*," he said, handing Lew a mug. "Bottoms up!" Lew smiled. He hated how Sal brewed coffee but didn't quibble, needing the caffeine jolt. He'd only slept an hour, if that.

Sal motioned at Lew's gear. "So, them's travelin' bags?"

"Off on a little trip."

"Ah, good timing for a little getaway," Sal chuckled. "That is, seeing how there's not much going on right now, just some existential crises and stuff."

Lew played along. "Yup. Gonna visit a little dream hideaway, deep in rural Southeast Asia."

"Not Amazia, perchance?"

"The same."

"Nice. *Juarez of the East,* I think they call it." Sal patted Lew on the back. "But seriously, Hoss, why now? We're just getting up a head of steam on Uzzi's to-do list."

Lew fired up his computer and showed Sal his email queue full of bounced messages. "Last day or so, we've been doing a lot of *sending,* but on the other end nobody is doing any *receiving*. Our little Kingdom seems to have gone missing."

Sal whistled low. "Mmm. That's bad juju."

"The worst. So I'm off, on Uzzi's explicit command, to personally deliver our demands. Assuming I'm even able to find Lotus."

"No problem." Sal whipped a yellow tennis ball off the far wall and Lew snatched the rebound one-handed.

"While I'm gone, Sal—maybe a week, max—stay close with Uzzi and the business, even if that mainly means opening brown envelopes with new lawsuits each morning."

***

The sleek black limo glided to JFK with Lew lounging in back, studying the itinerary on his smartphone. Laid out like that on the screen, it looked pretty straightforward, almost easy:

British Airways nonstop to Dubai, connecting on Thai Airways to Bangkok. A few hours layover at Suvarnabhumi and then an Air Amazia shuttle flight to Ruangbang, capital of Amazia.

While awaiting departure, Lew nosed around the JFK bookshops but found no travel handbooks for Amazia. Closest was a thick paperback guide for all of Southeast Asia, with a mere three of its six hundred pages devoted to the tiny Kingdom. Better than nothing! He bought it, separated the Amazia pages and ditched the rest. Then he got comfortable in BA's first class lounge and started to read.

"Welcome to Amazia, the Land of Seductive Chaos."

What an odd way for the guide book to begin, promising and a bit threatening at the same time. Seductive Chaos? No thank you.

"Count yourself lucky if ever you get the chance to visit this hidden gem of Asia! Few tourists—perhaps one in thousands—have the insight or nerve to visit here."

Nerve?

"Amazia is so remote a backwater that few outsiders tour the Kingdom, especially the mountainous upcountry region.

Perfect. 'Upcountry' was the Lotus stomping grounds.

"This lush green land is populated by gentle people with a mellow, laid-back national mood. Wealth and poverty peacefully coexist and crime is virtually nonexistent. The Amaza people are

slight in stature and uniformly attractive. The men are handsome and self-effacing, hiding their strength while outwardly quiet and humble. The women are beautiful and have a reputation for being flirtatiously friendly."

The place was starting to sound cool. In his imagination, Lew could hear happy, sing-song voices, clanging gongs and trumpeting elephants. If only the circumstances for his visit were different, like for vacation, not a business hit job.

European powers never colonized Amazia, so the Kingdom is unspoiled by any traces of Western influence. In recent years, wealthier Amaza have sent their offspring abroad for education, so a smattering of English is now spoken in the capital, mainly in government and the very limited tourism sector."

"The Amaza are naturally friendly and hospitable to their infrequent foreign guests, delighted to show off their cultural treasure house. The Kingdom incorporates elements from many surrounding lands: stunning temples, thrilling cultural dances, delicious food and so forth. While in Amazia, one is often reminded of its neighbors—Thailand, Malaysia, Laos, Cambodia, Myanmar, Vietnam, even India."

"No visitor ever leaves Amazia disappointed, as long as he adjusts his personal clock, calendar and expectations."

"Get in tune with the relaxed pace prevailing in this unique and eccentric land and prepare yourself for the experience of a lifetime!"

PART TWO:

Welcome to Amazia!

CHAPTER TEN
Seductive Chaos

The flight to Dubai and connection to Bangkok went off seamlessly. For some twenty hours, Lew luxuriated in first class pampering. Slippers, champagne, and Chateaubriand. But the final leg—the Air Amazia shuttle from Bangkok to Ruangbang—would be starkly different.

The plane was an ancient propeller-driven Boeing, hand-painted in the Kingdom's royal colors of purple, green, and orange. It shook after take-off and buzzed like a giant mosquito while climbing to cruising altitude over the Golden Triangle. Fewer than twenty passengers sat inside the dented fuselage, two on each side of the aisle. The seats were woven plastic webbing like cheap 1950s patio chairs and all carpeting had worn away so metal flooring showed through, blackened by soot and age.

Not hearing a peep from the captain, Lew assumed the speaker system no longer worked. Once at cruising altitude, a bell rang and pair of smiling young stewardesses leapt into action.

Sweet and charming in tight purple sarong outfits, with a flip of gauzy material over one shoulder, they began a frantic dash down the aisle to pass out little boxed drinks and tiny cello packets of fried peanuts.

Despite flight turbulence, they moved as surely as grizzled hot dog vendors at Yankee Stadium, deftly tossing items right and left, always with ravishing smiles. Then, having finished ten minutes of work, they disappeared for the rest of the flight.

About an hour in, the plane entered Amazia airspace. Lew had already been journeying nearly a day. He peered through the Plexiglas window scuffed nearly opaque and brown with age and began to make out rooftops of Ruangbang, the steaming smoky capital. It looked like a small to medium-sized town at best, with just a few asphalt arteries snaking away from the city center. Branching off those were tiny red capillaries, twisting roads of pounded clay.

He was shocked. How could so insignificant a place be the capital?

And Ruangbang from the air appeared remarkably green for a city—a pleasant hodgepodge of palm trees and myriad small farm plots, even in the 'downtown' district. His eyes flitted about, spotting huts, gardens and occasional buildings, mostly simple but some almost modern. Ornate temples, shrines, and gold-domed *stupas* dotted the landscape. And as the guidebook promised, Buddhist pagodas were everywhere.

The plane abruptly shuddered and began to drift lower. More discrete features came into view, like the assorted traffic on the dirt roads.

Whoa, elephants! Pachyderms lumbered alongside squeaking ox carts, bicycles and compact cars. Swarms of zippy little Japanese motorbikes zoomed around odd little trucks that appeared constructed entirely of duct tape and rust.

Music suddenly blared from the cabin intercom he'd presumed dead—a Muzak-style cover a 1980s Madonna song. Lew assumed that was to put passengers at ease while landing, always the trickiest part of a flight (especially on a plane that might lack brakes).

A minute later, the tires slammed into the tarmac with a squeal and passengers let out an audible *ahhh*! The plane bounced down the runway while the pilot reversed propeller direction and hit max thrust. The aircraft swung around and finally halted at the tiny airport's only building, a one-story terminal. Lew waited as a creaky metal stairway was wheeled to the plane.

Both stewardesses bounced to their feet and with plastic smiles pointed at the front door. All passengers immediately jumped up to bolt for the exit, like the plane was on fire. It might as well have been—with the air con off, the cabin quickly soared to sauna temperature.

Lew patiently worked his way toward the front and stepped down the creaky metal stairway, sweating like never before, his armpits slick and shirt sticking to his back. Swarming flights taught him to keep his mouth closed. He glanced back and noticed other passengers ad-libbing a faster exit via the tail door, hopping down the last few feet to the ground.

A large yellow sign with red letters across the rusty terminal roof proclaimed: WELCOME TO AMAZIA! Next to it was a large photograph of the royal family, decked out in over-the-top, Hollywood-style costumes.

Lew moved along with the flow of passengers and once inside the terminal witnessed pure chaos, heads bobbing and baggage sloshing around. It seemed an omnibus mosh pit catering to all travel functions, from check-in to customs, immigration, baggage handling and a waiting area for the terminal's only gate, with only a few airport employees. Many were meeting family members and others were taxi touts pushing unlicensed rides. But the majority appeared to be there for the entertainment value, like couples on dates. In so sleepy a place, Ruangbang Airport seemed a must-see attraction.

His first impression was that, indeed, the Amaza were a handsome people. Many were clothed in traditional sarongs but younger locals wore casual Western attire—breezy, button-down shirts and lightweight slacks though nary a pair of jeans anywhere. Some women covered up in Muslim-style *hijabs* but others pranced about in unabashedly sexy, curve-hugging batik outfits. One caught Lew's eye and smiled, her dark hair dangling in luscious curls, lips glossed pink and big eyes painted to stun in blue mascara and black eyeliner.

Wow. *Welcome to Amazia*, indeed.

Lew located the money exchange kiosk and queued behind an old man balancing live trussed chickens from a pole. After Chicken

Man finished, Lew stepped forward and slapped down a crisp $100 bill.

The clerk looked shocked—either by the US currency or the denomination—and summoned his supervisor. The two ran odd authenticity tests involving no technical gear and seeming made up on the spot, like spitting on a corner and rubbing it with a thumb. Finally the clerk handed Lew a brown paper sack overflowing with a gaudy rainbow of multicolored Amazian currency, called *Arysai*.

Lew smiled. Probably didn't need to change so much.

Sweat-dampened clothes adhered to every inch of his body. Though only early afternoon in Ruangbang, his body clock still ran on New York time and insisted it was the middle of the night. Killer jet lag squeezed him in its fierce grip. Desperately exhausted, he fought to keep his eyelids up and stay awake. Hopefully he'd reach a hotel soon.

But just then, he would have given anything—*anything!*—to sink to the ground and pass out for a short nap then and there for, oh, eighteen hours or so?

He exited the terminal to search for a taxi.

An endless stream of rattletraps, all unique, motored past on the circular airport road. Squarish old vehicles, kicking up dust, bounced past on puffy tires straight from an Elliott Ness movie. Beside them puttered yellow mini-taxis from Japan, seeming too micro to accommodate both a driver and passenger. Compact blue Chinese pickups and red Volkswagen Beetles chugged along beside asymmetrical orange sedans from India.

All taxis sported ornamental art and eccentric slogans honoring deities, football teams, famous holy men, film stars, and mysterious lovers.

Lew tossed a hand in the air and a purple Fiat Padmini zipped up next to him in a blur, its bald tires less than an inch from his shoes. The taxi displayed an English slogan in sky blue and lemon yellow: *The Spiritual Power of Celibacy*. Okay, wait . . . what?

Lew dropped into the backseat worn shiny by thousands of butts.

The car springs felt so weak he feared his tail might scrape the ground. Hanging from the rear-view mirror was a bouquet of religious medallions shining like metallic daisies. Crowding the dashboard was a scrum of tiny statues taped-down in a football-like formation—human figures with dog heads, multi-armed women and dancing elephant boys. He could only recognize the fat smiling Buddha, probably playing quarterback.

The driver's smile was intense and unnerving. "Welcome to Amazia! And Sir is going where? Sir is wanting girl?" It sounded like the fellow was offering him a *gull*. So much for the spiritual power of celibacy. "Nice girl, Sirrrr. All kind! Up to you."

Lew's smile contorted into a massive, involuntary yawn. "Sorry, and thanks for the kind offer, but no girl. I'm totally exhausted and just need sleep. Please take me to the Miracle Royal Pagoda Hotel."

The cabbie's eyes lit up. "Ah, Mir-a-cle Hotel!" Each syllable got a beat. "Oh, yes indeed, Sirrrrr . . . is best in capital city!"

Well *that* was a relief to hear. His guidebook pages offered no lodging details, so Lew chose at random from a list at the airport tourist desk. Only three hotels were deemed worthy of foreign visitors' money so he went with the best name. *Miracle? Royal*? How could it miss?

The driver gunned the engine, shifted gears with a *thunk* and the picayune taxi jolted off, rattling down dusty roads through blistering afternoon heat, snaking through traffic. The cab maneuvered through swarms of motorbikes, squeaky bullock carts and lumbering elephants camped at mid-road depositing whopping big brown turds. The cab passed families on bicycles, with fathers pedaling their entire broods perched atop handlebars and fenders.

Stray dogs lounged by the roadside, yawning and keeping watch under lush palm trees.

The squeaking taxi jiggled past rustic dry goods stores, greasy one-man auto repairs and bulging golden *stupas* squatting in courtyards. Those pagodas reminded Lew of the glass domes of ceiling lamps, but super-sized, painted gold and turned upside-down.

Or else, massive, upturned breasts.

And Ruangbang seemed to come with its own soundtrack. Distant soft clanging music grew ever louder until it reached ear-shattering volume when passing by street musicians hammering away on monstrous metallic xylophones. The music then faded with distance, until a hand-off to another roadside performance, always just ahead.

His first impression cast Amazia as a ramshackle, tumbledown place, yet exotic and even quaint. Ruangbang, the capital, was no one-horse town. Half a horse, at best.

Just as Lew's eyelids attempted another irresistible plunge toward sleep, the dinky vehicle shuddered to a halt and the driver intoned ceremoniously, "Miracle Hotel!" His voice quivered with importance.

Naturally the meter hadn't worked. So Lew reached into his sack of currency and grabbed a random assortment. Hmm, a couple purples, a yellow and a hot pink? He stretched a handful of assorted bills out toward the cabbie.

"Oh, yes, Sirrrrr!" the driver squealed, giddy as a big lottery winner.

The moment cash hit the driver's palm, the taxi doors flew open and a flock of hands started rummaging through the vehicle. Hotel attendants, Lew hoped. But he was too disoriented by jet lag to resist, even were it a band of thieves relieving him of everything. The invading hands then landed on Lew and nearly lifted him from the taxi.

As he half-levitated through the hotel entrance, his first look told him all he needed to know. This, the best lodging in town, was a ratty dump. The biggest miracle about the Miracle Royal Pagoda seemed to be that it managed to stay in business.

The lobby was dark and spare, with a simple front desk recessed into one wall and a no-frills beverage standing opposite and spilling out chalky white fluorescence. The only other light was a bare incandescent bulb that hung from a cord over the check-in counter. At the middle of the room stood a pair of aging cracked brown vinyl sofas, back-to-back and sandwiching a dirty white pillar.

After Manhattan's brute opulence, this all felt alien and nearly surreal, as if Lew might soon awaken from this strange dream. If this was the capital's premier hotel, how bad could it be upcountry in Biti, the remote location for the Lotus headquarters?

A short, slender clerk puttered around at the front desk. Milky tan skin covered his delicate facial structure and pronounced cheekbones, accentuating brilliant white teeth that sparkled like diamonds when he smiled. Continuously.

"Welcome to Miracle Royal Pagoda Hotel, sir," chirped the desk clerk in a sing-song voice with a wai. Every black lock of his hair as precisely oiled down in place. He wore a crisp white button-down shirt with a demure pink ID pin and dark green sarong from expensive-looking material. Lew knew the exorbitant price such fabric fetched at his Manhattan tailor. How could just a clerk in so impoverished a land afford such luxury?

"Sir is coming to Kingdom for business time? Or pleasure time?" As he spoke, his petite hands fluttered about hypnotically. Finely groomed fingernails floated through the air like snowflakes swirling in a winter breeze.

He pulled out a large leather-bound guest register with great ceremony and placed it atop the dusty wooden counter. He flipped the massive book open and laid it flat, displaying pages filled with blue ink entries in Amazia's odd circular script. Rows of squiggles, dashes and figures stacked up like hieroglyphics on a pyramid wall.

The clerk inquired, in limited but serviceable English, the usual check-in questions. He inscribed Lew's answers as a line of glyphs, floating dots and wavy lines. That's me, Lew thought, grinning. Reduced to a jumbled line of odd figures.

Perhaps a hundred visit entries filled the two open pages, covering the last two years. Dates were in Roman script. Lew did the math—just a couple hotel guests per week. That seemed about right from the looks of this sleepy place.

He took a room for three nights. His preliminary business with Asiatic Media there in the capital should take no longer. The clerk handed Lew a formal check-in card to sign. Amid the squiggles, blips and dashes, he only recognized the date and his name: *Khun* Lew Clarke.

Khun. He smiled at that honorific title, remembering it from the video conference. It effectively meant something like *Sir* and was often combined with a first name. A nice mix of formality with friendliness.

The smiling clerk selected a room key from a pigeonhole behind him. It was anchored by a length of chain to a heavy black ebony wood fob the size of a fist, intricately carved to the shape of an elephant. He held it gently in two hands as if a precious, delicate gift and presented it to Lew.

Lew dropped the bulky key ring into his green khaki satchel. Too big to pocket.

The desk attendant suddenly looked considerably relieved, his challenging transaction with the giant foreigner now completed. "And is other way we are helping Mr. Clarke?" A single gold tooth highlighted his smile, surrounded by snowy-white companions.

Hmm, what else? Good question. As Lew marshaled his thoughts, he realized his blur of jet-lag fatigue was dissipating. It must be about that time, back home in New York, when he would awaken most nights to urinate but then lay there and ponder work issues, rejiggering plans.

"Yes, actually there *is* something you can help me with. Does this hotel have a concierge?" His words were not even halfway out before he felt foolish and regretted them. Come on, this place, a *concierge*? Barely had functioning lights.

"Oh my, Sir. A what? *Con-see-er-jee*?" The clerk frowned. "Haha, maybe not yet, I think. Amazia still new for tourist business."

"Sorry. I just meant a help desk, that's all."

The clerk immediately brightened. "Help? Oh, yes indeed, Sir! Miracle Hotel is always helping customer, all possible way." He pointed across the room at a disheveled young man asleep atop two folding chairs, beneath the beverage chiller's ghostly white light.

"That fellow, Sir, we are calling him *Gob*—ha, nickname meaning 'Frog'. Khun Gob helping all important visitor. Also, Sir can please visiting me." The clerk handed Lew a crisp white business card with no hotel logo, just the words *Wongrat Smith, Inquiries.*

"Wow, your family name is Smith?" Lew smiled, feeling sudden relief. "Are your people originally from Europe or America?" Finally a ray of hope, something familiar amid the confusion of this alien place. It felt promising, a foothold.

But Wongrat laughed and looked embarrassed. "Oh no, Sir! Wongrat family is being Amaza people, only. Smith is friendly name for Sir, only. Foreign guest cannot pronouncing *real* name. Amaza people new at tourist business, but trying hard."

Lew certainly agreed. A Western alias? That *was* quite a nice touch. Amazia might seem like an economic disaster or a shuttle back in time, but its friendly people were sure trying hard.

Lew mounted the squeaky wooden stairwell at the rear of the lobby and climbed to the second floor. A threadbare carpet ran the length of the unlit corridor, with aqua doors facing each other in pairs. His room was halfway down.

He keyed the lock, entered and laid his precious leather suitcase on the narrow bed, already second-guessing the wisdom of bringing it. The pink bedside table wobbled as he reached out to turn on the tiny lamp. It didn't work. Then he spotted a candle in a simple brass stand and lit it using the provided box of *Elephant Brand* wooden matches.

Lew squeezed into a pair of child-sized rubber flip-flops from the little cupboard and padded into the damp bathroom. There he found a simple sink and a squat toilet, basically a hole in the floor with two footprints for targeting purposes. He filled the tiny reservoir with dark urine—man, was he dehydrated!—and wondered how to flush the thing. No yank cord or handle anywhere. So that was a good first question for his Amazia-style concierge, Mr. Frog.

He squeaked open the cold water spigot but nothing happened. Great. Didn't bother trying the hot. Then he spotted a small laminated wall sign bearing unwelcome news:

Water daily to circulating, 7-9 a.m. only

Lew sighed and began to peel off his travel clothes, sweated-through and molded to his shape. He'd been wearing them for what, thirty hours now?

He used the blue plastic dipper to draw water from the large cistern and give himself a simple splash bath. Anticipating the chill of cold water, he instead found it lukewarm and comfortable and fast found a happy rhythm, splashing and lathering and rinsing.

Insight struck. He ladled a couple scoops of water directly into the squat toilet and the dark urine disappeared. Voila! Manual flushing. Hey, look, just like a local: he was Khun Lew Clarke, being amazing in Amazia.

It was early afternoon. He could still productively spend the day. Find Khon and Asiatic Media, get this rolling.

But waves of fatigue, along with a headache and general dizziness, began to roll in again and muddle his thinking. The shoddy little room shifting in and out of focus. Damned jet lag!

What he needed was a quick lay down, a cat nap of just a few minutes to recharge. Then he'd head out. Smart plan.

But the moment his head hit the thin, hard pillow, his eyeballs rolled upward into his head and his lids descended, to stay shut the next twenty-two hours.

CHAPTER ELEVEN
Hopping Around with Mr. Frog

He opened his eyes, hazy and confused. What was this horrible room—where was he? It all came racing back and, judging from the bird songs trilled outside his window, it was still morning.

A quick rummage through his bag told him everything he'd packed was flat-out wrong, uncomfortable for the tropics or inappropriate for so primitive a place. Nice going, Lew. He settled on a pastel blue dress shirt, worn untucked with top buttons open, and rolled up his sleeves. He added light tan slacks and loafers.

Perhaps if—God forbid—the visit stretched out, he could hunt down a local tailor. Get something more suitable for an equatorial steam pit.

He shuffled down to the lobby and stopped at the front desk. Wongrat Smith was totally immersed in a meditative game played with pebbles and sticks on a pink silk cloth. When Lew coughed politely, several precariously balanced pebbles tumbled to the desktop and Wongrat looked up, frustrated. But upon seeing Lew, he smiled broadly.

"Ah, Mr. Clarke! Good sleep, yes? Sir is needing Wongrat help?"

Lew grinned, already really liking this fellow, his first real Amaza acquaintance.

"First off, please just call me Lew." Lew assumed American informality would be a refreshing change, perhaps even impressive, to members of a more restrained culture.

But Wongrat remained deferential. "Yes, Sir! So Wongrat now calling you *Khun* Lew, not Mr. Clarke." Apparently he was only comfortable if bolting *Khun* onto first-name intimacy, adding the respect and formality of Sir. Good enough.

"Excellent. I hope we can be friends. Is there a friendly nickname I can use for you? Perhaps *Wongie*?"

The clerk looked startled, almost shocked. "Oh no. My name *Wongrat*."

"*Khun* Wongrat, then?"

"Heh, just Wongrat, all by self, that okay."

Lew shrugged. "Fine. My first question: why is my phone getting zero network bars? And no Wi-Fi."

Wongrat's face went blank. Lew held up his sleek titanium smartphone and wobbled it at him. "You know. For my phone?"

The clerk's mouth fell open and he just stared goggle-eyed, as if the large Westerner was a talking dog. At last, a grin stole across Wongrat's face.

"Oh, my goodness, Sir is having modern pocket telephone! Isn't it? Wongrat never seeing close at hand before in Amazia! Only on film." Sounded like *fill 'em*. "Sorry, but is possible for my holding?"

Wongrat reached out and cradled the phone in both hands, caressing it like a bejeweled chalice containing the Buddha's very own blood. He explored rounded edges with his fingers and rubbed the cool shining glass surface. He hefted it and seemed pleased by its weight and solidity.

Lew reached over and pushed the side button. The screen sprang to life.

"*Aieeee!*" Wongrat launched the phone, which bounded off the countertop and hit the floor with a sharp impact.

"Oh no! Wongrat very sorry, indeed, Sir!" His hands flew into that familiar prayer-like stance, but the wai this time was pressed against his forehead as he bent low, a version dripping with humility.

Lew scooped up the phone to examine. Luckily, no damage. "As we say back home: No harm, no foul.*"*

Wongrat squinted at first, befuddled, but soon smiled to understand his mishap with the magical device would have no adverse repercussion.

"So you don't see many personal phones here?" Unbelievable: the front desk clerk at the Kingdom's best tourist hotel (yes, all was relative) seemed awed by a simple iPhone.

Wongrat giggled. "Oh my, Khun Lew! Pocket telephones in Amazia? No, we are not having. King or crown prince having, yes. Also maybe rich business man. But pocket phone almost not working in Kingdom. Only one or two place."

Wow. Lew's mission was getting harder by the minute. This phone revelation was nearly as shocking as the Kingdom's allergy to lawyers and contracts. With just a handful of smartphone users, perhaps supported by satellite, the Kingdom was even more backward and reclusive than he'd suspected.

Wongrat cleared his throat and reached out an open hand. "Please to give again, Khun Lew? Wongrat can storing valuable pocket telephone in hotel safe."

Easy decision. It was all but useless there anyway, so Lew handed it over. Wongrat gave him a little numbered orange plastic chip and taped its twin to the phone, which he then placed inside a small metal container like a child's tackle box. Plastic handle and all. He snapped a flimsy padlock through the clasp and stowed the box under the front desk, atop a stack of old newspapers. "All safe now!" he triumphantly announced.

I'll bet. Lew already regretted the surrender and wondered how he could retrieve it, soon, without embarrassing his host. He nodded thanks to Wongrat and headed across the dim lobby toward the beverage stand, the domain of Khun Gob . . . aka Mr. Frog.

Frog sprang up from the metal folding chair before Lew got halfway there, brushed off his lime green shirt and licked a palm to hand-comb hair down. He tightened his dark green sarong, inhaled deeply and stood at attention, ready for anything.

"Excuse me. Mr. Gob, yes?"

The hotel man smiled, snapped his fingers and slapped arms rigid down his sides.

"Yes, Sir, absolutely!"

"My name is Lew Clarke, from New York."

"Yes, Sir, absolutely!"

Lew hoped those weren't his only three English words.

Smaller and darker than Wongrat, the young man jiggled, visibly bubbling with enthusiasm. "And please, Sir is to be calling me *Frog*. Means same-same as Gob." The fellow had decent English, maybe even better than Wongrat, and certainly aimed to please.

"Thanks, Frog," said Lew with a smile.

"And look, do you see?" The man chuckled. "Frog is always wearing green. Like real frog, isn't it? Haha." He pronounced his nickname like *Flog*. Lew found that charming.

"Frog, I need to contact a PR firm here in Ruangbang."

"Pee-yar? What is this *pee-yar*?"

"Never mind. But the business is called Asiatic Media, operated by *Khun* Khon. Maybe you know him?" Ruangbang was so small it seemed worth a try.

But Frog only chuckled. *"Khun* Khon? Really? Sir is telling Amazia-style joke . . . yes?"

"I don't understand."

"That name, *Khun Khon,* is sometimes joke here. *Khu*n mean Mister. *Khon* mean man. So *Khun Khon* mean *Mr. Man*. Isn't it?"

Lew bristled. Damn. So the name supplied by the Texas blotch fellow was no doubt a fake, the Amazia version of John Doe? Wonderful. Nothing here was going to be easy. Lew had envisioned Khon as a helpful initial contact—an English speaker, presumably easy to find in the capital, for directions to the Lotus headquarters in rural Amazia. Hope was evaporating fast.

"Maybe this will help." He handed Frog the mailing address for Asiatic Media, torn from an envelope. Frog studied the address, pursed his lips and then smiled.

"Yes, this place I am knowing. Not far." He pointed a thumb at his chest. "So I am taking Khun Lew there, please?"

The offer was very kind but Lew reflexively did the usual American false demurral. "Thanks, Frog, but I don't want to impose. Don't you need to stay here for your job? Drinks for customers?" Lew motioned at the beverage cooler and only now noticed it was empty.

Frog waved a dismissive hand across the vacant lobby. Even the front desk was unattended. "Business today is already finish, Sir! You see? Mr. Wongrat already going home."

Wow, just moments earlier, not yet even noon, Wongrat must have already clocked out. Lew then at last understood—that week, *he* was the entirety of their business. That, in Amazia, was evidently enough already.

"So no problem, Khun Lew. We go that place, together."

Out front of the hotel, clouds of dust swirled around the incongruous duo, a tall blond American towering over a short, deeply tanned local. Frog raised his hand and a baby-blue pedicab instantly glided up, as if materializing from the hot air. The colorful vehicle, covered with garish decorations, was a converted bicycle, fitted with a wide passenger seat under a canopy, above a two-wheeled front axle.

They climbed aboard and squeezed into the cracked vinyl seat. A tight fit.

"Oh my! American people are large size, isn't it?" Frog shook his head, amused. "Bicycle taxi here is usually fitting three, maybe four Amaza people. Entire family, sometimes can."

The metal framework and canvas canopy crawled with extravagant art. Volcanoes spewed orange lava above a mint-green forest with troops of hairy monkeys at play. Colorful curlicues wriggled down the metal frame. On the canopy was a crest that resembled the brand logo from an old-fashioned ketchup bottle, but with Amaza words.

Frog anticipated Lew's question. "Sign is saying it *Wonderful to Live.*"

The driver clicked the bell on his handlebar and pedaled down the red clay road. Motion provided an instant cooling breeze to banish the scorching heat. This was a totally new experience for Lew, like cruising through his own private 3-D travelogue of Ruangbang.

Most buildings were shacks or huts, making the occasional modern building appear strange and out of place, usually a royal commission or government ministry. And for every motor vehicle— mainly toy-like pickups from India or China—hundreds of bicycles or bullock carts plied the roads.

But above all, foot traffic dominated. Pedestrians jostled along the road but always managed to miraculously part just as vehicles plowed through.

Lew studied the crowds. He especially noticed the women, many highly attractive with big eyes and complexions like milky tea, and some in sexy outfits but others hidden in nun-like garb, though with eyes still bewitchingly painted up.

"Holy shit, Frog, from this vantage point, I'm loving Amazia. Incredible." Seeds of affection were being planted by the odd place's mix of utter economic simplicity with a sweet but confounding culture. How could such a place have manufactured those amazing exports? Absent the modern world's enabling technologies, it seemed rather impossible.

Frog's eyes sparkled. "Ha! Frog happy Sir is liking our Kingdom. Good! Yes, Ruangbang nice . . . but rest of Amazia very different." He waved off toward the distance and shook his head. "Out there."

Hmm. Lew braced himself. "And is Biti that way?"

"Yes! Biti." Frog shivered with disgust. "How is Khun Lew knowing Biti? A very alone place, far away, behind mountains." Frog made a face. "But Khun Lew must stay in Ruangbang, only. No Biti! Okay?"

Lew shrugged noncommittally.

Frog leaned closer, as if sharing a secret. "Long time ago, our king is cutting off Amazia. Protecting from outside, Khun Lew. Many years alone."

That explained the isolation.

"But Amazia like bamboo fish trap."

"What does that mean?" This should be good.

"Fish trap is letting fish go in. But out, cannot. Amazia is letting ideas enter and keeping. Many words and foods here coming from Thailand, India and other. Amaza people joking how Asia visitors already having enough words for enjoying. Maybe enough, also, for trouble."

Lew chuckled.

"And so many different Amaza faces! Sometimes like Cambodia people, other times like Laos or China. Vietnam, too. Yes? And many religion, too, but most Amaza following Buddhism or Hindu."

"Any Christians?"

"Yes! Today, we are having one—you!" Frog giggled at his own joke. "But above all, everyone is worshiping spirit gods."

Ah, those same pesky buggers now ruining his life? "Yep, already heard about them."

The pedicab driver jingled his bell three times and squeaked his brakes. The vehicle jolted to a halt and searing heat and humidity suddenly returned to engulf Lew.

"And now, Sir, we are please going down from pedicab. This our place."

Lew stared at the long one-story building and double-checked the address—yes, this dirty retail mall was it. Ever since arriving in Amazia, his expectations had been sliding . . . but this established a new low.

"Shopping center," remarked Frog. "Hmm. Maybe not so busy today."

Or *any* day. It was hard to imagine the empty, derelict place *ever* abuzz with shoppers.

With an open-air front, the building was constructed from uneven, handmade bricks with little shops on either side of a central aisle that ran to a back wall, deep inside. They sauntered down the hallway and studied abandoned remnants of shuttered businesses. The shallow rooms behind smudged glass fronts were littered with broken stools, crushed cardboard boxes and scraps of wrapping paper. Of the twenty cubicles, only three were still active: a beauty parlor and two shops, one selling religious supplies and the other, tobacco, sweets and lottery tickets.

A worn decal stuck to the glass of the final shop at the very end of the hall: ASIATIC MEDIA AGENCY.

"Here it is, Khun Lew," Frog exclaimed happily and aimed a chin at the empty space. "But no your friends! Maybe nobody home."

The sad little space shocked Lew, so jarringly different from his preconceived image of a professional media consultancy in an Asian capital. This was just a hovel, a small reception desk and red fiberboard wall with company name cut from thick white Styrofoam.

The glass door was ajar so they entered and headed for the makeshift passageway beside the fiberboard wall. Lew parted the hanging bead strings and found a cramped work space in back, barely enough room for a computer desk and chairs. Just off to the side was an open area with an X taped to the floor in front of a green wall.

Lew immediately understood. This was the work area for video recordings—green screen magic. Probably where that Khon character had linked in for the video conference. Conduit and cable ran through a small window up to an empty wall mount outside, probably for a compact satellite dish. So that was how Asiatic rigged up their private internet feed.

Frog coughed, seeming embarrassed. "Sorry, Sir, but nobody here. Maybe your friends forgetting Khun Lew visiting?"

Lew chuckled mirthlessly. "Yeah, something like that."

"But Frog *very* sorry for your disappointing. This not good. Not Amaza style. Not polite to guest." He smoothed his lime green shirt, looking irritated the home team had let Lew down.

"Thanks, but no worries." Buddy, if only you knew.

Heading back to the street, they stopped at the surviving shops, seeking information—anything—about Asiatic.

At the religious goods shop, a comely shopkeeper greeted them with a wai that they returned. Her curious eyes scanned Lew. She looked like five feet of dynamite in a tight purple sarong and rainbow silk shirt, her hair bundled tight atop her head and held in place by a wooden skewer. A shining black ponytail emerged from the knot and dangled all the way down to her waist.

Punk smoldering in the air tickled Lew's nose, triggering a colossal sneeze. Frog and the woman both laughed. She gurgled something and they both chuckled again. "Khun Lew, she is saying your sneeze excellent. Meaning good luck."

Lew's eyes drifted to a line-up of small, happy Buddha figurines that filled the shopkeeper's shelves, along with angels, demons and various other wild mythological creatures. Geez, Lew thought, like straight out of a nightmare.

Frog and the storekeeper chatted amiably until he raised an eyebrow and gestured toward Lew. The shopkeeper nodded with a compassionate noise and a moment later offered Lew lukewarm tea, urging him toward a folding chair in the corner. But Lew preferred to stand. He smiled and sipped the tart amber liquid.

"Well she seems friendly enough, Frog. Anything about Asiatic?"

Frog gave a soft sigh. "She saying this whole place is finish. All business go away. Kingdom building new water plant here."

"And Asiatic Media?"

"Yes, also going away. Last week."

Lew felt a tiny flicker of hope. Finally information, anything, even if just a disappointing sliver. "Did she know Khun Khon?"

"Khun Khon?" Frog laughed.

"Yes, I know, it's some kind of joke here. But please ask her anyway."

Frog dropped to a low, earnest tone and the shopkeeper matched it.

"She say only one man and reception girl ever working that place, Sir. But no *Mr. Man*." Frog chuckled. "And she not knowing names, or where they go."

Naturally.

"But once, two old man—country people—are coming and visiting shop."

New hopes rose. Perhaps the Eternity Brothers, owners of Lotus? "Frog, did those country people come from Biti, maybe?"

"She is not knowing."

On the way out, they also stopped at the tiny beauty shop and the tobacco stand. Neither produced any information.

Lew felt powerless. The Ruangbang visit had been a total washout, with Asiatic and Khon eluding him. But the hotel workers' cheerful assistance gratified him, so he offered to buy them dinner.

"Oh yes, please!" Frog and Wongrat sang back in unison. And they knew just the place.

The three walked down the center of a clay road through the heart of the capital, as if daring traffic to appear. They passed a shop selling black gongs edged in gold filigree, some large as a table. And next door, young girls practiced temple dances, leaping about and striking poses while humming their own accompanying music.

An occasional bullock cart lumbered by.

And now that he knew to look, Lew couldn't stop spotting those simple spirit houses. Scores of them *everywhere*, just off the road, atop poles, tree stumps or the ground.

They arrived at the restaurant, a simple whitewashed shop with an open front, surrounded by palm trees and green metal tables that spilled out on the roadside. The trio selected one and plopped down in once-white plastic chairs. Flies immediately attacked. Lew furiously batted them away but his local friends just ignored them.

A group of children approached, giggling but hovering a safe distance from the odd foreign visitor. Drenched in sweat, Lew knew he must look other-worldly to them. A pale, giant devil man.

The meal commenced instantly—no waiting in Amazia! Waves of delicious, freshly-cooked food arrived on dingy blue plastic plates, astounding Lew from the very first taste. After years dining out in Manhattan's finest restaurants, this humble dive was serving up the finest meal of his life! At first he suspected this only reflected how famished he was, but after the succession of incredible courses continued, the verdict was clear.

This meal was perfection itself, including delectable, spicy coconut-flavored chicken; fiery, mouth-watering chili prawns; a crisp, shredded green papaya salad; and impossibly sweet steamed fish wrapped in tidy triangular leaf packets. Every dish was savory and fresh, fried up in woks or boiled in cauldrons. Some burned like edible lava, heated by fiery little chili dots that defied swallowing. But other dishes were as sweet and comforting as Mom's apple pie with vanilla ice cream. The dessert was a luscious chilled coconut and mango pudding that Lew all but inhaled, topped with blobs of rich cream.

How had those two sweating men in white tee shirts, manning woks in a simple kitchen, produced such a miracle? More Amazia magic. Lew closed his eyes with a satisfied smile.

"Gents, about this food . . . I mean, whoa!"

That startled Frog and Wongrat. Their faces appeared confused and sad.

"Oh, Khun Lew!" said Wongrat. "Sorry to esteem guest! Our humble Amazia food—"

"No, no, you misunderstand. I mean it's *wonderful*. Absolutely amazing!"

Both instinctively responded with abrupt wais, hands clasped high overhead. Lew blushed—that gesture got him, every time.

The trio sat contentedly after the glorious meal, stuffed to burping and chatting over steaming cups of hot black tea. Lew told them he needed to depart Ruangbang soon and head upcountry to somehow track down Lotus in Biti, in the Inner Amazia hinterlands.

"Go *Biti*?" yelped Wongrat.

Frog raised a finger, instructing. "Biti no good, Sir! When Ruangbang people angry, we are saying: *You go Biti!*"

Wongrat nodded. "Yes. Is very insult here."

Lew put his head in his hands and sighed. Great. This Biti place, where Lotus was apparently hidden, was so remote and awful that it served as part of a local curse.

The two Amaza jabbered away and from their tone, Lew surmised his audacity had genuinely shocked them. The idea of a Biti trip seemed to fascinate and horrify them, in equal measure, like a plunge off the end of the earth. Neither Wongrat nor Gob—both capital city slickers—could help, having never traveled in rural Amazia . . . and certainly not to the distant and horrific Biti.

Lew persisted trying to pull information from them. Anything. They responded with old wives' stories that made Biti sound like a downsized, low-grade version of Mogadishu or Kinshasa, but on risk-enhancing steroids.

"But seriously, gents, how do I travel there?"

The Amaza exchanged wary looks. Frog drew in a breath and spoke in a tone laden with regret. "Khun Lew, every night, express mail train is going Biti. Late." Right. Khon had mentioned that.

Well that was more like it! He'd be fine. He needed to just keep taking his shots.

He made an instant decision to leave for Biti at once. That night. All the Amaza he'd met so far had been welcoming and enormously helpful; surely that would be the case up in Biti, too. If he stayed resilient and just kept plugging away, he'd surely hit the mark. Eventually.

"Fellows, can you help get me onto that train, tonight?"

They smiled back, sadly.

"Can," they said with low voices.

Back at the hotel, Lew peeled off another set of his sweat-drenched clothing for a quick splash bath at the cistern. Man, he'd really messed up back home when packing and already was nearly out of wearable clothing. He shook his head. Why did he pack suits? And what was he thinking, bringing those expensive lizard skin cowboy boots to the tropics?

He decided to wear jeans for protection against who-knows-what on the train seats and pulled on his cowboy boots—might as well use 'em. He grabbed the Stetson for sun protection upcountry and headed for the lobby.

Wongrat grinned to see this new, Western Lew and proffered him a hand-written statement, carefully detailed in the psychedelic-looking Amazian script. Below an impressive blue hotel logo, lines of ciphers, squiggles and dots danced down the page. Lew could only read the two items not written in Amaza: his name (more drawn than written, looking like *Lez Clak)* and a balance due.

The number floored him.

Seven million *Arysai*!

But once he fished around in the paper sack bulging with local money, he realized his cash bankroll reached into the hundreds of millions. The hotel stay had cost him just pennies.

"And what about magic pocket telephone of Khun Lew?" Wongrat's eyebrows levitated.

"Keep it safe for me, okay?" Lew motioned at the tackle box under the counter.

Wongrat nodded back, glowing with pride.

Lew marched out the front door, his friends hovering close behind and smiling sadly, like relatives already missing a departing family member. Lew pawed in his wrinkled brown paper cash sack and fished out an inch-thick slab for each. "For your families," he announced to cut off any refusals. Major-league wais exploded back his way, new versions also involving semi-genuflections along with praying hands and bowing heads.

"Khun Lew now like brother for Wongrat," the clerk said with a sentimental sniffle. "Good luck," he said, his face souring, "in Biti."

Frog insisted (over only half-hearted objections) on chaperoning Lew to the train station. "Frog making sure Khun Lew safe and getting on train." The journey north was supposedly only twelve hours of snaking around brooding mountains. So how difficult could it really be?

Frog loaded Lew's leather suitcase and khaki satchel onto a trishaw and joined his American guest aboard a second vehicle and then they were off.

Just being on the move lifted Lew's spirits.

After a twenty-minute ride through cool night air, surrounded by the chirping chorus of evening insects, they rounded a corner and arrived at the train station, Hualambang Terminal. The place was utterly inundated, the most people Lew had seen yet since arriving in Ruangbang.

As they climbed down from the pedicab, Frog grasped Lew's hand, tight.

"Please coming now," Frog said as he pulled his tall friend into and through the festive crowd milling around the modest depot. Lew, standing a head taller than all rest, drank in an unobstructed view of the carnival-like atmosphere. A happy, barely-controlled pandemonium boiled away under yellow flood lamps.

Departing travelers toted huge bundles and trudged forward with loved ones trailing. Entrepreneurial vendors operated slapdash instant stalls to hawk everything from pocket knives to aluminum woks and rainbow-colored woven goods. Little one-pot restaurants popped up like mushrooms after a good rain, the cooks squatting upon hard-pounded clay to fan smoky wood fires. Swarthy farmers in coveralls guided squeaking wagonloads of cabbage or sugar cane.

A few unsavory characters hovered at the fringes, scanning the crowd. Opportunistic dogs scrounged everywhere, nosing around for food scraps and experimentally licking anything that fell to the ground. More than once, Lew's fingertips felt the sudden wet of a canine nose, causing him to recoil reflexively.

A red wooden station house stood at the center of all this commotion and beside it crouched a black antique locomotive, huffing up great clouds of steam and growling like a beast straining at the leash.

Behind it, ten rail cars sported cheerful paint jobs that failed to hide brownish rust scabs underneath. Three were brilliant cherry red, two a cool aqua, and the others lemon yellow, gravy brown, vitamin-packed Florida orange and lime gelatin green. The sight made him hungry. Overall, the vision summoned memories of circus trains in Lew's childhood picture books.

Loading appeared well underway, having commenced perhaps hours earlier.

But the next sight stopped Lew cold. Passengers were shinnying right up the outer walls of train cars and onto the carriage tops, where families staked out space. Crowds undulated up there like ants teeming atop colored sugar cubes. And despite the rooftops all being jammed, riders continued relentlessly ascending with khaki bags, trussed live fowl and anything else.

"Look, Frog! Why they going up there? The train already full?" Lew shivered at the prospect that he might also have to ride up top.

Frog chuckled. "Train not full, Khun Lew. All are being travelers, same-same like you, going Biti."

"Good Lord! So am I . . . going up there?" Lew held his breath, picturing himself perched in the darkness, wind and who-knows-what for the entire precarious journey.

Frog burst out laughing and rubbed his palms, savoring that. "What, you, Sir? Oh my, no! Only local people up top, not foreign visitor! Is Amaza way." He smiled. "Free."

Lew heaved a sigh of relief.

But if nearly *everyone* rode up there, free, how did the business turn any profit? Another Amazia mystery. As for himself, he certainly didn't begrudge Rail Amazia, or whatever they called themselves, the price of a ticket.

Frog led him into the station house. It was even more crowded than outside but with a mellow and patient atmosphere, despite the jumble of bodies. Bless 'em, even in situations like this, the Amaza peaceably coexisted.

A long, untidy line started just inside the door and snaked back and forth across the room until eventually reaching the small ticket window on the far wall, behind jailhouse-style bars. A black chalkboard provided schedule updates. Frog read it, nodding.

"Tonight, sir, Biti express mail train is scheduling seven or eight."

"But Frog, it's already past ten."

Frog smiled. "Yes, indeed, Sir. So train leaving soon."

Great. Lew's odds of navigating that long ticket line in time to board looked about nil. So why was Frog grinning?

"Sir is please now coming with Frog, and following closely."

Frog gripped Lew's elbow and began to steer him through the throng. They drifted forward through the crowd like magic, silently maneuvering around and through the line as the mob mysteriously parted and then seamlessly closed in again, right behind them. No pushing or shoving, no raised voices. Frog smiled or bowed at complete strangers and obstructions (people or their packages) magically disappeared.

It was utterly shocking.

Geez, just try a stunt like that at the Port Authority terminal back home? Get your ass kicked. But all along the way, Lew saw only smiling faces of kindly strangers, gesturing him forward, *please*, toward the ticket window, which they reached in just minutes.

Frog spoke in a loud, officious voice to the ticket vendor behind the bars, repeatedly pointing at Lew. Amid the pleasant, now-familiar gurgle of spoken Amaza, a few English words popped up: *Mister Clarke . . . America . . . businessman . . . Donald Trump.*

Trump? Where'd that come from? Lew suppressed a grin and just watched as arms waved and heads shook, though neither Frog nor the rail agent ever stopped smiling. But the tone sounded off somehow, not quite right.

"Hey, Frog," Lew whispered, "we good here? Some hang-up?"

"Sir?"

"Some trouble, I mean? A problem?"

Frog smiled brightly. "Oh my goodness, Sir, yes! Very serious. Is *big* problem. I'm sorry but train already fully booking tonight. Mr. Beaver, sales captain here, is only selling ticket for Sir, maybe next week."

Damn! So why the smile? "But tell him it's urgent, Frog. An emergency! And that I—"

With an abrupt stern look, Frog shut Lew down in midsentence. Now where did *that* come from? Lew felt stunned.

Frog spoke in a new, no-nonsense tone, though gently patting Lew's hand. "Now please to be waiting, Khun Lew. Frog is handling . . . Yes?"

In this land of boundless courtesy and friendliness, Lew could not recall ever being interrupted before, much less reprimanded. He felt chastened and a bit humbled.

Lew nodded and stepped out of the way, to watch the minuet of negotiation between his friend and the stationmaster. It played out for several minutes, yet the throng of ticket seekers behind them all remained patient and waited without complaint.

At last, Frog turned back to Lew with an electric smile, holding a paper with numbers scribbled on it. "And now, Sir is please to paying this amount. Also providing passport."

Wow. They'd won?

Having cut the entire line, Lew tried to be as nonchalant as possible while thumbing through his rainbow stack of *Arysai*. He handed a few bills over to Frog, who passed them through the iron bars.

Then, as if a starter's gun had been fired, the station master launched into the bureaucratic dance of Third World officialdom. In a blur of motion, he slipped tiny squares of carbon paper between flimsy pages of a massive book and penned in Lew's name and passport number. That accomplished, he hefted a rubber stamp and rocked it back and forth across a dried-out pad, seeking to coax forth a little ink. Then, taking firm grip of the fat black wooden handle, he raised and slammed down the stamp with a flourish, whacking the book and ticket in multiple locations. *Thwack, thwack, thwack!*

Next—in striking contrast to the stampings' kinetic violence—he delicately retrieved the carbons and copies, and politely handed one to Lew, plus a bright orange ticket on flimsy paper. He counted out Lew's change and handed over moldy pieces of currency so blackened by dirt, grease and perspiration they'd lost most of their color.

Lew did the conversion—he'd paid out about a dollar but received ninety-cents back.

Lastly, the clerk handed Lew two short, fat red candles, each about two inches long. Why? But before he could ask, Frog hustled Lew out the station door.

They paused on the platform beside the huffing locomotive. An endless flow of bodies passed them, like a fast-running brook parting around protruding rocks.

"Frog, thank you. That was simply brilliant! Your negotiation skills . . ." He shook his head. "One day, maybe we go into business together? Haha. How did you ever pull that off?"

"Pull off?" Frog then understood and proudly grinned. "We are chatting and learning brother of Mr. Beaver is matriculating from same secondary school as my cousin! Many year ago. So now we being friends and station master is helping us. Maybe later, too, I am helping him. Giving free room at Miracle Royal Pagoda Hotel." Frog paused and winked. He lowered his voice. "He is having *acquaintance* downtown."

Did Lew get that right . . . his problem was fixed in exchange for an expense-free tryst? Too funny, this Amazia . . . what next?

"And my ticket was so cheap. Only ten cents. I can hardly

believe it. Did you get me a special discount?"

Frog frowned, pursing his lips. "Oh, no. Standard price."

Lew drank everything in, this amazing scene and the stunning turn of events. Things were finally going his way. "But please don't tell me that, as part of the bargain, I have to ride up top." He pointed at the nearby luggage car roof and, thus encouraged, several smiling rooftop riders waved back and began calling out greetings.

Frog chortled at Lew's question. "Khun Lew, riding up top? Oh, my goodness, never! Honored foreign guest is always traveling top grade." He paused a beat and then intoned, with great ceremony, "First class compartment!"

First class, for ten cents?

But still clamoring for attention, the rooftop riders showered friendly catcalls on Lew as he and Frog walked down the platform. "Hello, America!" yelled one. "Mr. Cowboy!" another hollered. "Welcome to Amazia!" Lew tipped his leather Stetson, which only further amped up the frenzy.

But who could blame them? Not Lew, who understood what a unique sight he must be, as a tall, fair American in cowboy hat and swirling lizard skin boots. Thus far, the only Westerner *he'd* seen in Amazia was in the hotel's rippling bathroom mirror.

Shrill whistle blasts warned of imminent departure and the engineer began to gun the steam engine. Frog seized Lew's hand and doubled their pace, dragging him toward the front of the train. With every railcar passed, surprised topside riders cried out from above, cheering Lew on and urging him to hurry.

"First car is engine," Frog said over his shoulder, breathing heavily. "Second having coal. Next having restaurant. And number four is having Khun Lew. First class carriage!"

Lew dragged his bulky leather suitcase, bumping it along the cement platform, scuffing and scraping its sides. The two red candles (their purpose still a mystery) clicked in his pocket.

Just as they reached the fourth car, the train jolted and started to inch forward. Frog pulled Lew on board through the open door and into a dimly-lit hallway surfaced with once-fine mahogany. There were three doors, each in polished stainless steel, with small Plexiglas windows. Three first class compartments for the entire train.

They matched a cabin number against Lew's ticket and opened the door. Frog gently pushed him in. "And now, Khun Lew, Mr. Clarke, my dear friend and kind Sir," he said, adding an endearing little salute, "Frog is having to leave. Must go, fast."

Out the cabin window, people, luggage, and trash barrels began slowly passing by.

"No Biti today for *Gob*!" His smile disappeared for a moment, when saying *Biti*. "But Frog wishing you most wonderful good fortune there! And Sir is always please to remembering, always being careful!"

With that, Frog backed into the hallway and leapt down off the train. The cabin door hissed and closed with a metallic *click*. Lew was on his way.

But . . . *Always being careful—of what?*

CHAPTER TWELVE
The Overnight Mail Train to Biti

Lew turned in the doorway and saw other passengers were already settling in. A single ceiling bulb flickered, barely lighting the cabin. Suddenly, the candles in his pocket made more sense.

The first class cabin was a quad with two pairs of facing bench seats. Above each, flat against the side walls, were hinged cots able to swing down on chains to a sleeping position. And still higher up were luggage racks.

Everything was painted a muted aqua, like the hallways at an old-time children's hospital, with crumbly rust patches showing through. By reflex he slapped at his neck and then noticed the window had been left partially open. Damned mosquitoes!

So this was Amazia first class: hot, dim and bug-infested. He searched for positives. Well, those long padded seats and matching sleeper cots looked quite adequate, perhaps even comfortable. He had to hand it to them—the travel dime sure went a long way in the Kingdom.

The vacant bench by the window was surely his, with the other three already occupied. Sensing envious eyes, he strode briskly over and tossed his briefcase on the last empty bench to stake his claim and preempt a cabin turf war. He hoisted his heavy suitcase up onto the wall rack and dropped into the seat, sensing others' hopes deflating like air hissing from a balloon.

He nodded at the young family across from him. They flashed back radiant smiles and continued to unstack plates and utensils while setting up a small cooking device on the floor. Barely into their twenties, the parents juggled three small children. A newborn happily suckled at its mother's breast while a son, about four, played peek-a-boo with his father. Lew overheard the boy's name was something like *Tik*. Their third child, a toddler, had already crawled off to explore the far corner of the carriage.

She knelt at the feet of two middle-aged monks, a man and a woman with fully shaved heads, even eyebrows, who beamed indulgent smiles as the child played with the hems of their brilliant orange robes.

Lew watched it all like a TV show, almost unaware he was staring, so it jarred him when the monks looked directly back at him and wai'ed. He felt that familiar rush. Should he wai back? No, perhaps they'd enjoy something more colorful from so foreign a curiosity. Why disappoint them? He rose, tipped his cowboy hat and nodded.

"Howdy, y'all," he drawled in his best Deadwood imitation, "The name's Lew." Everyone in the carriage tittered appreciatively. But that, sadly, was the extent of his impressions repertoire. Style-wise, Lew was more Central Park West than Old West.

A grandfather and two teens squeezed into the final bench seat. Grandpa dozed while the boy rolled a tiny steel ball around obstacles in a wooden handheld puzzle. His sister pored through a local comic book.

It felt odd but refreshing to see young people not glued to electronic screens. But along with that came a sobering realization that none of the technologies he'd championed at Mega meant *anything* there in the Kingdom! It was as if his illustrious track record, all that precious skill and knowledge, did not exist.

Once the train cleared the rail yard, the overhead cabin lamp blacked out and the hallway also went dark. "Hey!" complained Lew. But his cabin mates seemed unsurprised and only chuckled. The lady monk rose and lit one of her candles and placed it in a small holder high on the wall. The young father pantomimed an explanation—

each would take a turn lighting a fresh candle as needed. Lew did the math . . . at two candles per bench, they'd get through the night.

Swaying and lurching, the train attained walking speed. The overnight express to Biti was on its way! This was going to work.

Lew sat back and propped up his legs, putting those extraordinary lizard skin boots on unintended display. Despite already being sweat-drenched and darkened, the intricate swirls of green, yellow, and red on the tan base riveted his cabin mates' attention. They buzzed with interest, commenting in their popping dialect.

Lew slapped at another mosquito. He glanced over—window was still open. Why didn't somebody close that thing?

But then he noticed something just *beyond* the window, so strange and unexpected that, at first, it didn't register. But a second look confirmed it. Indeed, two heads were hanging down outside the window, staring straight at him. Behind them, town lights skittered by like fireflies.

They were rooftop riders, no doubt, but how on earth did they achieve that? And though it had been entertaining before, on the platform as they cheered him, this was altogether different and unacceptable. How long was he to endure their scrutiny, like an animal in the zoo?

"Hello, America!" called out one of the dangling young men, waves of his long black hair swaying in the breeze. "Welcome Amazia," added his partner, pointing at Lew's boots. "Mr. Cow-boy!"

Not knowing what else to do but play along, for now, Lew again tipped his hat, Western-style, and they laughed. But how long would they hang there and watch? Surely not all night. It would be too dangerous, once the train picked up speed, right? He hoped so. But for now, the train only rolled slowly through the Ruangbang outskirts, as if sneaking away under cover of darkness. Higher speeds seemed a long way off.

Soothed by the hypnotic, clickety-clack of wheels on rails, they left the capital behind and soon plunged into unremitting blackness.

Whatever the speed, it wasn't fast enough—those upside-down heads still bounced outside the window.

Lew began to think of them, for shorthand, as *The Boys*. He'd never seen anything like this before except maybe on a PBS documentary. But now, with his attention fully drawn, he couldn't stop checking the window or monitoring the constant footsteps overhead. But it was getting late, so hopefully they'd soon settle down.

At least The Boys all seemed to like his attire. And that Mister Cowboy nickname? Pretty funny.

A tornado of insects circled the cabin's flickering candle, with singed bits of moth wings and exoskeleton slowly accumulating on the floor. Lew slapped his arm and left a tiny splatter of blood. "Oh crap," he sighed.

"Tsk." The young mother across from him clicked her tongue and smiled sympathetically. She then set fire to the tip of a blue-green coil and blew it out. The glowing edge smoldered and began to issue a sickly, sweet smoke that drove the mosquitoes away. Evidently they hated the odor even more than Lew did.

But his American DNA favored a more direct approach, so he rose to shut the window and cut off the insect problem at its source. "*Aieeee,* no!" the others howled as he first touched the window frame. What, they preferred smoky, buggy air? He then learned the window was permanently jammed open and sat back down, feeling sheepish.

The carriage rocked gently back and forth and lulled Lew, over time, into a peaceful, semi-awake state. That abruptly ended when the quad door banged open and a silver-haired conductor entered. This visit by officialdom spooked The Boys, who withdrew to the rooftop.

The conductor's deep blue uniform included magnificent epaulets, braided gold ropes and a chest full of medals. His over-sized cap would have suited the proudest of airline pilots and overall, his outfit could have passed muster with the most vainglorious of Latin

American generalissimos.

Lew handed over his ticket and the conductor shone a tiny penlight at it before punching a hole with a shiny clicker. Lew then watched with idle curiosity as other passengers followed suit. But they surrendered only three tickets in total, one per bench, for ten other passengers.

Hmm. So train travel in Amazia was something like an all-you-can-eat buffet. But more a case of all-the-asses-you-can-squeeze-in.

Once the conductor left, a comfortable atmosphere returned and gentle, relaxed conversation filled the cabin in the low candle light. All of it flew right past Lew, of course, but the mellow gurgle of spoken Amaza sounded clearly friendly and somehow comforting.

The lady monk casually glanced over at Lew and smiled.

"Love your robe, madam. That hot orange is fantastic." He meant it—it was indeed gorgeous. But she looked quickly away, nervous or embarrassed by his attention. Others just stared.

Had he been too direct? Well there was another lesson for him. In rural Amazia, even innocent American friendliness might come across as creepy. This place was a cultural minefield and Lew seemed intent on blowing himself up.

The cabin door flew open again and this time, in barged the next railway employee, an older, short-haired woman in a mannish white suit with a purple beret. She chirped something that stirred up all the passengers, who jostled in their seats. Now what? Lew raised his eyebrows in confusion at the young father and amused laughter erupted.

He sensed these Amaza liked him, even if just for the amusement of seeing a strange foreign man in a cowboy suit. Whatever.

The pretty teenage girl fiddled with her long black hair, perhaps working up nerve, and then smiled and pantomimed an answer to Lew's apparent question. She forked imaginary food into her mouth. Ah, the dining car was opening! Good, he needed an evening snack.

But then her little mime show continued as she put her hands together under her head, like a pillow, and feigned sleep and then, awakening, she held up six fingers before play-acting another meal. He got it—tomorrow morning, the dining car would open for breakfast at six. He smiled his thanks.

The parade of visiting railway employees rolled on. Now a cranky old couple came in, wearing frayed white T-shirts, sarongs and rubber sandals. They moved fast and in a brusque manner, speaking nary a word. The man headed straight for Lew's bench seat and, with the thinnest of smiles, motioned for him to rise. Now what?

He unbolted the padded sleeper above Lew's seat and lowered it to horizontal, supported by rusty chains, and locked it in place via linchpins. Then the severe, gray-haired matron unfurled crisp white sheets, snapping and cracking them in a show of no-nonsense efficiency. After dressing Lew's instant bed, she magically summoned a pillow and fluffed it—*thwack, thwack!*—with harsh punches

Within minutes, all four overhead sleeper units were ready for the night.

Flopping back down onto his bench seat, Lew banged his head against the protruding metal bed. The rail car dimensions reflected design for more diminutive riders. And indeed, the locals all sat in comfort beneath their sleeper racks while Lew had to slouch. He rubbed his head, wondering if there would be a welt.

The teens tittered at his predicament, earning a speedy reprimand from their grandfather. He looked over at Lew with a silent apology. Lew smiled back.

"Yeah, kids, right? I know." Well, not really. He and MJ never had any.

The old man shook his head and shrugged.

CHAPTER THIRTEEN
Movie Night in Amazia

The train chugged along through the steamy night, squealing against the rails with every curve. A brownish-red gecko clung to the metal wall above Lew, clicking hungry approval at the dizzying vortex of insects circling the candle flame.

Lew sat there wide awake at 11 p.m. in the still-uncomfortably warm cabin. His biorhythms demolished by jet lag, he wondered when he'd ever sleep again.

He found himself growing fond of the Amaza. Yes, their culture was bewildering at times and his learning was molasses slow. But he was already no longer a cultural infant—something more like a toddler now.

But the climate was something he'd never get used to. The Kingdom was a humid green oven where heat constantly smothered and pressed down on him, sapping his energy.

Nearly everything he'd packed for the tropics was wrong. He dug into his bag and put on his retro Yankees cap. Then on pure impulse, Lew summoned Tik, the small boy, busy capturing bugs on the floor. Lew handed him the massive hat. "Here you go, pal."

The youngster squealed with glee and pulled it on. It sat huge, dark and square on his shoulders, totally engulfing his head. He blindly shuffled about, growling with his arms outstretched like a movie monster. The entire carriage, including The Boys dangling outside, howled with delight at the headless miniature cowboy. Their outburst riled up two trussed chickens stowed under the monks' seat.

Lew pulled off his soggy cowboy boots and changed into dry

socks. He slipped into his custom Italian loafers. Inspired by the big hit created by the Stetson, he stretched an arm high out the window and dangled the boots aloft. A flurry of hands snapped at them like hungry bass striking at a lure. The boots disappeared up into the night and the rooftop resounded in delirium.

Soon the *clip-clopping* sound of boot heels rained down from the ceiling. What had he done? What a mistake. How would he ever sleep with all that racket? But a moment later, a surprising sight confirmed he was better off without the boots: a half-dozen heads dropped down outside the window and thanked him with a group wai.

He fidgeted about, not the least bit sleepy, and looked for a way to kill time. He unzipped his khaki briefcase and pulled out that futuristic gift from Apple, the sleek titanium tablet the size of a coffee table book. He propped it on the chipped Formica ledge jutting out from the window.

With a cutting-edge battery, the solar-powered computer could run for days. But in Amazia, with no internet or cellular networks, the miraculous invention was stripped of its most impressive powers, reduced to merely a word processor or video player. Lew couldn't miss making the painful analogy to his own situation in the Kingdom.

But such thinking was unhelpful. He decided to busy himself with a computer game or some company documents. But on looking up, he found his fellow passengers had crowded around him for a closer look at the contraption. Pungent exhaled aromas of recent meals floated through the nearby air. With chatty curiosity they rubbed against their adopted American friend and, before long, hands rested on his shoulders. The Amaza put a low premium on personal space, a lesson Lew learned soon after stepping off the plane in Ruangbang.

In an unexpected move, the Buddhist nun reached out a finger and traced the glistening monogram engraved on the titanium square. She remarked something as the others huddled closer to study the shiny mystery, their eyes wide with wonder. The sight reminded Lew of a 1950s team photo baseball card . . . but a team with two monks, a spry grandfather, two hip Amaza teenagers, a pair of young parents and their impossibly cute kids.

Lew hoisted the unit high for all to see. In so primitive a setting, the sleek device surely looked like serious magic from the future. He fully unfolded it, first opening it like a book and then a second time along the other axis, expanding the screen to four times the original square. Like a conjurer's trick, it made his fellow passengers gasp.

He laid it flat on the ledge. An army of small fluttering bugs instantly landed and marched across the smooth glass face, rolling around in small circles and paying special attention to Lew's sweaty fingerprints, where they dropped translucent wings and specks of unidentifiable goo.

He softly pressed a nearly invisible button at the edge and a brilliant red hologram keyboard snapped into existence, projected mid-thigh on his jeans. He started to type away.

"*Alamak*!" chirped the grizzled male monk while the others also mumbled in amazement.

Lew smiled—they'd seen nothing yet. He waved a hand through the air like a priest blessing a crowd and the computer, tracking this gesture, responded by flinging a brilliant orange rectangle against the far wall. A cheer rang through the cabin while The Boys outside also hooted their appreciation, banging the wall with Lew's boots.

He motioned for calm. All moved into position, facing the illuminated wall, stretching out at their seats or on the cabin floor after scooting away lizards and crawling bugs. Tik, the wee headless cowboy, took off his Stetson and skittered over to the light to cast hand shadows.

Lew swirled his wrists like an orchestra conductor. The sequence of extravagant gestures caused the far wall to explode into the brilliant colors of a Looney Tunes cartoon. The carriage also filled with sound. Lew didn't know how the tablet achieved such an audio trick, but when Bugs Bunny flattened a frying pan over Elmer Fudd's head, one felt the resulting *clang!*

The slapstick animation transcended language and culture and, for the next ten minutes, all shared this innocent escape. Soft applause greeted the conclusion. For a moment, Lew considered showing them a Three Stooges short, but better judgment prevailed.

All drifted back to their seats—time for sleep.

Lew leaned back, enjoying the temporary afterglow. His euphoria dissolved when he recalled he still had unread emails, downloaded at the Dubai airport lounge. Did it matter to stay at all current, despite being incommunicado there in Wonderland? He'd only been in Amazia a few days so far, but it sure felt way longer.

He folded the computer back down to compact mode and placed it on his lap, gesturing for secure private viewing. At the top of his downloaded email queue was a message from Emily, tagged *Urgent* with a subject line: '*60 Minutes*.'

The video was a rough cut of work in progress, currently going viral at the network. Obtained from her friend who was dating a CBS producer, the piece was entitled "Mystery at 99 Pacific Cliff Heights" and reported on the inexplicable disappearance of an entire California seaside estate. "Please watch this. Possible Avian connection," was all Emily wrote.

Goosebumps polka-dotted his arms.

The piece opened with the familiar ominous stopwatch and hand-wringing by Scott Pelley, who explained the network had obtained video shot by an Amazon driver whose phone had been out, ready to snap a delivery confirmation photo.

The images displayed an impossible event, even zooming in for close-ups of dirt boiling like water and ultrahigh-speed vibrations that transported an entire luxury estate downhill and into the ocean. Everything—the mansion, car port, patio, pool house, and boundary walls—moved offshore and took a coordinated plunge, disappearing in only a few feet of ocean water.

But only after Lew saw the sole surviving structures did his stomach clench. Both were early Avian products, unscathed.

Good grief, why *60 Minutes?*

Down through the years, their infamously harsh coverage had

destroyed political careers and misbehaving companies. So far, luckily, CBS made no connection with Avian, nor had any other media picked up on the goofy internet rumors.

Drenched in sudden nervous sweat, Lew gestured to shut down the tablet. The bizarre nightmare seemed to be gathering steam, seeming more possible. Had that been proof, seen with his own eyes, of a connection to Avian? His previous cocky Western certainty was growing shaky.

But still, come on: rampaging terrestrial spirits? That made no sense. Right?

Then what had he just seen on that video? Whatever the case, he felt trapped in a horrific mess he'd done nothing to deserve. His intentions had always been innocent, just business—import and sell a product, that's all. But it now felt as if the Fates had targeting him to be as the unintentional villain in a horrible fantasy.

Regardless, his priorities remained clear. Save his company, himself, and others at risk, like beloved friends who depended on Avian. He had no clever solution, not yet, but the first task remained unchanged: As Uzzi ordered, track down the supplier. Lotus.

The train grew quiet and by midnight the footsteps on the roof all died away. By consensus, the lone cabin candle was extinguished as enough moonlight bled in through the window.

The young parents somehow cadged extra pillows and put them to good use. The mother and baby slept in the cot overhead, with the infant buffered by pillows. Her other two children slept on the bench seat, also pillowed-in, with the father resting on the floor below, attentive as a hockey goalkeeper.

The male monk stretched out across his bench seat and allowed the nun to use the sleeper unit.

At the final position, Grandpa staked out the bench while his granddaughter slept up top, and her brother sprawled on the floor.

Utterly exhausted, Lew climbed into his sleeper, a tad short but okay if he curled up. The train's frequent stops woke him, accompanied by squealing brakes, screeching wheels, and the engine's loud gasping sighs. Around 1 a.m., he noticed the teenage boy had abandoned his floor position and commandeered Lew's empty bench seat. Fine.

Lew climbed down, stepping gingerly around the youth, and lit one of his candles to go off in search of the lavatory. Creaking a door open, he found a miserable little toilet at the end of the hall that made the Ruangbang hotel facility seem luxurious. Squeezed into the compact chamber was a squat podium with a lid above a hole in the floor. Beside that stood a drum full of water with a bucket on a wire hook.

A bright round spotlight, apparently with no switch, shone straight down from the ceiling at the tiny squat toilet. Perhaps the only permanent lighting anywhere in the first class carriage. Lew smiled—were the Amaza keen bathroom readers? Good, he hadn't yet lost his sense of humor.

He swung the lid open and a sudden shocking blast of motion engulfed him, millions of white dots swarming in an abrupt, buzzing kinetic mass. "Good God!" he yelped. Pain from countless bites instantly assaulted his hands, neck and legs. He slapped wildly at the army of insects roaring up through the hole in the floor, attracted by the bright light.

He slammed the lid down and burst free from the tiny bathroom, feeling invasive little legs skittering everywhere beneath his clothing and in places he wouldn't have guessed possible. "Damn!" he yelled, whacking at his legs, buttocks, arms, and torso.

He pushed the carriage back door open and fled out onto the sizeable platform where a group of Amaza men were gathered. They watched, their eyes merry and knowing, as he swatted and cursed. "Welcome Amazia!" sang out one with undisguised pleasure.

Lew knew that voice. Perhaps one of The Boys, down for a late night smoke? He knew for sure after spotting his sweat-distorted lizard skin boots sticking out from under a sarong. Mr. Boots pointed toward the bathroom and shook his head.

Lew, his bladder ready to burst, mimed unzipping his pants with a questioning shrug. Mr. Boots smiled and ushered Lew to the back corner where he opened his sarong and directed a urine stream downwind into the night. Lew followed suit, letting loose a veritable water cannon. The Boys hooted appreciatively at his powerful stream.

Lew returned to his cabin for a few more hours of sleep. With no desire for insects shooting up his rear end, he could hold off defecation until morning. He gingerly climbed past the snoring teen, curled up on his wall cot and fell unconscious. Pattering footsteps continually disturbed his sleep, the sound of topside riders disembarking. The train would slow but not stop, and barely-visible silhouettes jumped off to vanish into the night.

Around 2 a.m., a new pattern began. The train would decelerate, stop and then begin to back up. After a while, it went forward again, only to later reverse direction. This back-and-forth pattern confused the semi-conscious Lew, but once awake he understood.

The train was using switchbacks to climb steep hills or near-vertical mountain walls. No wonder this trip to Biti took so long—they were crossing mountains the hard way. As the train barely crawled along, more people jumped off amid goodbyes and shouts of encouragement.

At one point late that night, aggressive food hawkers boarded the train and ran down the aisle, yelling out offerings of eggs, chicken drumsticks, and tea to sleeping passengers. By the time Lew woke enough to realize what was going on, they were already gone. Nice.

By 5 a.m., a crisp mountain chill penetrated the rail car. That amazed Lew—wasn't this the tropics? He shivered and hugged himself for warmth. The railway supplied no blanket, just a flimsy cotton sheet he pulled up to his chin. By dawn, total fatigue compounded by jet lag finally knocked him out, plunging him into utter oblivion.

A harsh racket startled him awake and he bolted upright in his cot, confused and blinking his eyes in blinding daylight. He smacked his head against the metal ceiling. "Ow!" he cried, rubbing his head and wondering where he was. He winced from his throbbing skull and collected himself. He'd been out cold for hours of heavy sleep.

He realized the hellacious uproar that woke him was the furor of wildly cheering people. Scores, maybe even hundreds of passengers along the entire length of the train were whistling, hollering and banging on walls. He pantomimed to the others: *Why all the noise?*

They mimed back that after a night climbing ever-higher switchbacks, the train had just crossed over the route's highest point. They were finally on the downhill run.

"Ce-le-bra-tion," wheezed the grandfather in a high voice. "Always like that."

Whoa! The grizzled old dude spoke English? Shocking! He'd been holding out. Grandpa shot Lew a one-toothed grin, looking proud over his fragmentary recall of English. Rubbing his chin, he looked up at the ceiling and tried again.

"Hap-py!" he exclaimed. Explanation complete.

Lew climbed down from his sleeper. The moment his feet touched the floor, the cabin door burst open, as if a hair trigger had been pulled, and in shot those two surly bedtime attendants. In a blink, they gathered Lew's sleeping linen and bolted his unit up against the wall.

Geez, they'd been waiting all this time for him? Poor folks needed the lazy American to wake up his dead ass so they could finish their work? Lew felt chagrined. Only then did he also note the monks were already gone. Must have just jumped off during the night. Grandpa's teens already claimed their vacated bench seat.

Lew pulled on his jeans and loafers and headed to the hall toilet, fearing no bug cyclones in the safety of broad daylight. He stood over the hole, swung open the small lid and sent down a dark stream of urine, painting the slowly passing gravel and railroad ties below.

Whoa, that color. Too dehydrated. He needed to drink more water.

Then he turned around, peeled off his jeans and squatted, just as the decelerating train jolted to a full stop. Of course, that was the invasion signal for a new insect army, which quickly located the now-stationary entrance and began filling the small lavatory and Lew.

He jumped upright and slammed down the lid, hurling curses. The complex rules for evacuation on Amazia trains were now clear: nothing at night and, in the day, only when in motion. For such an apparently simple place, Amazia was proving an intricate muddle.

When he returned to the quad, he discovered the small family had departed. He scrunched his eyebrows, finding it hard to picture the young couple jumping down from a moving train, hugging three little ones.

Foot traffic from topside riders, overhead, also sounded vastly diminished.

The sun was high in the sky, noonish, meaning they'd already been rolling along for fourteen hours. So much for the promised twelve-hour trip. Hopefully they'd soon reach Biti.

Starving, he mimed an invitation at Grandpa and the teens—the only remaining first class passengers—to join him for lunch.

"Yes," chirped Grandpa, the new English linguist. "*Eating!*"

The four of them sat at a wobbly table in the dining car under an old sepia photo that showed the king when still a teen, decked out in gaudy military dress and wearing a crown that shone like the sun. Tassels dangled from his golden scepter.

A stumpy waitress in a stained pastel shirt and yellow sarong waddled over and handed out wrinkled menus, all yellow with age. Three were in Amaza and one in English. Numerous entries were crossed out and new dishes penciled in, reflecting menu evolution.

Grandpa spoke with the attendant and then slapped down his menu in disgust. The teens followed suit, so Lew played along and dropped his, too. The waitress collected them all and sped away.

Lew raised an eyebrow to just shrugs and ironic smirks from his companions. Soon all became clear. The server returned with four bowls of plain steamed rice topped by boiled egg slices, with cello packets of soya sauce, on the side. To wash down this banquet, each received a tall steaming glass of tea, speckled with black leaves.

Grandpa and the teens raised the bowls to their faces and began shoveling rice into their mouths. Grandpa, looking perplexed, nudged the daydreaming Lew. Concentrating hard to dredge up more English he barked, "Eat!" Then explaining, "Is *only!*"

Ah, the dining car had run out of food. But Lew was famished so the simple bowl of rice tasted delicious. While he sipped tea and casually examined the dining car, the train suddenly stumbled and began to decelerate. That clearly panicked Grandpa and his teens, who jumped up like actors in an old-time comedy, grains of rice still stuck to the corners of their mouths.

They anxiously hustled back toward the first class carriage. Near the door, the old man stopped and turned back to face Lew, who was still sitting there, oblivious and relaxed, nibbling at his breakfast rice. Grandpa shot him a stern look.

"Fast!" he commanded, waving Lew to follow.

Back at the first class carriage, a scramble was already underway. Doors for all three quad compartments were bolted open, releasing the hub-bub of passengers gathering up belongings.

Out the window, the outskirts of a humble village rolled into view, clumps of ramshackle straw huts and dusty, rutted roads patrolled by stray dogs. Tropical vegetation grew thick here and the humid air exuded a pungent muddy smell. This backwater made Ruangbang, the primitive capital, seem regal and modern by comparison.

The few remaining rooftop riders climbed down and hung off the sides of the moving train before dropping off, losing their footing and tumbling to the ground.

So this was the infamous Biti? Looked like nothing.

The teens were nearly vibrating with joy to be home as they helped Grandpa stuff his belongings into an old drawstring bag. Lew pulled down his leather case and adjusted his Yankees cap, ready for the next phase in this weird adventure.

It bothered him, absolutely winging it like this. Not like him, ever. And even worse, for perhaps the most important endeavor in his life. Yet there he was, blindly rushing forward and operating with zero information. Just pulling it out of his ass. Not good.

But thank goodness Grandpa and the teens had semi-adopted him. He'd already learned how critical local help could be. Without guidance he'd never track down Lotus or its mysterious owners in Amazia, where all basic information was missing, along with phones and the internet.

Lew smiled and pointed out the window. "Home, eh?" They grinned back.

The train bumped to a halt beside an empty passenger platform and all went silent, save for the exaggerated gasp of air brakes. Lew picked up his things, happy to escape this rolling garbage can. He followed their lead.

They walked the length of the train and exited from the rear. Along the way, it surprised Lew to see how empty the train already was. Most passengers had disembarked en route, at night during impromptu rolling stops. He jumped down onto the platform and in a forced cheery voice, called out a lame attempt to amuse his friends.

"Okay folks! Biti, here we come!"

But with that, all three stopped dead in their tracks, as if hitting an invisible wall. Frozen, they questioned him with confused frowns. Now what unwritten local rule had he broken?

"No *Biti*," the old man clarified, shaking his head. He waved a stern finger in the air and pointed at a small sign on the dilapidated station house. The placard was so insignificant it might have said *toilet* in the local language. "*Momuk*!" Grandpa correcting him. "No Biti!"

Hmm?

"Momuk," he repeated, patting his chest to signal ownership. Clearly *his* home. "Biti . . . no good!" Now having sorted *that* out, he motioned Lew to follow and enter the paradise on earth known as

Momuk.

Lew slammed an angry fist against the train's metal wall. "So, *not* Biti?" He rubbed his throbbing hand.

The codger hacked up a generous gob and spat it on the ground in a dramatic show of disgust. "Biti . . . like that!" he snorted.

Well *that* was pretty clear. Compared to the endless magnificence of his Momuk, Biti was like a greenish glob of sputum. Lew thought fast, scratching his head. He needed to get back on that train and fast, before it left without him.

He wai'ed his friends and pointed a thumb at himself. "Sorry, friends, but me? Biti."

The trio looked distraught as funeral-goers, unable to hide their pity or scorn for Lew's piss-poor decision-making. The lovely teenage girl sadly patted Lew's hand. *"Goo luhk."* The three clearly looked worried for their new friend, destined for that hellhole, Biti.

Luck? Yeah, think I'm gonna need plenty of that.

As they waved goodbye, Lew hurried back to reclaim his cabin. The train was now totally quiet and depopulated as a ghost town. Out the carriage window, he watched the trio cut across a rice field, the teens merrily skipping ahead while grandpa followed at his own pace.

Oppressive midafternoon heat baked the compartment, now down from the mountains and back at sea level. Lew waited and sweated profusely, saturating his clothes. After twenty minutes, the engine whistled and the train again began to roll. Motion created a meager warm breeze through the carriage window but afforded no relief.

"Overnight mail train, my foot," Lew mumbled. Billed as a twelve-hour run, the journey was now pushing sixteen and counting. Bored crazy, Lew strolled through the train and was sobered to learn only a handful of stragglers remained.

The few, the brave . . . those mad enough to endure the wilds of Biti.

CHAPTER FOURTEEN
Rock Star a la Cart

The engine chugged a hypnotic rhythm, propelling the train through lush countryside that shimmered in the equatorial heat. Lew mopped perspiration from his neck and brooded. It felt like he'd been mired in Amazia a decade already. Was it really only days?

He began dreading Biti, a place too disgusting for even residents of a tropical dung hole like Momuk. Yikes. But it was too late to worry. He folded up his shirt into a pillow, leaned against the metal wall and drifted off to sleep.

Hours later, he was roused from deep slumber by a rude whistle blast. It was late afternoon when he opened his eyes to a confusing sight. A green wall of jungle vegetation drifted slowly by, dangerously close, only inches outside his window.

He stared through that foliage and began picking out previously hidden details, like birds flitting from branch to branch or troops of monkeys scampering on tree limbs. The train crawled past the carcass of an unidentified animal where insects swarmed, some as large as small birds, and other furry scavengers feasted.

He headed to the outside platform for a better view. There it became clear the train was crawling through a narrow ravine, hemmed in on both sides by thick tree-covered slopes. On one side, just beside the tracks, a narrow, frothy, stone-studded stream spilled over cascades. Occasional gaps through emerald hillside walls allowed a view of distant mountain ranges, boxing them in.

He inhaled deep and filled his lungs with thick, damp air. It was pungent and organic and smelled of decaying vegetation and life. The train burrowed further into this remote recess, making Lew feel increasingly cut-off from civilization and hidden from the outside world.

Inner Amazia seemed tucked into the rear end of nowhere. Perhaps in the local language, Biti meant *suppository*?

Hours dragged by until, finally, the gorge began to widen a bit and the pristine landscape slightly transformed. Minuscule hints of human habitation started to pop up—a miniature garden with onions and cabbage here, two humpbacked cows in a pen over there. Small, uneven dirt roads began to appear, though little more than footpaths connecting a series of pot holes.

Regardless how meager, any signs of civilization were a godsend. Perhaps as they neared Biti, things would improve. But that looked hours away. Just as Lew settled in again, the engine bellowed a series of angry toots and the train began to slow. A railway worker in a sarong and bandana poked into Lew's cabin and burbled something, sounding excited.

Did he just say *Biti*? That was all Lew picked up.

Moments later, Bandana Man again stuck in his head, this time looking more agitated. He waved his arms. *Hurry up* was the clear message. But for what? Biti was still hours away—this was the middle of nowhere.

But to appease Bandana Man, Lew pulled his suitcase down from the rack and noticed, for the first time, the shocking deterioration in his fine leather bag, dotted by the unwelcome souvenirs of hard travel: cuts, fresh scuffs, and scars. And glancing down, he discovered his once-fine Italian loafers were also ruined, now soft and misshapen and stained by rings of dried salt that leached through the leather after multiple rounds of sweat.

It was time for a quick change. He peeled off clothing glued to his skin by perspiration and changed into a clean tennis shirt, khakis and his favorite sneakers, the bright red pair of Air Jordans packed for hotel gym workouts. Only now did the critical flaws in that plan become apparent: there were no gyms in Amazia . . . and hardly any hotels.

Various train workers passed by his cabin and pounded on the wall, taking turns sticking their heads through the door to hound Lew and keep him moving.

"Biti! Biti!" they hooted.

"Okay, okay," he muttered. What happened to all that famous Amaza hospitality?

Lew stepped down from the train, still in disbelief, and onto a sad, rickety wooden platform. Slowly, he slogged forward through air so thick it felt like wading through gravy.

But how could this be Biti? There was no *there* there, just mangy dogs and stray bullock carts. No way could this be a worldwide export center. But a rotting signboard on the tiny depot clarified it all. Below a block of indecipherable squiggles was a single line of English text:

BITI, CAPITAL OF INNER AMAZIA.

Lew laughed. What else could he do? But a nice touch, adding some English like that. He spied a few rickety wooden houses propped against coconut tree trunks for support. The construction looked improvised and amateurish, with wood bleached gray by the sun and walls leaning at crazy angles.

The valley here was narrow, maybe a city block wide. An ever-present hiss announced the river close by and proclaimed its dominion over the entire area, hemmed in by forested hills and even steeper mountains.

"Holy crap," Lew muttered with a sad laugh. "Welcome to the Greater Biti Metro Area."

Three small, conjoined buildings formed the ramshackle station house. Lew stooped to enter the low front door and immediately noted a wide, hand-drawn area map on the far wall.

About ten feet wide by three high, the playful and cartoonish map showed Biti sprawling down a long, narrow valley that followed the twisting Mobiti River. Colorful illustrations in faded yellow, red, and blue lifted his spirits—they depicted a school, some temples, and even a downtown area with a post office and a tourist center.

Good! Maybe this place was neither a ghost town nor a basket case.

Lacking a distance scale, he guessed the place probably wound along for five, ten miles at most. The entire way, Biti settlement never left the side of the river, like a faithful companion or jealous lover.

"Hey, anybody home?" But the only response was the river's muffled hiss.

He passed into the second connected building where wooden benches sat splayed at odd angles in irregular rows. Okay, the Kingdom's general lack of geometric precision was really offending his innate sense of order. As a detail-oriented perfectionist, all these cockeyed walls, angling doors, and haphazard layouts were upsetting his equilibrium.

How could so haphazard a place, characterized by sloppiness and imprecision, be the manufacturing source for his marvelous imports?

He moved on to the third building where an old poster celebrated the ruling dynasty. And right beside it, behind a barred ticket window, a man slept peacefully.

Lew remained unclear on accepted protocols for waking snoozing officials in the Kingdom and the station agent looked so comfortable, perfectly at rest with his chin snuggled in the cup formed by his thumbs and fingers. He snored softly with a pleasant wheeze and a tiny puddle of drool accumulated on the ticket counter. It seemed shame to wake him.

Lew tried a few loud coughs and throat-clearing *ahems*.

Nothing.

Then he spotted a button—perhaps for service?—and pushed it. No sound.

Finally, in a flash of comprehension, he deciphered the function of the two wooden blocks atop the ticket counter. He picked them up and clapped them together.

The stationmaster jerked bolt upright and reached under the counter for an officious blue cap crowned by a badge emblazoned with a golden eagle clasping arrows. Bleary-eyed, he gazed up at the tall, blond foreigner standing before him. His initial reaction of pure shock soon morphed into amused disbelief.

"Oh, my goodness!" he yelped. "Welcome Amazia, sir! Welcome Biti!"

Good. An unexpected command of at least *some* English.

The man looked mid-thirties, like Lew. And other than that marvelous cap, he only wore a white undershirt, shorts and flip-flops while still managing to appear professional. Smiling, he scampered around the partition and wai'ed Lew, who returned it.

"And hello to you, sir," Lew said. "Sorry to disturb you. My name is Lew Clarke from America and I'm here on business."

"Oh, yes, sir!" The man bubbled with excitement, fiddling with his fingers and shuffling from foot to foot. "Welcome Amazia! Welcome Biti!

"Err, thanks again. I need some help booking a hotel and getting a taxi to downtown Biti."

"Yes, Biti! Welcome, mister!" The petite man's eyes sparkled as he repeated permutations of his welcoming mantra. It became clear, Lew's communication problems hadn't ended, after all.

The elfin railroad man made a show of looking at his cheap Chinese watch and chuckling. Then he shrugged, walked over to the wall and flipped some switches. The lights all flickered out and the ceiling fan slowed. He turned over the bilingual sign on the front door to display CLOSED and led Lew outside.

He locked the depot door and Lew sighed. Wonderful, screwed again. Stuck in the middle of nowhere and abandoned, with nary a taxi or another soul in sight.

The stationmaster shuffled over to a simple hitching post beside the station building, where he stroked an attractive white pony's mane and made comforting clicking noises while unhitching the creature. Then he unfolded a small vinyl canopy above the driver's seat and climbed aboard the small pony cart.

Lew had two thoughts. First, that this fellow surely had the easiest gig in all of Asia, sleep-waiting for infrequent overnight mail trains and then going home by mid-afternoon. And second, that Lew, now abandoned and totally lost in rural Amazia, was as hopeless as a one-legged man in an ass-kicking contest.

He approached the cart and raised a hand. "Sir, please, can you wait a moment? You're surely not going to just leave me here, are you? Middle of nowhere."

"Yes, sirrrr! Welcome to—"

"Yes, yes, I know: *Welcome to Amazia.* I gather you probably have no real English but still, please, just *look* at me." Lew summoned his most pathetic frown. "I need help, isn't it obvious? You *must* be able to see that. I mean, no taxis, no hotels . . ." Lew struggled to tamp down his rising frustration. "And for that matter, just where the hell is freakin' Biti itself? I see nothing here. And I've come so far . . . such a long, long way."

The stationmaster listened, concern evident in his eyes. Looking thoughtful, he dismounted and offered Lew a clove-scented cigarette. Though Lew didn't smoke, he gladly accepted it. The man scratched a wooden stick match against the station wall and it flared with a bitter sulfur smell. In an exaggerated show of courtesy, the man lit both their smokes and snuffed out the match between a spittle-wetted finger and thumb.

Actually, he seemed rather nice, just didn't appreciate Lew's problem. Maybe slow him down a bit and he'd eventually catch on?

They stood there filling the mid-afternoon air with thick clouds of sweet smoke. Lew caressed the white pony, a dappled beauty with tan and reddish-brown spots. The creature stamped its feet and whinnied, as if anxious to get underway and sensing familiar patterns being disrupted. The bells studding its red leather harness jingled in complaint.

Lew continued to pat the pony's nose, its tinkling bells reminding him of Christmastime when he was a kid.

"Pasha," said the pony's master, stroking the beast's side.

"Nice." Lew ran a hand down the animal's mane. "There you go, Pasha. Who's a good girl, huh?" The beast was sturdy and more than healthy, with clear eyes and a shining coat. "Yes, mister, Pasha seems like a real fine pony. Total sweetheart."

The stationmaster smiled broadly and tapped himself on the chest. "Sivarong," he said and then, after a pause, "*Siva*."

Lew understood and pointed a thumb at himself. "Lewis N. Clarke . . . *Lew*." He blasted out his friendliest, super-sized, American-style grin and Siva nodded back.

"Lew!" Siva grimaced with concentration, working hard to summon up something. Then out popped a stunning question. "Mister Lew . . . *ho-tel*?"

Whoa! In a marvelous and most welcome development, Siva *did* have another word of English, and a helpful one at that. Things suddenly looked brighter. "Yes, ol' buddy. *Hotel!*" Lew shook his head, looking sad as a Jets fan fresh from another blowout loss. "I need one, bad."

Siva took that in, squinting.

"Also, Khun Siva, I really need a taxi. *Taxi.*"

Siva shook his head. "No tax-i, Khun Lew."

Marvelous. Was he supposed to sleep in a ditch?

Siva's face brightened and then he clapped his hands like a croupier at end of his shift. What did that mean? Lew hoped for the best. Siva patted the pony cart seat and looked expectantly at Lew. "Sir?" he said, thumping it harder. Lew flushed with gratitude. An angel, it seemed, was saving him.

He placed his suitcase (once worth thousands, now rotted down to $2.99 at Goodwill) atop the bed of straw in back and climbed onto the driver's seat. Way too narrow, of course, for a typical American posterior, even Lew's now-skinny ass. But where would Siva sit?

The stationmaster gathered the worn leather reins in his hands, issued a soft clicking noise, and started to lead Pasha down the road.

Good heavens, there it was again—that absolutely stunning, world-class Amazian kindness. Lacking taxis, the Biti stationmaster himself was chaperoning Lew to a hotel. And judging from the cartoon map at the station house, it might be quite a *schlep* to the town center.

They were probably at one of the far ends so along the way, at least he would get a thorough overview of Biti . . . perhaps even spot the Lotus headquarters.

Things were looking up.

Siva sauntered on through the sultry humid air with Pasha following, her hooves sounding a gentle *clip-clop* cadence. The journey was lateral as much as forward, with the cart dodging frequent potholes. The pony's tail chased flies, flicking right and left like a metronome. Lew gripped the seat as the cart bounced over ruts.

Pasha made numerous unscheduled stops to nibble grass or berries on the roadside while her master just smiled.

The valley gradually widened and the rushing water sound faded as the dirt road looped farther away from the river. They passed through a lush sector studded by thickets of palm trees and swaying seas of tall stalks of sugar cane. Dozens of lime-green rice paddies glinted in the sunlight, off mirror-like surfaces.

Siva played tour guide, pointing out highlights—family huts here and simple mounded pagodas there.

The road undulated through forests, mango orchards and rice fields, past small barns and huts. Troops of monkeys hovered overhead in the forested areas, scratching hairy bellies and swinging on vines. One occasionally dropped onto the cart to investigate Lew's bag. No worries—it was locked and too heavy for so tiny a creature to steal.

The entire experience was magical. The repetitive squeak of cart wheels was hypnotic, lulling the American into a peaceful, hazy consciousness. Cocooned in total warmth, his brain flooded with alpha waves.

After maybe an hour, the valley further widened to display more signs of habitation. Simple paths and tiny roads angled off toward clusters of thatch huts and habitations on stilts. Simple but lopsided barns—in yellow or purple—stood proud beside compact fields under cultivation. Women hanging laundry were awestruck to see the large outsider but Siva just laughed and reassured them it was okay.

Picturing the cartoon map, Lew guessed they'd probably traveled maybe a third of the way down the valley. Soon, perhaps, they'd reach downtown Biti, whatever that meant.

The road widened enough for two carts. One approached from the opposite direction and its driver—in a floppy white linen shirt, sarong, and Panama hat—waved at Siva and did a double-take seeing Lew.

"Coca-Cola!" he called out with a laugh. Lew smiled back. When the carts passed, Siva grinned and shrugged, indicating *what could I do?*

Groups of monkeys, twenty or thirty strong, swung through treetops while birds of every color flitted about. Goats, oxen and water buffalo guided by farmers shared the road.

But then, just ahead, a massive elephant appeared, like a wild, impossible hallucination—Lew's first up-close, non-zoo sighting of a pachyderm. Ever. The gray brute lumbered along the side of the road and lifted logs, working under the direction of a slight man, nearly naked save for a loincloth and head covering. Lew waved at the beast's tanned boss and the *mahout* smiled back. Obeying a command, the elephant trumpeted a shrill salute to the international visitor.

Siva walked gingerly to avoid the immense elephant turds, scattered like boulders on the clay road.

All this felt like something out of National Geographic, seen on Lew's eighty-inch screen at the penthouse. Closest he'd ever come to raw Nature.

Biti had transformed into a feast for the senses, even giving off a generally attractive aroma that Lew couldn't quite place. After a while, he decoded a few elements in the mix: there was ever-present coconut; the sweet, delicious aroma of palm oil; and fragrant tropical flowers. Distinct organic bass notes surely came from those elephantine fecal boulders and manure clods he spotted everywhere, deposited by dogs, ponies, water buffalo, and cattle.

Siva seemed impervious to the heat as he marched on at a steady pace.

Lew suddenly cried out, "Siva, please stop!" The man halted the pony and turned back toward Lew. "Look, Siva, right there!" Lew stared at another spirit house and tingled. It was a local model, charming and totally basic. Vastly inferior to the US export models with none of the quality, glitz, or extravagant frills.

But once he spotted that first spirit house, he couldn't stop seeing them *everywhere*. On poles, on the ground, in trees and on porches. Always neat, clean, and honored by offerings. He'd probably walked right past hundreds more in Ruangbang.

Siva said something but Lew shook his head, not understanding. Then the stationmaster fluttered his hands through the air, flying them around like birds. Or rather, Lew realized, floating them like ethereal beings.

"Yeah, thanks, I know. Guardian spirits. Already learned about those buggers, now that it's too late."

But that was his opening. Did Siva perhaps know the factory that made them? Lew gestured at the structure and mimed fitting imaginary boards together, hammering nails. Siva watched with fascination before shaking his head with a confused grin.

Nope. Naturally. That would have been too easy.

They rolled along and by now, the valley was a few city blocks wide between the forested boundaries.

The people indeed looked like a perfect mix of Southeast Asian stocks and cultures. Take a variety of religions, people, cultures and attire. Put all that in a blender and *voila:* Amazia.

But the dominant cultural trait for these shy people seemed their consistently warm and welcoming attitude toward him, a stranger. He was utterly swamped by smiles, waves, and sing-song greetings from friendly faces. They seemed genuinely overjoyed to see him. Occasional shout-outs flew by in out-of-context English. References to Trump especially amused him. But oddly, when he responded, the shouters would look away, embarrassed by his attention.

Lew remembered the packs of mints he purchased at JFK and began to distribute them to any kids brave enough to approach his cart. They went wild. He laughed, feeling like a celebrity.

Pasha began to stop more often to nibble roadside greens, refusing to budge. Each time, Siva solved that by fetching a length of sugar cane from a nearby field for the animal to chew.

Dogs were a constant threat. Several raced up, barking ferociously and feigning attack until Siva threatened them with a long stick. After that, they hung back and trailed at a distance.

By late afternoon, the road surface dried out and was transformed into fine powder. Dust devils rose and swirled around wandering chickens that pecked and clucked. Entire families pedaled by, balanced upon single bicycles. "Hello, Mister!" called out the children.

This was all wonderful, no doubt, but Lew's tour of Biti had already stretched on for several hours. So where *was* the downtown section and his hotel? As if to answer that question, a large shack appeared, just ahead, fashioned from thick bamboo stalks lashed together and topped by a thatched roof. A small hand-painted sign hung on the front door:

POST OFFICE.

He remembered the cartoon map. Really? *This* was downtown Biti, the absolute center? Impossible!

But all doubt vanished when Lew spotted a second sign: HELP FOR OUR VISITOR. Ahah! The tourist agency.

The building was padlocked, already closed for the day. He resolved to visit the next day, first thing. But if this was indeed *downtown*, where was all the rest—the hotels, restaurants and shops? There was no sign of any commercial activity, just a few more buildings amid farm plots. Something was very wrong.

As charming as Amazia was, no way could so primitive a place have manufactured those stellar Lotus products. Lew feared this might be another Khun Khon fabrication, and that Biti wasn't the true location for Lotus. If so, he was fatally off track and completely lost. And meanwhile, back home, the clock was ticking on those ruinous lawsuits.

With nightfall approaching, Pasha clip-clopped onward. Lew knew darkness would descend around 6 p.m. But they were now leaving Biti's sad little downtown area, so where was Siva taking him?

The valley again narrowed and structures thinned out. Once-distant mountains closed in and the river drew closer, its frothy hiss growing louder. As the sun touched the treetops, the river was again right beside the path, with forest walls oppressively close on both sides.

Lew pictured the cartoon map. Good grief, they'd walked the entire length of the Biti valley and reached the other end. Had Siva completely misunderstood him? Lew needed a hotel, food and information. A staging point for his next steps. Not this.

Siva approached the cart, beaming with pride, and offered a hand to help Lew down. Only after the stationmaster pointed off to the side with his chin did Lew notice a small lodging tucked into the trees. Easy to overlook.

Siva tethered the pony inside a small barn next to the house and guided Lew inside where a tiny, bubbling woman came forth, all excitement and smiles. Siva held her hand and faced Lew. "Luam!' he said and she wai'ed. His wife.

Lew finally got it. There were no hotels in Biti. And the local stationmaster was personally hosting his spur-of-the-moment visit.

Luam seemed clearly astonished and delighted her husband had delivered so unusual a visitor. Wrapped in a sarong, she was lean and tan from the sun, her hands hardened by work and her hair pulled back tight. She gave off a pleasant fragrance. Coconut? Her hands danced about as her voice soared high like a tinkling bell. When she smiled, her teeth shone white and perfect.

"Wonderful to meet you, Khun Luam—and thank you for your hospitality."

They seemed a lovely couple, thirty-something, like him. No kids. They both grinned, not understanding his words. But once again, Lew had been adopted by friendly, trusting strangers. Serendipitous, to say the least.

But despite the pleasure of that, he couldn't block the unsettling concern that Biti might not be the right place, after all. He'd ridden from one end of the valley to the other and seen every nook and cranny. He saw no sign of any commercial buildings.

Certainly no Lotus headquarters or factory.

PART THREE:

The Monkey Dump and The Rama

CHAPTER FIFTEEN
Lew Clarke, Human Jungle Gym

Lew woke early in a makeshift bed of hay and palm fronds piled a foot deep and rubbed his eyes, confused. Oh right, Pasha's stable. The quaint barn smelled of fresh straw and dung. He was grateful—if not for Siva, Lew might have spent the night sleeping in a roadside ditch. Stretching, he gazed around and noticed his bunk-mate, Pasha, already gone.

Had Siva left for work? It was still quite early, judging from the morning cool and low angle at which sunlight spilled in. Roosters filled the air with insistent crowing that sounded like an argument. Funny, last night he didn't notice neighboring houses.

Then he recalled dinner, when Luam filled him to bursting with a magnificent fiery, sweet egg curry ladled over warm steamed rice, plus unlimited servings of savory, stir-fried greens. Simple, satisfying fare, all washed down with hot black tea.

Coming fully awake now, refreshed, he went outside to urinate against a tree. But back in Pasha's cozy stable, he groaned to discover in the clear morning light that his magnificent leather suitcase was now totally ruined by a black rot defiling the vanilla brown saddle leather.

He snapped it open to release a foul odor—the contents were fully-saturated and rotting. Wonderful. All had seemed okay just a day ago on the train, but an ugly yellow-green bacterial fuzz had now taken hold. His bespoke business suit was destroyed (waste of space, anyway). But thank heaven for small miracles: his passport, wallet, and cash were all safely preserved inside an industrial-strength ziplock. His shaving kit, too.

He examined the jeans, also slick and stinky with bacteria. Was it worth trying to scrub off the buggy mold and maybe cook them in the hot Biti sun? Perhaps Luam knew some local laundry magic?

He hauled the rest to the pit out back where the couple kept a flame alive to heat water for cooking and laundry. Fiddling around like a Boy Scout, he teased a roaring fire to life and fed it his suitcase and diseased clothing. The greedy flames consumed it all, spewing out a stench that eventually summoned Luam.

Siva's wife, wrapped in a green sarong with vivid tropical batik decoration, approached while wrinkling her nose.

"Yeah, Luam, I guess it does smell pretty bad." Lew laughed and mimed the situation to her. She nodded but then also pointed at the clothes Lew was wearing and made a face.

"These, too?" His cheeks burned with shame. He'd been sweating into those duds for days so white perspiration rings striped the shirt and grease blotches stained the pants. The cuffs were stiff with brown mud and dung, embedded with straw from his bedding.

Luam politely took his wrist and gently guided him to the simple facility behind the little house, with a water cistern and dipper for splash bathes. She also pointed at the small hole in the lavatory floor and then, shaking her head, toward the tree where Lew earlier peed.

His cheeks flushed again. How did she know *that*? "Sorry!" He wai'ed her. "Boys will be boys, eh? We American guys pee pretty free and easy, I guess, almost anywhere."

She wrinkled her brow, not seeming to understand, but then smiled. She guided his hand to the splash bucket and motioned for him to bathe. *Now*. He chuckled.

She turned her back and waited for him to strip down and surrender the befouled clothing. Even the Jordans and his Yankee cap. Modestly shielding her eyes, she gathered up his stench-ridden clothes, pinching them between fingertips to minimize contact and holding them at arm's length. Then she turned and headed off toward the rustic laundry area.

"Sorry!" Lew called after her, suppressing a chuckle. "I mean, for being so stinky. Not usually my thing. Oh, and I've also got more jeans . . ." She waved her arms in mock disgust and kept on walking.

But really, it wasn't entirely his fault, right? This place was just so gosh-darned hot and dirty. He cleaned up nicely though, already a fan of this Asian splash-bath thing, and enjoyed ladling cool water over himself. The tiny brown bar of laundry grade soap produced meager lather but still felt like high luxury to remove days of sweat and muck.

Luam returned, again primly looking away, and set down a plain towel and other items on the simple wooden slat bench. Upon her retreat, Lew dried off and slipped on a roomy pullover shirt with long, loose sleeves. Fashioned from rough cloth, a little granary logo revealed it was salvaged from a rice sack. Then he picked up a long rectangle of blue cloth, guessing it to be a sarong. But how did one tie it? After a half dozen failed attempts he invented his own method.

He slipped his pasty white feet into some primitive black rubber flip-flops cut from truck tires, with treads on the bottom, and headed into the house.

Luam had already prepared breakfast, much the same as the dinner—rice, eggs, veggies, tea. Hovering, she smiled as Lew politely shoveled in the food.

"And today," Lew asked, "Khun Siva go where?" He held his palms up in question.

She understood right away, laughed and pointed her chin in the general direction of the village center. *Hubby went that-a way. Work.*

Lew also needed to get cracking, back to work. Despite all this wonderful hospitality, he could waste no more time at Siva's home. "Me, too!" he said, motioning toward the city center, and began walking toward the door. "Thanks again!"

"No!" she cried, concern evident in her voice. Now what? Luam handed him a threadbare khaki cap, like what an Amazia trucker might wear. Did he really need to wear *that*? Oh, right, sun protection. He had already lost his Yankee cap to the Luam Laundry

Service and the Stetson was gone, too.

He wheeled around to depart but Luam seized his rice bag shirt from behind to stop him. "No!" she barked again, but this time with a small laugh and a beautiful smile.

"Okay, ma'am, now what?"

With the disapproving face of a mother scolding her naughty child, she motioned at the searing tropical sun, then at Lew's pink-white feet.

Yeah, good point. Until he could obtain some sun block or build up a protective tan, all pale uncovered skin was in serious burn danger. Not your mild, North American summer vacation type of sunburn. Nope, this would be the Welcome to Amazia and lose-several-layers-of-skin variety. His arms were already toasted red just from yesterday's pony cart ride.

Luam saved the day with a pair of Siva's old black socks to save the day. Lew barely squeezed in and then pulled on the flip-flops.

"Okay. Bye-bye again. This time for sure."

His hostess wai'ed and gave him friendly shove toward the door. It felt good to move forward again.

Lew started down the small path toward town for an initial exploration of Biti. In theory, every step should bring him closer to resolving his horrendous problems—assuming, that is, that Lotus actually *was* in Biti.

The tourist info kiosk at the town center seemed a great place to start, an invigorating hour's walk away. The morning was glorious with air still cool and stirred by a mild breeze. All colors seemed somehow richer in the early sunlight—flowers popped in yellow, white and red against deep green flora. The sky above the forest canopy glowed blue—none of that smoggy New York gray.

He tramped down the packed clay road, still damp from overnight sprinkles. It would later cook to a powder. He gazed at many simple homesteads and barns tucked into the edge of the forest—each apparently rooster-equipped— he'd missed on arrival.

A tornado of angry barking erupted from several huts ahead. Already taught by Siva, he found a thick branch, several feet long, and it worked. The dogs kept yapping as he approached, but none were brave enough to challenge the tall man with the long stick.

Soon a gaggle of schoolchildren, adorable in pristine uniforms, fell into step with him, but always keeping a safe distance. "Hello, Mister!" sang out a cute little girl, fearless as she was sweet. Angelic in a white blouse and navy blue sarong, she toted a pink vinyl *Hello Kitty* backpack that made Lew smile.

"Good morning, sweetheart." He tried to look friendly.

They all marched along in silence, listening to bird calls against the low hiss of the river. Up ahead, the road split around a massive banyan tree, and the kids began to swarm in what seemed a tighter protective formation. They glanced side to side, looking nervous.

What provoked all that? Lew didn't see any more dogs.

The answer came from the sky.

In a flash, Lew sustained a heavy blow to his shoulder, like the thump of a balled fist, and tumbled to the ground. A mysterious assailant, moving fast, had dropped from the banyan tree to attack him. He lay there stunned, frozen by shock. Assault or robbery seemed totally out of character for the gentle Amaza.

Then, only after a delay, did he notice a furry brown creature furiously rifling through his clothes and bag. The bandit monkey, no larger than a cat or small dog, treated Lew like a jungle gym. Clearly well practiced at this, it scrambled with blurring speed from one shoulder to the opposite foot, probing and tugging along his torso and legs.

And from above an ear-splitting chorus of shrieks and chattered encouragement rained down from a monkey troop in the branches, cheering on the simian thief. His tiny hands stayed busy, searching and probing at Lew's various nooks and crannies. At last Lew gathered his wits, rose to a sitting position and began to wave his stick at the beast, who instantly recoiled and scampered up the tree trunk to rejoin the troop.

Lew rose to his knees, still shaken and his heart thumping double-time, and immediately sensed something was wrong. He began patting himself down, his hands automatically flying to check rear pants pockets that didn't exist in a sarong. Oh, right, his valuables were in that little rice sack Luam loaned him.

Before he could open the flap, he caught sight in his peripheral vision of his blue passport, clutched in the bandit monkey's paws and disappearing up the tree.

Oh shit!

With a jolt of anxiety, he desperately began to search the shoulder tote and confirmed more was missing. Looking high into the leafy branches he saw his possessions being gaily passed around by little simian hands. Crap, there was his wallet! And that little hairy bastard swiped other things of value, too—money, identification, credit cards.

The tiny humanoids gleefully sorted through his valuables and then took off, swinging from branch to branch until jumping down from the banyan and scampering across the field to the nearby jungle edge.

Taking in the entire encounter, the schoolchildren giggled and skipped about, aping the monkey's antics.

"It's not funny!" roared Lew. The brats! But seeing real fear on their faces, he immediately regretted his outburst. They were just kids—no way could they understand the gravity of his loss. And hell, it probably *was* pretty funny, as long as you weren't the victim. The Amazia equivalent of an impromptu comedy skit. *Cute Monkey Robs Giant Foreigner.*

But it was too late for apologies: the kids smartly jettisoned the Western grouch and scampered ahead.

The temperature was climbing and his borrowed clothes were starting to feel scratchy. And ouch, that pain in his arm? He noticed a series of thin parallel scratches near his shoulder, dotted with blood and starting to ooze. Perfect. Back home that would trigger panicky talk about anti-rabies shots . . . but here in Amazia? Meh.

He stood up, a bit numb, and walked on, once again feeling like a total geographic incompetent. Back home he'd know *exactly* what to do after a robbery. He'd be unhappy, sure, but then get up, dust himself off and take action. Report it to authorities, replace missing items, and get on with life. But in this fantasyland, how did anything work?

This setback felt serious. How could he survive (much less execute his mission) without a passport, money, all that? Shaken, he resumed his march to the village center.

He saw the children veer off into a small schoolyard up ahead, joining several dozen others on wooden benches, shaded under a fabric canopy suspended from trees. A slim, elderly teacher scratched lessons on a portable chalkboard, calling out to students who parroted back her words. When the impossible sight of a large foreign visitor in a sarong, walking by, whipped the class into a frenzy, all Lew could do was wai his apology. The distraught teacher nodded back. And despite all his miraculous tech triumphs, Lew had to wonder who had a bigger positive impact on the world, him or that diligent teacher?

Shortly afterward, he finally reached the 'downtown' sector. If Lotus had an office or factory in Biti, common sense argued it should be nearby. But nothing remotely resembled that.

He pulled open the rusty screen door and entered the modest post office. A fan in the corner swept the long, poorly-lit room, the warm breeze stirring dust balls on the floor. A large sign above the counter displayed a golden crown and Amaza script. At the bottom was a small deck of words in English: POST OFFICE - BITI REGIONAL STATION.

A middle-aged man with slicked-down brown hair stood and smoked a crooked cigarette. From his looks he could have been Siva's elder brother. He wore an official-looking badge, like a marshal from the Old West.

Lew drew in a breath, removed his khaki trucker's cap and

approached, smiling wide and thinking: *Here goes nothing*. "Excuse me, sir. I am looking for Lotus Creations, a company in Biti. Can you help?" Unblinking, the man shot back a nervous grin, a bead of perspiration trickling down his brow. "Lo-tus," Lew repeated with painful clarity. "Spirit houses?"

The clerk slowly shook his head. Finally a voice emerged from his rigid smile, just above a whisper. "Wel-come Amazia?"

Oh boy. "Okay. Thanks anyway." Lew stepped back and noticed an alcove down the wall contained a small wooden desk with a pyramid-style wood block sign that said: TOURIST BUREAU.

Ahah! Though nobody seemed home, surely the tourist bureau could help—maybe somebody even spoke English. Lew pointed at the alcove. "Sir, is Tourist Bureau open?"

The postal clerk squinted back and smiled, then sprinted over to the small desk. He changed caps, sat down and waved Lew over. Behind him an old poster showed a globe and bold words in purple: *AMAZIA? TOURISM? OK!*

The agent rummaged for a scrap of paper from a drawer, carefully pressed it out flat and handed it to Lew. A blurry, umpteenth-generation photocopy of that Amazia cartoon map. Lew inhaled slowly. "Gee, that's great. Thanks, really helpful." Another thought struck. "Can you perhaps help me find a police station? PO-LICE? I need to report my wallet and passport being stolen. By a monkey, of all things, and I, um . . ."

"Yes," the man said, nodding sagely. "Welcome Amazia!"

Well, he *was* trying and for that, Lew was grateful. He flapped his thumb and fingers in the universal sign for *talking* and pointed at himself. "No speak Amazia." He shook his head sadly. "English?"

The clerk's face lit up and he played a talking hand back at Lew. "In-griss? No Amazia?"

Lew smiled. "Exactly. Our problem."

The postmaster-tourist bureau manager flashed a confident smile and motioned Lew to sit down at the alcove desk. He trotted out the door and crossed the road to where a shirtless, bespectacled young man was painting an old picnic bench. The painter looked in his twenties, lean and well-muscled with tightly cropped black hair that ended in a rat-tail tassel down his neck.

After an animated conversation with hands flying, the young man nodded and wiped yellow paint from his fingers. He carefully balanced his brush atop the bucket, slipped his shirt back on and followed the postmaster across the road.

Smiling through his round specs, the young painter reached out and shook Lew's hand, revealing a small geometric tattoo on his inner arm. "Good morning, sir. Mr. Gul says you need some help translating Amazian?"

Holy shit, English! Finally, he could communicate. A giddy blast of gratitude coursed through Lew.

"Sir, my name is *Boonyarit Phu.*" His English was crisp with an unusual intonation—choppy and staccato, a touch of British inflection. Given his hairstyle and the tattoo, he seemed way jazzier than the average Amaza. As he spoke, he flicked at and played with his tassel, a harmless nervous habit. "But everybody here just calls me *Boo.* My grandfather was *Big Boo.*"

"*Boo* will work great. I take it I won't be running into your grandfather?"

"Doubtful, *lah,* as he's gone to his next life, sir."

"Oh, sorry."

"And sorry why?" The young man's face was dead earnest.

"Never mind." What a stroke of luck—imagine, fluent English! Lew couldn't stop grinning. "So, Boo, are you some kind of translator or what?"

The youth smiled and passed a quick comment in Amaza to the postmaster, who shook his head and wheezed out a shy chuckle.

"Me, a translator? Oh my goodness, no, *lah!*" He was handsome when his face brightened. "No, sir. At this moment I am just a lowly, mainly unemployed, unpaid bench painter." He fiddled with his tassel. "Actually, I am thinking to reopen my friend's tiny diner across the street. It closed after financial difficulties and was offered to me, free, so . . ."

Lew nodded. "I understand. A no-risk opportunity. But if I may ask, what's that *'lah'* thing in your speech—Amaza slang?"

"Why no, sir. That's Singlish." Boo winked.

"I don't follow."

"You know, *Singapore English*. Years ago, during hard economic times, my family sent me to live with wealthier relatives in Singapore. I learned English there and picked up lots of non-Amaza habits." He shrugged. "Like that *lah* thing . . . a fun verbal tic, I guess, never managed to shake it off."

With services of a fluent English speaker at hand, Lew's mind raced with questions, but the first was obvious. "Boo, I'm searching for a company here called Lotus Creations."

Boo's lips tightened. "Sorry, sir, never heard of them. Probably no such thing here."

That landed as a direct gut punch. In microscopic Biti, everyone should know everything about everybody. So if an intelligent, tuned-in young man never heard of Lotus, that was a horrible development. He had Boo interrogate the postmaster, with the same result.

"Maybe they just use a different name locally. Lotus only for international operations?

"Maybe." The youth looked doubtful and fiddled with his tassel, double-speed.

Lew refused to give up. "Okay, next question: Where is the nearest police station?"

Boo rubbed his face and sniffed. "Sorry to disappoint you yet again, Mr. Lew, but we have none of those in the Kingdom. Not *per se*."

"*Per se* meaning . . .?" Lew vaguely recalled something like that during the video call, but had brushed it off. No police? It just seemed impossible.

"Well, there are no stations. The entire Inner Amazia region has only one officer, Khun Ta, a one-man constabulary. We have so little crime, you see. Usually Ta is out and about, making his rounds. So he finds *you,* not the other way."

"Hmm, interesting." But unhelpful. This frigging place!

"But Khun Lew, if I may inquire, what is your problem requiring police assistance?"

"My passport was stolen."

"Alamak, so unfortunate! Very sorry, *lah*."

"Also my wallet, cash, and credit cards."

"Dreadful stuff! But such robbery is incredibly odd, here in Biti. Almost impossible."

Lew paused, suddenly a little embarrassed. "Well, it was a robbery *of sorts*, just up the road. I was walking underneath a large tree—"

Boo abruptly threw his hands in the air and chuckled. "Ah, I see!" His face was gleeful. "It was a *banyan* tree, correct? And your thief was a fuzzy little monkey! Isn't it?"

What an astounding, prescient guess! The youth's wild though accurate hunch amazed Lew but his cavalier attitude was irritating. Really, what was so friggin' funny?

"Yeah, Boo, a whole gang of monkeys up in the tree. One dropped down, knocked me over and picked my pocket—my bag, actually—while I was dazed. Then he ran off with my stuff. Whole troop disappeared up into the woods toward the mountains."

Boo translated the story and Gul, the postmaster, melted in hilarity. Skittering his hand across the countertop to simulate an animal in flight, he mimicked a small monkey snatching something and scampering off. The two Amaza leaned against each other, heaving with mirth and weak with delight.

Lew's anger finally burst free—not funny! His face flushed hot and his blood pressure zoomed. "Hey, men. Really . . . stop it already! It's no joke. I'm in big trouble and need help, not mockery. Police or an embassy."

Boo reeled in his attitude and bowed his head. "Khun Lew, sorry we upset you. You are right. Your problem is not funny—not for you." His tone was humble. "But you are in luck."

Lew silently waited for more, his arms folded and fingers drumming.

"Actually, sir, that monkey family is quite infamous. So many people have lost things to them! Purses, wallets, lucky charms, keys, anything. But they are mainly seeking food. All the rest, they don't want. Or usually keep." He smiled. "Lucky!"

"Lucky, why?" Intrigued, Lew unfolded his arms.

"Well, they dispose of pilfered objects they can't eat, often in the same particular vicinity. In the hills, deep in the jungle, near their home. Not far from the elephant logging camp."

Now *that* sounded better. Promising. This lad's possible usefulness was climbing. Lew calmed further. "Boo, I'd like to make you an offer."

Boo caressed his rat tail. "Oh ho . . . yes?"

"I'd like to hire you for a couple days. As my translator and guide in Biti."

Boo's grin melted a bit. "Oh, sorry, sir, but cannot, *lah*. Not really my thing. But thanks."

Lew grinned. "I understand, but any chance could you *make* it your thing for, say, $500?"

"Singapore dollar?"

"No, US dollars. Worth twice as much."

The young man looked absolutely stunned and doubled the pace toying with his hair. "*Aduh!* Five hundred dollar US for just a few days' work?"

"Maybe three or four. Five days, max."

Boo bounced his shoulders. "What to do? More than a year's pay here. So, putting this in my best Singlish: Can, *lah!*"

"Wonderful. Consider yourself already on the clock. Now first, I need a place to stay, closer to this town center. I temporarily bunked last night at the house of Siva the stationmaster. About an hour's walk away."

"Nice! Khun Luam is an excellent cook. But yes, quite distant from here. But chief, there's bad news. Biti has no hotels."

Lew's shoulders drooped. "I was afraid of that."

"But no worries," chirped Boo. "Do like us Amaza, when we travel. Get a dormitory bed at the local temple."

"That works—beggars can't be choosers."

Boo gave him a strange look, obviously unfamiliar with the Western maxim. "Anyway, chief, first we'll arrange your bed at the temple. Then, we'll attack your most pressing issue, to retrieve your money and passport. Very critical, no?"

"Indeed."

"Otherwise, you can't pay me." He winked.

"Good thinking."

"And then we'll take a shot at your Lotus mystery." He seemed confident, almost cocky, and his attitude was infectious.

But to find Lew's valuables in the middle of the jungle? That sounded like an odds-against proposition.

Boo eased right into his role as Lew's right hand, like he'd done it all before. First he borrowed two bicycles so they could pedal back to Siva's and collect Lew's laundered belongings. The jeans were scrubbed clean but deeply bleached by the sun. His Yankees cap was also laundered and his once-crimson Air Jordans had faded to a lovely pink.

He thanked the couple for their hospitality and pressed a colorful wad of *Arysai* bills into Siva's palm. Then they cycled back to town to purchase cheap local clothing at a shanty shop. After that, the remaining task was to secure Lew a place to sleep and, just as promised, that proved easy. By mid-afternoon he was checked-in at the Srivanastra Temple, having secured a rock-hard dorm cot far from the Biti post office. Free.

Boo rubbed his hands with cheery satisfaction. "First few missions accomplished, sir! Now, get a good rest. Tomorrow I'll collect you early to fetch your passport, wallet, and money."

"You're *that* confident?"

"Absolutely. Otherwise, wouldn't have taken this job." Boo scratched his chin. "And since we'll be near, I'll also show you the elephant logging camp."

"Might be interesting." Actually, not. But perhaps that might help unearth a lead on Lotus. After all, the logs went to a sawmill; maybe some of the resulting lumber might find its way to a spirit house factory. A long shot, lots of *mights,* but all he had for now.

Lew moved into the small temple dorm with a dozen young monks. While maintaining respectful silence, they teased and horsed around like typical young men anywhere—typical, that is, but dressed in holy, flowing robes in hot orange. Most were just on a temporary stint, a month or two, a normal part of growing up in Amazia. Not unlike in America, where Catholic kids went on retreats and Mormon youths traveled on mission trips.

At dinner time, he followed them across the courtyard to an open-air pavilion. The numerous dogs prowling the temple compound yawned and did not threaten, having mellowed out there just like the humans.

A pair of chanters droned on endlessly, during meals, praying in an ancient language while Lew gorged on plain rice and greens.

Bedtime came early with lights out at 9 p.m. Lew's thoughts rolled around as he drifted off. This trip was unfurling like nothing expected. What was possibly next? Regardless, his life absolutely hung in the balance.

CHAPTER SIXTEEN
The Monkey Dump

Temple bells began to tinkle well before dawn, along with the sonorous moans of bassy gongs. Neighborhood roosters—AKA the temple alarm clock—roused the young monks. The youths dressed, gathered their brass begging bowls and headed out the door. Half-awake, Lew lay in bed watching the bustle of activity.

Once the dorm emptied, he performed morning ablutions using a pitcher of water and washing bowl on a wooden table. He pulled on his new local clothes, liking the loose powder blue long-sleeved shirt. The slacks (biggest in the shop) were sturdy but too tight—apparently the Amaza had super-skinny hips and no butt to speak of. So he again went with the sarong and put on his baseball cap, socks and flip-flops.

The sun's early rays painted the morning sky pink and purple. He found Boo crouching outside the door in a relaxed Asian squat, cleaning his metal spectacles on a shirt hem. The youth brightened upon seeing Lew and jumped up, his rat tail flying.

"Morning, captain!"

"Already here? Good man, Boo."

"Your fellow monks left without you, sir. You not hungry?" Lew didn't understand but knew when he was being teased. "Early each morning, townsfolk line the street and donate food and offerings while the monks parade by with their begging bowls."

Lew rubbed his stomach. "Actually, I'm starved, dude. Bet I could eat an elephant."

Boo didn't miss a beat. "*Aieeyah*, elephant steak? Why yes sir, can, *lah!* Or perhaps elephant curry, though that's rather heaty. Later on at the logging camp, we can try."

"Really?" Lew grinned uneasily.

"No, lah, of course not! Just kidding." Boo rolled his eyes. "I thought you got my jokes. Elephants are the work crew, chief—nobody dares to eat them! What kind of people do you think we are?" Boo fake-growled a smile. "We'll rustle up some rice or bread, on our way."

Lew enjoyed Boo's sense of humor and positive attitude. A bit of Sal in him, a playful young Amaza version, kidding around. An idea struck—later, after he'd resolved all his Lotus issues, maybe he'd hire Boo for bigger things.

"Two stops on today's agenda, sir. Very productive! First, off to the jungle to retrieve your valuables."

"Easy as that, eh? Awful lot of trees. You really think you know where my things are?"

"No, sir. But we've got a good shot."

"Okay. And after that?"

"Continue on to the elephant logging camp. You expressed some interest, right? Not far from the monkey dumping ground."

Boo had returned their loaner bikes the night before, now making them pedestrians. After a steady walk away from the town center they approached the crime scene, where a large banyan tree divided the dirt road.

"Yes, here. This is where that monkey bandit got the drop on me. Furry bastard."

Boo grinned. "Perfect!"

"Glad it makes you happy."

"It does! Your confirmation raises our odds. So now, we must head *this* way." Boo motioned toward a small opening in the thick flora off the road, the entry to a nearly invisible, overgrown trail through trees, bushes, and grass. "This heads toward the mountain wall, Khun Lew, at the far edge of our valley. Off we go."

They plunged in, wading through the green thicket, and got

scratched by prickly weeds and swiped by branches. Lew constantly swatted at mosquitoes and other biting insects.

They trudged beyond where Lew anticipated they should already have hit a mountain wall. The valley wasn't that wide. "Boo, where the heck we going?"

"Khun Lew, we've already switched off onto another path through a break in the mountains, on our way to the next valley over."

Whatever. All Lew knew was he was being eaten alive, raw, like North American sashimi. "Why aren't those damned things feeding on you, too? Just me?"

Boo laughed. "Probably your rich American diet, boss. You know: beef, dairy, sweets? Once that works its way out of your system you'll smell more local, not as uniquely tempting or delicious."

Hiking through ever-deepening vegetation, Lew kept falling as his rubber thongs lost their grip on the slippery, stone-strewn path. Just as they were hitting peak jungle density, Boo turned to Lew and clapped his hands. "Okay, good!" he exclaimed. "Here we are, chief."

But all Lew saw was a green hell of leaves, vines and tree trunks. "Okay, Boo, and where exactly is this?"

"Why, at the Monkey Dump, of course!" He flicked his tassel and motioned Lew to follow. They veered off the primitive path and waded straight into the thickest vegetation.

"Shit, Boo, we're totally swimming in this stuff!"

"Sorry, sir, but you *do* want to recover your valuables, right?" Boo pointed off in the distance, at a large boulder the size of a Volkswagen Beetle. "Should be over by that big rock."

After minutes slogging chest-deep through the green tangle, ducking vines and branches, they reached the boulder. Breathing hard, both leaned against big rock to catch their wind.

"Boo, I'm sure you know what you're doing, but do you mind explaining?"

The Amaza youth grinned. "Not much to it, sir. Over time, the monkeys learned to pick pockets and bags at that banyan tree, seeking food, chocolate bars, and whatnot. Their colony is close to here, so upon returning home this way, it became their habit to settle upon this big rock to pick through their stolen treasure."

Lew's eyes grew wider. "How does anyone even know that?"

Boo chuckled. "I suppose a theft victim once chased after them and somehow tracked them to here. Then found his stolen goods discarded near that boulder and word traveled. Later, others also found lost possessions here. By now, everybody in Biti knows this."

"So now we just—"

"Yes! Start looking."

They methodically combed through the area, Lew on one side and Boo the other, parting chest-high grass, fern and other leafy plants. Foot by foot, they moved along. Not hard work but after twenty minutes in the thick humidity, Lew was totally drenched by perspiration, despite it being cooler in the shade, shielded under the jungle canopy.

He leaned against the huge stone for a break and Boo, also huffing slightly from exertion, came up beside him.

"Sorry this is so hard for an old guy like you, chief."

"Old?" Lew bristled. "Who says I'm old?"

"No offense. I mean, even myself, I'm a little gassed. So for you, twice as old as me—"

"The hell? You got that wrong, Boo, no way I'm twice as old."

"Want to wager?" Boo cocked his head, inviting a response.

"You're on. What's the bet?"

"Well, if I'm right, perhaps you double my salary this week."

Lew nodded. "Done! But if you're wrong?"

"Then I suppose I work for free."

Lew enjoyed the banter and tiny challenge. What was another measly five hundred bucks, anyway? Nothing to him but maybe the world to this kid. "Okay, Pancho, you're on. So how old are you?"

Boo briefly stared off in thought. "Well, I am just past eighteen, sir. So that means if you are at least thirty-six, I win and am suddenly wealthy, a least in local terms. Let's confirm this." He reached into his cloth tote. "Okay, see right there on the identity page, there's your birthday. Do the math and . . . *alamak*, I win! In a few months, you'll turn an ancient thirty-seven!"

Boo smiled, fanning himself with the small dark blue booklet, a US passport.

Lew exploded in laughter. "Give me that, you no-good cheater!" Delirious with relief, he yanked the booklet from Boo's hands and grinned. "Where did you find it?"

"Over there," Boo said, smiling. "Under a mound of ripe, smelly monkey turds! See the brown stains on the cover. *Aduh!*" Then he reached into the tote and returned Lew's wallet. "You probably also need this, chief. To pay my double salary. You know, our bet."

Lew grinned at the lovable scoundrel.

"Same monkey fecal problem, sir, but they don't eat currency so all your money should be there." And it was, along with credit cards, traveler checks, and some personal papers.

"How can I ever thank you, Boo? Even at double pay—"

"Oh, no, Khun Lew! That bet was just playing, not serious. To make the revealing more fun. Our agreed wage of $500 is already far too generous."

"I understand, but sorry, I have already made an executive decision. Your salary for this week is hereby revised to $1500. And no arguments."

The lad appeared dazed. "B-but sir!"

"Case closed." Lew patted him on the shoulder. "Now, I think you promised me an elephant cheeseburger, or some-such. Lunch at a nearby logging camp?"

They marched along the slippery path formed at the bottom of a twisting crevice where forested mountain walls joined. If Lew spread his feet wide enough and straddled the narrow rivulet, in theory he'd be standing on two mountains. He continued to slip and fall as his rubber flip-flops repeatedly lost traction. His black socks from Siva were soaked and separating at weak spots. Why didn't he buy more pairs at that little shop? Next time.

The path began to widen. "Almost there," announced Boo. "We're nearly through this pass in the mountain wall. Soon we'll reach the next valley."

"Funny, Boo, but seems no animals in this jungle, just bugs."

The youth popped his eyes, playing comedy. "No animals? Ha, Khun Lew, they're all around us." He spread his arms wide. "Watching."

Lew didn't particularly like that. "Really? What kind? Monkeys?"

"Yes, monkeys, of course. But also tigers and wild boar. Crocodiles! Also other big reptiles along with cobras and vipers, giant centipedes, scorpions and more. But most of the danger is asleep right now, though."

Tigers? Yikes. "Still, it feels pretty safe to me here. Luscious and green, drippy wet. Mainly full of pretty birds."

Boo shrugged. "Don't be fooled." He cast his eyes downward. "In fact, I see you've already been attacked."

"What?" Lew glanced around in panic.

"Sir, if you would kindly lift your sarong?"

Lew pulled up the fabric to reveal legs dotted with numerous fat, slimy black lumps adhering to his skin, each a bit larger than his thumb.

Lew began to hop about, kicking and shaking. "Christ almighty, what in the goddamn shit *are* those awful things?" Dark shiny blobs bulged with his sucked blood, a disgusting sight that nauseated Lew and left him woozy. "Help, please! Get 'em off."

Boo chuckled. "Relax, boss. No big worry, heh. Just some leeches."

"But I didn't see anything, a half hour ago, when I lifted my sarong to urinate." Lew's heart thumped like a bass drum.

"Maybe some were already there, sir, but still thin and small. So you didn't notice." Boo pulled out a box of Elephant Brand matches from his tote bag. He gave Lew a whimsical smile, fiddling with his rat-tail. "See, after generously drinking your blood they expand a lot, sir. Isn't it?"

His blood! Hearing that word was all it took to push Lew over the edge. The world started to pixelate, all color bleaching out, and the jungle began to slowly revolve.

"Khun Lew!" Boo caught Lew in mid-collapse and sat him on a stump. He scooped up cool water from the rivulet and splashed his face. Then he squatted down to work on Lew's legs. "Really, sir, please. No big thing. Just try and relax."

Boo lit a wooden match, blew it out and touched the still-hot match head to one of the glistening, worm-like creatures. The leech abruptly recoiled and fell off, wriggling on the ground with a flexibility and speed that was stunning. "This is the only proper way to remove them, boss. If we just pull them off, their little beaks stay stuck in your skin —"

"Beaks?"

"— and get left behind. They quickly grow infected in this climate."

Boo made a show of counting the wormlike creatures, one by one. "Hmm, about twenty in all. Lucky!"

Nausea and disgust still gripped Lew but he was coming around. "Lucky, how's that? Is twenty a propitious number in your local superstition?"

"No, not at all," Boo scoffed. "But I only have nineteen more matches, sir. Just enough, if they all work!"

"But I never felt a thing," Lew complained, "nothing biting into me—"

"Of course, sir. Nature's anesthesia."

Bloody dots marked all the punctures up and down Lew's calves and lower thighs. Boo used his handkerchief to apply pressure and stanch the bleeding. "That will slow it down, sir, but those little buggers inject an anti-coagulant that keeps the wounds flowing freely. So it will take a while before your wounds clot."

Lew shivered with revulsion. "Really, Boo, what kind of place *is* this? Leeches crawling up my legs and I wasn't even in water?"

"Yes, sorry about that. A spot of bother." Boo said. "But on the plus side, they *are* rather tasty in a stir-fry!" Lew almost gagged to imagine eating the slimy things.

As promised, after fifteen minutes the wounds only wept slowly and Lew's senses were fully restored. Time to resume their jungle journey. He rose from the stump but an abrupt, shrill trumpeting sound stopped him cold. Terrifying, it blared through the trees, loud as a freight train, recalling those Jurassic Park films. Surely not a good development.

He poked Boo. "Hey man, so *now* what the fuck?"

Boo held his sides and jiggled with laughter, small tears forming at the corners of his eyes. "Ah, you *gweilos*!" he chuckled under his breath and put a hand on Lew's shoulder. "Relax, sir. Just a big bull elephant. Remember, we're getting close to the logging camp."

With every step the footpath widened until they at last walked out from under the leafy canopy and under a brilliant blue sky. The primitive path ended in a T-junction at another small, hard-pounded clay road that followed along another river, much wider and calmer than the Mobiti, with no cascades or hiss.

"Welcome to the Rama River Valley," Boo said. "The logging camp is just ahead."

Rama River? Lew liked that coincidence—he'd just been musing about those old *Ramar of the Jungle* episodes on the classic TV channel. They walked along and tossed stones into the water, competing for distance or accuracy.

More shrill elephant blasts thundered from up ahead and camp activity became visible in the distance, on both sides of the river. Large patches of forest canopy swayed and shook as entire trees crashed to the ground. Sudden cracking noises were followed by monstrous, ground-shaking thuds and the sporadic, harsh shriek of chainsaws ripping through the air.

Lew counted ten elephants in all, four brutes working belly-deep in the river and six more scattered up the angling river banks, completely under the control of just a handful of tiny men.

"Those are the elephant masters. The *mahouts*," Boo said, pointing at the lean, shirtless men in loincloths and crude turbans for sun protection. Lew shook his head. Wow, how did just a few small fellows control that pack of massive brutes?

High up from the riverbank on a hillside, a heavyset middle-aged man sat in a folding chair near the edge of uncleared forest. He wore dark sunglasses, a Hawaiian-style shirt and sarong, and appeared to be overseeing the entire process. He waved.

Boo grinned. "*Aduh!* Inpanh is summoning us, Khun Lew. Let's go."

They maneuvered through an obstacle course of stumps, ditches, and underbrush to ascend the hillside, dodging limbs, boulders, and massive heaps of elephant dung. Boo and the man embraced, burbling on in Amazian. The overseer smiled and folded his hands to wai the tall foreign stranger. Lew returned the greeting.

"My uncle asks you to please be very careful in the camp. Quite dangerous for visitors. Please stay up here, close to him, where it's safe."

"Your uncle?" Lew chuckled. "You never mentioned."

"Ha! Why spoil the surprise? But yes, Uncle Inpanh is my dad's brother. Biti is so small that many people here are related, somehow."

Lew experienced a glimmer of new hope. And frankly he was desperate for *any* reason to be optimistic. But perhaps his growing local network might help him track down Lotus.

Inpanh offered Lew his seat, a picnic-style folding chair with blue and yellow woven slats, several broken. Lew tried to refuse but his host insisted.

From that perch, one assayed a grand, almost cinematic view of the work—a thrilling sight of massive beasts, crashing trees, and trimmed tree trunks tumbling down the red clay jungle slopes toward the river below. Lew watched intently, finding the process fascinating.

Up the hill, at the edge of uncleared forest, men with chainsaws cut deep angled notches into tree trunks as easy as slicing apples. Then, under the dominant direction of the mahouts, elephants pulled those trees down, tugging on enormous chains or just using their trunks. The trees tumbled amid the ear-splitting violence of cracking wood and booming thuds.

Once down, chainsaws then descended upon the trees like flies alighting on rotten food. Limbs were buzzed off and the stripped trunks were then rolled down the slope to the river where other pachyderms, working as if in slow motion, collected and grouped them. Small teams of men with vines loosely lashed them together like huge rafts.

A sudden commotion broke out at the river, disrupting normal patterns.

The mahouts shouted, flapping their arms and trying to discourage a pair of elephants who had taken the first steps toward copulation. The massive bull had risen up on hind legs behind his partner's rump and unsheathed his monstrous organ. The mahouts, jabbering and hollering, descended and began to peck away at the amorous male's thighs with little wooden hand tools. Trumpeting loudly in complaint, the bull dismounted.

"Holy crap, what are those little thingies?" Lew asked. "Like hammers?"

"Boss, those metal picks are several inches long and sharp. Not enough to seriously injure, but they sure get the brute's attention, *cepat-cepat.* Fast."

Inpanh babbled something.

"My uncle says that big amorous fool, Khun Samson, was confusing work time with love time. But it's probably the lady's fault. Matilda is such a tease. Quite the hot number, sir."

Lew looked at Boo, who read his mind and smiled. "Yes, sir, *Matilda* and *Samson*? Of course our workers all have names. Why not?"

Lew scratched his head, looking all about. "So where do the logs go from here?"

"Those makeshift rafts float down the river to the sawmill."

Okay, now *that* was interesting. Was it possible Lotus was hidden away somewhere in this *second* river valley? That would explain why no trace of it in Biti. Lumber from this sawmill could feed a spirit house factory.

Excitement bubbled in Lew's breast but he played it cool—no sense spooking the locals. After floundering so far, perhaps his Amazia mission was getting back on track.

"So just how far away is the sawmill, Boo?"

"Never seen it myself, sir, but not far. Five kilometers or so."

A few miles downriver. "Can you ask your uncle—?"

A sudden, blood-curdling scream split the air, the heart-rending cry of a human in enormous pain. "Down there!" Boo said, pointing at the river bank, where a worker lay pinned under a giant log.

Inpanh stomped down the hillside with stunning speed for one so hefty, maneuvering between tree trunks and loose branches, to oversee extraction of the man's leg. At his command, a mahout guided an elephant to lumber over and lift the tree while others pulled the victim free.

For the first time, Lew noticed a lithe woman with dark, flashing eyes, there at the camp and responding to the emergency. Absolutely gorgeous, she delivered a bucket of steaming hot water and clean towels to the accident scene before scampering back to a tented cooking area up the opposite river bank.

Lew tossed his chin in her direction. "Hey, Boo, who's *that*?"

"My cousin, sir. But no time to get into that. Uncle has ordered us to leave, immediately, and get out of the way while they deal with this."

Sure, Lew understood. But he had questions for Inpanh, plenty of them. As a member of the area's business community, the old man was potentially a pipeline to Lotus. "Okay, but I really need a good chat with your uncle. He might be able to answer many of my questions."

"Questions? Hmm." Boo shrugged, a funny look on his face. "Not sure what you're up to, sir, but I'll try. Wait here." Boo picked his way down the hillside and sidled up beside Inpanh, still busy with the injured worker. Inpanh waved his arms, looking fierce, but before long the two men were smiling.

Boo climbed back up the hillside. "Khun Lew, we *really* have to leave, right away. They have too much work to do and the stoppage for this accident just makes it worse. Precious little time for visitors."

Great.

"But Uncle Inpanh is happy to chat with you. Later, at dinner tonight. *Boleh?* Can?"

Lew brightened. "Perfect. But I didn't spot any restaurants in the whole Biti valley, only that little closed diner where you were painting."

Boo chuckled. "Restaurant? Nonsense. You're in for some family hospitality, chief. My mom is one of the best cooks in the Kingdom. We'll host you and Uncle Inpanh for a family sit-down dinner. Can or not?"

Lew's appetite heated up just recalling that extraordinary dinner in Ruangbang.

"You'll enjoy my family, sir. My father co-owns this logging camp with Inpanh. When those two get together, it's a real hoot!"

That sounded promising. With just a little more patience, Lew might soon learn plenty about business in the Biti-Rama river valleys . . . and therefore Lotus Exports.

"One more idea, Boo. Can you invite your cousin, too?" That just popped out and Lew didn't know why. Okay, he did, but immediately regretted sounding like a lascivious fool.

Boo chuckled. "Nong? Sure, easy to arrange. She *is* rather a knockout, eh? But fair warning: she recently became engaged."

Hmm, so it's *Nong*? Just as well she was taken, he had no time to lose focus over romantic nonsense. Dinner would be both a hello and a good-bye.

CHAPTER SEVENTEEN
Fateful Dinner at Boo's

Finally over his jet lag, Lew slept in late at the temple dorm. To kill time before that night's dinner with Boo's family, he decided to further explore Biti and acclimate himself. Armed with a hefty stick for ill-tempered dogs, he strolled down the main road and turned off onto a footpath where he soon discovered a whitewashed brick building huddled between coconut palms. Compared to the usual local standards, it was an impressive construction with a bright orange tiled roof.

The sign out front shocked him, indicating some sort of telephone service. Could this be real? Considering the Kingdom's utter paucity in that regard, this place should have been busy as a Popsicle salesman in Hell. But instead he only found a sleepy, small-time operation with two smudged Plexiglas phone booths. One was empty and in the second an old monk was making a call, with muffled bits of his conversation leaking out.

Reigning in his excitement, Lew approached the front counter and wai'ed the stylish attendant whose name badge said *Tina*. She looked mid-twenties, with a skewered ball of dark brown hair and almond eyes shining through slim black spectacles.

"Good day, Miss Tina. Is it possible to phone America from here?" He tried English, hoping the shop sometimes served foreign tourists. She smiled silently, her teeth white and beautiful and brown eyes alive, before waving a hand through the air in some sort of negation.

"Sir?" she said with great effort, "no *Inggris*."

But she handed him a crude laminated card that outlined available services and prices, with a section in charming English. Good. Once he obtained the lowdown on Lotus, at dinner with Inpanh and Thant, he could return here the next day to phone Sal and exchange updates.

The clerk smiled and passed Lew a ledger. Though the clipboard of registration sheets overflowed with Amaza glyphs, he could suss out some of the contents. Call records went back years, in columns for dates, times, names, and phone numbers dialed.

Now what was the exact date of that video conference? This shop was probably the only phone service in Biti, so perhaps the Eternity Brothers had phoned from here. He ran a thumb down the pad, scanning dates.

"Sir, please, no!" gasped Tina, waving a forbidding hand although clearly uncomfortable reprimanding a customer.

"Tina, my friend," Lew uttered reassuringly while skimming fast as he could, "relax! Wow, look at all these customers. Good job!" He fanned the pad. "Impressive for your little shop."

In a calculated move, he placed the pad on the counter and started to pencil in his name and fake data for a call. It worked. Instantly relaxed, she puttered off to prepare the empty booth for her newest customer.

He had to work fast. Quick now, what was that date? *Think!* He remembered to factor in the half-day Amazia was ahead of New York and, about fifteen sheets down, found the correct date range. There he spotted two names in the bouncy Amazia script, the only multiple entry. Moving fast, he tore off the bottom of that sheet and stuffed it into a pocket. Closing the pad just as Tina returned, he acted sheepish and feigned embarrassment.

"Oh, sorry, Tina, my mistake. No money!" He rubbed his thumb and fingers together in the universal shorthand for cash and made a show of carefully erasing his name. "What a dope, eh? Forgot it at the temple." He comically slapped his forehead. "Be back tomorrow."

Tina seemed to get the gist and watched him leave, smiling but a little wary.

Lew explored more of Biti before making his way back to the temple to clean up before dinner. Boo had promised to fetch him around sundown.

The family home was a simple wooden structure in forested foothills, at the end of a rutted path. Under a thick thatched roof, it nestled comfortably between coconut palms and vine-tangled trees. All day long, a constant medley of tropical birdsongs provided an idyllic backdrop, replaced at night by the raucous chitter and buzz of insects.

Lew entered to find a comfortable home larger than it looked outside, thanks to several side and back rooms hidden by forest. Nice. He could get used to something like this. Not that he ever would—his plans were to soon be back on a plane to America.

Boo's family squatted beside him around the low-rise dining platform while Lew sat on the carpet. The colorful batik tablecloth dazzled him. To his sides were Boo and his parents; and across were Uncle Inpanh, cousin Nong and a silent old monk whose presence went unexplained.

Boo's mother, Tuk, served an exotic multicourse extravaganza that was both delicious and visually attractive. It began with a spicy shredded green papaya salad and moved on to sweet and fiery curries, rich with coconut milk and chilies. Everyone ate off green place mats cut from large banana leaves, devouring the fare with gusto. All used their right hands (no utensils) to scoop up food, soaking up sauces with little balls of sticky rice.

The loving family atmosphere was equally sumptuous, with lively nonstop conversation amid laughter and applause. Boo translated for Lew in real-time, ultra-abbreviated snippets. When Thant and Uncle Inpanh debated local business issues, Lew knew he missed a lot and wished he spoke the local dialect.

But more than once, he unintentionally locked eyes with Nong, the ravishing cousin, and felt himself flush, his mouth running dry. Probably in her late twenties, Nong looked glamorous with long, silken hair, hypnotic green eyes, flawless skin and pronounced cheekbones. Something like a cover model for *Asian Vogue*. She glittered in a shimmering purple blouse that swished as she gracefully reached for platters, sending her floral scent wafting by.

But her demeanor was odd—sweet, even shy, but with a hint of sadness. Or was Lew imagining that? And if she was already engaged, why did she keep stealing glances at him? Strange. And why wasn't her lucky fiancé invited?

Lew reminded himself to focus on what mattered. He didn't need a potentially massive, counterproductive distraction like Nong.

The wizened old monk sported a brilliant vermillion robe and crude rubber sandals and just ate, never speaking. Finally introduced as *Pak Mo*, his connection to the family was unclear. Lew missed that part of the translation because his brain was increasingly becoming fogged by the mysterious, electrifying glances being lobbed across the table by Boo's sizzling cousin.

Each time the meal seemed to have run its course, the serving area was cleared and yet another course emerged from the kitchen. The idyllic evening floated along until it was finally time for dessert. Out came platters of succulent mangoes they gorged upon along with chewy glutinous rice, topped by heavenly sweet coconut cream.

This had all been wonderful, yes, and Lew felt sated and euphoric, but he was impatient to start pulling information from Inpanh and Thant. When could he start?

Tea glasses were all refilled and eyes settled upon him. He sensed it was time for the foreign visitor to sing for his supper. Predictable questions began to roll in, translated by Boo:

"What do most Americans think about Amazia?"

"Will you visit our King at the royal palace?"

"How tall is the building where you live?"

"Are you friends with movie stars?"

"Are you friends with Donald Trump or Michael Jordan?"

"Are all Americans millionaires?"

"Do all New York people carry guns?"

"Does winter snow bury houses there?"

Lew gamely answered each, simplifying and carefully framing words to ease translation. Where possible, he shaded answers for a favorable spin that would please his hosts. For instance, why tell them virtually no American even knew Amazia existed?

But then Nong, so quiet all evening, surprised everyone by asking a question. Boo bantered with her. Did she just blush?

"Khun Lew, my cousin asks if you are married. And if so, is your wife beautiful . . . and do you miss her?" Boo sighed, shaking his head. "Sorry, chief, but that's just Amaza women for you. I asked her, *Why so nosey, lah*?"

"It's okay, Boo. I'll answer but then she has to do the same. My questions." Boo translated and the negotiation was quick. Nong looked over at Lew, softly bit her lower lip and nodded, suppressing a shy smile.

"It's a little complicated," Lew started. "Back in America, I had a wonderful wife but we stayed married just a few years. Only now do I fully understand why. We loved each other but our jobs probably more, and grew apart. Eventually she took up with somebody else."

Boo's eyes flashed. "Oh, wow . . ."

"But it wasn't all her fault and I no longer blame her. If I'd given more of myself, more attention and consideration, maybe none of that happens." Long-buried emotions welled, forcing Lew to stop for a beat. He drew in a deep breath and, regaining control, forced a little laugh, as if false levity might fool them. "But as to Nong's second question? MJ was absolutely beautiful. A total knockout. And I miss when we were happy."

Boo patted Lew's shoulder. "That's a bit involved, sir, and maybe a tad depressing for the dinner table. If you don't mind, I'll simplify my translation. But still, sorry. Hope you're okay."

"Oh, more than okay by now, Boo. This probably sounds crazy, but lately it almost feels like I'm finding the real me. Knowing my true self better. Even this visit to Amazia is, oddly, spurring growth. But I'm dealing with some difficult issues and hope you all can help."

"I'll certainly do my best, chief." Boo's smile couldn't mask his concern.

Lew realized that curious eyes, all around the table, were intently trained on him. Boo smiled and began his abbreviated translation. The group sighed and clucked little sounds that Lew took as comforting and empathetic. He watched Nong's wistful reaction from the corner of his eye. When it was over, all softly clapped and a few wais came his way.

"Okay, Boo, Now time for my question for Nong."

"*Boleh*! Can, *lah*."

"I understand your cousin is engaged. When is the wedding and who is this luckiest of men? Her fiancé is surely a man to be envied."

Boo inhaled deeply and his face grew serious. "Damned good questions, sir." He burbled a translation and Nong's eyes grew wide. She looked down for an eternity and played with the hem of her blouse. When she finally looked up, she answered in just a few syllables, her face blank and her voice a strange monotone, her prior mysterious sadness redoubled.

Now *that* was downright weird. Where was the usual glee of a bride-to-be?

"She will marry soon, sir, this month or next. To a very important man. But it's all quite involved. Complex."

Boo's father, Thant, abruptly cut in, wielding his authority as host and household head. He spoke with great animation, waving his hands as his tone rose and fell, in an amusing speech that tickled the others, though the bewitching Nong only stared down at her lap.

Lew had no idea what he said but could tell the subject was being changed.

"A funny story," Boo whispered.

"I guessed."

Then Thant gazed directly at Lew, muttered something and the rest murmured in concurrence. Boo leaned closer. "Father apologizes and says we Amaza are rude to focus like that on ourselves. Nong's wedding and so forth. It is better we should learn more about our distinguished guest, such as why you visiting our humble Kingdom."

Finally, this felt like his opening. Having mentally rehearsed, he was ready to smoothly segue into his Lotus pursuit. But before he could start, Boo leaned over to speak privately.

"I should mention, sir, they *only* know you as my temporary employer, nothing more. But between us, I've already figured it all out. My guess is you're an anthropologist, correct?"

Lew couldn't stifle a grin.

"Ah, you're smiling. I knew it! Cultural anthropologists occasionally pass through here."

Lew grinned. "Sorry, way off the mark. Tell them my company sells estate decorations in America. Magnificent yard ornaments like spectacular birdhouses or gazebos."

Boo knotted his eyebrows. "It does *what*?"

"Go on. Translate."

Boo relayed that and the group burst out laughing. Thant immediately hushed them. The old man is smart, Lew thought. The others may think I'm joking, but he knows better and doesn't want me insulted.

"It's true. I'm here in Biti to visit my manufacturer."

Boo's translation stirred up a buzz. "But chief," he said, narrowing his eyes, "there are no big, modern export factories here for America."

Lew inhaled deeply on that news, finding it far bitterer than the astringent brown tea they were sipping. "After a serious business problem back home, I traveled here to visit the headquarters of the company called Lotus Creations."

The tone of the group's murmuring darkened. Oh, geez, was that pity? They felt sorry for him? They mentioned Lotus several times, pronounced like *Rotus,* while all heads shook *no*.

"Sorry, chief," Boo said in a flat voice. "Absolutely no such thing here. Trust me, Biti is so small, we'd know. And they are concerned—er, are you okay, sir?"

Oh boy, now they worried he was maybe delusional. Lew felt adrift but refused to surrender. Resilience had always been his major strength, and was now nearly all he had left.

"Maybe you don't recognize 'Lotus' because that's just the company's *international* name, for exports? Maybe a different local name in Amazia?" That felt like a stretch. Boo shook his head sadly. Great, now even the kid pitied him! Lew tried a different tack. "Maybe they know the company owners?"

Boo sighed. "Well, boss, considering how small Biti is, it's worth a try."

Lew locked eyes with them all. "I am desperately seeking two men, brothers. Their names are Apiwat and Bobo Eternity."

Before Boo could even start to translate, a loud, involuntary gasp hissed forth from Thant and he dropped his tea glass on the floor, shattering it, while Uncle Inpanh's eyes popped wide. The two elders began to fiercely whisper at each other and the room's emotional temperature soared, but why? Far more seemed wrong than just spilled tea.

They growled terse instructions at Boo, who appeared highly uncomfortable. He turned toward Lew with a clearly false smile, like someone with stage fright facing a large audience.

"Sir, they are inviting you to join them outside, later, to smoke some after-dinner cheroots and enjoy the cool evening air and festive silver moon." Boo lowered his voice. "They also want to privately chat with you about those two men, Apiwat and Bobo Eternity."

Whoa! Wham, blam, bull's-eye!

Lew's heart raced, pounding so hard it might break through his sternum. Finally progress, after so many disappointments and false leads. He smiled calmly and tried to hide his excitement. So close now, he didn't want to spook anyone. If they had *anything* worthwhile, he might soon zero-in on the elusive Lotus.

The dinner party dawdled another hour before breaking up. The men all rose and filed outside while Boo's mother and Nong stayed behind with the servant to clean up. Under an enormous full moon, high in the sky, the old monk placed a bony hand on Lew's forearm and raised his chin at the tall foreigner. A few quick Amaza words spurted out, the first Pak Mo had spoken all night. Then he smiled and pattered off into the night.

Boo sidled up. "Pak Mo cannot smoke, sir. Health, *lah!* So he's walking back to the same temple where you stay."

"Really? Never seen him there."

"Naturally. You are in the dorm, with low-level monks. Pak Mo ranks much higher."

"Makes sense." Lew scratched his head. "But just now, he spoke, first time all night. I'd presumed he was a mute or under a vow of silence. Did you hear what he said?"

Boo shrugged. "Just an old man's mutterings, Khun Lew."

"Don't play coy, Boo. His only words all night, so I can't help but be curious."

Boo sighed. "Well, if you must know, he said: *'Little brother, please be very careful now. There is danger.'*"

CHAPTER EIGHTEEN
Apiwat and Bobo Eternity

The four men huddled in the rutted field out front of the house, ready to fire up their long, Burmese-style cheroots. But local traditions were to be honored before anyone could blow smoky clouds into the clear night air. As master of the house, Thant lit each guest's cigar, one by one.

"Rude to light your own here," Boo explained in a whisper, his face bluish-white in the moonlight. "Bad luck, too."

Lew had never been much of a cigar guy. Sure, maybe a Macanudo while playing business golf, or a tangy Montecristo when out for drinks with an important contact. But from the first searing drag on this local cigar, it was clear these were altogether different.

Harsh, bitter smoke burned his mouth and throat membranes, making him cough. But he fought the urge to hack up phlegm and spit out the foul taste, fearing he'd insult his hosts. So close to obtaining crucial information, he must be careful. He would dispose of the darned thing nonchalantly, just letting it burn itself out.

The men formed a loose ring, each rocking back and forth while aiming smoky streams up at the moon's metallic gleam. They took turns issuing appreciative little grunts and post-meal burps to compliment the cooking of Thant's wife. Lustrous brilliance from overhead illuminated every detail of their faces. To Lew it seemed like being in an old black-and-white movie, with the plot growing weirder by the frame.

He bided his time but his patience was not unlimited. Hadn't they'd invited him out there to discuss the Eternity Brothers? After the commotion at dinner, it was certain they knew *something*, but what? Finally, Thant began to speak, with Inpahn interjecting, and the names of *Apiwat* and *Bobo* were mentioned several times.

Boo leaned closer and spoke low. "This is rather bizarre stuff, sir, things I've never heard before. But Father just explained those were *their secret childhood nicknames*! A private joke from grade school. Kidding around, even now, they sometimes still refer to each other like that."

Wait . . . what? *Those guys* were Apiwat and Bobo, the Eternity brothers? How could that be? Lew couldn't recall the sound of their voices on the conference call, and there'd been no video. None of this made much sense.

If Thant and Inpanh indeed *were* the Eternity Brothers, then they owned a world-class export business. So where was the factory and headquarters? And where did all Lew's money go—those two lived under the most basic rural circumstances. And further, what about all those heartfelt denials during dinner? They claimed to know nothing about Lotus, and seemed absolutely truthful. Thant and Inpanh were good folk who probably couldn't lie if they tried.

Lew was totally bewildered but soaring on an adrenaline rush. Until that moment, his entire visit to Amazia had been one of endless frustration. He'd been lost in a slow-motion world where everything was vague and mired in cultural ambiguity, with no clear answers.

But now, suddenly, out of nowhere, here was a rock-solid lead!

Boo continued to translate. "So yes, they readily admit they *are* Apiwat and Bobo Eternity. Their very little secret joke. So imagine how absolutely stunned they were when you dropped their private nicknames at dinner! And then announced you were hunting them."

"Now wait just a minute—"

Boo held up a palm. "Please, sir! Try, just for a moment, to imagine how totally shocking that must have been. Frightening! Some giant pink stranger from overseas turns up at dinner and suddenly starts revealing their secrets. Personal things—private things. Perhaps threatening things."

"But Boo—"

Boo's father waved an insistent hand at Lew, to let his son to continue.

"Khun Lew, amazed and terrified as they were, they didn't want to frighten my mother or my cousin. So that's why they wanted to speak in private. And now, they demand to know what this is all about, this unspoken threat to them you represent."

"What, *they* demand?" Lew flushed an angry red.

Thant muttered something in a low, menacing tone, his face etched with concern.

"Father asks what kind of trick are you trying to play? What do you want?"

The nerve of these guys! Lew was the aggrieved party, not them. He pulled out the paper scrap from the Tina's phone shop log. "Have them to look at this. Ring any bells?"

The old men studied the paper and, anew, angrily threw their hands into the air.

"Yes, their secret nicknames again. But what is this?"

"This is proof, in their own handwriting, that they are lying." Lew's voice rose. "I tore this from the call ledger at the Biti phone office, where they called me in America. The Lotus meeting. So their denials insult my intelligence. Tell them to stop already."

Boo translated and the two brothers' outrage soared higher, their voices huffing with disagreement. After storming a full minute, they fell silent.

"Let me intercede," Boo said. "Sir, with respect, they say your story is impossible. Yes, you have mysteriously learned their secret childhood nicknames. But the rest of your information is entirely wrong. They have absolutely no international business. Why, the very idea is laughable! As you saw, they run only a modest elephant logging camp."

This was going in circles. "Tell them stop this foolish game and just admit they own Lotus. They schemed to export spirit houses overseas, to unwitting buyers under false pretenses, and have caused terrible harm to many. Allegedly. Plus huge potential damage to me and my business."

Boo burbled a translation and the elders stood rigid with arms folded, disbelief wrinkling their faces. Lew tossed his cheroot to the ground and crushed out the vile thing in a puddle.

"Further, they must indemnify my company against losses caused by their reckless behavior." Lew realized he was barking, his voice loud and out of control in the quiet night. He reined it in. "Please remind them I myself was on that same phone call, when we negotiated the partnership. So they just should stop the lying, now. This paper proves they participated in the trans-Pacific business call. Linked in to the conference by Khun Khon, in Ruangbang."

At that mere mention of Khon's name, a second round of shock blew through the old men. Boo rendered a very careful translation, met by sounds of comprehension but not agreement from Inpanh and Thant. Animated discussion again broke out and Lew clearly heard them bandying about the name of 'Khon'.

Boo inhaled deeply and placed a hand on Lew's shoulder. The old men bowed toward Lew, as if in reverence. "Sir, my elders asked me to convey their apology. They are only now beginning to realize something very strange is going on."

"I should say so."

Another flask of spirits appeared. Thant broke the seal, spilled some on the ground, as was customary, and passed the bottle to Lew for the first swig, as honored guest.

With his disposition running hot as molten steel, Lew had little interest in any more of the local hooch. But he took a placating gulp after detecting a new earnestness on the others' faces. They followed suit. Another handful of cheroots materialized, again triggering the slow-paced ignition ritual while the flask continued to rotate.

For the first time, Lew appreciated a strange symbiosis. The Amazia liquor made the local cigars taste better, and vice versa.

Minutes passed in silence and tempers subsided. Finally, Thant issued a lengthy instruction to Boo, who nodded.

"First principles, sir," Boo said. "It is imperative that you understand it is absolutely contrary to our culture to lie. And my father *swears* he is being truthful. Therefore, you *must* believe that they have nothing to do with any Lotus, just the logging camp."

"Odd, then, to find their nicknames on that phone shop registry."

"True. And they do not dispute writing that."

Whoa, more progress.

"They can explain." Boo said. "Their logging camp has but a single customer, a very big monopoly buyer who is in control, in every way. Basically their boss. They send every last log downstream to the saw mill owned by Mr. Khon and his partner."

Khon? Ahah, more progress! Lew held off from triumphantly punching the air. So Khon was indeed real and these two admit a connection.

"And that's why they panicked at dinner. First you tossed around their secret childhood nicknames and then, even worse, you namedropped Mr. Khon, their ultra-powerful customer. This terrified and thunderstruck them. What was this strange, scary *farang* up to?

A *farang*, sure, but strange and scary? Lew smiled sourly. "Well, the way I hear it, the Eternity Brothers *own* Lotus and hired Khon as a PR consultant to kick-start their export business."

Boo translated that and the elders tossed their hands in the air, moaning. Wow, the Amaza might be slow to reveal emotion but once they did, the anger volcano went *ka-boom!* With lava spewing everywhere.

"That may be Mr. Khon's version, sir, but it's incorrect. Please hear the truth."

Lew folded his arms, chuckling mirthlessly. "Yes, high time for that."

Inpanh and Thant rattled on.

"Mr. Khon and his partner," Boo translated, "have a stranglehold on Inner Amazia. Very powerful. Men you do not cross."

Lew scoffed—this new version of the truth was becoming a muddle. His goal was to solve the mystery, not deepen it, and this was veering off course. But his gut said to stay quiet and keep listening. "Boo, their story has more holes than my Uncle George's underwear. First, they fully admit to being Apiwat and Bobo —"

"Indeed. The Eternity brothers."

"And that they were in business with Khun Khon —"

"Correct. Just selling him logs."

"And they admit to participating in that video conference —"

"Certainly."

"But, rather incredibly, they claim to know nothing about Lotus or its export scheme?"

Boo grinned wide. "Ah, there, you finally get it!"

"Bah!" Lew harrumphed. "I get *nothing*. How would that even work?"

Boo translated and his elders sighed and answered.

"Mr. Khon only sent them a command that morning, just before the video meeting, to phone his Ruangbang office. They *had* to obey. As their sole customer and owner of most of Biti, Mr. Khon is like a dictator. So they went to the phone shop with no idea what was going on."

"So why did they sign-in with the Eternity name?"

Boo asked and the old men shrugged. "No particular reason. Just fooling around. A game they sometimes play."

"Hmm." Lew shook his head.

"Once they called Khon, they discovered another party was on the line, too. We now know that was you, in America."

"Right."

"Now please recall, they speak zero English. So Khon was their total filter for the call, translating *everything*. They knew *nothing* other than what Khon told them."

Lew knew Tina's shop had no video capability, either, so the brothers saw nothing. Lew's stomach started to feel a little weird. His mouth was dry so he took a sip of the whiskey.

236

"Khon told them you were an important timber broker in Singapore. An English speaker."

"What?"

"He completely deceived them, sir. They were on the line supposedly to answer any technical logging questions."

Lew's neck felt hot. "No, we were discussing an export arrangement for America. For birdhouses, or whatever those things are that Lotus manufactures."

But their twisted version of reality seemed eminently possible. Lew recalled all those sidebar discussions in the local dialect—he had no idea what they discussed. "To be honest, Boo, suddenly I'm no longer sure *what* I believe."

Boo's father motioned for all to get comfortable. Evidently, more was yet to come. "Father begs your patience, Khun Lew. His story is somewhat complex."

Lew nodded.

"In the past, Mr. Khon only operated his sawmill half the year, during high season when the river was deeper. Other months, the water downstream from the mill was too shallow to send the cut lumber onward to market. The inevitable result was always six months of frantic work followed by a half-year shutdown."

"Very inefficient." Where was this going?

"Everything changed the day a foreign businessman arrived in Amazia to partner with Mr. Khon. This stranger was bold, with new and aggressive ideas. They built a factory beside the sawmill, to process lumber year-round."

Lew's blood stirred. "Not a factory for spirit houses, by any chance?"

Boo nodded. "Indeed. An excellent business here, something every household or business buys."

Bingo. Lew nearly tingled to be back on track.

"Lotus Creations, perhaps?"

Boo shrugged. "No, sir, that is not our way. There is no name for the sawmill and factory. Here in Amazia, we just say *factory* or s*aw mill.* No names like *Lotus.*"

"Got it."

"Once the local market was saturated, Mr. Khon began to send spirit houses to Ruangbang by train. From there, wholesalers sold them around the region, to modest success."

Made sense. "Just a wild guess, Boo, but was the next genius move to get into overseas exports . . . about a year ago?"

Boo translated but the elders just shrugged. "No idea, sir. They only supply logs and we never go there." But then Inpanh, visibly irritated, spat out a testy diatribe.

"Uncle says Mr. Khon and his partner have grown too rich, buying up businesses and property in the region. Many small-timers, unable to compete, are forced to borrow money from them under unfair terms until their companies are ruined."

Thant muttered more.

"Mr. Khon and his partner now control village life across Inner Amazia, as landlords, business owners and bosses. Very powerful and dangerous, reigning like kings. Brutal and ruthless, they are greatly feared. It's like they own us."

"Including your folks?"

"Especially."

Lew smiled some reassurance. "I don't completely understand, but it seems like our problems may somehow be linked." Lew then poured out his entire story, utterly astounding his Amaza friends.

"Sir, that is horrific!" Boo wrung his hands. "But worst of all, it is highly improper—a sacrilege!—to export spirit houses to unknowing foreigners. Enormously dangerous. The angered spirits cannot know the buyers' insults are unintended."

The old men scowled in disgust.

"Father and Uncle are very sorry for your misfortune . . . but even more concerned about your enormous obligation."

"My what?"

"You now have a huge, serious moral duty. And must take immediate action."

Those words battered Lew. "What do you mean?"

"You must immediately make sure all your customers know they are in mortal danger. And also advise them of ways to appease the spirits and minimize further danger. Right away! Today. No time to lose."

The old men's faces, heartfelt and deadly earnest, deeply moved Lew. Their insistence and sincerity—and especially their unshakable certainty—were not to be ignored. He didn't really buy into the reality-bending idea of terrestrial spirits, but rational or not, the righteous old Amaza were beyond fully convinced. He knew nothing about Eastern spiritualism but these people absolutely *lived* it. It was hard to just blithely ignore their warnings.

It seemed extraordinary, this new responsibility weighing down on him. If the assertions were true, countless lives were at risk and depended upon him alone. This new obligation felt huge, dwarfing the concerns that had propelled him to Amazia in the first place.

His ability to embrace their advice surprised Lew, usually a rational objectivist by nature. This inner change was not unlike the perceptual shift one experienced after gazing, long and hard, at an optical illusion and then suddenly perceiving the hidden second view.

"Tell them I vow to fix this, on my very soul." His voice rang out clear and strong. "Tomorrow, I'll go to Tina's phone shop and call my partner to make sure all customers are warned. But many have *already* been hurt, at least their properties, so I need to recover money to help repair homes and pay bills. Since Khon and his partner caused it all, it's proper they pay."

Boo and the elders agreed. "Yes, Mr. Khon and his partner are duty-bound to help those suffering people . . . but the trick will be in convincing them."

Lew seemed to have finally secured a footing, after days slipping down the Amazia rabbit hole. Now he needed to confront Khon and his mysterious partner, the masterminds behind the entire mess.

***

With midnight closing in, Boo chaperoned Lew back to the temple. The two quietly pedaled borrowed bicycles and rode single file, dodging potholes.

The evening's revelations unsettled and thrilled Lew, but he felt a nagging suspicion more was yet to come. The Amaza were still holding something back, but what? And Boo's current silence seemed really odd, totally out of character. Something was on his mind.

They arrived at the temple courtyard, dismounted and walked to the dormitory.

"Sir, I will leave now. Tomorrow you're on your own. I have family business all day."

That suited Lew. Already brewing plans, he welcomed a day alone. But Boo's face showed unmistakable, weighty concern.

"Boo, what's wrong? I can see it in your eyes."

"Boo flicking his rat tail. "Perceptive, sir. Well, it's about Mr. Khon's partner."

"Right, the mystery man with no name." He really had them freaked out—the Amaza seemed terrified to even say his name.

Boo shrugged. "Oh, he's got a name, all right, but that's not for me to, um . . . well, there's something more important."

Lew pursed his lips. "Out with it."

"Khon's partner, the Big Boss? He's the one."

"Which one?"

"The one Nong is marrying." In a night chock-full with surprises falling like dominoes, that one perhaps stunned and upset Lew the most, though he wasn't sure why.

Boo shook his head. "It's already fixed. Totally committed." Looking resigned, Boo waved good-bye and wandered off into the night.

Lew entered the darkened temple dormitory, his mind flying as he tried to piece together a logical summation of the evening's slew of bizarre revelations.

Khon and his mysterious partner were clearly his targets, the likely scoundrels behind Lotus, screwing people right and left—not only foreigners but innocent Amaza, too.

And though Boo didn't reveal more, his demeanor hinted something was very wrong about Nong's betrothal. Was she being forced into marriage with the Big Boss? The idea made Lew's skin crawl. None of his business, of course, but there was something irresistible about Nong and he couldn't undo his deepening feelings, much less understand them.

CHAPTER NINETEEN
Elephant Turds and Potholes

Lew joined the teen monks with their brass begging bowls early the next morning as they walked a gauntlet outside the temple to accept breakfast donations. Residents lined up on both sides of the path and smiled at the sight of the tourist monk in a Yankees cap. Lew, with a borrowed bowl, scored several triangular leaf packets of rice with curried fish bits, a box of sweet tea and a biscuit. After eating it all, he left for Tina's shop to phone Sal.

While heading down the clay road, early morning steam lifted off shimmering green rice paddies as he replayed the discussion from last night.

Though his deep-seated Western beliefs and values continued to argue that terrestrial spirits were a fiction, he was open to the alternate view and felt an undeniable moral obligation to take action.

After all, the Amaza (and another hundred million souls across Southeast Asia, for that matter) did believe such entities existed. And it went beyond just belief: they were certain, so who was he to say they were wrong? Moreover, as a Christian (though granted, not a great one) he already fully acknowledged the existence of an ethereal dimension to the universe—souls, angels and devils, heaven and hell. So what was the big difference?

It had been easier, back home, to dismiss Dr. Narathiwat's contentions as just talk. But now, immersed in this place and its culture, those claims overpowered him.

Dodging dogs, elephant turds, and potholes, he reached the phone shop at 7:30 and found it already open.

"Hey, Tina, remember me?" He flashed his most disarming smile. "Said I'd be back."

With a stern face, she nodded and picked up her clipboard. Hmm, no wai? Still a little pissed. "Yep, ready to call America now . . . and this time, even brought cash." He flashed the bag of *Arysai* and Tina smiled.

"*Ah-MEH-ree-ka*," she said, looking impressed. While he filled in the registry, she scurried off to prepare a booth, wiping clean the small wooden counter, metal seat, and clock. She ushered him in and handed him a black phone receiver straight from 1955, tethered to a wall via a black curly plastic cord.

It was already muggy in the shop—no air conditioning—and even worse in the booth. Lew started to sweat, waiting for Tina to make the connection. Five minutes later, Sal's husky and sleepy-sounding voice came winging across the Pacific.

"Yeah, operator, say what?"

"It *Meestah Cluck*," Tina said, "from Amazia." She shot a beatific smile and thumbs-up to Lew, through the Plexiglas.

"Hey, Sally Boy, good evening to you there in Gotham!"

"Christ's holey socks!" Sal exclaimed, "It's the late Lewis Nathaniel Clarke—and I do mean *late*, at this hour. Where you been and where exactly *are* you, man?' He cleared his throat and started to sound more awake. "Thought you fell into a volcano or something. Gave up on your cellphone long ago. *Nada* connection."

"I'm still in Amazia, but way upcountry now, in Biti—basically the ass-end of nowhere, where Lotus is supposedly headquartered."

"*Supposedly?* Been there more'n a week and you haven't met with them yet?"

"They seem to be hiding."

"Well, better step up your game, Hoss. You should be heading home already."

"Gee, thanks for all the usual support and empathy." Lew enjoyed their familiar banter. Sal's irreverent chatter somehow always helped him to re-center. It now reminded him of the entire world that existed beyond this quirky Asian wonderland. "Long story, Sal, but generally one miserable development after another. Would you believe Khon's PR office in the capital turned out to be an abandoned shop at a ratty strip mall?"

"Whoa."

"So now I'm hunting Lotus way upcountry and finally got a decent lead. But this place doesn't even have landline phone service, much less cellular, so I'm calling from a plastic cage in a little cockamamie shop and sweating like a pig. My clothes are saturated and downstairs, my boys are itching. I've got no idea how long this line will hold up, by the way. "

"You make it sound too fun, bro. I'm jealous! And are the women hot there?"

"Like gargling with Sriratcha."

"Well all righty then . . . enjoy!" Sal's tone then abruptly went all-business. "But while this connection holds, let's hit high points. You first or me?"

"Shoot."

Sal cleared his throat. "Okay, more legal papers arrived."

"Lawsuits?"

"Some. On the bright side, more customer orders keep flooding in, too, though we still haven't unloaded a container in a while. No new supply. Lotus on holiday?"

"Don't expect any more, Sal."

"Huh?"

"Just write this all down," Lew said, his tone going stern. "First, from this moment forward, we are accepting no new orders and dispatching no new product."

"What!" Sal's voice leapt high like a soprano.

"You heard me." The first step was to stop the problem from spreading. The Amaza elders had gotten through to Lew—lives sure seemed to somehow be at stake.

"Okay," Sal grunted. "I don't get it . . . but you're the boss."

"Next. Draft a letter. Run it past Steiner. And then immediately send it to every customer who has ever purchased a Lotus unit from us. Explain that only now have we become aware these items, from Asia, were designed as homes for powerful terrestrial beings. Spirit houses, not bird houses. So installing these, anywhere in the world, will attract dangerous beings who are easy to offend. Steps must immediately be taken to appease them."

Sal hacked up some phlegm and spat. "Lew, with all due respect," he growled, "have you lost your *fucking* mind? That's the crazy Dr. Narathiwat shit, all over again. The polar opposite of what our hot-shot lawyer advised us to do."

"Forget all that, Sal, and just do exactly what I say. Immediately."

"But Lew," Sal whined, "we'll just be screwing ourselves. Such a letter will create the appearance of guilt. With lawsuits already pending, the last thing we want to do is admit any of that. Remember, it's only an *alleged* danger, right? Come on, man! This is the twenty-first century. Spirits don't really exist."

Lew's felt his anger rising but ordered himself to cool down. Sal meant well and was just trying to protect them. He didn't understand, laboring under the same mindset of total Western disbelief that had also been Lew's, up until just a few hours earlier.

"Sal, believe me, I *know* where you're coming from. But this is all non-negotiable. We're dealing with some deadly serious shit here. You saw Emily's *60 Minutes* video, right?"

"Sure. That looked serious. But who says it's *our* shit?"

"Trust me, it's real and we probably own it. Unintended, of course, and we've understandably been in denial till now—I mean, spirits? But none of that changes our obligations now." Lew drew in a calming breath. "But to your point, yeah, why kill ourselves in the process?"

"Finally —"

"So look, our customers must be warned. That one hundred percent must happen. But work with the lawyers to see if there is a better way to communicate this danger, less suicidal to our personal interests. If not, then draft something today and mail it, posthaste. Human life is at risk and we bear a heavy moral duty."

Sal whistled low from 8,500 miles away. "Wait, who's this Mr. Moral Duty guy on the line? Pope Lewis? Where'd my partner go? But okay chief, your call. I'll look into this —"

"And immediately execute the warning."

Sal ended a long sigh with a chuckle. "You know, boss, It's actually kinda impressive, even admirable, this new un-prick-like version of you, all worked up over morality, even when it screws over our business."

Lew scoffed. "Ready for more? From what I can see, there's zero wealth *anywhere* in this Podunk place. So Uzzi's master plan, relying on Lotus to legally bail us out, seems a nonstarter."

"Dude, you're just a font of cheery news! Glad you woke me for all this. But there must be a lot of cash there, *somewhere*. After all, you paid five years of up-front money. And maybe other countries did, too."

The phone connection was clear and holding well. Lew and Tina exchanged smiles.

"Anything else, Sal?"

"*Nada*, chief. Any idea when you're coming home?"

"Nope."

"Well, Hoss, then go with God, in your extended travels through the Mysterious East."

Lew signaled Tina to end the call and went up front, where she frantically punched numbers into an old calculator and laboriously penned an invoice. Lew grinned. Tina probably didn't handle many international calls.

She handed the invoice to him with a lovely smile. He saw a long string of zeroes and felt a jolt. *Arysai* A100,500!

That seemed an extraordinary amount until a quick calculation revealed the total due was only around six bucks. He gave her A200,000 and motioned for her to keep the change.

***

Lew bounced out of the shop and down the clay path—connecting with Sal was always a tonic. He stopped at a small drink stand to buy a lukewarm bottle of Fizzo. The dark non-carbonated beverage was sour-sweet and tasted like cola with cloves.

As he sat on a wobbly plastic chair and nursed his soda, Tina jogged up, waving her arms and looking flustered. "Khun Lew!" she squawked, out of breath. "America!" She mimed holding a phone by her ear and waved for him to follow.

Back at the shop Lew untwisted the knotted cord and picked up the phone in the same booth. "Hello? Lew Clarke speaking."

"Clarke? I'm honored," the gruff voice growled, dripping with sarcasm. "About time."

"And who the hell is this?" Lew barked.

"Just your lawyer, the poor *schlub* trying to save your sorry ass. So just listen now, it's late here and I'll make this quick."

Wow, Steiner? He must have phoned Amazia immediately after Sal relayed Lew's urgent plans. "Ah, Uzzi! Nice to hear your voice, too."

"Kid, nobody likes a smart ass." The lawyer's gravelly voice hacked through the phone static like a butcher's cleaver lopping off a limb. Unmistakable hostility. "Sal just woke me up to pass along your asinine ideas."

"Listen, Uzzi, just execute my plans. Okay?"

"What, send incriminating memos to all your customers? Or hire that nut-case professor?" Steiner groaned. "That would be tantamount to admitting guilt. News flash, son: your company is absolutely innocent . . . your sincere new beliefs notwithstanding. And that's just a fact. Accidents happen every day, sometimes to people who just happened to buy your products. Coincidence! There are *no* evil spirits, only bad luck, and nobody can sue you for that."

Lew fully understood this utterly rational, Western line of reasoning. But an intense week in the Kingdom had had its impact.

And certain things were more important than money.

"Yeah, Uzzi, I know. But listen—"

"No, Lew, *you* listen. I could gather a pool of unrelated folk who went to Starbucks or McDonald's today and later wound up in car crashes. Nobody in his right mind would try to link their accidents to eating cheeseburgers or drinking lattes. Correlation is not causation. Thought you already understood that."

Steiner's tone made Lew bristle. "Right, I get all that, but—"

"*But* nothing! Your only job there is to force the manufacturer to provide indemnification. We on the same wavelength?

"We absolutely *were*, Uzzi, but there's been a change."

"Not at all. Our legal course is steady as she goes." Steiner's hard-edged voice could crack rocks.

"Actually," Lew said, "Avian's *new* top priority is to ensure every customer knows about the terrestrial spirit threat and what to do. Dr. Narathiwat was right. There is no other choice, Uzzi, it's life or death. Of course, we want you to keep Avian as legally protected as possible. So don't admit guilt, but make my new directives happen, please, and right away."

Steiner chuckled bitterly. "Now listen, son—"

"And I've also decided, as Avian's owner, the company should issue a full, immediate refund to any customer who wants it. No questions asked."

"Moses' holy beard, pal, you been brainwashed? What nonsense. Something happen?"

Lew paused. Steiner would never understand. "Doesn't matter. Just say I've received strong advice from some Amazia businessmen."

"Well, in my professional opinion they are talking prime grade, uninformed bullshit."

"That's your view, Uzzi. But my decisions are final."

"What you are ordering," the lawyer said, "would be, for me, tantamount to professional malpractice. So I must refuse."

"Sorry to hear that."

"Why?"

"Because if you refuse clear orders, I have no choice but to terminate your services."

"What, you're firing me? You ignorant pup!" Steiner was yelling now. "I'm not fired, I quit! And boy, will you ever regret this!"

"Don't you threaten—"

But the line was already dead.

Lew was totally agitated as he left the shop, his pulse thumping in his ears. Steiner was way off base, sure, but shouting matches with the hired help were for rookies, not the likes of him. Hot emotions rarely led to good business decisions.

But ever since arriving in Amazia, he'd been immersed in an alternate reality that seemed governed by previously imperceptible truths, where the spiritual was more important than the physical.

No wonder his views were changing.

He forced his mind to go blank and calmed himself, meandering down the jungle path. With his senses dulled, he lost awareness of his surroundings and just walked, enjoying physical movement as a form of meditation or therapy. He sucked in fresh jungle air and simply existed in *the now,* finding temporary release from his problems.

Naturally, that was impossible to sustain and before long, his innate rationality took back control. He realized he was near the Monkey Dump.

The snap of a branch behind him drew his attention. Then came the soft patter of approaching footsteps. He swung around, expecting to see those damned monkeys again . . . but instead, it was Nong, Boo's knockout cousin from the family dinner.

She approached, floating in grace, as her dark hair trailed in long cascading waves that bounced with each step. She closed in, sobbing quietly, and their eyes locked for an eternity. It felt like she was gazing into his very soul and he forgot how to breathe.

This connection felt like far more than mere physical attraction, like their very souls were somehow merging. Since the collapse of his marriage, he had forgotten such feelings could exist.

Tears looped down her cheeks in long trickles and she softly moaned, burying her face in his chest. "Khun Lew . . . please . . . can help Nong?"

So she knows English?

At least that's what he thought he heard. With most of his upper level brain functions fried, he wasn't sure. For minutes it was all he could do to just hold her and utter soothing sounds while she wept into his shirt. "Hey, hey there. It's okay," he whispered.

But nothing was okay. For God's sake, what on earth was going on? And why bring it to him, already confused, fairly overwhelmed and lost in Amazia?

But still . . . poor Nong! But what about her fiancé? Surely the Big Boss could fix nearly anything. He supposedly owned most of Inner Amazia, so the man could just snap his fingers and boom, all problems solved. No?

Her weeping finally subsided and Lew offered her a sleeve to dry her tears. Despite the storm of recent emotion, both were able to laugh at that. Good, that was better.

Lew pointed at his ring finger, hoping that was a universal. "Your fiancé?" he asked, bouncing his shoulders in question, "Maybe *he* can help?"

She immediately pointed at *her* ring finger and shook her head fiercely. "No!" she exclaimed, her face dark with fear or anger. Okay, maybe she didn't love the guy, after all. More typical Amazia confusion or what?

They locked glances again and he felt the electricity.

All that sizzling vulnerability just made her all the more intriguing and desirable. He was being taken prisoner, overwhelmed by a nearly irrational urge to protect this woman whom he hardly knew, and from what, he didn't know. But he was powerless to slow down this unneeded complication.

Nong stared deep into his eyes and they kissed, her warmth suffusing his entire being. She tasted of cinnamon and coconut and smelled like a tropical bloom. Monkeys in branches all around them observed, howling and chattering.

She again uttered words that, this time, enslaved him. "Please! Khun Lew ... save Nong! Only you can."

Only him, huh, but why? That made no sense. But she was fantastic and his brain was already short-circuiting. He pulled her closer and they kissed again and out came his reply.

"Sure, I promise." He was never much for intuition or playing hunches, but this connection was blowing him away. It felt real, love and his concern. He couldn't really understand but at a deeper level knew he had to help her. There was no other choice.

Nong broke free, turned, and glided back up the path toward the village, her lithe figure in retreat visible beneath rippling silk. Twice she stopped and turned back to see if he was watching. Both times, he returned her wave.

This new "Save Nong" obligation rose to the top of Lew's Amazia to-do list. But how, and from what? He probably needed to have his head examined, becoming infatuated with a woman with whom he couldn't even converse. He hadn't traveled to this tropical fantasyland, halfway around the globe, to find a soul mate.

Yet, at his innermost level, this felt right. For him, everything about Nong now mattered most. But what was the problem?

Boo had been holding out. It was time he came clean . . . about everything.

CHAPTER TWENTY
River Rafting on the Rama

Nong's scent stayed with him as he slogged down the muddy jungle path toward the elephant camp. While slipping along and keeping careful watch for leeches and simian assailants, he was unable to stop mentally replaying all the morning's surprising events.

He reached the tee junction at the Rama River, turned right and headed downriver, soon reaching the logging camp. Uncle Inpanh, perched in his director's station high up the hillside, waved Lew over.

"Great dinner," Lew called out. "And thanks for the cigars and drinks."

Inpanh didn't follow until the American playacted gunning down shots and choking on cigar smoke. They both laughed and shook their heads, agreeing: indeed, a tough night!

Down below, camp workers lashed together massive reddish-brown logs into floating bundles of three like loosely-bound rafts. The elephants, directed by yelling mahouts, shoved the floating bundles out toward mid-river where, jostling and bumping, they slowly rotated to align with the current and then floated downriver.

Lew tapped Inpanh on the shoulder, pointed downriver, and mimicked the shriek of a blade cutting timber.

Inpanh nodded: *Yes, sawmill that-a-way.*

Lew needed to investigate that, soon, quietly and on his own. A potential gold mine of information about Lotus, the factory and its owners.

Down on the river, a fearless worker danced across the raft tops, scampering from one to the next, using a long pole for support. His job was to ensure clean getaways, keeping the logs from getting clogged before they could pick up speed and head downriver.

A bold, probably reckless plan popped into Lew's head. It was even dangerous—he remembered that worker pinned under a log. But what else did he have? He wai'ed Uncle Inpanh and climbed down the slope, working his way toward the riverbank.

His approach alarmed the elephants, who began trumpeting their concern. But upon seeing Lew, the mahouts only smiled and whacked the hairy beasts with those little sharp picks. Immediately obeying, the animals ignored Lew and returned to work.

Lew moved quickly. He hopped aboard a log raft in the shallows, an outrageous sight that clearly amused camp workers. Imagine, a *farang* playing like one of them! They babbled and laughed but just as Lew suspected, no one bothered trying to stop him. After all, only moments earlier, they'd seen him up there, buddying around with the boss.

His makeshift raft rotated into the current and began to crawl out toward midstream. A worker on an adjacent bundle, closer to shore, waved for Lew to follow him off. *Quick!* But Lew only grinned back and motioned for patience. *Just another minute.* The Amaza chuckled and shook his head. *Crazy farang!*

Lew crouched down and held tight to the binding, watching his fingers and toes. Before long, his makeshift vessel picked up speed, heading downriver.

By this point, all the timber workers and mahouts were going berserk, roaring as if they'd never seen anything so funny. But high up the hillside, an angry Uncle Inpanh yelled and waved his arms at the runaway American. Lew feigned unknowing innocence, smiling back with a dramatic shrug, his arms spread wide as if saying: *Well, what could I do?*

The crude raft bobbed and floated around the bend and left the elephant camp behind. Lew leaned back to make himself comfortable as he wound through pristine jungle. Cool from movement and shaded under the dense, interwoven jungle canopy, he felt as if teleported into a BBC nature documentary, something beyond fantastic, engulfed by vegetation and dwarfed by trees with leaves the size of men.

Brilliantly colored tropical birds serenaded him and flowers carpeted the river banks, perfuming the air like a fancy lady's boudoir. A strangling crisscross of vines looped overhead as trees from both banks merged their branches. A haven for Tarzan.

He stared deep into the green backdrop along the river and, focusing hard, began to discern previously unseen wildlife—monkeys and wild boar, but also predators like the occasional jungle cat. At one point he glided past a coven of mighty Asian crocodiles, lolling on the opposite riverbank, their nostrils sniffing the air. He lay rigid and flat on the logs, afraid to even breathe until he'd safely passed by.

To be honest, he knew diddly about jungles and feared as-yet unseen creatures like thick, giant snakes and flesh-eating fish . . . or was that just in South America? He didn't care to experiment to find out.

This, he decided, was probably totally effing dangerous! What on earth was he thinking? But it was too late now, no turning back.

After drifting along for an hour on his own real-life Disney Jungle Cruise, but without the lame jokes, a strange sound started to pierce the jungle aural backdrop of birds, insects, creaking trees and rushing water. It was a shrill new noise, intermittent and violent—the high-pitched mechanical roar of sawmill blades ripping through logs.

As the river drew him along, the racket grew louder. When he at last rounded a final bend, a monstrous complex faced him, just ahead, sitting in a clearing carved from the jungle. It looked totally alien in this verdant setting. Dozens of log rafts meandered around, jamming the entry chute.

Okay, now what? Time to wing it again. He'd ad-libbed more in a week than the past five years, but Amazia seemed to reward flexible creativity and risk-taking.

He double-checked his wallet and valuables, still dry and secure in a plastic bag in the pocket sewn into his sarong. He tightened the laces on his Jordans and clicked his Yankee cap a notch tighter, in case he had to abruptly jump in. But remembering concerns about flesh-eating fish, crocodiles and snakes, he prayed it didn't come to that.

As Lew's primitive raft drifted closer to the sawmill, intermittent mechanical noise pounded him with greater violence. During quiet periods, after his ears stopped ringing, he could hear workers singing at the riverbank while they directed a smaller elephant to free logs from their bindings and aim them at the entry chute.

Crouching low to avoid being seen, Lew began to carefully work his way toward shore, leaping from one raft to the next like an Eskimo maneuvering across ice floes. Then the inevitable happened—he slipped and fell in. Unable to touch the bottom, He was surprised the river ran so deep. He clung fast behind a log.

All hands heard his ill-timed splash, occurring during a machinery silent period, so all singing stopped. Heads in unison swiveled in his direction.

Lew stayed low, hidden behind an enormous log, afraid to even breathe. Remaining concealed behind rafts, he gradually worked his way to shore, the entire time terrified of being crushed. Only luck prevented serious injury as the pampered city boy dodged monster tree trunks in an Asian river.

He scampered up the riverbank and disappeared into the dense jungle. The air was thick with insects and full of their metallic whine. The damnable creatures immediately began to feast on imported meat as Lew slapped at his arms and legs, to no avail.

He stripped off his wet clothes, wrung them out and put them back on, damp. They'd dry fast in that climatic oven. Thankfully, his wallet and passport stayed dry inside the plastic bag.

The jungle seemed impenetrable, with visibility penetrating

barely a few feet into the organic tangle. For Lew, this challenge was also a blessing, rendering him near-invisible to the mill workers. He squirmed through the undergrowth, staying near the riverbank, until he reached the edge of the sawmill clearing. Then, following its perimeter as it looped away from the river, he stealthily crept along to assess the complex, always staying hidden just inside the jungle.

The cleared area seemed about the size of several football fields, stretching out beneath a single, enormous thatched roof suspended between a nest of tall trees trimmed free of branches. The massive roof was alive with twittering birds and small, scampering animals.

Beneath that, laborers were divided into separate areas by tasks: for timber cutting, sorting, and stacking of planks by size. Most wore simple sarongs but some sported recycled American team jerseys, sold across the developing world by American charities for pennies a pound.

Shining with perspiration, they flashed around manning gas-powered saws that emitted angry burps as they sliced giant planks into smaller boards of precise measurements. An elderly man laid a yellow metal tape measure against each, rejecting as many as half.

In another work area, men guided a trolley down hard-packed earth paths, selecting boards according to predefined packing lists, looking like an old married couple out shopping. Lew wasn't sure what all the precise cutting and sorting was for, but hoped it had something to do with Lotus.

Moving quietly under jungle cover, Lew reached the far end of the perimeter loop, where it met the river, and completed his surveillance.

Crouching down to rest and gather his thoughts, he was disturbed by a woman's shrill cry that pierced the jungle buzz. It emerged from still further downriver, below the sawmill site. What was that? A man's angry response followed, triggering a chorus of whimpers. Such strange verbal fury, confusing and out of place among the gentle Amaza.

He headed downriver toward the sound, following the riverbank, parting tall grass and weeds like a curtain, and soon reached a second clearing . . . the factory complex.

He sat on a boulder and stared for a full minute, stunned and unable to process what he was seeing. Was this the same jungle factory site as in that Lotus video? Maybe. Couldn't be sure. Perspiring freely, he plucked a large stiff leaf and fanned himself.

This second site was huge, several times larger than the sawmill complex. A honeycomb of work stations stretched off into the distance, each with an individual thatched roof, where a mixed work force labored in near-silence. Many appeared malnourished or sickly and some of the women were pregnant.

But most chilling of all was the large number of children, some young as four or five, all wearing a haunted look as they toiled. Lew soon realized each work station contained a nuclear family.

It all made his blood boil.

Crews pushed trolleys down aisles and delivered presorted 'kits' of wood pieces to vacant cubicles where, soon thereafter, a manager would usher in a fresh family. Wasting no time, the emaciated parents began laying out pieces to match assembly diagrams while the others, even the youngest, started to hand-smooth the wood using coarse sand, pebbles, and crude files.

At the closest cubicle, Lew drank in a good look at a family that was far along in the process, their output indeed resembling a marvelous, export quality spirit house. They had probably already been working on it for many months, no way to tell how long. A grandmother was joining final pieces, using the thinnest of nails and a special glue from saplings planted around the factory compound.

The angry hollering Lew previously heard resumed and his eyes locked onto the source. It was a beefy Amaza man wearing swank Western clothing and sunglasses, snapping a ferocious-looking whip at a cowering family of cowering workers. The sight was outrageous, unbelievable in today's world, and it conjured up deplorable chapters of history long-thought to be closed—images of forced servitude, slavery and masters.

Lew shuddered at the implications. This wretched beehive, founded upon near-slave labor, was the Lotus factory! And as a major importer, he had unintentionally been complicit in this immorality.

A cold fury percolated through to his core. At that moment, he would have gladly crushed the skull of the unknown villain who'd landed him in this mess. His previous hypothesis (or perhaps, hope) had been proven ridiculous, that the amazing Lotus exports were perhaps founded upon some secret Amazia technologies. No, this was actually manufacturing via brute force; not even low-tech, it was *no*-tech, like construction of the pyramids. Provided enough free manpower and adequate time, nearly anything could be achieved.

There was no denying the natural artistic genius of the families, turning rough-hewn wood into such sublime artifacts. But their incredible workmanship came at the unspeakable human cost of enslaved families working night and day, their unremitting lot of shattered lives and sapped health.

Though absolutely innocent in his intent, Lew felt tainted by his involvement. He felt coated in impurity, his anger exploding. As if abandoned by the Fates, he'd unwittingly enabled a slave camp and profited from that labor. And this oppressive new moral responsibility piled on top of his other worries, like those crushing lawsuits or helping Nong.

He crept ahead along the jungle perimeter and spotted several spirit houses being painted and polished in other cubicles. Each glowed with that familiar, immeasurable beauty of the Lotus export products. Proof positive, all right.

Up ahead, a wide, new-looking gravel road led away from the factory complex, heading off from final work stations where those amazing Jenga-like wooden shipping cartons were created and packed. He watched a family transport its creation—perhaps a year of painstaking labor—to this area, where they collaborated with a family of dedicated box-makers to fit their artwork into a perfectly-sized, handmade crate. Sealed, it was then hoisted onto a cart pulled by a young elephant.

Lew deduced the gravel road was to transport boxed spirit houses to the Biti train station, in the next valley. Staying under jungle cover, he crept up far along the road and then jumped out and sprinted back to Biti.

That evening at the temple, famished, he wolfed down bowl after bowl of steamed rice while reliving the day's events. He looked at the young monks and wondered if they knew about that factory. Had some even worked there?

He scribbled a note to summon Boo next morning, painstakingly tracing the squiggles of his name in Amaza script. Inspired by a new cross-cultural respect, his days of smirking at English misspellings on menus in Asia were over.

He sealed the envelope and passed it to a small boy squatting in the temple kitchen, washing pots in a low basin. Lew handed him a few *Arysai* notes. The child looked at the name, smiled, nodded, and scampered off.

CHAPTER TWENTY-ONE
Secrets of Khon and the Big Boss

The daily rooster concert commenced just before dawn. Lew opened his eyes and his heart jumped as two forms hovered over his dormitory bed, barely visible in the dark through his sleepy blur.

"W-what . . .!" he gasped.

A gentle hand touched his arm. "Sorry, sir. It's just us."

Squinting, Lew could make out Boo and his father. That was fast. He'd only sent the note a few hours earlier. But why did Boo bring Thant along?

"Khun Lew, let's go outside, so we don't disturb the others." Lew nodded, though the boyish monks were already waking and getting busy with their early morning activities—prayers, ritualistic ablutions, and assigned chores.

The three slipped out to the courtyard and sat on a wobbly bench under an ancient banyan tree. Several temple dogs wandered over, heads cocked and tails wagging like metronomes, hoping for scraps of food.

Out of Thant's earshot, Lew said, "I only summoned you, Boo, so why'd you bring your father?"

Boo's lips tightened. "Because from your note's timing, I guessed what this was about."

"Oh, reading minds now? Must be handy."

Boo rubbed his hands in the morning cool. "With all due respect, Khun Lew, you are the talk of every morning market today across Inner Amazia! Did you really believe a *farang* could pull off a stunt like that and not draw attention? No foreigner has *ever* ridden logs down the Rama River. Much less, alone."

Geez, everybody already knew? No secrets in this tiny place. That must be why the kid monks were winking at him last night. "Yeah, rode a log raft down to the sawmill. So what?"

Boo's eyes popped wide. "What, you reached the sawmill? Nobody said anything about that. Anybody see you?"

"I don't think so. I was able to study the sawmill and the gigantic jungle factory compound, just beyond it. Looked like a Uighur work camp in China. Forced labor, complete with angry guys cracking whips. Last thing I ever expected here." Lew searched Boo's eyes.

Boo translated, in a voice tumbling low, and his father appeared jolted before hissing out a terse response. "Father asks you to describe what you saw."

Lew bristled. What was this, a memory test? "Tell him I saw the whole sordid mess, beyond ugly, that he and your uncle are involved in. Maybe they own some of that operation? By providing lumber for Khon's factory, they are party to a slave labor operation."

Though surmising a lot, Lew felt pretty sure he had the story straight. Checking his rising anger, he reminded himself that as the duped foreign buyer, he was *also* complicit. Perhaps he should save the uppity pronouncements.

After Boo translated, his father looked shocked, numb, and broke down weeping. Boo gathered the trembling old man into his arms and patted his back.

Pity welled up in Lew. How could it not? But a stronger emotion soon swamped that. Anger. Thant and Uncle Inpanh probably deserved any pain they felt.

The sun crested on the horizon and more neighborhood roosters joined the dawn chorus as families of other birds fluttered overhead. Several minutes passed before Thant regained his composure. Finally he rubbed his eyes and directed a short speech toward Lew.

Despite the language barrier, the tone sounded heartfelt. "I suppose," Lew muttered, "that was his litany of excuses and justifications."

Boo frowned. "No, actually, he says you unfortunately have completely misunderstood almost *everything*."

What, Lew being mistaken in topsy-turvy Amazia? Imagine that.

"You only see the surface, sir, and therefore hurry to incorrect conclusions."

Lew resented what felt like an attack. "I see. So now I'm the bad guy? A typical American, drawing hasty conclusions—"

"Sorry, sir, but with so much of the background hidden, naturally your understanding must be seriously flawed."

That was enough. "Your father is an accomplice to slavery, Boo. Tell him to stop ducking the blame."

Boo's cheeks flushed with anger and he pointed a finger straight into Lew's face. "No, sir, now *you* listen! You have it all wrong, I am telling you." Boo stopped a moment to calm himself and continued in a lower tone. "Yes, he agrees the conditions at that jungle factory are wretched. But Khon and his partner exert an iron grip on the region, one so strong that *everyone* is forced to obey. And that includes my father and uncle, imprisoned by their crushing debt. Their elephant camp is already effectively under the control of Khon and his partner."

"Hmm." Lew folded his arms. Now *there* was a new wrinkle.

"Khon and his partner, as monopoly buyers, dictate prices they will pay for logs. No surprise, that keeps going lower and there is no other buyer. Worse yet, Khon drags out paying them. So many Biti businesses have already been choked into near-bankruptcy this way. And then, Khon and his partner buy the assets for almost nothing."

Thant and Inpanh were also victims? That landed like a slap.

"It's just a matter of time before the logging camp inevitably goes under."

Lew felt his head spin. The entire world had again flipped.

"That's just dreadful, Boo. I really want to believe it, but . . ."

Boo's father pulled out a wrinkled piece of paper and handed it to Lew. The usual Amaza jumble of dots and squiggles. Lew shrugged and pushed it back. "Don't read Amazian."

Perhaps misreading Lew's response as disdain, the elder seemed really set off. Thant tossed his hands in the air and growled noisily while Boo pulled in his head, like a turtle.

"Sorry, sir. He's sure to regret that later, so I'll just say *sorry* right now for him, in advance."

Lew forced a smile. "No sweat but yeah, that was quite a show. Your dad's usually mellower."

"Sir, we Amaza pride ourselves on not showing emotion, especially anger, but even my father has his limits."

"Tell him sorry I made him pop his cork." Lew placed a consoling hand on Thant's shoulder but the old man just looked sad.

"That paper was his copy of a promissory note, sir. He and Uncle now owe Khon a huge amount, with the logging camp pledged as collateral. After already pouring in their life savings to keep the business afloat, Father and Uncle Inpanh had to borrow even more to cover wages, hire elephants and mahouts, buy fuel, pay license fees, and taxes. And that only delayed the inevitable. Soon they must repay it."

Wait, what? Lew squinted, a bit confused. "I thought there were no contracts or laws here. So what enforces debts?"

"It's true, no contracts or courts are needed. But of course we *do* make agreements with one another, every single day, as people do everywhere. That is how society functions! But the common law that binds all such agreements is far more than courts or laws. The highest authority here is our Amaza sense of morality. The strictest of obligations, the most powerful of all."

Lew could not help but admire the Amaza and their sweet society, kept under control by honor and mutual trust. Seemed to work great until it didn't work. "So what comes next?"

Boo sniffled and wiped his nose on a sleeve. "Well, Father and Uncle won't be able to pay. So Khon and his partner will soon take over their logging camp, just like most other area businesses, already. Steal it for next to nothing." His voice trembled. "They will lose the business, our livelihood, our family itself."

Now what did *that* mean? Fully immersed in their dread, Lew now regretted his earlier mild insolence. "Boo, tell him I'm sorry, accusing him like that, before, as being party to that slave labor camp? I really didn't know—"

Boo waved a hand. "But just wait, sir. As bad as that seems, there's more and it's even worse. Months ago, the loan was first due for repayment. To secure a delay and stave off collapse of the logging camp, Father and Uncle struck a deal with Khon." Boo shivered with disgust. "A truly horrendous thing, actually, but they had no other choice. Desperate, right down to their very bones, they accepted an offer from Khon's partner."

"The effing Big Boss." A wave of revulsion swept through Lew and he prayed his hunch was wrong. "Please tell me this doesn't involve your cousin, Nong."

Boo dropped his head. "To forestall the payment, Khon's partner pressured my uncle for Nong's hand in marriage. He promised after both sides were united by marriage, everything would be better."

"All debts erased?"

"Not clear," Boo scoffed. "But the loan repayment, *that* is due again, and soon. That hasn't changed." So much for the groom taking care of his new in-laws.

Lew pictured the beautiful and innocent Nong, her purity being bartered like chattel, and a hatred flared within him, directed at two men whom he'd never met but who had destroyed his life and those of so many others.

"Boo, I'm not sure why, but I sense that Khon's hidden partner is the actual villain, much more than Khon."

"Could be, Khun Lew. Khon seems just a businessman, amoral, not a monster. But once he hooked up with his partner, everything changed. The Big Boss is like the devil himself. Though in at least one way, he's like you."

Lew's face tingled red. "What the hell does that mean?"

Boo held up beseeching palms. "Sorry, nothing personal, I just meant he's a *farang* like you. A foreigner. A white man."

What? That curveball came from nowhere.

Boo leaned closer. "And his name is Khun Napoleon."

Jeez, a freakin' Frenchman was behind this mess? "What's the bastard's full name, Napoleon what?"

"We don't know. Father never met him, sir, and Uncle only saw him just once, back when Khon and Napoleon were finalizing their partnership. My folks only deal with Mr. Khon, the local connection, the front man."

Another twist and down was once again up. When would it ever end? "And as for your cousin—"

"Yes, so very sad, *lah*. Heartbreaking. Nong's wedding is very soon."

"How could your uncle ever agree to something so horrendous?"

"Desperation." Boo sighed. "No other explanation or options. And Nong herself insisted on making the sacrifice, perhaps a way to save the family."

Lew sensed all stakes had just multiplied, with everything kicked into higher gear. The only positive was that all these problems somehow seemed interlinked, including his own. If he solved one, the others might fall into place.

But he felt pitted against a true monster, a man who ruled an enslaved population by fear, one who even took brides by force. The only way forward seemed to first track down Khon and then hope for a path to the ultimate villain.

As if reading his thoughts, Boo handed Lew a scrap of paper. "Uncle wants you to have this, Khun Lew." A string of digits. "It's a phone number in Ruangbang. Maybe you can speak directly with Khun Khon."

PART FOUR:

Jazz Master at the Mango in Love

CHAPTER TWENTY-TWO
Railway Return to Ruangbang

Lew stowed his few possessions at the temple and set out in the blistering afternoon heat for the Biti rail station, for a return trip to the capital in search of Khon. Finding Khun Siva dozing behind the barred ticket window, Lew rumbled a loud cough and the stationmaster opened his eyes. Lew pushed a warm bottle of Fizzo through the bars and Siva, grinning at their one-week reunion, took a swig.

They mimed a surprisingly detailed conversation. Lew was getting quite good at that. Siva reminded him that Luam still had some of Lew's clothes, now freshly laundered, and how much the townsfolk had enjoyed Lew's visit. Lew replied how he'd come to love Biti and described the twin thrills of seeing live elephants and riding atop logs in the river.

Minutes later, a shrill whistle pierced the air and the black locomotive arrived from Ruangbang, halting its eight colorful cars beside the station house. As soon as the train shuddered to a stop, a mahout and his elephant materialized to push a rail car from the side track to the end of the train, where it was attached.

Lew casually reached for Siva's clipboard, having spotted a Lotus logo on the manifest. The final destinations were listed as Sydney and Frankfurt. Too bad no Lotus cargo had been dispatched the day he'd arrived—would have really cut his investigation short.

He slid a fistful of multi-colored *Arysai* across the counter to Siva for two first-class tickets to Ruangbang. He wai'ed, boarded the train, and settled back into the empty first class quad, anticipating a journey of anything from eighteen to thirty hours.

Departure was imminent but where was Boo? Unlike him to be late. To expedite things on this trip, Lew had negotiated a special per diem rate for Boo, though the youth needed little convincing to accept an expenses-paid trip to the capital.

An hour passed and still the train sat beside the station house, not budging. Boo suddenly cruised into the carriage, toting a small khaki bag, and before he could even sit the train jolted into motion. His timing was exquisite. Suspiciously so. Had Siva held the train for him?

"No, *lah*! Nothing like that, sir." Boo grinned. "I just waited at my house until I heard the arrival whistle. The return train always leaves an hour later, so I had plenty of time to walk here and get on board." Local knowledge.

Lew shook his head wistfully.

They stretched out in relative luxury, the entire first class quad to themselves. The run down to the capital went off like clockwork, at least in Amazian terms and compared to Lew's first train ride—no bugs up the butt or friendly, upside-down stalkers outside the window. And Boo seemed to intrinsically know everything, like when to head to the dining car, how to unjam windows, and when toilets were safe to use.

"And going in this direction, Khun Lew, the trip is faster. More a downhill run."

As the lush countryside slid by, Lew peppered Boo with questions on a wide variety of topics. But one in particular made the youth smirk.

"Now, Boo, about your cousin . . ."

"*Aduh*! I thought maybe I picked up on something, sir. Ha! Are you by chance smitten?"

Lew blushed. "Nah, me? Well, maybe a teensy bit infatuated, sure. I mean, let's be frank. Nong is pretty incredible. It's ridiculous but I keep thinking about her, like a high school student. We can't really communicate well, and I know so little about her, too, though my feelings run deep. Spock on Star Trek would warn I'm probably thinking too much with my glands, not my brain."

Boo nodded. "But chief, your intuition is spot-on the mark. She is indeed an amazing person. A truly beautiful soul. After my aunt died, poor Uncle Inpanh pretty much went to pieces. Nong canceled her departure for university in Singapore and shouldered the burden, keeping the family and the business together. Huge sacrifice."

"College?"

"Business studies, actually. She has a brilliant mind for that. But instead she stayed in Amazia. It took a few years for Uncle to totally recover. During that time, she ran the logging business almost by herself."

Lew's heart and intuition had been five-star. Nong combined stellar brains and heartfelt compassion all in a single stunning package.

Sixteen hours later, Boo leaned across the carriage and nudged the dozing Lew. "Best to gather your things, sir. We'll be arriving within the hour."

That couldn't be right, it was too soon.

Lew looked out the window and saw no sign of civilization.

But of course Boo was correct and by early afternoon, the pair were wading through the bustle around Ruangbang terminal, the patina of familiarity rendering it slightly less chaotic and intimidating this time.

Lew tossed a hand in the air, seeking to show off his local competence, and a hot pink and yellow Padmini taxi rattled up and screeched to a halt. Boo opened the rear door and jumped in, leaving the honored front seat for his boss. Lew slid in and fumbled around for a nonexistent seat belt.

The driver made eye contact. "Sirrrr . . . welcome to Amazia! Number one taxi! Change money? Sir is wanting nice gul? Massageee?"

Boo blasted the unsuspecting cabbie with a gale of words. The shocked driver, looking crushed by an unexpected betrayal, shrank behind the wheel and switched on the motor.

"Alamak!" Boo chirped. "Chief, this fellow mistook me for, um, *another* type of tour guide. Straightened that out." Clearly, there were to be no more offers of girls, Japanese cigarettes, or bootleg whiskey.

"Thanks, Boo." But feeling sorry for the shell-shocked driver, Lew smiled and gave him a pity wai. "Sir, please take us to the Miracle Royal Pagoda Hotel," he said in a humble tone.

The driver smiled back but added a quick scowl at Boo in the rearview mirror.

As before, the ride slowed to navigate around potholes and ox carts, packs of dogs, kids, and wandering elephants. After the isolation and sleepy rural poverty of Inner Amazia, Ruangbang this time felt modern and downright frantic, an astonishing urban tangle.

Lew understood: *he* was changing, not the Kingdom, and in a good way.

As the taxi braked in front of the hotel, Boo shouted orders out his window in a strong but friendly tone, before urgent hands could descend upon the taxi, and the pending storm of overly intrusive service dissolved in the tropical air.

They exited the taxi under their own steam and marched through the front door of the dilapidated hotel. There in the lobby, as if time had frozen, all remained precisely as before. Wongrat and Frog holding down their appointed stations and looking bored, until one glanced up and spotted their returned friend.

"Khun Lew!" squealed Wongrat.

"Gentlemen!" Genuine happiness washed through Lew.

Bowing low, the Amaza wai'ed the American and laughed, giddy as drunken chickens. But then noticing Boo, hanging back at the entrance, they exchanged suspicious glances.

Lew eased their concern. "That over there is Khun Boonyarit, my assistant from Biti." Lew waved him over. And that was all it took.

Delighted, the hotel men peppered Boo with endless questions in the Amaza tongue, his responses triggering surprise and hilarity. Lew let it go on for a while, his patience already expanding in Amazia.

While they chatted, Lew worked on Frog's paper bag of fat, crunchy brown nuts—addictively delicious with a salty, crackly outer texture while moist and flavorful within. Lew couldn't stop nibbling and, only slightly embarrassed, finished off the entire sack. He apologized but Frog just smiled with pleasure that Lew had enjoyed the local treat.

"So, Boo, what was all that chitchat just now?"

"So many questions, sir, mainly about Biti! For Ruangbang folk, my home has a strange reputation. So for them, this was like the chance to question a newly-landed Martian."

"Heh, I figured. Anything else?"

Boo stared up at the ceiling, carefully weighing his next words. "Yes. A lot about you, too, sir." He looked down and giggled. "Rather unusual ideas, like that you were CIA or an associate of Donald Trump."

"What, Trump again?" Lew chuckled.

"But now they understand you are just a New York businessman, though still a hero to them, brave enough to journey solo into the wilds of Biti!" Boo snorted a laugh. "As if Inner Amazia was beyond the civilized world! Foolish Ruangbang city slickers."

Right. Lew grinned at that oxymoron but then turned toward Wongrat, speaking slowly and carefully enunciating. "Wongrat, may I please have my phone back, and the other things I gave you for safe-keeping?"

Wongrat's face blanked out as he stared off into the middle distance, thinking. Just before Boo could intervene, Frog muttered something harsh, jolting Wongrat, whose eyes popped big with comprehension as he jumped up and ran to the front counter. He retrieved the phone from the tackle box on the floor and fished a manila envelope from a casual heap of paper on the front desk.

Trotting back, he handed both items to Lew with a courteous flourish and collected back the matching plastic ID token from Lew.

The phone seemed fine. And on opening the envelope, it was all there—roughly ten thousand dollars in traveler's checks and a thick packet of high-denomination *Arysai* currency.

Losing the checks would not have been fatal, as money seemed fairly unimportant in this strange land. But the phone? That might have been a blow. In their effort to track down Khon, the phone might still prove useful, if they could only find a network.

"Friends, I am still searching for Khun Khon and Asiatic Media."

That triggered the three Amaza to chatter, filling the lobby with sounds like typewriters clicking or bubbles popping.

Boo turned to Lew. "Sorry, sir, they didn't search any further for him. They just assumed you'd just fallen for an old Amazia joke. Did you know *Khun Khon* actually translates as *Mr. Man?*"

Lew sighed.

"But I straightened them out, sir, that Khon is real."

Lew's stomach growled. Talk about starving, he was still famished after the long train ride, again with an unprovisioned dining car. "Hey, Gob, those nuts were wonderful! Got any more of that delicious snack?"

Frog pursed his lips with a puzzled look. "Nut snack? Khun Lew eating nut?" He turned and spoke to Wongrat and Boo. Soon all three were giggling uncontrollably.

Okay, now what?

Wongrat wiped little tears from the corners of his eyes. "Wongrat happy Sir enjoying our Amaza snack."

Lew nodded.

"And Wongrat already sending small boy, running to buy *keyla krikee.*"

"But what's so freakin' funny, Boo?" Lew rubbed his stomach and smiled. "Just about the juiciest cashews ever."

Boo shrugged with an embarrassed smile. "Well, yes, *lah*. But actually, they're not really *that kind* of nut, sir."

"Mmm?" Lew's smile faded, ever-so-slightly. "So what *kind* are they?"

Boo just looked down.

Frog tried to help. Smiling, he began to crawl his fingers across the sofa, by way of explanation.

"Hey, stop that, Frog, it's creepy." Lew looked to Boo. "What the heckworker's he doing?"

Boo frowned. "I suppose he is demonstrating, sir. You see, *keyla krikee* aren't nuts at all." A tingle of concern tickled Lew. "They're insects, actually. A type of cricket! Deep-fried in palm oil and nicely seasoned!" Boo licked his lips, smiling. "Delicious, no?"

Color drained from Lew's face. "Bugs…? I ate *bugs*?" A wave of visions engulfed him: the whirling insects on the train, the crawling bugs in the jungle and the engorged leeches fastened to his calves. His stomach began to clench and rotate.

Lew's friends, oblivious to his distress, grinned as they continued to walk fingers atop the leather couch like fleshy tarantulas.

"*In-sec!*" Frog chirped, proudly repeating his newest English word.

"In-sec!" Wongrat happily mimicked.

His gut churning, Lew kept smiling but urgently needed a bathroom. "Wongrat, please give us your two best rooms. And right away. I am very tired."

"This way," Wongrat said, leading them up the squeaky back staircase to the end of the hallway where a sign proclaimed MAHABHARATA SUITE. They swung the door open and entered a dark common room with a dank smell. The ceiling fan didn't work. Lew threw open drapes on the far wall, revealing wide windows facing onto whitewashed brick, only inches away. Bedroom doors opened to simple rooms on both sides, each similar to Lew's first visit.

So this was their best? Didn't matter. What he needed, and immediately, was a toilet.

He dashed into the suite's small loo but the door kept creaking back open. He spotted a filthy wooden wedge in the corner and made use of it for privacy.

Then, for the next hour, he alternated nonstop between bouts of explosive diarrhea and yakking up stomach loads of fried crickets and digestive acid.

CHAPTER TWENTY-THREE
Mango in Love!

Mosquitos kept him awake past 1 a.m. until inspiration finally struck. He lit a match and set fire to the end of that odd green spiral thingy atop his bedside table, like the young mother's coil he saw on the train. The tip glowed and began spewing a twisting trail of smoke that meandered and filled the room with a god-awful, cloying odor. But it chased the bugs away.

Lew plunged into total blackout and slept until late next morning when odd noises, seeping in the window, awakened him. Bleary-eyed and half conscious, he drank in the mysterious concert of random clicks, whistles, and chimes.

He slipped on the rubber flip-flops from the bathroom and entered the dingy common room where Boo was already jotting notes onto a legal pad. The youth had passed on the pink rocking chair and torn red vinyl sofa, instead comfortably settling into an Asian squat beside the wobbly rattan table. With drapes wide open, tropical sunlight rendered the place cheery and bright.

"Already been up for hours, sir. Too many ideas bouncing around in my head, *lah*!"

Lew smiled. "Great. Eat yet?"

"*Belum*." Not yet. "But breakfast is at hand!" He explained that all those odd noises from outside were the identifying calls of itinerant neighborhood food vendors announcing their wares.

All day long, a disorganized caravan of roaming food carts offered every treat one could ever desire—sweet, ultra-dark coffee in little rubber-banded baggies; fresh fruit cut into artsy slices; chewy pancakes drizzled with red bean syrup; mixes of salty nuts and tiny dried fish; or boiled egg halves in yellow-brown curry sauce.

Boo stretched out a palm and Lew filled it with crumpled yellow and purple *Arysai* bills. A good color combo—a foreign currency salute to the LA Lakers.

Boo dashed off.

Lew considered how happy the Amaza were, despite having so little, and contrasted that with his own, relatively unfulfilling life. He'd never been so unremittingly happy, himself, not even at the peak of his glorious career when drenched in wealth, status and comfort. No question, this weird little backwater was sinking its hooks into him.

Minutes later, Boo returned with local delicacies wrapped in newspaper sheets and stuffed into pink plastic sacks. Four rubber-banded baggies hung off his wrists, bulging with the potent local coffee. He spread the feast across the rattan table.

Lew munched away, his mind wandering.

This hotel would serve well as their Ruangbang nerve center for hunting Khon. Frog and Wongrat would provide excellent back-up, too. And with so few leads, the entire process shouldn't take long. It would be quick, either progress or a complete dead end. If they succeeded in locating Khon, Lew might be well on his way to solving everything. If not, he'd be a plane back to America. Total failure.

Boo scrunched his eyebrows in concentration while pressing a cheap local pencil against the yellow pad. "Ideas for our investigation, boss."

Our investigation. Good man. Lew gave him a thumbs-up.

During their train ride down, Lew had laid it all out and Boo absorbed the details like a sponge. He clearly found it thrilling to hunt down a mysterious company and its immoral agents, and also had a personal stake, a chance to perhaps address his family's horrific problems.

Boo scanned his notes. "First off, Uncle Inpanh's old phone number for Khon is key."

"Absolutely. But how do we get a phone line here?"

"Maybe a Ruangbang version of Tina's phone shop?"

"Right. And what if we phone and Khon won't answer?"

Boo nodded sagely. "He may pick up once, the first time, and never again after he knows it's you. So straightaway we might consider Plan B. I say we visit AT&T."

Lew scoffed. "You crazy? Ma Bell only operates in America."

Boo smiled, bemused. "No, sir, the Amazia Treasury and Taxation is a government ministry. Phone owners here pay a special tax to AT&T."

Lew felt his cheeks redden. Duh!

"And perhaps they have a registered address for Khon's phone number."

"Excellent idea," Lew said, though suspecting it would be for that abandoned strip mall. But he loved the kid's positivity. "Okay, so AT&T it is. How good are your contacts there?"

"*My* contacts? *Alamak!*" Boo grinned. "Khun Lew, I'm just a country boy from Biti."

Lew sighed. "But in Amazia, there's always a way, right? Perhaps Gob or Wongrat can help."

A feeling began to sink in that although the endgame was near, too much remained unclear. Suppose they succeeded in finding Khon, then was Uzzi Steiner's way still the plan, to demand legal indemnification? Fat chance getting that. And even if the Big Boss agreed to pony up the funds, was his word worth anything? Especially with all the money already vacuumed up long ago and transferred out of Amazia.

Worse still, with the Kingdom's total absence of contracts, courts, and law enforcement, everything would depend upon morality and honor, two items in short supply for slime balls like Khon and the Big Boss.

And as for saving Nong and all those enslaved workers, not to mention solving the existential issues vexing Boo's family, Lew hadn't a clue where to begin.

One thing, though, did seem certain. Amazia appeared immune to complex, multi-staged plans, so the best way forward was to take it all just one step at a time. That meant first, *find Khon.*

Down in the lobby, feeling a bit guilty, Lew nudged Frog and interrupted his afternoon nap. He then inquired about phone shops in Ruangbang—or *any* place in the capital, for that matter, with network service or the internet, which immediately brightened Frog. He gabbled across the hotel lobby with Wongrat.

Both seeming instantly energized by the idea and pleased to close up shop. Singing and laughing, their excitement contagious, they led Lew and Boo out to the street to hail pedicabs.

"So where we going, gents?" Lew asked.

Frog grinned. "To Amazia number one headquarters for foreign guest!"

Tantalized, Lew poked Boo, who only shrugged back.

"Famous place," continued Frog, "and always having phone service, Sir!"

"Get outta here! In Ruangbang? Where?"

"Wait. Is surprise." Frog mimed zipping his mouth shut.

Three bicycle taxis pulled up and Lew climbed into the deep blue pedicab with images of stars, planets and zooming rockets with the title HELLO SPACE MAN! Ha. Space? Lew could have used more of that, barely able to squeeze in his Western-sized bottom.

Frog and Wongrat shared the next vehicle, comfortably sitting side by side. Called COCONUT DREAMTIME, it was lime green and pink with blue cartoon coconut trees.

Boo luxuriated in the third under a canopy with art honoring the Buddha.

Wongrat barked out directions and his leather-skinned cabbie jingled the handlebar bell three times and stood on a pedal to initiate motion. He headed off and the other two trishaws followed in hot pursuit.

As they coasted down back lanes of the ramshackle capital, palm trees and small buildings flew by, with road dust churned up into trailing, billowing clouds. After wheeling a sharp turn around a swaying thicket of green sugar cane, the destination came into view.

A sprawling red multi-story building sat far back off the road. Numerous small balconies irregularly studded it like barnacles on a ship's hull, each with a dining table, chairs and simple wrought iron railing. A network of ladders and simple stairways reached them all. And at ground level, yellow wooden picnic tables surrounded the building.

A large sign above the front door canopy resembled an old-time movie theater marquee. Bright yellow words in black borders announced the unusual establishment's even odder name: MANGO IN LOVE! A second deck of words, below, added more detail: INTERNATIONAL! COFFEE, INTERNET, PALM WINE, TELEPHONE SERVICE.

Whoa. This was unlike anything Lew had seen before in the Kingdom. It gave off an almost big city vibe, but Amazia-style. And at the very peak of the roof was an absolutely stunning sight: a nest of electronic dishes. Antennae for phone and satellite TV.

And there were plenty of customers.

"And look!" exclaimed Boo, pointing at a high balcony table, "even some *farang*." A pair of Western backpackers rested their bare feet on the iron railing, sipping iced coffee and thumbing their phones.

This, of course, would be a total magnet for elites and paradise for foreigners stuck in Ruangbang. Coffee, snacks, and communication. In a funky way it simulated a Western feel, sure to lure homesick travelers.

Lew pulled out his phone. "Jackpot! Look, three bars!"

Frog frowned. "No, sir. Mango in Love having only *one* bar. But maybe best in all Kingdom."

Lew didn't bother to clarify. "And over there, what's that?" Across the street hunched a stark run of unpainted cinder block buildings with no signage or identification. People streamed in and out. "Hardly an attractive view while drinking your coffee."

"Oh, that Ruangbang foreign district," Frog said, inflating with pride. "What is word? Ah, yes! Embassy row." He pronounced it *low*. "Vietnam and Myanmar having office. China coming, maybe later."

Lew remembered his State Dept. contact. No, there would be no official US help.

The foursome entered the complex and found business bustling, with still more tables inside plus a small tavern playing recorded music, and a retail shop. Choosing from a small array of kitschy souvenirs embossed with the restaurant logo, Lew bought a silk-screened T-shirt showing the red building and movie theater sign.

Exiting the rear, they encountered an unexpected scenic view of the lush Ruangbang valley, refreshing to the eye. The entire back wall was dotted with even more balconies and, attached to the building was an elevated walkway overlooking the vast valley beyond the capital. Attractive, roaming young women in pink hot pants rented out binoculars by the minute.

One could easily become lost there for hours, just sitting and sipping coffee, gazing out across the landscape, picking out details. Tidy little farms and compact homes dotted the landscape around the capital with laundry flapping on clotheslines and children at play. Small processions of elephants marched down distant paths. Quite a place, this Mango in Love!

They went back inside, placed an order and then recessed to a vacant balcony perch high up the back wall. Their food and cold drinks quickly found them.

"My God!" Lew gasped, wiping his lips. "Best freakin' coffee ever!"

His Amaza hosts smiled broadly. "We are loving you, Khun Lew, as good friend of Amazia," said Frog.

Their sentiment made Lew blush and feel conflicted. After all, he was only there because he was a businessman, and an avaricious one at that, who'd unknowingly preyed upon this place. But now

Amazia, like an exotic woman, was starting to infatuate him. Ever since he'd arrived, kind people had gone out of their way to help, no catch, just motivated by good will.

To an American, all that seemed nearly impossible.

Furthermore, *their* problems now felt increasingly important to him, heavy new bonds of obligation, perhaps even more crucial than his own issues. But how could that be?

Sitting at a balcony table, Lew pulled out his phone. "Holy smokes, guys, four bars."

Wongrat quizzically scrunched his eyebrows.

"Never gonna be better." Lew surrendered to impulse and keyed in the number from the scrap of paper. The connection was immediate.

"Hello?" came a familiar-sounding voice.

"Mr. Khon?"

"Yes, Khon here. To whom am I speaking? I don't recognize your number."

Lew's heart raced. He drew in a deep breath. "Sir, this is your partner from the US. Lew Clarke, remember? I've been having difficulty reaching you, so it's great to finally—"

The line went dead.

"Damn it!"

In a blink, all that Lew most feared seemed confirmed. His Amazia supplier was absolutely giving him the shake—the absence of email replies was no error. Fat chance Lotus would ever legally stand behind his company in US courts.

Lew's instincts flashed amber and warned him to play this with utmost care. No sense immediately redialing, trying to wear Khon down until he answered. Were Khon to panic and shut down that phone number, it would forever sever this flimsy connection.

No, with the line now confirmed, they could try ministry records to physically track down Lotus. But time was the enemy. Khon had no reason to suspect Lew was in Ruangbang, but in a place so compact, nothing stayed secret for long.

"Finish your snacks, gents," Lew bubbled. "Time to move."

"Going where, Khun Lew?" Frog finished the last of his pancake with bean paste.

"AT&T."

Boo explained his idea to Wongrat and Frog, hoping they had friends at the government ministry. That launched a wave of spirited chatter among the Amaza trio. As Lew waited, a little bored, he thumbed his phone and thought.

Hmm, maybe take just *one* more shot at Khon? What was the harm? Perhaps last time, the line accidently cut off. He redialed, almost on impulse, and the line connected. Khon's phone rang once, twice, six times before it shunted Lew off to voice mail.

Shit.

He scowled but, upon looking up, noticed his friends had all gone silent and were pointing with amusement toward a balcony a few decks down.

Boo giggled, his eyes happy. "Khun Lew, it's *so* funny! See that Asia businessman down there? His ring tone is so loud, *lah*, we could all hear. *Hotel California*, the Amazia version! Haha, it made us laugh."

Even at this hotspot for foreign elite, perhaps only one customer in ten carried a phone. So when a ring tone went off and serenaded nearby tables, it was an event.

"Eagles song! Too old," Boo clucked with mild disdain. "But so funny, sir, the coincidence. His ring tone sang out right after you dialed! Almost like you called him, haha." All three tittered at that observation.

But Lew's heart momentarily fluttered. Was it possible . . . ?

He squinted down at the man eating stir-fried veggies and furiously punching things into his phone, a possession that already labeled him as privileged and worldly, perhaps an Amaza businessman or tourist from beyond the Kingdom. A diplomatic dignitary from across the street? He sat alone, preoccupied with work in those pleasant surroundings.

For the longest time, Lew could only see the man's shining bald dome. But finally, he lifted his head to momentarily gaze out across the valley vista and Lew briefly got a clear view of his face.

And there it was.

Just below his right cheekbone was a large, purple-pink blotch. A birthmark shaped like the state of Texas or the Indian subcontinent, as seen during the Lotus video conference.

Khon! And of *course* he was there. Mango in Love was a natural go-to spot, with its communications links and comfort, a simpatico environment to get work done.

He was resplendent in sunglasses, fine slacks and a brilliant white polo shirt, with a thick gold chain loosely hung around his neck, looking like straight off a California golf course. But what happened to the monk outfit, his flowing vermilion robe?

CHAPTER TWENTY-FOUR
Silk Orchid Interrogation

Lew stared down at his prey, thinking hard. How best to corner Khon and get him somewhere private to talk? A direct approach, right there at the restaurant, seemed too risky. Lew's surprising appearance would no doubt threaten the man and if he fled, Lew might never locate him again.

That would be the worst possible outcome, total mission failure, and Lew would find himself on a plane back to New Jersey, empty-handed and his life irreparably in shambles.

As a cultural neophyte, unskilled in this alien setting, he didn't trust his own instincts. His Amaza friends were infinitely better versed in local nuances so to succeed now, Lew needed to place his full faith and reliance upon them. For a prototypical alpha male who typically relied only upon himself, this was humbling.

"Hey Boo," he whispered. "Got something to tell you. Now stay cool and don't over-react, okay?"

Boo fiddled with his rat tassel. "Can, *lah*." He leaned closer.

"That dude with the Hotel California ring tone? Pretty sure it's Khon."

Boo's face lit up as Frog and Wongrat looked on curiously.

"I need to get him somewhere private and secure, to talk," Lew breathed. "And right away. But this is delicate. Gotta be super careful because if he runs, it's a disaster."

"Understood," Boo said, nodding.

"Our advantage is he's got no idea I'm right here on his tail. He must assume I was calling from America, right? But if he sees me and bolts, I might lose the trail forever."

Boo stared confidently into Lew's eyes. "Okay, boss, what do we do?" They both studied Khon, his bald head gleaming as he calmly sipped wine and munched on crackers.

Lew shrugged. "Well, much as I might like, we can't just kidnap the dude."

"*Tak boleh.*" Boo agreed. "Cannot, *lah.*"

"And he mustn't see me. So far we've been lucky."

Boo nodded.

"Can you three lure him back to the hotel, somehow, and keep him there for me? As to how, I don't know. Will leave that in your good hands." Lew's heart sped up a little. Trusting and relying this much was tough, especially with the stakes so high.

"A bit tricky, sir, like a game." Boo's mouth spread into a sly smile. "But I like games."

Frog seemed out of patience and loudly put his iced coffee down. "Sir is having problem?"

"Let me handle this," Boo told Lew.

The trio of Amaza leaned in across the table and launched into an animated, whispered discussion. After several minutes, all heads bobbed in agreement and the table went silent.

"Okay, sir," Boo said. "We have a good plan! Now please remove that US baseball hat and wear this instead." He handed Lew a Mango in Love! souvenir cap. "Pull it low to hide your face and quietly go down to one of the picnic tables, far off to the side, where you won't be seen. Stay there until you see us leave with Khon. Then wait fifteen minutes and catch a pedicab back to the hotel. We'll be there with him." Boo smiled. "Can?"

"Can, *lah*," Lew chuckled.

What was their plan? He didn't ask. It was all in their hands.

Lew made his way to a vacant picnic table at ground level and hunkered down.

Within twenty minutes, a big honkin' Rolls Royce Phantom pulled up, a cream-colored beauty, maybe the sole Roller in a nation of rusty old sedans and tiny coupes from India or China.

The mammoth luxury vehicle looked as out-of-place as an arriving spaceship. Its windows were tinted dark to shield passengers and large black tires glistened despite the Kingdom's ever-present dust. A chauffeur probably cleaned them by hand, every few miles.

That chauffeur emerged, looking powerful in sunglasses, a tan military-style suit and aviator-style cap. He swung the rear door open and stood at attention as a group emerged from the restaurant's front entrance. Khon led Boo, Frog, and Wongrat, all chattering and laughing.

Amazing! How had they done it?

Playing host, Khon made a grand show of ushering his guests into the sumptuous vehicle. The trio slid into the rear seat and the driver gently pressed the door closed. Khon climbed into the passenger side front seat. Lush strains of classical music began to bleed out from the cabin, shrill-sweet sounds of Vivaldi as the vehicle sped away.

Lew waited the agreed quarter hour and then hailed a trishaw. His arm was still rising when the bicycle taxi driver spotted him and sped across the clay road, jingling its bell.

"Yes, boss!" the driver cried, lurching to a stop.

Lew climbed aboard. "Miracle Royal Pagoda Hotel, please."

He jumped down at the hotel entrance and handed the driver a random wad of bright blue and red *Arysai* bills, a Chicago Cubs feel this time. The driver grinned like a tiger, pocketed them and pedaled off, jingling his bell several times extra. By now, Lew had already given up converting local currency prices to dollars. Seemed hardly worth the effort. He was still living off that rainbow sack of cabbage bought at the airport for a single hundred dollar bill and hardly dented the pile. So lately, he just grabbed a pleasing color combo. If it came up short, the recipient was sure to say so. And if he overpaid, fine.

The hotel lobby was empty. No Wongrat or Frog at their usual stations. But a smattering of faint voices caught Lew's ear and drew his eye to a slit of light leaking out under a previously unnoticed closed door behind the front desk.

Swinging it open, he found all four men squeezed into an office the size of a large walk-in closet. Wongrat sat behind a small metal desk with Khon facing him, perched atop a flimsy visitor's chair. Frog leaned against the back wall and Boo squatted comfortably in the corner.

All four looked over and smiled. Lew's pulse raced. Khon, at last! He struggled to remain calm. "What's up, gentlemen," he said, trying to keep his voice steady, though to his own ear it sounded hyper and squeaky.

Boo stood. "Ah, good, sir, you've arrived!" He motioned toward the chair. "This is Khun Khon, a businessman exploring the possible purchase of this hotel from Khun Wongrat and Khun Gob." They all smiled. "Due to family matters—an urgent need for cash—they must sell quickly, at an attractive price."

Lew suppressed a smirk, admiring their cleverness. Good story. From up close, he examined Khon's one-in-a-million birthmark. The bastard clearly didn't recognize him. Yet.

"Hello, sir," Khon said in his odd, clipped English accent. "I missed your name. You are, I take it, somehow connected with the sale of this hotel? Friendly advisor or perhaps another partner?"

Lew kept his expression neutral and searched Khon's eyes. "I am indeed the one you need to speak with, Mr. Khon. And since your English is quite excellent, we can handle this directly, in private. We don't need the others." Lew motioned and his associates immediately rose to leave.

Khon's face slumped in confusion. "I don't really understand."

For just a split second, Boo shot a malicious look at Khon before turning to Lew. "We'll stay close, sir. Just outside the door."

Perspiration beaded Khon's forehead. "Forgive me, friends, but I'm a little confused now. Sir, exactly what is your role in this negotiation?"

Lew pulled the door closed with a click. "Relax, Khon, and save your breath. You won't be stealing any distressed hotels today."

Khon eyes went wide. "I'm afraid you have the advantage on me, sir. Just who did you say you were?"

Lew reached out to shake Khon's hand, gripping hard. "I didn't. But I sure am pleased to *finally* meet you, Khon, in the flesh! My name is Lewis N. Clarke. That should be familiar because I'm the owner of your sole North American distributor, Avian Luxury. And I flew to beautiful Amazia from northern New Jersey, just to see you. But, spoiler alert: I am one *very* unhappy customer."

Khon was so startled, his eyes bulged. Coughing and fidgeting, he pulled a purple silk kerchief from his pocket and mopped up perspiration that glistened on his bald head. Then he methodically cleaned his golden spectacles.

Lew understood the man was stalling as he took all this in. Thinking.

"So whatever happened to that beautiful monk's robe, Khon? Or do you only wear it during video conferences, when conning foreigners?"

It was amazing how unimpressive the man was in person. Petite, bland, no aura. How could one like him be responsible for so much damage? But this was indeed Khon, all right—that outrageous purple blemish was better ID than fingerprints.

Khon was fast to collect himself and when he next spoke, his voice had returned to firm and measured. Friendly and reassuring. "Mr. Clarke! Why yes, indeed, what a pleasure to *finally* meet you in person. Allow me to wish you the warmest welcome to Amazia, sir. I trust your travel was smooth."

"Mmm," Lew grumbled. This guy was smooth, but absolutely full of shit.

"It's wonderful you decided to visit," Khon continued, "though the circumstances are a bit unclear. If only you'd advised earlier—"

"That'd be difficult, Khon, considering how Lotus has been ducking my emails and phone calls for quite a while already."

Khon smiled blandly. "Goodness, no. There *must* be some mistake. As you no doubt have already gathered, heh, we have serious communication complications here. I had actually been planning to reach out to contact *you*, Mr. Clarke. Absolute top of my list. North America is so critical for us, you see. But with the recent crush of business, well, we've just been so very busy. I'm sure you know how it is."

Lew's blood pressure was zooming and he'd had enough. He slammed a fist down upon the small metal desk and Khon cringed.

"Okay, asshole, let's cut the B.S. already. Because yes, I *do* know *exactly* how it is."

Khon's face went ashen.

The door cracked open. It was Boo. "Everything okay in here, boss? Heard a noise."

"Yeah. Under control," Lew mumbled as he pushed the door shut again. He sat on the edge of the desk, crowding Khon. "Anyway, Khon, if that's even your real name —"

"Of course it is!"

"My company is facing a barrage of lawsuits because of the goods Lotus sold us, under false pretenses. Spirit houses, not birdhouses or lawn decorations, and they have triggered enormous damage to customers who installed them. Horrendous attacks by the beings attracted to those things."

Khon cocked his head. "But you don't *really* believe all that, do you, sir?"

Good question. "Doesn't matter. I'm not sure what I believe anymore. But I am certain what of I don't. Like Lotus' integrity."

"Hmm," Khon said, rubbing his face, "I see."

"This is the bottom line: My company demands that *your* company," Lew said, poking Khon in the sternum, "accept total legal liability. Lotus knowingly and intentionally misrepresented its products, so we expect you to keep us whole."

"Meaning?"

"You pay for it all. The lawsuits, everything." The words felt cathartic as they burst forth, unloading some of the burden crushing him.

Khon sat silently, eyes downcast. "All right, Mr. Clarke," he said in a voice little more than a whisper. "Time for a very serious discussion. But I'll need a drink. And you may, too, before we're done."

Lew didn't like the sound of that. But so close now, why not play along? Give a little, get a lot. "Okay, I'll find us a bottle."

Khon wrinkled his nose. "Thanks, but instead, let me take you someplace comfortable and quiet. We have a lot to discuss. This closet —" he wrinkled his nose "— is hardly conducive."

Lew didn't trust the man but why jeopardize their chance at their establishing a rapport? To deny so simple a request might seem petty. "Okay, but I'm bringing my man along. Back-up."

Khon inhaled deeply, pursing his lips. "No, I rather think not. Just us, please?"

Despite misgivings, Lew agreed but privately arranged for Boo to shadow them.

The flashy Rolls idled outside and Khon ushered Lew into the backseat, climbing in beside him. "Silk Orchid," he muttered to the driver through the privacy partition. The limo sped off and Khon turned with an ingratiating smile.

"Mr. Clarke, I have a theory. Please indulge me."

"Yes?"

"You strike me as a sophisticated man, cultured, with varied tastes."

Maybe true in some ways, but coming from Khon it was just a line. Lew wondered if it ever worked on anyone.

"So anyway, Khun Lew—may I call you that, please?—my hunch is you are a fellow aficionado of fine music. Jazz and/or classical."

Hmm. Right out of nowhere, but a damned good guess.

"Maybe."

"I am getting a strong Thelonious vibe from you. On the right track?"

Involuntarily, Lew snorted a surprised chuckle and nodded. Clever fellow, this Khon. Lew had forever been hooked on jazz, with a broad range of favorites, but Thelonious Monk was his private addiction. How had Khon read him so perfectly? Caught totally off-guard, Lew couldn't suppress a smile.

"So while we drive, Khun Lew, I have something special for you. A digitally enhanced, perfectly remastered 1957 performance from the East Village. A private recording of a session at the Five Spot."

"Back when Coltrane was still with Monk?"

"Yes." With a knowing smile, Khon fiddled with a remote and hidden audiophile speakers suddenly bathed the luxury sedan in rich, vibrant sound. Tropical Asia fell away and Lew was transported back to a New York City jazz club, a half century earlier. Endorphins kicked in. This stuff was simply irresistible, an aural narcotic and Lew was a total junkie.

Did he have Khon right, after all?

This meek, cultured, soft-spoken jazz aficionado in the fancy car seemed a walking contradiction, far more complex than just a simple Asian business cheat. And hadn't Boo's elders earlier alluded that Khon had previously been legitimate, until being corrupted by his new partner?

Lew stopped himself before distributing too much forgiveness. It was undeniable that Khon had fronted for the Lotus con job and was absolutely involved, somehow, in that gruesome jungle labor scheme. So where lay the truth?

Despite so much being unresolved, Lew allowed himself the slightest (if guarded) optimism.

The Rolls floated up to a small building in an empty sector of 'downtown' Ruangbang. Though constructed mainly from cinder blocks, it was stylishly painted an elegant white and lime with precise purple trim. Out front, a sign announced: THE SILK ORCHID.

They entered a small lobby where a white jacketed man instantly recognized Khon and extended effusive greetings. Khon slipped him a folded-up crimson *Arysai* bill and the grinning maître d swung open the door to an inner chamber. He led them up front to a VIP alcove, clearly Khon's regular spot.

With lights low and incense wafting through the air, the atmosphere in the little club was intoxicating. There were no chairs beside the alcove's low table so Lew followed Khon's lead and made himself comfortable, nestling against large silk pillows and reclining like a sultan on the thick padded platform. Blissful comfort.

Every table in the room was private, either tucked into an alcove or screened off. Clever. A secret meeting place for Amaza elites.

A small musical group played, but not loud enough to deter conversation. The music was fresh and new but pleasantly dissonant. Rhythmic and jittery, it fluttered forth from unusual indigenous instruments. The sound box for one looked fashioned from a gourd. Another, like a xylophone with dampers, impelled a soft metallic percussion that paced the melodies.

A voluptuous woman in a tight purple sarong and silken waist-length hair arrived hoisting a large platter and spread snacks on the alcove table. A waiter in impeccable Western business attire arrived unbidden to deliver a bottle of Johnny Walker Blue Label, an ice bucket, and bottles of soda water. He poured drinks, already knowing Khon's preference for whiskey with soda and lots of ice.

"This is the most civilized place in the capital," Khon said. "Local music, but jazz variations."

"Thanks for the hospitality, Khon, but can we get down to business?"

"Yes. But let me start, please. You just relax and listen." Khon gestured toward the snacks.

This story should be good. "Fine. But don't waste my time or insult me with lies. I need the truth, and all of it."

"Yes, Khun Lew, truth. And believe me, I now have no reason to withhold anything." Khon took a long swig of scotch. "So, straightaway, to the heart of the matter, about your lawsuits in the USA? I strongly doubt Lotus will help you . . . at all."

He doubts? He should *know*. Wasn't he a Lotus head honcho? It felt like Big Boss excuses were about to start rolling in.

"Now were it up to me, yes, I would want Lotus to help you. But frankly, sir, I no longer have *any* real power in the company." Khon's voice broke and he dabbed at his eyes with a cocktail napkin. Then he flashed an incongruous smile. "I am . . . oh, what's the word? Ah, yes: a corporate *eunuch*."

Oh, brother! But the tears were a nice touch.

"Mr. Clarke, I was forced out from my Lotus holdings more than a year ago and no longer own any of my former company. My partner has completely taken over."

"The so-called *Big Boss*."

"Ha, that name. How he hates it! But yes, many locals still call him that. His actual name is Elders. Napoleon Elders, but he refers to himself as *Nap*."

Lew bristled, recalling Elders' many transgressions.

Khon shook his head. "Actually by now, Mr. Elders has absorbed *all* my former businesses, along with most of the other wealth in the region. Citizens of Inner Amazia, like me, all work for him. Mr. Elders relentlessly expanded, like a powerful force of nature, pushing businesses into bankruptcy and then buying them for nothing." Khon drummed his fingers and smiled ironically. "So your friends tricked me with that hotel offer, eh? Clever. But I *had* to look into it, you see. It's exactly the kind of situation Mr. Elders loves."

"*Mister* Elders? Please stop with that already. Too respectful for such a scumbag."

"Sorry, but that's a habit I must be careful to maintain. For my own survival."

"Mmm."

"Truly! To oppose or displease that man, in any way, can be fatal. And I speak from observed experience." Khon's face went grim. "Naturally, for both our sakes, he must never learn of this meeting."

"Sure." Lew remained wary. "But *Napoleon Elders*? Odd name for an Amaza. Or is he French?"

Khon sipped his scotch. "Actually, like you, he's a *farang*. An American! Or at least born that way. He acquired Amazian citizenship some years ago."

Holy shit, an American? This was really getting weird.

"Okay. Elders calls the shots, not you. But just for the sake of argument, let's say he agreed to my demands. Would Lotus/Elders have enough resources to provide the needed legal backing?"

Khon chuckled. "Sir, Mr. Elders has more money than the King of Siam. He arrived in Asia thirty years ago, worked at a Singapore hedge fund, and quickly learned the rules of the game—how to acquire companies with leverage and dismember them, selling off bits and pieces for massive profits. Then he struck out on his own." Khon munched a green papaya slice and shrugged. "Always ruthless, he met with incredible success and now resides in an enormous estate outside Chiang Mai, in northern Thailand. He operates his massive business empire from that palace, dominating the region."

"And how often does he come here?"

"Rarely. Almost never."

"Relying upon you instead, as his eyes and ears?"

Khon shot a thumbs-up. "But back to your question. Despite his enormous resources, there is a less-than-zero chance of him agreeing to financially backstop your company."

Lew crunched an ice cube. "Sort of figured. No principles."

"Nary a single one." Khon leaned closer. "He approached me, a few years ago, with the idea to build a spirit house factory beside my sawmill. Create year-round demand for my lumber. An excellent idea. But unbeknownst to me, he already planned to expand for global exports. Later when I learned, I warned him of the potential danger. But it was too late and he simply didn't care at all. And once he seized total control of my business—a long sad story I won't bore you with—he just made his own decisions. Like his labor 'solution'. Totally immoral but for him, typical." Khon sighed. "So no, Khun Lew, Mr. Elders cares not one iota about your suffering customers or your lawsuits. Your company be damned."

Did Lew correctly understand that? "Are you saying the danger to overseas customers was anticipated?"

"Of course! Any Amaza schoolchild could foresee that."

"And you warned him?"

Khon looked frustrated. "Yes, repeatedly, and in the strongest terms. But he only became enraged and finally ordered me to drop the issue or suffer the consequences."

Lew understood. "But once the trouble began—"

"It amused him. Your reports from America made him laugh, uproariously. He really couldn't care less."

"And in other countries . . . ?"

"Only very few incidents. A handful. Nothing on the US scale. Your sales are vastly larger." Khon raised his glass. "So here's to your business intuition, Mr. Clarke. It was spot-on."

Lew grunted. "Thanks, though I never suspected this was a ticking time bomb."

Khon shrugged. "How could you?"

"And that must be why Lotus wanted five years' payments up front, right? All was anticipated! Elders set a trap with irresistibly low prices and demanded that huge prepaid lump sum. Take it or leave it."

"Exactly. And now that he has all your money, he won't be refunding any of it. Believe me, I know the man."

What a total hosing!

Lew's pulse quickened and he angrily kicked the low table, sending ice, peanuts and bitter green mango slices flying. The bottle of blue label wobbled but was salvaged by a quick-moving waiter. The band momentarily halted until Khon nodded for them to resume playing.

He softly touched Lew's forearm. "Sir, I am but a pawn, a lowly businessman caught up in things far beyond my scope." For Lew, too, that hit close to home. "A victim like you, Khun Lew, so please don't vent your anger at me."

Lew grumbled, wanting to believe Khon but not able to fully trust him.

Khon brushed broken peanut shells off the silk cushion. "Here in Amazia, Mr. Elders controls everything, including me. Like a god."

"Or a demon."

"And what he has done absolutely disgusts me." Khon wrung his hands. "Turning my sawmill and factory into a virtual slave labor camp! He owns all human life here, with those workers as trapped as if wearing iron manacles. I live in utter shame for having played even a remote role."

Remote? Now wait just a minute. He was Elders' key enabler, the brain who ran video conferences and did the sales pitches, providing fuel for the engine. He designed the website and acted as the local conduit and was now the villain's eyes and ears in Amazia. And now that it was too late and he was haunted by guilt, he claimed to be trapped and forced to execute immoral orders.

Yet, if Elders *was* the true opponent, Khon could be a useful ally, an information source inside Lotus. A bridge to fortify, not burn.

But no way could Lew drop his guard and trust this guy. Not yet.

"So basically, Khon, you're saying I'm on my own." Lew searched the man's eyes.

"There isn't a single way I can help you," Khon said, his face as straight as a laser beam. "From deep within my heart I am sorry, but every advantage lies with Mr. Elders."

Something inside told Lew to concede nothing. "And all that rigmarole about there being no courts or contracts in Amazia —"

Khon scratched the Texas blotch. "Absolutely true. Those Western concepts don't apply here."

That still seemed impossible, a reality warp like time running backwards or gravity reversing.

"So is that why Elders changed his nationality to Amazian? One can't be sued in courts that doesn't exist."

Khon bounced a shoulder. "Excellent insight. But it doesn't matter really anyway. The money is all gone. All funds are immediately siphoned out of Amazia. Elders leaves nothing here."

Wonderful. "Where does it go?"

Khon waved his hand. "Oh, banks in Singapore, Switzerland, or the Caymans. An anonymous account in Luxembourg. Suffice to say, there are no assets here for you to recover."

Lew threw back his scotch and poured another. This was even worse than he'd imagined. "Related topic. About your pals, Thant and Inpanh—you know, the Eternity Brothers from that video conference? How deep are they stuck into this mess with you and Elders?"

"What?" Khon's eyes flashed. Lew had landed an unexpected blow. "Hmm, interesting. So you've learned their real names . . ."

"And spent a lot of time with them in Biti, so be careful. Stick with the truth."

Khon grinned. "Heh. Wonderful chaps, actually, business associates. But in this entire matter, pure innocents. They were my log suppliers in the old days, unaware of the more recent changes. They knew nothing about Mr. Elders' export plans, or even that a company called Lotus exists. Alas, they also will soon lose everything to Mr. Elders. Their business, and much more."

It delighted Lew to hear that exoneration. "But the video conference . . .?"

Khon shrugged. "I am not proud of this, Mr. Clarke, but during that entire meeting, they hadn't a clue what was going on." He echoed the ruse about a Singapore timber broker, confirming Thant and Inpanh's story.

"But why use their secret childhood nicknames?"

"Just a coincidence. Being cheeky, I suppose, playing around." Khon chuckled. "But secret? Ha, there are no secrets in Amazia!"

Khon offered Lew a mango slice. "They were on that video conference only because I ordered it. Mr. Elders worried about American courts and wanted an additional buffer, as worst case protection. So we positioned those two as figurehead owners of Lotus. They had no video, only a phone link, and didn't even see their nicknames on screen. And I was careful to never actually say their names, or even Lotus, for that matter. Did you notice?"

"No, I didn't." Lew's guard rose. Wow, this guy was pretty devious. Lew's guard went up again. "You are an amazing actor."

Khon bowed slightly. "Rather like an improv role, quite challenging to keep everything straight! I would speak to them about one thing, in Amazian, and then to you, sir, in English, an entirely different subject." Khon visibly inflated. "Actually, *professionally* I am proud of my work creating the Lotus website and running those video conferences. Easy tasks in your modern Western world, no doubt, but nearly impossible here."

Information was fire-hosing at Lew. But one thing remained clear: he needed to confront the mastermind, Napoleon Elders. Nothing else could move the needle. And while Khon had sounded helpful, so far, he hadn't offered to make that happen.

"So where is Elders now? I want to get him alone in a room." Lew pounded a fist into his palm.

Khon laughed softly. "Wish I knew. There are no schedules or advance notice for Mr. Elders. He comes and goes as he pleases. Just shows up and, no matter where, I must immediately drop everything and make myself present."

"Surely you have an address or phone number to contact him."

"As already stated, sir, *he* contacts *me*."

"But how do you reach him in an emergency?"

"Through intermediaries, at phone numbers that frequently change. A go-between would contact Mr. Elders, who later phones from a secure, untraceable line. What they call, in American movies, a 'burner' phone? But mostly he stays at his Chiang Mai estate, protected by a small army and electronic security."

Great. Khon had surrendered plenty of information but none that made Lew feel particularly good. By this point, he felt ready to forget it all and just head back to the hotel to retreat into sleep or perhaps hide at the bottom of a liquor bottle. "One final question. When might Elders next turn up in the Kingdom?" Perhaps Lew could ambush the monster.

Khon looked off into the distance, considering his words with caution. "Well, I must be very careful what I say here, but Mr. Elders *should* be coming to Amazia fairly soon. I don't know exactly when, but he will travel to Biti on a very personal matter."

"Why?"

"Please do not press me. I can say no more." Khon's eyes brimmed with anxiety so Lew stopped pushing, already knowing at gut level what this was about.

Nong's wedding.

CHAPTER TWENTY-FIVE
The Rise of Lew 2.0

Lew slept fitfully, haunted by Khon's revelations. When he woke late the next morning, he found that Boo had already left their decrepit suite. Lew padded down to the hotel lobby and rapped on the front desk, where Wongrat was lost in a weekly news tabloid, *The Ruangbang Rumor*.

"Wongrat, is there phone service closer than that coffee place?"

"No, sir. Mango in Love! having best phone in capital. Also is phone shop near train station, but more far."

Lew hustled out front and hailed a hot orange pedicab decorated with Rambo cartoons. Stallone resembled a Buddhist monk in fatigues. Twenty minutes later, he was back at the colorful caffeine refuge, already feeling like a veteran.

Pantomiming hard, he ordered a big mug of local coffee, fruit, and a heavenly bowl of full-cream rice pudding. He climbed to the highest balcony deck out back, took a table far from other customers and waited for his purchases to find him.

He thumbed an icon on his phone and seconds later, Sal's rough voice boomed through from New Jersey, clear as crystal.

"Lewis Nathaniel Clarke!" Sal bellowed. "Sweet Mother of God, man, *great* to finally hear your voice again! Though you *do* realize it's like 1 a.m. back here in civilization, right?" He sounded miffed but happy.

"Oops, sorry. My bad."

"Fuhgeddaboudit!" Sal laughed.

"I'm finally learning the ropes here, Sally Boy. Ready for this? I tracked down Khon."

"Whoa, all right! Nailed that slippery fuck. So, Lotus gonna cover us or what?" Sal was instantly midday awake, adrenaline gunning his voice.

"Long story. You ready?"

"Listening and frozen with anticipation, like Han Solo in that black stuff."

Lew laid it all out.

"So you mean," Sal summarized, "we're up against an evil overlord with no moral compass? So at least my *Star Wars* analogy continues to hold true. What do we do?"

"I'm hatching a plan." Lew sadly shook his head. He had almost nothing. "But write this down. First thing tomorrow, send a formal written notice to Lotus to terminate our contract. Cancel everything and demand full refund of our prepayment. Hit this every way you can—by email and overnight registered letter to their old mailing address. I'll also give you a Khon phone number you can text."

It was probably all useless CYA, of course. But with Elders being an American, there was the slightest glimmer of a chance this might reach US courts. So Lew wanted to tick all the boxes.

"What else, bro?"

"Courier a formal letter to every last customer and offer a full refund. They don't even need to ship the spirit houses back."

"What? Good Lord, Lew, we may have a lot in the bank from sales but could burn it all. Come close to breaking us."

Sal was right. It was not just a bad business idea, but probably one of the worst ever. But Lew's way of thinking was being rewired, his priorities shifting and adjustments being made to his very sense of what was right. Not long ago, just the notion of terrestrial spirits seemed like utter nonsense. A fairy tale. Utter nonsense. But the Amaza philosophy and mindset was making inroads. Big time.

He took another sip of Mango's miraculous coffee.

"Another thing, Sal. Top urgent."

"Shoot."

"Cut yourself a cashier's check from the company treasury and buy out your share of Avian. I forced you to pony up what, a half million? So write yourself a check for two and get a proper return on your investment."

"What —?"

"That way, no matter what happens, at least I know my best friend is safe."

"Come on, Hoss, I—"

Lew clicked off at mid-sentence to truncate useless debate. He knew Sal's good heart all too well, and his mind was already made up. Pressing moral issues were clarifying and some of his existential fog was lifting. Avian's legal woes were undeniably important, of course, but no longer his sole or even primary focus. He somehow needed to clean hands sullied by involvement with enslaved workers, crushed local businesses, women taken into bondage.

He decided to walk back to the hotel. He didn't really know the route but Ruangbang was small and long walks were good for thinking. He had a load to sort out and would surely find his way.

Those fresh directives to Sal should staunch the bleeding and limit the lawsuits to the dozen already filed, though even a single ruling could destroy the company, considering the heavy hand of American juries when dispensing defendants' dollars to punish perceived bad guys. All his wealth, reputation, and future prospects might be sent swirling down the drain.

At least he'd now protected Sal, his dearest friend. That felt good and was only right. After all, Lew had lured him into this wretched mess.

Striding past a run of coconut palms, he mumbled to himself, shaking his head. It seemed unfair and his odds looked slim. And Elders, with more money than Elon Musk, could easily afford to do the righteous thing. But fat chance of that.

Gaggles of children gathered to trail behind him before dropping back and handing him off to the next neighborhood pack. He rounded a corner and spotted the ruined strip mall he and Frog explored the first day, with that squalid little office where Khon operated Asiatic Media. Hmm, really . . . how could he trust that guy?

All businesses there were now shuttered and halfway down the corridor, mangy street dogs had moved in. Hearing their growled warning, he made a careful retreat.

Now on foot, he absorbed far more of the capital than before. What stood out, and jarringly so, was the absolute profusion of spirit houses. The blasted things were *everywhere*, in every farmyard and beside every house or shop. Simple, modest, whitewashed things. Similar in design to Lotus' ultra-luxury exports, but this was like comparing a Volkswagen Beetle to a Maserati.

Without exception, all were graced by offerings—small, delicate woven platters, candles and little bananas or other symbolic gifts. Lew sighed. Unlike his American customers, the Amaza all fully understood their end of the bargain with cohabiting terrestrial spirits. He still found it near-impossible to believe in their existence, but it increasingly felt like utter hubris to continue denying what millions across Asia insisted was true.

As he wandered Ruangbang's overgrown lanes, his mind floated free and a vision of Nong settled upon him—her long, silky hair, perfect latte skin, and hypnotic green eyes. She was draped in that same shimmering purple blouse from dinner. Indulging in the pleasure of his daydream, he relived their jungle path meeting and her plea for help.

Well, of course he'd love to help her, but reality was colder. Her father had already committed her hand to Elders. Lew could do nothing about that and, furthermore, it was really none of his business, was it? Other than that he was downright infatuated.

There was no denying the linkage among all these problems. Elders. In fact, a single overarching, successful negotiation might solve everyone's problems. What an audacious masterstroke *that* would be.

"Dream on, you dope," he muttered to himself.

He exhaled quietly, knowing his life could never again be the same. Not just because his high-flying career had crashed and his new venture imploded. Nor because of the legal problems threatening to crush him.

No, the main reason was a stark change transpiring at his very core. His vision of life—call it philosophy, morality, whatever—was definitely evolving. The world just felt different, along with his role in it. Values. Whether it was personal growth or madness, ever since landing in Amazia he'd experienced far too many jarring sights to un-see, too many revelatory moments to erase from his memory.

This stunning new perspective, almost like a fresh take on existence, seemed like a gift. Sal's lame joke suddenly seemed meaningful. He indeed now *was* Lew 2.0, describing his growth as a human being, not just code for the next phase in his business life.

Sunset in the tropics always came quickly and in just minutes, Ruangbang's streets became a darkened maze. Lew stubbornly pushed down side paths and alleys for another half hour before admitting he was lost.

He raised a hand, heard the familiar jingle of a bicycle taxi bell, and climbed aboard.

Five minutes later, they pulled up in front of his hotel.

The empty hotel lobby looked eerie at 8 p.m., illuminated in the beverage cooler's chalky fluorescence. No surprise, Frog and Wongrat were long gone.

As Lew reached his upstairs suite and squeaked the door open, a power outage pitched the place into sudden darkness. "Yo, Boo, you here?" But there was only silence. Odd, where'd he go? Nighttime in Ruangbang, most everything shut down.

Lew shrugged and lit a candle. The past twenty-four hours had been emotionally draining. Luckily, what he now needed most—sleep—required no electricity. Ripe with sweat and dust, he took a quick splash bath, ready for slumber's sweet oblivion.

He shuffled into his bedroom and in the flickering candlelight spotted a flimsy square of paper atop his pillow. He recognized Boo's ultra-legible handwriting, a message clearly scribbled in a hurry:

> *Dear Khun Lew—*
>
> *My father just sent urgent word summoning me for Nong's wedding.*
>
> *I regret I cannot wait any longer and must immediately depart. I am getting a ride to Biti with a friend, in his overland vehicle. PLEASE find your own way to Biti.*
>
> *The ceremony will take place at the sawmill complex, perhaps as early as tomorrow! This is also our chance to finally meet the Big Boss.*
>
> *We desperately need your help, sir.*
> *Cheers,*
> *Boonyarit*

Lew's heart raced.

Elders was on the verge of taking delivery of his hostage bride. If Lew was to ever help Nong, it had to be now. And if he was to succeed convincing Lotus to provide legal cover for Avian Luxury––or do anything, for that matter, like help Boo's family or the enslaved workers—this would be the moment.

He stuffed his meager possessions into a small duffel, bolted down the stairs and out to the street where he flagged down a bicycle taxi. "*Train station*," he barked in one of the few Amaza phrases he'd absorbed by osmosis. The grizzled driver looked shocked.

Lacking any real plan, Lew buzzed with a mix of excitement, worry and confusion. But he would have plenty of time to mull over his next steps. Like eighteen to twenty-four hours on the mail train back up to Biti.

CHAPTER TWENTY-SIX
Peeing with Khon and The Boys

They reached the train station well past 9:30 p.m. and the usual pandemonium reigned under yellow floodlights. Amid a sea of bubbling chaos, the stodgy black steam engine huffed and sighed beside the modest station house as passengers climbed aboard its circus-colored cars.

Thank God, the train hadn't left yet.

Everything felt more familiar this time and Lew smiled at his luck. With the Biti 'express' running late, as usual, Amazia inefficiency was for once working in his favor. Had he missed this train, he would have lost a full day and probably missed Nong's wedding, his best chance to intercept Elders.

He slithered through the crowd and barged into the depot to find, just like before, passengers milling about, packed as thick as beans in a can. Again, a long line zig-zagged back and forth between the front door and the ticket window.

Lacking hours to stand in line, Lew slapped a huge goofy grin on his face and began to knife his way through the crowd, modeling Frog from last time. He nodded sweetly and smiled, tipping his Yankees cap. "Sorry, folks! American! Don't speak the language."

But this time the sea of people didn't part like before, when Frog slipped Lew through as if he'd been greased with Crisco. Bumping shoulders and into bags, Lew only slowly nosed forward amid irritated grunts and scolding hisses. So different now, without his friendly, enabling host as blocking fullback. He finally neared the ticket window, stirring complaints from frontline customers.

"Sorry, folks, very sorry. Emergency!"

But it got even worse. An unfamiliar ticket seller stood behind the window, not Frog's eighth cousin, three times removed, or whatever their shared fiction had been. The short woman behind the bars just scowled at Lew and pointed toward the back of the line.

No way! The train could pull out at any moment and Lew couldn't afford to lose a day. He wai'ed the testy ticket seller and sped out the station door.

Jogging down the crowded platform, he heard those familiar hoots and jovial cheers raining down from the train tops. But once he set hands on the metal ladder bolted to one of the cars, making his intentions clear, all went deathly silent.

He began to climb, all the while wondering if a *farang* was even allowed to ride up there? Would that violate some unwritten local cultural tenet? He'd soon find out—he had to get to Biti and so he *was* riding up there that night. Period.

As he grasped the top rung, a flutter of hands pulled him up. His arrival on top triggered a wave of murmured commotion that finally morphed into a rousing welcome and massive group wai, which he returned.

From up top, the surrounding view was remarkable, a delightful panorama illuminated by candles and torches and bleeding out from the rail yard's fiery jumble to the rustic city beyond.

The carriage roof was packed like Times Square on New Year's Eve, with nearly every inch claimed by the likes of smiling moms, pops, and kids; gaggles of young soldiers heading home; groups of monks chanting evening prayers; and farm families traveling with various trussed-up livestock, mainly goats and chickens.

Piled at the center of the rail car roof was booty from big city shopping in the capital. Items destined for upcountry included car batteries, disassembled bicycles and Chinese transistor radios, even a small cast-iron stove and a flat-panel television set. Did Inner Amazia even have television broadcasts, or did they just nick signals from Thailand, Myanmar or South China?

A toothless farmer in a conical cap waved Lew over to sit with his family, motioning with his palm down and fingers spread, like raking the air. A cozy sitting space miraculously opened up, like waters receding to reveal a small island. The mother folded a checkered blanket into a cushion for Lew to sit upon.

And just like that, he'd been adopted. Again. He chuckled and his fellow passengers, seeing him happy but not understanding why, laughed along with him, just being friendly.

Snacks floated around, passed hand to hand, like biscuits, brown sugar lumps and pickled vegetable bits. When salty bits of unidentified protein arrived, he demurred, remembering the fried crickets.

A large ceramic beverage container floated on a mass of hands, straight at him, and he shivered recalling the harsh local liquor. The jug jumped over intervening victims and soon arrived, forcing him to take a fiery gulp to accommodate his hosts. At least he was spared the cigars.

All in all, it felt delightful, like a mobile block party, company picnic or country cocktail hour. Amazia style. Atop a train.

The thrilling night sky hypnotized him, a blanket of deep blue-black pocked by a billion discrete dots of light, extending infinitely toward the horizon. But at close range, the view was equally pleasant, a candle-lit mosaic containing every color of the rainbow. Muted by darkness yet visible in the candle flicker were monks in orange and deep vermilion robes; blue and yellow sarongs; green army fatigues; white shirts; yellow straw hats; and multi-colored blankets.

An unknown party squeezed through the crowd to approach Lew. "Hello, America?" said the smiling young Amaza man with long curly hair, perfect white teeth and twinkling eyes. He wai'ed and tapped his chest as if to say, *Remember me*?

Gazing down, Lew was astonished to recognize his old lizard skin boots! What were the odds? They looked miraculously restored on their new owner, the tooled leather and luscious swirls more spectacular than ever. Back when Lew had hoisted them out the first class window, they seemed irreparably ruined. Lew pointed at them and smiled. "Well done!"

Grinning fiercely, his new Amaza friend lunged forward and gave Lew a sudden, macho hug. The young man then interlocked fingers with Lew and, along with his chattering friends, guided Lew toward the roof's edge. Mr. Boots pantomimed, forming binoculars with his hands.

Something to see?

He knelt down and Lew followed his lead. Then both sprawled forward on their stomachs and seized metal handles protruding from the train's outside wall, just below the roof line. Strong hands suddenly gripped Lew's ankles and began lowering him over the side.

"Hey, wait a minute!" he cried. They laughed but didn't stop. Was this a test?

Hanging beside him, Mr. Boots gave Lew a nudge. *Look in the window.* Lew gazed inside and his brain began to process and sort out the inverted perspective. As luck would have it, it was a first class cabin and three of the four bench seats were already claimed by two families and a pair of soldiers, colorful ribbons and medals decorating their breasts. All ignored him and Mr. Boots, dangling outside the window.

But then the final passenger entered the car—Khon!

Utterly shocked, Lew signaled for The Boys to quickly pull him back to the rooftop, where he pondered this development.

No doubt, Khon was hurrying to Biti for Nong's wedding. At first blush, this felt like betrayal. All that time at the Silk Orchid, while professing and proclaiming honesty and integrity, had Khon been withholding news of the wedding ceremony? Could Lew ever again trust *anything* that man said?

He tingled with nervous excitement, realizing Khon's presence all but guaranteed Lew would reach Biti in time for the wedding. Also, he wondered if Elders might be aboard.

The train finally jolted into motion, departing hours late, as usual. Lew's fellow rooftop riders purred with delight as the steam locomotive began to pound out a quickening cadence, peppered by shrill whistle blasts. Dozens of candles flickered in the breeze from motion and many were extinguished, only to be re-lit and shielded inside makeshift lanterns recycled from glass jars.

The farmer's wife offered Lew a bun, which he nibbled while lost in thought. What should he do about Khon? There was no hurry. The man, captive to the whims of this mail train, was going nowhere soon.

The Amazia landscape rolled slowly past, under the moonlit sky. In the dark, figures constantly jumped on or off the train. Several times Lew crawled back to the edge of the roof for another peek at Khon, just to make sure, and each time found the man still there.

By 2 a.m., the train began to ascend switchbacks. Blankets and sweaters appeared from nowhere, to cover his fellow riders. Lew would have frozen but for the kindness of his farmer godparents, who passed him a scratchy blanket and squeezed in closer for extra warmth.

He woke deep in the night, his bladder filled to bursting by all the black tea he'd drunk. Discharge was urgent and he certainly couldn't just let fly a stream from atop the train. Nor would he again chance the train's bug-infested lavatory at night. So, the question was where? The platform at the rear of the carriage would do.

He stepped gingerly around sleeping bodies, through the night's chill and descended the iron ladder. The train was just crawling along, so he had no fear of falling.

On the rear platform he found an impromptu stag party had already broken out, with a dozen young men smoking, laughing and sharing the inevitable bottle of local spirits. He recognized many of The Boys from up top, including Mr. Boots, who invited their favorite *farang* to join in.

Someone popped the cork on a porcelain jug and offered Lew a swig. The stuff was potent with a near-chemical taste and packed a wallop. What on earth did they distill to make such rotgut? But after a few quick shots, Lew's taste buds went numb and he felt warmer. Then he made his way to the rear corner and released an explosive torrent downwind into the blackness. Ah, sweet relief!

Upon rejoining the heart of the gathering, he noted a new participant: Khon, who looked out of place in his businessman's attire, placidly smoking a cigarette in the moonlight. Glowing embers from other smokers drifted around him like fireflies.

Lew came up from behind. "So, did you pack a tuxedo, Khon?"

Appearing stunned to hear his name, Khon turned and came face-to-face with Lew.

"You know," Lew continued, "I mean for the wedding. Elders and Nong. What's the dress protocol? Am I okay in jeans?"

The shock on Khon's face melted, quickly replaced by a suave, knowing smile. "Ah, Khun Lew! Such a nice surprise!" Man, this guy was smooth, all right.

Lew fought to contain his rising anger. "Just cut the crap already, Khon." No more *Khun* honorifics. "Funny, but when we were chatting the other night, you forgot to mention this wedding in Biti was coming up. Slipped your mind?"

Khon bit his bottom lip, thinking, and then smiled. "Oh, dear me, Mr. Clarke, I fear you have badly misjudged me yet again. When we last spoke, I had no such information. I only learned about the wedding early today, when Mr. Elders ordered me to arrange everything. I immediately sent word to Nong's father and am now proceeding to Biti."

Well, maybe that was plausible but Lew still bristled. "Sure. And what about Elders?"

Khon knitted his eyebrows. "What?"

"Is he on this train?" Lew held his breath. *Please say yes*.

Khon laughed, as if the very proposition was outrageous. "Goodness! That's amusing, sir, just the thought of Mr. Elders ever riding on *this* mail train? Highly entertaining. Thank you."

"I'm not laughing."

Khon sighed. "Please understand, sir. Mr. Elders travels the region in total luxury by private aircraft—a Gulfstream jet—and maintains a fleet of Sikorsky helicopters, including one at Ruangbang. So perhaps tomorrow morning, he will jet to Ruangbang and helicopter to Biti. An afternoon arrival is possible."

"But this train may not even reach Biti by then."

"True enough." Khon shrugged. "But no ceremony can be held until I arrive. After all, I am Mr. Elders' translator, intermediary, and general source of legitimacy in Amazia."

Thank goodness! So Lew *would* arrive in time.

"But I don't understand. Why didn't Elders just bring you along in his helicopter?"

Khon pursed his lips. "Clearly, sir, you still don't quite grasp the nature of our relationship."

Lew pumped him for more information. "I've heard the wedding is at that sawmill and factory complex."

"Almost correct. Near there, actually, at a grand, custom-built ceremonial stage plus floating honeymoon cottage. The most talented artisans worked more than a year. It's quite astounding."

Probably just beyond the area Lew had already explored. He further tested Khon's integrity. "So, the bride . . . Nong, is it? How is she doing?"

Khon cocked his head, challenging. "Sir, please don't play the fool with me. We are adults. Miss Nong is essentially being bartered into slavery. How would *anyone* feel?"

Ten points for honesty. Okay. "Yes, but she'll at least have a wife's rights, right? Not too horrible a deal, considering how rich Elders is. Correct?"

Khon shook his head with a sad laugh and then spoke slowly, as if to a child.

"At his various estates across Asia, Mr. Elders basically maintains harems for his own pleasure. The most beautiful women, each one personally selected. When it comes to making a prime new addition to his stables of concubines, Mr. Elders will do *anything* necessary. He reckons Nong is one of the finest women he's ever seen so, to get her, he agreed to participate in a sham marriage ceremony in rural Amazia. Very unusual. But not surprising as he absolutely *wants* her."

"What do you mean, *sham ceremony*?"

"Ah, Khun Lew. Never forget, Amazia is generally a place without laws and for Mr. Elders (unlike the Amaza) vows, obligations, and honor are all meaningless. The final result of this elaborate charade is just that he can take Miss Nong back to Thailand, where she will be mere chattel, a slave, with no rights. Certainly not a true wife."

Cold fury spread through Lew. He studied this character. Who was Khon, really? This pathetic little man or the sophisticated, jazz-loving businessman of the other night? Or the heartless fraud who impersonated a monk on that video conference? Perhaps all three? But Lew couldn't reconcile him as hatchet man for the ghoul, Elders.

"You're an intelligent man, Khon. Cultured. How can you live with yourself, enabling Elders' evil?"

Khon looked down, his mouth aquiver. He pulled a silk kerchief from his pocket and swiped at a single tear near the corner of his eye. Then he reached for the bottle circulating among The Boys and took a mighty swig. All an act?

"Actually, sir, little is as it seems to you." His voice wobbled. "My real name isn't even *Khon*."

What? Damn it, when was this flip-flopping of the truth ever going to stop?

"In truth, I am Arthit Thongkam and originally from Thailand. But I started to use the *Khon* name to shield my identity, once my work for Mr. Elders deepened and its unsavory nature became clearer." He stared at the ground.

"Unsavory? Better words might be *depraved* or *horrific*."

Khon remained silent.

"So, you basically made a deal with the devil."

"Lucifer himself," Khon said, with a bitter grimace. "But, well, the money is truly excellent. By the way, my assumed name is a bit of a joke. *Khon* is the Thai word for *man.* Did you know that?"

Lew bristled. "Yes, actually, I did." So the damned name *was* a fake, all along. "But don't expect me to start calling you Khun Arthit. To me, you'll always gonna just be fucking Khon."

"As you wish." The man shrugged. "But let me explain. Long ago, my father worked as a chauffeur for Mr. Elders in Bangkok, when he was young and just starting his business. Father was promoted to work at the Chiang Mai estate. I was still just a boy when my entire family moved there. We lived in the servants' quarters."

Lew studied him closely. Seemed to be telling the truth.

"When I came of age, Mr. Elders sent me off to school in Singapore and paid for everything. Saw something in me so it was always understood that one day, I would work for him. After graduating I returned to Chiang Mai and was taken under wing as his personal aide. I saw *everything*."

"Flunky in training?"

Khon rubbed his face. "He later staked me in my own business, as my silent partner. I purchased a little sawmill near Biti and later expanded by adding a modest spirit house factory. The business thrived and I became close friends with Inpanh and Thant, relying on their logging camp for all of my wood. They, in turn, completely depended upon my purchases. We were very friendly business associates. They believed me to be a local from Amazia, and I never discouraged that erroneous assumption."

"I married and had three children. And my career with Mr. Elders really took off as he assigned me to also run other businesses for him. Life was beautiful! But the demands of Mr. Elders increasingly began to conflict with my values. Nothing major at first, but later, more serious."

Lew shuddered, fearing where the story was heading.

"He started to push me to find a way to force out Thant and Inpanh and absorb their logging business into our sawmill company.

I took a stand and resigned, planning to go off on my own." Khon's eyes brimmed with tears. "That was when Mr. Elders made clear my family, living comfortably at his estate, were essentially hostages. As long as I complied with his wishes, they would be treated well, though never allowed to leave."

"Holy shit," mumbled Lew, shaking his head.

"The threat stunned me. I was confused and frightened. A few months later, it all came to a head when Mr. Elders announced *his* plan to massively expand the factory and export spirit houses. He also had a strategy to obtain essentially free labor. I told him my conscience wouldn't allow me to be party to any of that." Khon trembled, the tears now flowing freely. "The very next day," his voice shook, "my sweet daughter, Lek, only a toddler, disappeared."

What? "Oh my God."

"My wife went entirely to pieces, as you can imagine. I pretended to be strong but was crushed. Mr. Elders' brutal message was clear."

"Comply or else." Lew's skin crawled. "The bastard! But as for your little girl, did you ever—"

"Never, to this day, years later. But Mr. Elders insists Lek is fine and being treated well."

Good Lord. Poor Khon!

"Better off, in fact, than if she were still living with us at the estate. She lacks nothing, we are told, and no longer even remembers her family, so she feels no grief. And our child will continue to do well, Mr. Elders promises, as long as I ensure all his commands are executed smoothly."

"Your full cooperation and continued employment."

Khon sighed bitterly. "My wife is absolutely terrified for our child's welfare, of course, so she's become Mr. Elders' chief enforcer of my compliance. For the best of reasons, naturally." He bowed his head and spoke in a weak voice. "So, as to your question, as to how I can be party to such evil, sir? The answer is easy. The man's power over me is absolute"

Khon began to rhythmically sob, sucking in air. The Boys and the other men on the rear platform stopped chatting to stare. Mr. Boots gently pushed the uncorked bottle toward Khon, who seized it and greedily chugged more of the liquid fire. He wiped his mouth, said thanks and headed back to his cabin.

Lew climbed back up the iron ladder and settled in under the stars, his mind ablaze. The bigger picture was clarifying. This was no longer just about lawsuits in America or stolen businesses in Amazia. It was about more than a forced marriage or a child being kidnapped. No, this was a battle against pure evil.

Just like before, the stop at Momuk siphoned away most of the remaining passengers, leaving the train nearly empty.

Sore and achy after a night on the hard, chilly rooftop, Lew went down to first class and joined Khon. Why not? There he found the man spread out in relative luxury and appearing to have fully regained his composure.

"Ah, Khun Lew, a pleasure. Do come in." He smiled.

Lew rubbed his backside and carefully dropped onto the padded bench across from Khon. "Man, what a colossal butt ache."

Khon nodded in sympathy. "Rooftop riding is not meant for *farang*, sir. But we will reach Biti in just a few more hours."

Lew smiled. "Hey, listen, about your little girl . . ." Khon's face darkened. "Surely somebody knows where she is. One of Elders' people, somebody like you."

Khon sighed. "Yes, sir, I even suspect whom that might be, but nobody would ever dare cross Mr. Elders to tell me. He is too vicious and rules by terror. To even ask would be dangerous and doomed from the start."

"Understood. But what if Elders was removed from the picture, somehow? With fear of him gone, somebody could tell you, right? You'd be able to find your child."

"*Removed?*" Khon spat the word out like rotten food. "Highly risky talk, sir. You can't imagine."

Lew shrugged. "Maybe. But if Lek was *my* child, I'd be sorely tempted to kill that man." He searched Khon's face but saw only a blank slate.

The train pulled into Biti station by late afternoon.

"Have a place to stay, Mr. Clarke?"

"Don't worry about me, Khon." Lew played it safe, still unsure whether to trust him. "But I'll see you at the ceremony, in the jungle."

Khon's eyes widened. "Extreme danger for you. Be warned."

"Don't worry about me."

"Khun Lew, I still sense you don't fully trust me. Why not?"

"Want to, Khon, but . . ."

They exchanged curt nods and Khon walked off. Lew then entered the station building. "Khun Siva!" he boomed.

The stationmaster, dozing behind the counter, jolted awake. "Khun Lew!" They exchanged wais.

On a scrap of paper, Lew drew a stick figure of a man and a simple house. Then he walked his fingers across the desktop and tried one of his few Amaza words: *"Rumahbaan . . . Khun Boonyarit?"* Boo's house?

Siva laughed and summoned a small boy who'd been playing on the road outside. Siva burbled instructions and handed the boy an orange *Arysai* note. Lew smiled. Probably all of five cents.

Siva warmly grasped Lew's hand and guided him outside to his pony cart lashed to a tree. He unhitched Pasha and helped Lew climb aboard the stout creature. The child grasped the pony's leash, announced *"Rumahbaan* Khun Boonyarit," and led Pasha down the road.

"Goodbye," said Siva, waving.

Wow. What a surprising world. His man, Siva, was speaking English, and Lew, the Amaza dialect!

PART FIVE:

Wedding Bells in the Jungle

CHAPTER TWENTY-SEVEN
Hooch and Cheroots, Redux

For the next hour, the sweet-natured Pasha clip-clopped behind the young guide toward Boo's home. Lew reached his destination just as the sun set. Before Lew could dismount, the entire family spilled out the door, somber and upset.

"Khun Lew!" cried Uncle Inpanh, furtively wiping away tears. Thant stood there silent and brooding.

"Chief," Boo said, "thank goodness you've arrived." He tossed an arm around Lew's shoulders. "I knew you'd make it. We need help, all we can get."

"So the wedding is definitely on?"

"Yes, sir, sometime tomorrow, *lah*."

"And the bride . . . ?"

"Very upset and hiding away, alone in her room. Talking to no one."

"And the bastard, Elders?"

"Arriving tomorrow, we believe, direct to the wedding site. So there is only tonight, to plan." Good: at least Boo, unlike Khon, didn't yet accept the marriage as a done deal.

"Hey chief, no offense, but uh . . ." Boo fanned the air with a hand.

"Mmm?"

"Maybe you want to clean up a little?" Lew hadn't bathed since the previous morning and then sweated his way across Amazia. Must've smelled like an old shoe. Boo handed him soap, a towel and a shaving razor straight from the 1900s. "My dad's. Plus laundered clothes Khun Luam sent over for you. But hurry. Soon as you're done, we eat."

Lew returned to the dining area freshened and revived after sudsing off a layer of crud.

The entire family already waited at the table—Thant, Inpanh, Pak Mo, Boo, his mother, and the bride-to-be, immersed in her own private misery. All ate quietly, heads down. After the previous chatty family affair, festive as a carnival, this meal felt funereal.

Lew stole looks at the sniffling, grief-stricken Nong, her eyes puffy from tears. Heart-stoppingly beautiful, as always, she was rendered all the more endearing in this forlorn state. She made brief eye contact, telegraphing an unspoken message, and then mumbled some excuse, abruptly stood and bolted off.

Glances flew around the table and Boo's mother jumped up to chase after Nong.

Lew felt overcome by the compulsion to save her, though it was all madness, of course. Nobody flies halfway around the planet and finds their one-in-a-billion soul mate, hidden away in a random backwater. But all other methods of finding happiness had failed him, so far, so why *couldn't* this have been fated, to find his life's love this way? The split with MJ had opened a hole in his soul, and only now with Nong did he feel the possibility of true healing.

Nobody had eaten much, except Lew, but all the men rose and dinner seemed over. Uncle Inpanh whispered something to Boo and motioned toward the door.

"Khun Lew, meet us outside for some air? Uncle and Father." Boo tossed a knowing look and Lew groaned softly. Oh God, no. The cigars and booze were killing him. "Just an excuse, chief. They want to talk with you, alone. We all do."

They filed out of the house and right on cue, a brilliant silver moon crested above the rim of neighboring mountains. Cigars were distributed, the familiar gray porcelain jug appeared, and now-familiar rituals began to play out in silence. As always, the old brothers made a great show of tending to Lew, according him special honor.

The Amaza finally relaxed into squatting positions and Lew sat on a woven reed cushion. Inpanh spoke first, stopping only to puff his cigar and knock down another shot. His voice wavered but he otherwise stayed in control. Impressive, considering how he was set to lose his only daughter into bondage, the next day.

"She is his only daughter, Khun Lew," Boo translated," but he had no other choice, up against Elders' massive power. Still, sadness and guilt are destroying him. If Uncle refused, Elders would then have just called in the promissory note and forced the family to immediately lose our business and homes. Our lives. Everything!"

"A wretched choice," Lew muttered, "but no real choice at all."

"And Nong insisted to make this sacrifice, her chance to perhaps help save the family."

Lew weighed a concern that still vexed him. "I still don't quite fully understand something. Isn't Elders' enormous power over them, frankly, just legalistic? But there are no contracts in Amazia, right? So, it stands to reason —"

Boo frowned. "Listen, sir, please. Of course we all make agreements here, each and every day. Mutual promises. That is how life works! But all are enforced by a higher authority, not just words on paper, laws, or men in courts. One's honor is all important."

"Even if the other side in an agreement has no honor at all?"

"Irrelevant. It is about one's *own* personal morality and integrity. So defaulting on a commitment, even to the likes of Napoleon Elders, is a catastrophe."

Lew grunted and shook his head, still not really getting it.

But if that was reality for the Amaza, who was he to argue? They embraced a strict, profound personal morality that defined their existence. He found himself both admiring and pitying them for that, in equal measure. "Okay, if you say so."

"Also remember," Boo added, "Elders has powerful ways to totally enforce his will."

"If honor fails, use brute force?"

"Something like that."

Thanh and Inpanh yawned and stood. Boo also stretched. "We're exhausted, chief. But you've still got half your cigar left and plenty to think about, so here's the jug. Maybe stay out a little longer and enjoy this beautiful night?"

Odd. After luring him out there they really said nothing new and were now abandoning him. He soon stubbed out his cigar and rose to retire. Time for him to sleep, too.

But something stopped him—a sweet floral fragrance, familiar and lovely. Had night-blooming flowers just begun to release their perfume?

He turned and caught a breathtaking sight. Nong stood there, an arm's length away, outlined in the moonlight. She wore a long, light gown draping against her curves and rippling in the breeze. His heart all but stopped. It was certain: she was the most perfect being in all of creation.

She bowed her forehead to the tips of her fingers and gently wai'ed him.

"Khun Lew," she purred, her sweet, high voice like music.

He moved closer and wrapped his arms around her as she buried a tear-soaked face into his shoulder, trembling as he stroked her long, silken hair. "Hey, whoa there," he softly mumbled, "don't cry. It's all going to be all right. I'll make sure." He trusted she understood his tone, if not his words.

But how could *anything* ever be okay again? He had no plan and the woman he was irreversibly falling in love with was just hours away from a lifetime of sexual bondage.

Considering all his other massive concerns, this was a complication he didn't invite but was powerless to resist. Sharing no more than a dozen words in common, they communicated at the level of their souls, existences merging as one.

He had detected her inner beauty, from the very first moment, outshining even her magnificent exterior. And now, her soul-wrenching vulnerability entrapped him even deeper.

Sure, it was crazy. But all his life he'd been rational and organized, methodical, and look where that got him. Was it now time to embrace a new life, one more emotional and intuitive?

Her trembling dissipated as she pressed tightly against him and he buried his face in her hair, feeling her softness and warmth and inhaling her scent mingled with that of sweet perfume.

She raised her head and their eyes locked for an eternity.

"Khun Lew," she pleaded, using her few English words, "please to help Nong?" A delicate hand touched her heart and then moved to Lew's chest. "Is love, yes?"

Her simple gesture and words astounded him, confirming their mutual feelings. "Yes, my darling, incredibly, I think it is." He kissed her forehead. "And I will protect you."

Their lips pressed together and they lowered themselves to the ground, oblivious to the dirt and vegetation. Lew fashioned a pillow for her, as best he could, from his shirt and there, hidden away in the black Amazia night, they surrendered themselves to their passion.

Afterward, he stroked her face. "Don't worry," he whispered, "I won't let us down. I can't. Somehow, we'll fix this."

Nong rose and disappeared into the tropical night while Lew drew in a deep lungful of evening air. Had that been a dream? Surely the Fates weren't so cruel as to allow him to finally meet the woman of his destiny, only to lose her straightaway.

A smile flickered across his face. Had Boo and his elders known? Did they spot a budding, mutual attraction? Or had Nong asked him to set up the rendezvous?

His smile grew wider.

CHAPTER TWENTY-EIGHT
Unholy Sacrament in the Jungle

Silence blanketed the household the next morning, as each personally prepared for that dark day. Nong stayed hidden while Uncle Inpanh sat on a stump outside, quietly bemoaning his daughter's fate. Thant provided mute support.

Boo disappeared well before Lew awoke but returned midmorning with a pony cart splendidly garlanded with red, purple, and yellow tropical flowers. "Transport for the bride," he said, his eyes sad. "Borrowed from my friend. Took us a while to pretty it up."

Lew feared his head might explode from the contradictions. This was no normal wedding. That very day, his precious Nong was to disappear forever into slavery. And her sweet family would march toward this doom while locked in a charade of normalcy, meekly accepting this horror for reasons of moral obligation.

Nong in particular appeared willing to accept the self-immolation, on the remote chance it might save her family. Yet she also confided her hope that Lew might somehow swoop in and save them all. But how could anybody do that? They were pitted against a fire-breathing monster, an absolute tyrant who was choking life out of the entire region.

A small crowd of friends and well-wishers began to gather around noon and serenaded the bride and her family with a sentimental, multilayered Amaza choral song. The tune, appropriately bittersweet, dampened any eye that had thus far managed to stay dry.

"Our tradition, *lah*," Boo said, his voice cracking. "Amaza bridal song, for good luck and happiness." He quickly turned away to wipe away tears.

The bride, at that moment, made her first appearance and a hush fell over the singers. The only sounds were from trilling birds and clicking geckos. Eyes downcast, she marched silently to the flower-bedecked pony cart and climbed aboard the silk-padded seat.

Lew drank in this heart-stopping spectacle.

Nong had been stunning before, even without makeup, but now in full wedding regalia she was astounding. Local make-up enhanced the bride's facial perfection to a near-impossible beauty, marred only by blurry mascara streaks below her eyes, at which she daubed with a frilly pink handkerchief.

Her dress was a confection of gauzy-thin layers with intricate floral patterns in bright colors—reds, yellows, and deep purples, all perfectly blended. A princess's diadem perched atop her head, trailing a veil of white fabric, pure as morning mist. She hugged to her bosom a bouquet of orchids, frangipani, and other local flowers.

Destiny had provided them a sunny, magnificent day with a deep blue sky and perfumed air. A mild cooling breeze kept the equatorial heat at bay.

As if rehearsed, everyone now fell into line behind the pony cart, to process toward the nuptials site. Lew joined the grieving family, walking beside the cart like bodyguards. The chorale resumed, creating a heart-rending backdrop as the procession flowed through central Biti, with new participants continuously joining, their additional voices making the music louder and the harmonies more intricate.

Lew tingled with a sense of déjà vu, recalling a similar procession in a mountain town in Guatemala, while once on vacation with MJ during Holy Week. Throngs of the devout bore a statue of the Blessed Virgin along the hilly town's streets, serenaded by an amateur brass band playing oompah-flavored hymns. Same emotions.

Boo leaned closer, to be heard over the singing. "You okay,

chief?"

Lew stole a glance at Nong, rocking side to side in the cart, stoic as a martyr. "Yeah, guess so." A lie.

After an hour dodging potholes, the procession climbed aboard the new private jungle road from Biti to the factory compound.

The pony cart wheels squeaked in counterpoint to the chirping of birds, high overhead. The music and setting lulled Lew into a trancelike state, marching along to deliver her up as a perfect sacrificial victim, volunteering to save others.

Enough already! Snapping out of it, Lew committed: he *would* stop this travesty, as he'd already promised. No plan? No matter. How? No idea.

But if necessary, he would kill Elders. Right?

As the parade traversed the new jungle road, Lew recognized some of marchers as small families who worked as indentured laborers, evidently summoned to applaud their owner's grand achievement. Lew's outrage sizzled hotter.

Upon reaching the Rama River Valley factory complex, a noticeable chill descended upon the crowd and all singing stopped. The work site, seen for the first time unobscured by jungle foliage, impressed Lew even more. The place was as big as a dozen football fields.

"Where are the special ceremonial structures?

"Somewhere nearby, chief, I suppose." Boo said. "But I've never seen them." That surprised Lew. "Sir, I often visit the logging camp, several clicks upriver, but this sawmill and factory area is prohibited. Dangerous and off limits except to workers."

Most of the procession members dropped away and disappeared into the factory complex. Despite the wedding, it was evidently still a work day, until the ceremony.

Nong, her head down, nervously fussed with the bouquet in her lap as the cart skirted past the last of the work stations. Then, with Lew and the family still in tow, it turned off the road and headed further downriver atop a wide, trampled-down path through grass and weeds. Soon they arrived at a separate cleared area.

The wedding site.

The pony cart wobbled to the edge of the river and Nong dismounted, careful to not soil her frothy gown or silk slippers. She stopped and gazed back at the dramatic stage-like structure on the riverbank, where her fate would soon be sealed.

The magnificent ceremonial stage was a pyramidal wooden platform stacked three layers high, with steps on all sides. A creamy white canopy rippled overhead in the breeze. Maidens and spry grandmothers flitted about, covering every square inch with floral decorations.

Just behind the stage and floating on the river was the ornate honeymoon cottage. Resembling an enchanting magical abode in a faraway fantasyland, it sat atop pontoons and was tethered to posts thick as tree trunks. But Lew shivered to realize the stage and barge had also been created by enslaved artists, for an utterly foul purpose.

Uncle Inpanh, with his face grim as a mourner at a loved one's funeral, took Nong's hand to assist her as she stepped onto the barge. She then disappeared into the pink and white cottage bedecked with festive silk streamers and flower garlands, and closed the door.

"Now what, Boo?"

"Amaza tradition. She stays in there until the ceremony. Nobody can see her, especially the groom."

"Speaking of which, where *is* that bastard?"

Boo checked a nonexistent watch on his wrist. "Should arrive soon."

All momentum seemed to argue this impossible abomination would indeed go forward. Other than by murder, how could Lew stop it? Time was short and he needed help, information, anything. "Boo, can we talk to some of the workers?"

Boo pursed his lips, weighing the risks. *"Alamak,* sir! Okay, but just for the shortest time, before Mr. Elders—"

"Oh, screw Elders already!" But he knew Boo was right. "Hey. Sorry."

Boo shrugged.

They cut back through the forest to the factory site and secretly watched a young family working at the closest station—a father, his plump wife and a boy of about six, bare-chested in shorts and flip-flops. Looking diligent and totally consumed by their current tasks, they rubbed outer wooden surfaces smooth, using handfuls of sand, starting with coarser grit and proceeding to ever-finer grades.

Lew's heart sank. So *this* was the secret formula to achieve such perfection. Brute force applied over unlimited time! Not an artisanal technology unknown to the West.

He felt searing guilt and ached for this sweet family, seeing hands scarred and blistered, and wounds where hatchets or saws had gone astray. It crushed Lew to witness so innocent a child, trapped like that. Childhood was a time for joy and discovery.

An infant's sudden whimper drew the mother's attention toward a cradle hidden at the edge of the work station. Looking up, she then also spotted her surprising, partly-hidden observers just beyond the jungle edge. She smiled and waved them over, mostly staring at the large foreigner.

Boo laughed. "She can't believe seeing you, Khun Lew."

She offered them a cool drink from a beaten-up water jug.

"Please ask her to just take care of the baby, not us."

Boo relayed the message but the thirtyish woman shook her head. "No, she says it's her honor to host a Western visitor."

Boo chatted briefly with her. "The family has worked here about a year, sir. At first just the husband, but as the family fell deeper into debt, she soon followed, along with their son. A few months ago, she stopped only briefly, to deliver their little one."

Lew gazed at the lovely Madonna, an infant cooing in her arms, and his outrage exploded. "Boo, this is just too horrible for words. Surely not work for women, children nor even most men. Why would anyone put up with such conditions?"

The husband stopped sanding and joined them.

"He says, sir, there are simply no other choices. Nearly all property and businesses in Inner Amazia have now been looted by Khon and his partner so prices for everything have skyrocketed. Rents climbed so high that people needed extra money just for a place to sleep. Hard to pay even normal bills. When the opportunity came for extra money, working at night under lantern light at this factory, there was little other choice. Most residents were forced, one by one, to take employment here."

Lew fumed. If ever a man needed killing, it was Elders.

"But then things only got worse. When people and businesses fell further behind on their debt, Mr. Elders lent even more, at outrageous rates. So eventually, most became trapped and unable to *ever* repay their debt. No way out. So now, via cruel economic power, Elders now owns everything, all the region's businesses *and* the people."

"Christ Almighty." Lew studied the endless hive of work stations, in a jumble spilling off into the distance. Each contained a family like this one, lives crushed and hopes destroyed.

Boo sniffled. "And Khun Lew, soon our family logging camp business will go under. Then our family will be forced to work here, even me. And Nong, of course, will be lost."

Lew snorted. "Not if I can help it."

Boo's eyes brightened with a dash of hope. "Really, Boss, what can you—?"

With a quick gesture, Lew cut him off. Yes, this was all an outrage and had to be stopped, but face it: he was no murderer. And would the death of Elders (and Khon?) solve anything, or were other villains in line, ready to take over?

Once Lew met this devil and looked into his eyes, perhaps he could better assess things and an answer would emerge.

A thumping mechanical racket began to thunder at them. Boo

shouted through cupped hands, right up against Lew's ears. "Must be Elders' chopper from Ruangbang, landing in Biti."

"Sounds close."

"Well, it is. Only the next valley over."

"Sure felt farther away, on foot by jungle path," Lew said.

The deafening noise died away, only to be replaced by a second malevolent roar, a loud low growl that made camp workers cover their ears and jungle creatures scatter. Lew could feel it physically pound his stomach.

"The hell, Boo—motorcycles?"

"Sounds like it. Coming up the new road."

They scurried back to the wedding site and sat in two of the bamboo seats by the stage. Moments later, a trio of muscular custom three-wheeled motorcycles rolled into camp, magnificent Harley-Davidsons without mufflers, roaring like dinosaurs.

Each driver did a curving power skid and sprayed red dirt on the watching crowd. The engines switched off but Lew's ears continued to ring like he'd been front row at a rock concert.

Three cyclists and a helmeted passenger, riding pillion, all wore ear plugs. Two of the drivers were burly Asians in mirrored sunglasses and heads shaved like Odd Job from the Bond films. Wearing dark, ill-tailored suits and hard-toed boots, perfect for shit-kicking, they were clearly bodyguards. When one raised a hand to motion, his jacket slid aside and revealed a holstered automatic.

The passenger removed his helmet and revealed himself as Khon, appearing dapper and professional in a fresh suit and tie. Could Lew really trust the man? It felt they almost shared an understanding, almost a secret alliance.

But it was the last man of the four who riveted everyone's attention. Napoleon Elders, the diabolical businessman who controlled their destinies. Lew stared, drinking in the details. But how could this disheveled runt be the arch villain? He looked nothing like the impressive businessman that was expected.

He appeared grizzled and burned-out, maybe in his late fifties and dissipated after years of hard living. His haggard face was marred by various scars and his drinker's swollen nose squiggled with meandering burst capillaries.

Instead of an $8,000 suit, he wore denim and aviator sunglasses and his head was wrapped in a dirty blue bandanna from which dangled long strands of greasy hair. Tattoos covered his arms and piercings violated a cheek, an ear and a nostril.

Overall he looked repulsive, like a dissipated biker.

At one time he no doubt dressed in the expensive attire common to financial titans—he started out at a Singapore hedge fund, right? But now he was so powerful it now no longer mattered what anyone else thought. He made his own rules.

Looking humble, Khon made brief eye contact with Lew and shot a barely perceptible warning shake of the head. Hmm, so *that's* how they'd be playing this. As if they don't know each other. Okay.

Almost immediately, Elders spotted the out-of-place Westerner.

"Hey, guys," he shouted. "We got us a real wedding surprise here. A *farang!* Now ain't that a hoot. Maybe he can be my best man." Elders dissolved in laughter but the surly bodyguards just scowled.

Grinning wide, Elders ambled over and Lew's heart began to speed up. Stay calm and play it smart, he told himself. Just be quiet and listen. Don't escalate anything. Not yet.

"Hey there, buddy," Elders murmured, moving close. He needed a bath and smelled like bad cheese. "Don't see many white dudes around here. Like ever, actually."

Lew just smiled.

"Silent type, eh?" Elders looked amused. "Fine. Well here's my reading. Tell me if I got ya, dude! You're some kinda hippie bro on the drug trail, roaming around Asia. But mid-thirties? A little old for that."

Lew nodded and chuckled amiably. The bodyguards closed in to an arm's length away.

"Well, hombre, this seems to be your lucky day!" Elders

laughed. "You've wandered to here, the absolute ass-end of Asia, and on my frickin' wedding day!"

"Really?"

"Hell, yeah! And gonna be big fun. Plenty of party favors." Elders gave Lew a quick peek at the drugs stashed inside his leather zipper pouch. "I'm getting pretty good at these Asian wedding days, too. Musta already had a dozen by now." He laughed.

Lew tilted his head. "I guess I don't understand."

"Course you don't." Elders squeezed Lew's shoulder. "Hottest women in the world here, but from very traditional backgrounds. So to get 'em, sometimes you gotta marry 'em! You follow?"

Lew stayed quiet.

Elders sighed blissfully. "See, it's worth the effort to marry the bitches. Wait till you see the bride today, name is Pong or Bong or something, I forget. But who cares? She's the best one yet, even compared to dozens back home." Elders' scratched his stubbly chin. "But I'll bet a foreign overland traveler like you gets a lot of local poontang, no?"

Lew just shrugged and kept listening, hoping for something—anything!—useful to reveal itself. Elders appeared delighted by his unexpected audience and clapped his hands. "Hey, Arthit, get over here!" Khon trotted over, avoiding eye contact with Lew.

"Arthit, fetch us a bottle. The good stuff. Ice and glasses, chop-chop." Lew noticed he used Khon's real name.

"Yes, sir," replied Khon, a study in humility. He continued to carefully ignore Lew, who returned the indifference.

"Brilliant fella, that Arthit. Reliable, too. My right-hand man." Elders pulled Lew closer. "Catch that Texas pigment map on the poor mofo's cheek? Nope, I didn't tattoo it there. Ha! But first time I saw it, I knew it was a sign. You see, I'm originally from Texas."

"Oh. I see."

"Arthit knows Amazia inside out, just every fucking thing possible. He runs businesses for me here, and elsewhere. Would you believe his family lives on my estate in northern Thailand?"

Lew kept his face blank. "Generous employer?"

Liquor, glasses and ice appeared. Elders poured Blue Label right up to the rims.

"So anyhoo, here's to my newest bride." Elders raised his glass. "And to my next honeymoon, coming up real soon!" He leered theatrically at the floating cottage and clinked Lew's glass, draining his own. Lew took a modest sip and set his down.

Elders stared at Lew's glass like a turd on the dinner table. "Aw, come on, dude. Drink up! Don't go insulting my bride like that, not on her wedding day." He smiled but his voice had a clear edge. "Go on now, kill that." It was unmistakably a command. And alerted by his tone, the two bodyguards eased closer.

Lew gulped it down and shivered from the alcohol bomb. Smooth but fiery and way too much, too fast. As soon as he set the glass down, Elders refilled it.

Had to slow this down, keep the man talking. "So, mister, what'd you say your name was?"

The greasy degenerate smiled and flashed a mouthful of golden crowns and bridges. "It's Elders, Napoleon. But just make it *Nap*. How about you?"

"You can call me Lew." Something told him to retain some anonymity, for now. He changed the subject. "But those three-wheelers? Absolute freakin' monsters, musta really set you back."

Elders shrugged with evident false modesty. "Just north of $350k apiece, that's all."

Lew whistled low. Christ, a million bucks for three bikes?

"Total custom jobs, first class for everything. Largest engines, fastest transmissions, best suspensions, wheels. Luxury all the way. Flew 'em here from the States." Elders moved his chair closer. "And their cousins are stationed all across Asia, waiting for me in Chiang Mai, Singapore, KL and Shanghai."

"Wow."

"Listen, honestly, that kind of expense is nothing for me. I could wipe my ass with thousand dollar bills, amigo, but I hear they're scratchy." Elders howled at his own joke. Lew smiled. Just let the asshole talk. Another round was poured. Elders went full strength again but Lew was quick enough to dilute his.

"Been here in Asia more'n three decades, Lew, and in that time, I've seen and done things that would blow your mind. Not bragging, just being real." The man searched Lew's eyes.

Lew nodded, sipping. "I'll bet." Looking away, he caught Khon's eye for a moment and decoded a warning. *Be careful!*

Elders lit a cigarette and blew the smoke skyward. "Just a pup when I started out at that Singapore hedge fund, but soon realized I could do better on my own. Took me years, but I've now got an absolute empire and live like a king. Armies of servants and employees at a dozen palaces across the region. I own a shitload of companies, private jets, helicopters."

Lew studied the face of pure greed.

"I'm on first-name basis with every generalissimo or dictator in Asia! When I pick up the phone, kings and presidents all jump."

"Quite successful," Lew offered.

Elders scoffed. "Successful? Ha! *Successful* was twenty years ago. Way beyond that now. More like a god."

Lew raised his eyebrows. "Well surely that's going a bit too far, no?"

"Not really." Elders lit another cigarette and smiled. "After all, who but a god decides life or death? Look, I get it. You can't understand my situation, yet. All my power. After all, you're just another vagabond doper, some rootless failure." Elders hovered close and his bloodshot eyes peered into Lew's. "Not judging! But here's the truth: in your life, you've never before met anyone like me."

That was for sure.

"And just like a god, Lew, I *do* exercise absolute power. My every desire is instantly gratified. Personal harems at all my homes. The world's most beautiful women attend to me." Lust glowed in Elders' eyes. "Sometimes it feels like I could command the sun to rise or set."

Anger bubbling inside Lew threatened to explode, but he somehow reined it in and just let the blowhard pontificate. "That's incredible, Mr. Elders."

"*Nap*, remember?"

"So, presumably, you must be some kind of business genius?"

Elders' ugly face melted in crude laughter. "Not really, but I do have a secret. If you take it to heart, it may not be too late for you."

If only you knew, you stinking bag of manure.

"You see, nobody out here stands a chance against me."

"And why is that?"

"I'll show you." He waved Khon over, whispered something and a moment later, Khon returned with a bowl of peanuts. "Now watch carefully."

Elders tossed a peanut to the ground, several feet away. A delicate yellow bird flitted down from the rafters to snatch it up and Elders smiled. *"Tik–tik-deet!"* it chirped, seeming delighted. Elders dropped a second nut, this time closer to his feet, and the same bird hopped over to again retrieve the nut. *"Tik–tik-deet!"*

Elders next stretched his arm out far, a third nut in his palm. And again, the same result. His face broke into a broad, nearly joyful smile. "Now, still watching?"

Lew nodded.

He held out a fourth nut in cupped hands, just inches from his chest. The little bird fluttered down and alighted. Elders instantly clapped his hands together, crushing the tiny creature like a paper bag, with a small *pop!* He opened his hands to reveal smashed feathers, a flattened carcass and the peanut.

"Works every time," he laughed, searching Lew's face for comprehension. "Get it?"

Lew just frowned. Stunned.

"People here are like that little bird, innocent and too trusting. If you are ruthless enough, they simply never have a chance." The man's limitless, unfeeling cruelty sent shivers through Lew.

Elders straightened his bandanna and combed greasy locks of

hair with his fingers, leaving behind bits of yellow feathers. "Maybe this'll help. Ever play football as a kid?"

"Sure." Now where was he going?

"Tackle or touch?"

"Both."

"Well, what would happen if one team played full-on tackle, while the other just played touch?"

"Tackle team would demolish them."

Elders nodded. "Exactly! Every time. Fuck 'em up real good! And that's regardless of either team's skill, size or speed. Tackle would always demolish touch."

"And your point is . . .?"

Elders' face soured. "You're a little dense, eh Lew? See, people everywhere constrain themselves, but especially here. Call it morality or ethics, their self-imposed rules set down harsh limits. Not free to do all they could."

"Whereas you, on the other hand, are completely unconstrained."

"Bingo!" Elders grinned like a teacher pleased by his prize pupil. "Like Sean Connery in that old *Untouchables* movie. When I go to knife fights, I always bring a gun." Elders made a pistol with his hand and fired it at Lew.

"Nothing ever out-of-bounds?"

"Never. Do *whatever* is needed to win, always. Imagine how well that plays in a place full of sweet people bound up by silly rules. My victories are always inevitable. Just a matter of time."

Having digested that, Lew was now certain: this man was pure evil. Like Lucifer himself.

Elders rambled on, his tongue lubricated by alcohol. "Consider today. To score such a prime piece of ass, I'll have to 'marry' the bitch. So I just do it. Means nothing. Just another way to export some prima pussy back to my estate."

Lew growled under his breath. "But she'll be your wife, right? At least *one* of them?"

Elders looked at Lew like he was crazy. "Haven't you been listening? No, knucklehead, she'll just be another whore or concubine or whatever they call it. But my wife? Please."

"No rules."

"Correct. Never. None whatsoever."

Everything made perfect sense. Elders was *precisely* the type of uncaring businessman who, in pursuit of a huge payday, would have not hesitated to unleash that spirit plague across North America.

But to vanquish such evil, must one play by the same twisted rules—total reciprocation, unconstrained by ethics? Should Lew, that moment, just reach out and choke the bastard? He wrestled with the question and the idea made him shudder, violating the moral code that defined him. Anyway, with Elders' burly security detail hovering nearby and packing heat, Lew would probably be dead before his thumbs could begin pressing into Elders' windpipe.

Factory workers began to assemble in front of the stage. Lew continued to secretly spill drinks at his feet, fighting to stay sober, though Elders already appeared too buzzed to notice. He leaned over and wrapped an arm around Lew's shoulders.

"Know what, Lew? I *like* you." Elders was badly slurring his words and fumbled trying to light a cigar. "Kinda remind me of myself, when I was younger."

Good Lord, I hope not.

"Hey, betcha I could use a sharp young fella like you." Elders' pupils were unfocused black pools, hovering above a goofy grin. "Partner in training, maybe? You'd learn lotsa valuable stuff, working under me."

Lew answered with a noncommittal grunt.

"Said you're American, right?" *Murr-i-kan*, it sounded like.

"Yeah. *Murr-i-kan*." The mocking slight didn't register. "From New York, but my company is in Jersey."

Elders looked knocked off balance. "*Your* company? Whaddya

mean?"

Though alcohol surely swayed Lew's judgment, this felt like a cue. Time to act. He had no better idea than to play a longshot, now, and confront this greedy businessman. As his father used to say, *if you never ask, you never know.* So he stuck out a hand, grabbed Elders' filthy paw and firmly shook it.

"Yeah, *my* company: Avian Products. Your sole distributor in North America. I'm Lew Clarke. That name ring any bells?"

Looking confused, Elders scowled at the suddenly talkative young man.

"Anyway, Elders, you're a hard man to find! I've been tracking you a while."

Elders looked dazed and although seated, seemed to visibly stumble. "What? Clarke?" He rubbed sweaty palms on his forehead and stared back while Lew pushed ahead.

"I've traveled here to insist Lotus Exports do the honorable thing. We are getting our asses sued off, back in the U.S., due to your shoddy business practices, selling dangerous products under false pretenses. Your lawn ornaments are actually spirit houses, causing horrible outcomes."

Elders breathed heavily, flushing crimson. His eyes darted to and fro and a fresh coat of perspiration beaded his forehead.

"Helluva story," Elders said, suddenly smiling. He peered into Lew's eyes. "So exactly what the fuck do you want?"

Adrenaline surged in Lew and his voice grew strong. "Absolute financial back-up. Lotus must refund our entire prepayment and take full responsibility for any future legal judgments."

Elders grinned like that was the world's funniest joke. Then he jumped up and threw down his glass at Lew's feet, shattering it. "This some kind of joke?" Smiling, he drained the last of the bottle.

Lew boiled inside but still projected calm. "It's no joke. What I am proposing is essentially your only moral way forward."

Elders now seemed to have entirely regained his bearings after Lew's surprise attack. "Clarke, didn't you hear a single word of what

I was saying? You must be some kind of fucking idiot. What kind of fool do you take me for?"

It was clear a businesslike solution was out of the question.

Lew was down to his final option. Unable to save himself or his company, could he at least strike a blow for Nong, her family or the enslaved workers of Inner Amazia? It was now or never.

He jumped to his feet, snatched the empty whiskey bottle and slammed it against a canopy support pole. The neck broke off, leaving shards that transformed it into a deadly weapon that he waggled threateningly.

"What kind of fool? The kind, Elders, that deserves to die."

But before Lew could attack, much less even move forward, Elders' two powerful bodyguards pounced and, in a flash, grabbed him from behind, pinning his arms. The jagged bottle dropped harmlessly to the dirt.

While they restrained him, Elders launched a knee into Lew's groin. He collapsed to the ground and curled up in pain. All three worked him over with fists and steel-toed boots until he lost consciousness.

When Lew came to, later, he found himself alone and secured to a tree, bound and gagged with a clear view of the ceremonial platform and honeymoon barge. The crowd milled about and cast sympathetic glances his way.

Well, so much for *that* weak-assed plan. What was he thinking? He was a tech geek, not some Navy SEAL fighter or martial arts black belt. Perhaps he should have moved earlier to kill the guy, while he still had the element of surprise. No talk, just action? But now it was too late.

So much for the Hollywood action movie ending. He'd botched everything, so now the marriage ceremony could begin. And he was completely at Elders' mercy, something surely in short supply.

CHAPTER TWENTY-NINE
Intervention

The jungle air was thick with incense as beautiful damsels tossed pink and white flower petals around the stage. They fluttered down like snowflakes and settled in small heaps. Tiny green lizards skittered and darted about while brilliant-colored tropical birds pecked at seeds.

The muffled thumping of drums began, along with the low clanging of gongs. At that signal a dozen garlanded elephants began to parade into the ceremonial grounds, trudging forward and leading a procession of monks and musicians. A choral melody arose from the hundreds of assembled workers, accompanied by percussive instruments.

For so damnable an occasion, it was a heavenly backdrop. But Elders, already bored by the pageantry, began snorting lines of cocaine off trimmed banana leaves along with his bodyguards. He occasionally dispatched them into the crowd to retrieve unlucky targets to briefly molest, only to then dismiss moments later. Lew read his sick actions more as displays of power than lust.

Stumbling and intoxicated, Elders and his men mounted motorcycles to engage in some drunken horseplay. The mahouts, worried their elephants might be provoked or worse, stampeded, yelled out warnings but were ignored.

The assertive rumble of engines drowned out the music as they zoomed around the pachyderms, spinning wheelies on the dirt. Elders finally tired of this foolishness, parked his bike under a tree and went back onto the stage. His men, as if to profane the sanctified wedding platform itself, drove straight up the steps and parked on the ceremonial stage.

"Whoo-eeee!" Elders whooped, loving that and pumping a fist at the shocked crowd.

Lew was gagged by a rag stuffed into his mouth and strained against his bonds. Powerless and securely anchored to a tree, and having already failed in most every regard, he watched the nightmare play out. Surely all was lost. Why did the heavens allow such horror? And soon, Elders would surely have him killed, to erase an unnecessary complication.

At a flick of Elders' wrist, the ceremony and sweet choral harmonies resumed. Atop the honeymoon barge, Khon pulled open the bamboo door and Nong emerged. She stood there momentarily and took in the extravaganza.

Despite pain oozing from his every fiber, Lew was overwhelmed by her sadness and beauty. He now knew with certainty she was all that mattered in his life, yet he was powerless to help.

When the bride spotted Lew, beaten to a bloody pulp and tethered to a tree, she shrieked in Amaza, "*Oh no! My love!*" Her emotion infuriated Elders, who scowled at Lew and drew a dagger line across his neck.

The embodiment of grace, Nong glided across the barge and stepped onshore. Then with cheeks shiny from tears, she ascended the tiered platform.

Elders swaggered over, smoking a cigar and clutching a can of Beer Lao, laughing and coarsely joking with his men. The bridal couple moved to altar center stage, surrounded by ritualistic dancers who moved sensually to the beating drums.

Monks carrying lit candles were next to file on. All music ceased when they sat down pads across the back of the stage. The crowd then also sat and a wonderful, absolute silence prevailed. The deep quiet was broken only by stray tropical bird songs or, occasionally, Elders' gruff voice. The orange-robed monks began to chant a monotonous, almost hypnotic melody, evidently a holy prayer in some ancient language. It droned on for ten minutes, seeking blessings for the impending nuptials as audience members prayed, dozed or meditated.

The entire time, the bride made pitiful, beseeching eye contact with Lew, in a tortured plea for help. But he was powerless to help and easily foresaw how this would end. He would be forced to watch Nong's defilement and then himself be killed.

In the crowd, many eyes glistened, but wet with rage or fear, not the usual happy wedding emotions.

After the monks finished chanting, several girls sprinkled flower petals on the nuptial couple. Nong wept while Elders, oblivious, wrapped an arm around her back, his hand wandering. A withered monk rubbed balm on their foreheads and dipped a frond of palm leaves into a bucket to sprinkle holy water on the couple.

Elders, looking bored, scratched his crotch.

A white silk sheet was then stretched tight above the bride and groom and large candles were lit. Finally, the elderly monk struck a large gong three times and the low booming triggered a mournful groan from the crowd. The old monk sighed, turned and abruptly walked away.

Nong sobbed quietly, her head buried in the crook of her arm, her breast rising and falling. Elders, on the other hand, roared with delight. He nodded his head and raised fists into the air like a victorious boxer, waggling his bandanna-covered head before launching into a profane, hip-thrusting dance around the stage. His thugs pounded him on the back and offered congratulations amid shots of whiskey.

Lew didn't know Amazia religious ceremonies, but he certainly recognized a man in celebration. The deed was done. Nong had been stolen. And Elders, legally married, had just added a trophy concubine to one of his harems.

Women singing like heavenly nymphs escorted Nong back onto the honeymoon barge. Elders turned to stare across the field at

Lew with a taunting grin. Laughing, he grabbed at his crotch and then rubbed his hands in anticipation, like a cheap movie villain.

He waved over at his lieutenant and, pointing at Lew, issuing instructions. Khon nodded and, face grim, walked over to the captive. He removed Lew's gag. "Careful, Mr. Clarke," he muttered, "Mr. Elders is watching. But I'm so sorry."

"This whole thing is disgusting, Khon. An outrageous farce! What's happening now?"

Khon sniffed, his face dark. "The bride is readying herself, Mr. Clarke, to consummate the marriage."

That hit Lew like a body blow. "What? You mean right away? Now, on that barge?"

Khon nodded. "And it is also my unpleasant duty to advise that Mr. Elders plans to deal with you soon, sir. Right after, uh, his honeymoon."

Lew understood. His death. "Khon, you've gotta help me. It's in your own best interest, too. Then I could also help you."

Khon heaved a sigh and looked helpless. A single tear trickled across the map of India. "If only I could, Mr. Clarke. Truly, I want to. But Mr. Elders is in command. I can't risk crossing him."

Lew shrugged. "Yes, I remember. Your daughter, Lek, and your family. Hostages."

Khon nodded.

"So now we just wait?"

"Yes."

Khon squatted beside the tree where Lew was bound. They watched Elders jump aboard the honeymoon barge, a spring in his step. His bodyguards trailed and stopped at the riverbank, where they turned and scowled ferociously with crossed arms, standing guard over the floating pleasure cottage.

In less than ten minutes, the cottage door burst open and Elders stormed out, leering and making a show of zipping his jeans and straightening his bandanna, mugging shamelessly like a high school boy after scoring his first bottle of liquor.

His braggadocio made clear the demon had indeed defiled Nong. At least Lew's beloved had already gifted her virginity to him, her first, as if that was any real consolation.

Grinning cruelly, Elders stared over and made a gun with his hand, firing it at Lew. He jumped down from the marital barge and jogged back onto the wedding platform with his two thugs trailing and waved for Khon to bring Lew on stage.

"I'm sorry Mr. Clarke, but your time has come," Khon said. Apparently Lew was to be executed on the same sacred platform. "It's probably no great comfort, but my fate is likely to be the same once Mr. Elders learns of our private conversations. It's inevitable. There are no secrets here."

Khon began untying the tough, thin vines lashing Lew to the tree, but was stopped cold by a loud, puzzling noise that began to issue from the river. It was a mysterious hiss that steadily gained in volume and seemed to be generated by the strange, foamy base building underneath and elevating the wedding barge. Though secured to thick logs driven deep into the river bank, the barge rose and rocked, side to side.

"Hey, Khon!" Lew pressed against his bonds. "Nong is still on that thing! Somebody has to —"

But from just inches away, Khon could not hear him amid all this noise. Already white with shock, he held hands to his ears against the deafening roar. Elders and his bodyguards, watched from onstage, befuddled and frozen in wonderment.

The honeymoon cottage soon elevated atop a foot-thick bed of creamy foam and broke free from its mooring, snapping the logs like toothpicks. It processed out onto the water at a stately pace, moving contrary to the current, until stopped still at mid-river, like it was anchored. The hissing racket suddenly, like a cosmic mute button had just been pushed.

"Hey!" Elders yelled, pointing at the barge, "my new wife's on that fucking thing!" He ordered his men to fetch Nong but looking terrified, they didn't budge. Raging and frustrated, Elders hollered for Khon to return onstage.

"I'll leave only your wrists tied," Khon told Lew with imploring eyes. "But please don't get me into more trouble. If I can't trust you, just tell me now, and I'll refasten your other bonds."

"You have my word," Lew said, stunned. "Going nowhere. I'm riveted here with fear, anyway."

The moment Khon departed, a hand abruptly dropped onto Lew's shoulder. Someone hiding behind the tree and had reached around. "It's just me, sir," came Boo's familiar voice. "But don't turn. I'm pretty well hidden."

Thank God—help at last. "What the hell, Boo? The foaming and hissing barge tricks, is that kind of stuff normal here in Amazia? Sure ain't back in New Jersey." Lew forced a grin.

"No, *lah.* But we'll weather it together, sir." He squeezed Lew's shoulder.

Grayish-black clouds began to swirl overhead, flowing and churning in a murk like film running at high speed, with electrical discharges flickering at random. The day—sunny and bright just minutes earlier—had gone dusky and cool. Winds whipped the jungle canopy, making Lew shiver in the instant chill. Heavy branches swayed, cracked and thudded to the ground.

In a bizarre display that seemed impossible and hallucinatory at best, vines as thick as anacondas began to slither up onto the stage, creeping in from all sides to close on Elders and his bodyguards, who howled in pure fear. A frightened murmur also erupted from the audience, frozen in place by the spectacle. The assaulting greenery wriggled its way around the men's ankles and curled up their legs, writhing crotch-high and then grasping tight, immobilizing the trio.

Paralyzed by fear, the men cowered and cried out to the heavens for mercy, imploring for help as tears streamed down their grubby faces.

Khon, for his part, stood at a back corner of the stage and appeared dazed, but thus far not targeted.

Lew felt himself drowning in cold anxiety and had trouble breathing. What was going on? This was all beyond comprehension, like being trapped inside the terrifying finale of a Spielberg movie. Even more troubling was that his beloved soul mate remained trapped out there on the river, her fate unclear.

Boo suddenly shrieked. "Chief, look!"

An apparent mass of slow-moving goo—sluggish and brown like maple syrup—began to ooze up onto the stage from the jungle floor and creep toward the captives. Whatever the weird stuff was, its flow defied gravity. It began to coat the bodyguard on the far end, climbing up his calves, knees and beyond, while the man wriggled and howled.

Elders and the other bodyguard, both untouched, watched close-up in rapt horror.

"What *is* that slimy stuff, Boo?"

"Not sure, chief." The youth stared hard until his eyes popped wide. "Holy Buddha! Khun Lew, it's a sea of ants. Millions."

The countless insects were conjoined into a horrific, throbbing, ravenous mass that began eating away at the man. His form steadily shrank on down until, after several minutes, not a morsel of flesh was left. The nightmarish living ooze then slowly retreated, flowing off the stage and back into the ground.

Was that it? Horror show already over? Not so fast.

The second act soon began, one even more revolting than the first, launched when an endless mob of brown long-tailed jungle rats began to mount the stage from all directions. The crowd cried out in disgust and concern. The rodents circled—sniffing, snapping and tumbling over each other—while Elders and the other man yelled wildly to frighten them away. But the rat army, now maybe a thousand strong, were undeterred and filled the stage.

At last, a leader made the instigating move, a remarkable leap from the floor up onto the head of the second bodyguard. That, like a signal, triggered the rest to immediately attack. They streamed in and piled onto the poor man.

Elders, just a foot away yet untouched, watched the horrible carnage from close range. The rats scrambled, bit and gnawed upon every inch of their victim, transforming him into what resembled a writhing, screaming brown creature that eventually went limp. In only minutes, the feasting animals finished him off and, like the ants before, left not even a bone. After licking the stage clean of pooling blood, the creatures scampered back into the jungle.

Elders, still bound by his viney green manacles, looked horrified but also relieved to have survived. Watching from afar, Lew wondered why the wretched villain had been spared.

A frail little yellow bird fluttered down from overhead and landed onstage, at Elders' feet. The tiny creature sounded out its charming call, one Lew perhaps recalled but wasn't sure. *"Tik–tik-deet! Tik-tik-deet!"* it chirped. A warm chuckle rose from the crowd, clearly welcoming a return to normalcy.

A second tiny yellow bird—of the same breed—then oddly flitted down from the forest canopy to join the first, immediately followed by a third, fourth and then a fifth. Their delightful, high-pitched calls of *"Tik-tik-deet"* intermingled and bounced off trees and summoned even more of their flock.

The wee creatures began to arrive by the dozens and soon, as if avian floodgates had been opened, by the hundreds, a yellow swarm stampeding. Their calls at first had been sweet, when singular, but now combined into a shrill roar that grew louder and harsher by the second. Before long, the stage undulated with thousands of the yellow birds surrounding the stunned Elders, stiff with fear and hardly breathing.

At last, a single bird fluttered onto Elders' shoulder.

That was all it took.

Like a starter's pistol having been fired, myriad other birds followed suit, in the blink of an eye. Amid their ear-piercing group cry and the growling thunder of flapping wings, they attacked.

Loose feathers fluttered through the air. The Big Boss, trapped inside the gyrating yellow mass, began to melt away under the assault of the countless minute beaks that pecked away at him. His shape grew ever smaller until finally nothing remained, not even bone. The meal concluded, the yellow horde then departed, cheerfully flitting away through a hole in the jungle canopy.

What had just happened? Lew wondered how any of that could have been real, like Biblical vengeance being meted out by an angry, Old Testament-style God. Hollywood all the way. The impossible visions left Lew overwhelmed and numb, his brain refusing to work. His pupils were dilated, as if under hypnosis.

For his part, Boo seemed more lucid. "Oh, look, sir. There in the far corner, Khon is still okay."

Daylight returned and the air warmed again to its usual temperature. Jungle creatures resumed their frolicking as a wave of nervous laughter rippled across the crowd. At mid-river, the honeymoon barge began to slowly glide back to shore, still riding its bed of foam, and settled back at the original docking location.

Nong stuck her head out the cottage door, wearing an expression mixing terror with bewilderment. Lew tore free from his remaining bonds, sprinted across the field and jumped onto the barge to take her into his arms and hold her tightly, his heart racing.

"Nong, my darling! I don't know how or why, but you're safe." He kissed her forehead, a tear streaming down his own cheek. She remained silent, appearing in absolute shock. Her eyes were squeezed closed and face buried hard into his chest as Lew carefully guided her ashore amid delirious cheers from the crowd.

Hardly able to think straight, Lew could not comprehend what had just transpired, except for one undeniable truth: Nong had been safe all along. Whatever all that chaos was, she was never a target.

Khon approached, looking oddly perturbed for a man who'd just cheated death. "Mr. Clarke, I'm sorry, but I must immediately depart. It's crucial."

"Where to?"

"I will explain later. Please trust me."

Were that man's promises worth *anything*? Unable to force him to stay, anyway, Lew relented. "Okay, Khon, but stay in touch. Remember, I may still need your help."

He returned Lew's nod and sprinted over to Elders' three-wheeled Harley parked under a tree next to the stage. He turned the key, still in the ignition, and a sudden ear-splitting racket made everyone cringe. Shrugging an apology, he fed it some gas and rumbled off.

"That a good idea, boss, just letting him go like that?" Boo looked unconvinced.

"Don't know, Boo. But my sense is he's probably not so bad, just way in over his head, with real bad company. Not even his choice. With Elders now out of the picture, perhaps he can help us."

"Or not." Boo shrugged but then motioned toward the stage and barge. "But all that weird stuff just now . . . a lot to digest, eh?"

"I'll say." Yikes. If this day's dramatics were even difficult to process for a native Amaza, raised in the Kingdom's mystical ways, how could a Westerner like Lew even begin?

The Wedding Poltergeist.

That's how he began thinking of it over subsequent days, as memories replayed and knotted up his mind.

A wary mood settled in across all of Inner Amazia, driven more by practical than metaphysical concerns. As Boo explained, with the sudden demise of the region's primary employer, a deep fear spread that the local economy might collapse altogether. Fears swamped the population that all the businesses owned by Elders might now just disappear, along with their jobs and incomes. How would anyone put food on the table?

"You kidding me?" Lew challenged. "That's nonsense."

"It's quite real, sir." Boo's face was serious. "And please, try again to remember where you are, that there is so much you really cannot understand. At least, not yet."

Equally perplexing to Lew were all their concerns about the debt broadly owed to Elders by nearly everyone. To the righteous Amaza, the scoundrel's demise did nothing to diminish rock-hard ethical constraints that bound them all, forbidding debtors from just walking away from obligations. Core moral tenets governed all that was right and ethical and still held them all to their debts.

Lew continued lodging at the monastery during this strange period and traveled daily to the family house to soothe Nong, imprisoned in the throes of a deep depression.

One morning she finally displayed hints of an appetite, but with eyes still glazed like dark pools. He hugged her and was rewarded by a weak smile in return. She nibbled a few spoons of white rice and sipped warm black tea as he softly massaged her shoulders.

That moment brought a great awakening for Lew. All became blindingly clear. His love for Nong utterly consumed him. She owned his very soul and defined his entire existence, making her well-being his only priority. Nothing else mattered.

And the corollary was that, beyond all doubt, he would *never* leave Amazia. All meaning and fulfillment for him resided there; all other concerns, from elsewhere, faded in importance.

His lips brushed against her hair and he breathed words into her ear. "Dearest one, I love you and will stay here with you forever. My home is here, now and always." He trusted she comprehended his tone and intent, if not words.

But remnants of dread lingered on her face, reminding Lew that, as shocking and disorienting as the Wedding Poltergeist had been for them all, no one suffered that day as much as Nong.

A small voice wheezed out her first words in a soft monotone, directed toward Boo, whose face reddened. "Boss, um, my cousin wants me to tell you she loves you. More than life itself." Then Boo's face fell. "But she fears you can never really love her. Not anymore."

Such nonsense. Why would she say that?

"Boo, tell her she's as perfect as any angel in the heavens. And that I adore her."

Frowning, Boo shrugged sheepishly. "It's because of that marriage. It truly did happen. She actually did marry Elders. So now she's his widow. And confirms, to her great shame, the marriage was indeed consummated in that cottage. She fears that will always linger at the back of your mind. So you can never *really* love her."

His poor, darling Nong! He burned with a new, white-hot rage at the dead man, only taking solace in knowing Elders already received far worse punishment than Lew could have ever meted out.

He hugged Nong, unable to let go. "Boo, tell her none of that matters, not one bit. She was a victim but her nightmare is over. As my fragrant flower, she will stay with me forever, right here in Amazia. That is, if she'll have me."

"What, ho! So you *are* staying?" Boo's eyebrows danced.

Lew continued. "And to make it perfectly clear, tell her I want to marry her. When she feels better and is ready. I am proposing."

Boo's eyes popped comically wide. "*Aduh!* You serious, chief?"

"Absolutely. Tell her."

Boo chuckled in disbelief, shaking his head. "How can, *lah*? My boss becoming my new *matsalleh* brother-in-law?" He turned to Nong and translated.

Trickles of joy streamed down her cheeks and a smile stole across her face. Amid her emotions that were still a complex tangle, happiness had clearly taken root. She looked into Lew's eyes and touched a hand to her heart. "Love, Khun Lew," she whispered.

Boo's mother ushered her niece away for more rest and directed the men to the kitchen, urging them to eat.

There, Lew settled into his own thoughts. Her pain grieved him. How cruel was this universe, where one as pure and innocent as Nong could be so victimized.

***

Lew and Boo crouched at the low table with Thant and Uncle Inpanh. Boo's mother stuffed them with a tasty lunch of fried rice and curried fish, fresh-caught from the Mobiti River, with a banana and mango salad dessert. Inpanh raised his head and muttered something, pointing his chin at Lew.

Boo smirked. "Sir, my uncle heard a rumor you want to be his son-in-law."

This being just moments after his private discussion with Nong, Lew was caught well off guard. "Well thanks for keeping my secret, Translator Boo."

"Secret?" Boo blushed. "I didn't know."

Lew nodded at Inpanh. "Tell him it's true. I totally love his daughter and—"

Inpanh impatiently waved a hand to cut Lew off, not waiting for a translation. The old man rattled on and. Lew waited patiently for a translation.

"He has no objection to such a marriage. In fact, he says you may make a decent catch—even for a *farang*." Boo winked. "But planning a wedding is the last thing on anyone's mind right now. Weightier problems to solve first."

Lew nodded. "Fair enough. I'm listening."

"First off, they ask, you are supposedly some kind of Western business hotshot, right?"

"Yeah, but that feels a lifetime ago. It's a little embarrassing actually, but the bosses at Mega used to call me their 'new young Edison of tech.'" Lew blushed.

The Edison reference was lost on the Amaza, but the old men still smiled upon hearing Boo's translation.

"Well, Khun Lew, the Inner Amazia elders need help sorting out the post-Elders economic mess. No one quite knows where to start."

Fair enough. "My honor, Boo." Lew rubbed his hands. "But

rather than just give advice, I would want to formally partner with this community. After all, I plan to permanently reside here with Nong, so I have a huge vested interest in Inner Amazia."

Boo translated the news of the proposed partnership, causing the old men to burst into joyful smiles. Laughing and talking loud, they jumped to their feet. Inpanh ran to fetch glasses while Thant opened a rickety family cupboard and pulled out that familiar gray porcelain jug. He popped the cork.

"Oh, no," groaned Lew, laughing. "It's hardly past noon. And next it'll be those foul cigars, like smoking a piece of rope."

The Amaza men grinned at Lew's good-natured apprehension. Uncle Inpanh looked warmly into Lew's eyes. "*Cel-e-brate*?" he said, appearing uncertain about the English word.

Ignoring Lew's friendly grousing, the old men hoisted him to his feet and guided him outside to a pair of canvas hammocks hanging under a thicket of trees. The temperature plunged refreshingly when they passed into the shade.

As always, several minutes were consumed lighting cigars and pouring drinks, but soon all lay back, side by side in the wide hammocks. Bathed in cool, damp air and the rich fragrance of tropical flowers, they surrendered to utter relaxation.

Finally, Lew spoke. "Boo, as Amazia's partner going forward, I need better information."

"Anything, boss. That's why we're here."

"I've got questions, both for you and the elders. For instance, that otherworldly scene at the wedding the other day, I mean, that was a total *mind-fuck*."

Boo laughed abruptly, snorting up some whiskey. "Not an expression we use here. But I completely understand."

"But right now, it seems you Amaza are way more concerned over mundane consequences—jobs, debts, all that—than the utter existential implications raised by that horror show. As for me, my bearings were totally shaken and I'm still struggling to recover my grip on reality, much less understand what happened."

"Hmm." Boo nodded. "Go on."

"You always like to say, *Khun Lew, don't think so much!* Well I've been trying to follow that advice but it seems high time to confront facts and stop hiding from the truth."

Boo relayed that to Thant and Inpanh, who discussed it animatedly while Lew waited and sipped his rotgut. He puffed on his cheroot and aimed a stream of smoke at a silver gecko on a tree limb. It flitted away.

Boo smiled. "Sir, to summarize. Yes, they agree that at the time, those events were very frightening. Shocking! But now, looking back, we all realize it should have been no surprise. Something that could have been anticipated."

Lew squinted in disbelief. "Jeez, how could a total freak show like that ever be, even in retrospect, *no surprise*? That was some scary, Stephen King horror type shit! I still get chills."

Boo sighed like an instructor having to reteach a lesson.

"Consider the facts, sir. That whole area was consecrated ground, sanctified for a religious ceremony. A holy place which Mr. Elders and his men profaned, right? Racing their noisy motorcycles through there, roaring and popping wheelies. Taking drugs, getting drunk, and even molesting local women on the anointed altar platform."

Boo drew in a deep breath.

"So, looking back, what eventually happened was as predictable as gravity. Offended, the local terrestrial spirits exacted retribution. Elders and his men only got what they deserved."

Terrestrial spirits . . . again? Okay, now *that* came as a surprise. "So this was the work of local spirits?"

Boo's face telegraphed frustration there was any doubt. "Well, of course, chief! Who else, *lah?* They were defending their own interests, with plenty of coincidental benefit for us Amaza, with whom they peacefully coexist."

Spirits? All that caught Lew by surprise. He felt stunned and a bit numb, even lacking the appropriate vocabulary to further discuss the matter. His Western hubris had essentially blinded him for more than a year, with serious consequences.

Boo continued. "So anyway, our people are now free but penniless. The local economy has fallen off a cliff, but all previous debts and obligations still hang in the balance. There are no jobs, no money, and nobody knows what to do about it."

Feeling humbled yet enlightened, Lew's mood rose. He swung his feet down from the hammock and stood, concerns burning away like morning mist in the sunlight. He laughed and embraced the three Amaza in a group hug.

"Friends, problems such as these are things this *farang* well understands. We can certainly fix this. One hundred percent! While I make my new home here with Nong, helping Inner Amazia solve its economic woes will satisfy my business genes."

Boo translated and the old men cheered.

"Wonderful, sir! And exactly how will we achieve all that?"

Lew smiled. "Good question." False modesty aside, he knew he could, just not yet how.

The following morning at the monastery, Lew carried on an amusing (mostly mimed) conversation with the young monks. The strength of their belief in terrestrial spirits surprised him, how much such entities were considered a given by the Amaza, just a routine aspect of everyday life.

As a result, the young monks (like Boo's family) were already quite blasé about the circumstances of Elders' death, considering them unfortunate but quite predictable. No longer of any concern. What else would anyone have expected?

Lew shook his head. His Western biases, or arrogance, had created a blind spot in him a mile wide. He had a lot to learn.

He wondered what else he was still missing.

A small hand tugged at his shirt sleeve. He turned to face a small child, all sinew and bone, with tan skin and bright eyes, who thrust forward a folded note. Lew handed him a turquoise *Arysai* bill and the child squealed with delight.

The message overflowed with the usual Amaza squiggles and dots, no English, so Lew handed it to a teen monk who mimed the contents—*phone shop, Biti, now.* But who could be calling at so early an hour? Surely not from within the region, so not Khon.

Lew realized he'd been lucky. Had Tina's business been one absorbed by Elders, it would now be shut down in the post-Elders business limbo gripping Amazia. So he would have been cut off.

He pushed open the phone shop's creaky door and received a broad smile and charming wai from the demure proprietress. For the first time he noticed a cot tucked into a corner, where Tina probably slept, and why she was able to receive the early incoming call.

"Somebody rang me, Tina?" He made a phone gesture with his hand.

"America, Khun Lew!" she chirped, directing him to a booth in back. He untwisted the black plastic cord and held the receiver to his ear. Moments later, Sal's familiar voice flashed across the Pacific.

"Aw right, aw right, aw right!" Sal bellowed in a fake movie star voice. "Our erstwhile explorer of the Mysterious East resurfaces!" He sounded way more upbeat than usual, almost giddy. "Been more'n a week, amigo, and I've got great news!"

Lew grinned. "Whatever you got, Sal, I can top it. Incredible stuff going on around here, too." The sawmill poltergeist flashed through his mind.

"No way. Wanna bet? How 'bout loser runs around Mega Tower at high noon. Naked."

"No, better yet, in a pair of tighty-whities."

Sal snorted a laugh. "Can't. Having seen you in your Jockeys, bro, I can't risk exposing Gotham to such trauma."

"Chicken. Ha. Well sit back and listen. I'll go first, Sal."

Lew spelled out his impossible tale in cinematic detail, including the evil Elders and his vile role; the plight of the beautiful

361

but wretched Nong; the jungle complex and the masses of enslaved workers; the story of his wonderful friend, Boo, and his lovable folks; and all the Amaza businesses that had been stolen.

He bewitched Sal, like a child absorbed by a scary fairy tale, rolling out the impossible nightmare climax of the *Wedding Poltergeist*, complete with villains being erased by massive teams of insects, rats and cute yellow birdies . . . afterwards sending the local economy into freefall.

"So, in summary: spirits are real, Narathiwat was right, and I've fallen fatally in love with a local woman. Oh, and I'm staying here with her. Forever. The end."

"Well, holy crap, Batman." Sal whistled low. "You're right. That's some really incredible shit. A regular world-class story, almost too much to absorb, especially that fun twist at the end, where tech genius Lew becomes enlightened and transitions into a Southeast Asian peasant. Gonna work in a rice paddy with what's-her-name, eh? Must be some hellaciously good poontang."

"Hey, watch it! You're talking about the woman I'm going to marry."

"Oops, my bad. But okay, I guess you win. That story's an all-timer. I can't top it. But, surprisingly, I *can* come close."

That startled Lew. "Whatcha got?"

"Mine's also way shorter, too. Pithy."

"Damn it, Sal, spit it out already!"

"Hoss, I still can't quite believe it, but a huge slug of cash was dumped into our company bank account. More than enough to pay all our customers and provide Avian legal cover. The funds hit our bank just this morning, with no explanation or accompanying details. I'm trying to trace the routing."

"Whoa." Lew's heart danced. "How much, exactly?"

"Remember that monster prepayment to Lotus, for five years of imports."

"Sure." His life savings. How could he ever forget?

"Well, a fraction more."

Khon! This was surely his doing. But how had he achieved that? And how could Lew ever thank him? A large portion, not quite all, of Lew's US problems had just vanished. Only a handful of lawsuits should remain, meaning he could stay in Amazia, largely free of haunting concerns from back home.

"Sal, get an agent to list my Manhattan condo for immediate sale, as-is, and grab the first reasonable offer."

Sal stage-mumbled, as if writing, "Put Lew's flat on eBay."

"Ha, very funny. Also, Avian Luxury has already paid you off. So now it's time we give Emily a big severance —"

"Beautiful."

"— and then you take her back to Mega, with you."

"What?" Sal screeched. "Go crawling back, just when things were tilting back our way? No way, man."

"Listen, forget about Avian. There'll be no Round Two for our company. We're totally finished and can never, ever sell those things again. And anyway, I'll never leave Amazia again."

"So all that stuff before was for real? Was sorta hoping you were just bullshitting me about staying."

Lew took a deep breath and momentarily pondered if he should raise deep metaphysical questions with Sal—concerns like the existence of other ethereal planes and hidden spirit worlds, morality or big questions like why we were all here, anyway?

Nah.

"Remember, Sal, when I insisted your exit from Mega be a friendly one?"

"Yeah, a good call, I guess." He was already calming down.

"Okay, so now that we have adequate funds, phone Steiner—"

Sal laughed. "Uzzi? Your brain must be going soft in the tropics, chief. Too much of that Amaza nookie. You forget? Steiner quit, or else you fired him. Whatever."

"Yeah, so now's time for your famous sweet-talking powers. Get him back on board and have him settle as many of the outstanding lawsuits as possible. Be generous with our newfound cash. Tell him to think *closure*, not *winning*. And execute nondisclosure agreements. Let's bury this thing and make it disappear." Lew smiled. "Then, if I'm not wrong, most of our problems are cleared, other than just a few lingering, monstrous lawsuits—"

"Any one of which being enough to ruin us."

"Yes, so those we fight to the bitter end. Uzzi can string those along for a decade, with delays and appeals, while earning himself a nice retainer."

Sal took notes in silence. Then he finally mumbled, "So our little Asian misadventure is truly finito."

"But big fun while it lasted, no?"

Sal grunted in agreement. "But Hoss, really: never coming home? That's a long time."

"I meant it, Sal. With my new life here, I'll never be happier or more fulfilled. To be honest, I've no idea how all this will work out, but I'll be busy. Plenty already on my plate." He outlined his upcoming role in helping restructure and revive the Biti economy.

"Wow. So the tech whiz of the Western world really is trading it all in. Must be a helluva place. You visit Amazia for just a few weeks and your life turns upside-down."

"But I know what's right for me."

"Of course. Still, amazing that you're dumping all of your stature here, just to become a *kept man* in Bumfuck, Asia?"

"Huh?" A kept man? Teasing or not, that grated.

Sal's tone went gleeful. "You heard me, bro: a *kept man*! After all, you *do* plan to marry and live off a super-rich widow there, don't you?"

"Damn it, Sal, you've got it all wrong. I . . . I, um—"

Lew's voice suddenly broke and he almost couldn't breathe, overwhelmed by a sudden and thrilling realization that flattened him like a runaway freight train. "Oh my God!" he finally muttered in stunned amazement. "That's it, Sal. That's it!"

"That's what?"

"The answer!" Lew's heart raced and he flushed bright red. Tina looked over to see if he was okay. "Old friend, you are an utter fucking genius!"

"Me, Sal Weissman, a *U-F-G*? Finally! Thought you'd never notice."

"Holy crap, I gotta go. Talk later, I promise."

Nearly panting with urgency, Lew slammed down the phone and sucked in a lung-bursting breath of stale phone shop air. He danced a little jig and Tina, still watching, giggled.

Previously bereft of any idea how to proceed in solving Inner Amazia's many problems, he was suddenly awash in options. All thanks to Sal's teasing little joke. His mind swam as he trotted back to Boo's house at breakneck speed, not even noticing the blistering tropical heat.

"Boo, something huge has come up." Back at the house, Lew was still catching his breath. "Gotta chat with the old dudes, right away."

Boo probed Lew's eyes. "Ah," he said with an airy chuckle, "the *Khun Lew has an idea* look. Know it well. Father and Uncle are down by the river, fishing. What's up?"

"Maybe the mother of all ideas. Amazia-style."

A brisk half-hour hike delivered them to the T-junction at the Rama River, where Boo then turned left. "This way, upriver, to their favorite fishing hole." The path eroded and soon they were wading through thick underbrush. The river narrowed and flowed faster, its waters swirling and foaming over scattered decks of rapids and large boulders.

They rounded a bend and encountered a small jungle clearing where Inpanh and Thant lay placidly atop a large woven bamboo mat at the riverbank. Overhead, a homemade canvas awning was rigged to trees to shade them. Grasping dark, gnarled cigars, they passed a bottle and laughed. Down in the river, a series of cylindrical bamboo fish traps were staked in a line.

This was fishing? Lew laughed. More like a splendid way for two elderly Amaza brothers to idle away time. Lew shouted out a greeting, startling the old timers who turned, smiled, and waved the younger men over.

They made room on the mat and before Lew's butt could touch the ground, a cigar was thrust into one hand and the whiskey bottle into the other.

"They catch anything yet?"

"Wouldn't know yet, sir," Boo explained. "Only been here a few hours so they haven't yet checked their traps. No hurry. Fish are going nowhere."

Lew grinned, understanding. Catching fish was no priority.

But this setting was perfect for the discussion he wanted. Seeing a lot of red in their eyes, he hoped the elders were still relatively coherent. "I need a super serious chat with them, Boo. If they're already too boozed-up, it can wait."

Boo asked and the old brothers harrumphed. "Drunk? That quite cheesed them off, sir," Boo laughed. "Go ahead and talk."

They settled into a comfortable circle and Lew looked each man in the eye. This would be tricky. "Inpanh, as soon as your daughter recovers, I plan to marry her. We'll be family. You'll be my father-in-law." Boo translated and Inpanh smiled.

"Her terrible treatment by Elders pains us all. Being forced to marry that man and endure that mistreatment on that barge. And if the bastard lived, she would have been trapped in a life of sexual bondage."

Inpanh's smile faded considerably. Lew hated being so indelicate but trusted it would soon all make sense.

"Not that it personally matters to me, at all, but she absolutely *was* legally married to that monster."

Boo translated and Inpanh's smile totally vanished, his lips drawing tight.

"But as his wife, Nong was just a pitiful victim. All my anger is directed at Elders, her first husband. None for her."

Inpanh's uncomfortable stare drilled holes through Lew.

Boo leaned over to whisper. "Sir, better stop. This is really going badly. You're only making Uncle hot, reminding them—"

"About the *truth*, Boo. Under Amazia law, Elders absolutely *did* legally marry her."

"Yes, but that's all in the past. And they prefer to forget."

"Sorry, Boo, but I have my reasons. And Inpanh is about to get even angrier, as this next part is *really* uncomfortable. But please just trust me." Lew sighed. "Now, ask if they believe Nong had sexual relations with Elders on that barge."

Boo's eyes jolted. "Sir! Oh, no, I cannot . . ."

"Please!"

Boo did the translation and the old brothers jumped up, shaking fists and cursing at Lew.

"Khun Lew," Boo said, "really! Nobody has even discussed any of that with Nong. No need. Too inappropriate and even cruel, for her to have to revisit that trauma."

"Sure. But even without confirmation, I am already totally certain Nong and Elders had sexual relations. Tell them that."

Boo rolled his eyes but did so. The elders flushed crimson with outrage. Furious, Inpanh poked Lew's sternum and yelled, his drunken voice scattering colorful birds from low hanging branches.

Lew tried to defuse that by calmly putting a hand on Inpanh's shoulder. He gently squeezed and tried to hold eye contact, but the old man looked away. "Sir?" Lew's voice dropped to a soft, reassuring tone. "Father? I absolutely love Nong. You know that. And I am so sorry to offend you now. But there's good reason I must raise these painful issues."

Boo chattered a running translation but the old men only growled.

Lew smiled brightly. Inexplicably happy. "Beloved family-to-be, don't you understand?" His words began to race in excitement. "We've been sent a solution. Like a gift from the heavens, the answer to all our problems. Everything is going to be okay, for everyone."

Boo relayed that but the elders only looked doubtful and confused.

Lew drew in a silent breath, raising the moment's tension. "Gentlemen, whether we like it or not, that marriage *was* consummated. Nong absolutely *was* married to Napoleon Elders."

A fresh wave of scowls rumbled.

"So now, in Amazia, she is his legal *widow*."

All three stared back, not yet comprehending.

"Which means that she inherits her dead husband's assets. Isn't that true in Amazia, whether by custom, practice or common law? Like everywhere else in the world?"

Boo's eyes opened wide as saucers as his translation gushed out. Startled, the old men bobbed straight up in surprise.

"There is no disputing Nong officially married Elders, gents. There were hundreds of witnesses! And the marriage was immediately consummated. That evil son of a bitch couldn't wait to get his hands on her."

The three Amaza gasped at the wide-ranging implications and their voices rose as they all jabbered.

Lew raised a finger, dramatically. "Therefore, our dear Nong now *owns* the sawmill, the factory complex and nearly every other business in the region. She also legally owns all that crippling debt Elders used to enslave the workers and companies. She owns *everything*."

Tears of shock and joy began to flow. Laughing, Inpanh rasped a few warm words while sniffling happily.

"Your future father-in-law," Boo translated, "calls you his own good son, the crazy *farang*.'"

Lew's ideas, still developing, poured out in a torrent. "Our beloved Nong is now the Business Queen of Inner Amazia." All chuckled at such an outrageous turn of events. "She has an absolute, undisputable right to the marital assets here. And with no courts or lawyers in Amazia, potential rival claims from outside the Kingdom will be out of luck. With her support, we have all the power necessary to correct all the ills vexing Inner Amazia."

The bottle of harsh brown liquor cycled double-time as the four merry men pounded each other's backs, joyful over a future that suddenly looked infinitely brighter.

Thant shot Lew an imploring look and muttered something.

"Father says we can't do this alone, sir. Indeed, Nong *may* possess such authority, but it's unclear how to best wield such power."

Lew wai'ed the old men. "No worries. It is my privilege to help sort out all the issues facing my new homeland. Luckily, I am pretty good at this sort of thing. Actually, I'm already bursting with ideas and together, we will turn Amazia into even *more* of a paradise. Everything that went wrong—the debts, the indentured servitude, the lost businesses—will be reversed, and more. I vow it."

That evening at dinner, Lew sat beside Nong, holding her hand. Her eyes remained downcast and she ate only sparingly, poking chopsticks at her food. But several times she looked up into Lew's eyes and broadcast the beginning traces of a smile.

Those signs fortified Lew's hopes that his cherished beloved would fully rebound. He vowed to see it through, no matter what or how long it took. Together, they had a lifetime at their disposal.

The next morning Lew hustled over to the phone shop and handed Tina a slip of paper with a cellphone number. Not waiting for instruction, he headed to the back booth and Tina nodded when it was time to pick up.

"Hello?" came a perplexed voice on the line. "Who is calling?"

Lew grinned with satisfaction. "Hello, Khun Khon! This is Lew Clarke, calling from Biti. I'd hoped your old cell phone number might still function and took a shot."

"Ah, Khun Lew!" chuckled Khon. "Last voice I expected to

hear, but lucky you called now. I planned to destroy this cell phone, later today. One of many changes underway."

"I see. And where are you now, sir, back in Chiang Mai?"

"No. In Europe." A smile brightened Khon's voice.

Whoa, Europe? That caught Lew off guard. Khon really moved fast, last seen maybe ten days earlier, blowing out of the *Poltergeist* scene on one of Elders' three-wheelers.

"Mr. Khon, my partner in New Jersey reported a considerable sum of money just landed in our company bank account. I'm guessing that was your doing, correct?"

Khon laughed. "Ah, good, the funds already cleared. I told you to not worry, Mr. Clarke. I was sure if I moved fast enough, I could finesse a lot of solutions for us both."

Lew shook his head in admiration. "What did you do, exactly?

"At Biti, I commandeered Elders' helicopter back to Ruangbang and from there took his Gulfstream back to headquarters in Thailand. The pilots know me as Elders' right hand man, so I was fine just as long as I could travel faster than any news of his demise." Khon drew in a deep breath. "Nobody ever questioned me, not even in Chiang Mai, where all just assumed I was acting on Elders' orders. Word from Biti never reached there."

"Bravo." Lew grinned.

"I found your lump sum payment in the Lotus system, added ten percent for your troubles and instructed the bank to pay you. Surprisingly easy when one operates with the authority of one like Mr. Elders. Like your American joke: I told the bank to jump and they said 'How high?'

"I am so grateful —"

"My pleasure. I keep my promises."

"Oh, and about your little girl? Anything?"

"Indeed!" Khon's voice rang bright. "I traced an odd, repeating payment in Elder's records, a hidden account that dated from just after when Lek disappeared. A tidy sum, wired monthly to a small bank in Laos, in the provincial town of Luang Prabang. That led to other files that corroborated where Lek was being kept. Immediately, my wife and I went to Laos, thanks again to Elders' wonderful private aircraft to retrieve our daughter. The foster parents were innocent. They believed their role was legitimate, unaware they were party to a kidnapping."

"Incredible."

"From there, we flew directly to Changi Airport in Singapore, and transferred to a commercial flight onward to Europe."

"But what about all your possessions?"

Khon laughed. "Who cares? Just abandoned."

Lew shook his head. "Wow. So to where, exactly, in Europe?"

"Switzerland. We're starting a new life in Basel with new identities. That's to head off any future complications, should authorities ever start chasing down Elders' corrupt operations. And I paid myself a generous separation payment on Elders' behalf."

"More than fair."

Lew updated Khon on the fast-changing Amazia situation.

"Marrying his *widow*? Bravo, sir, that's brilliant! And all the better, since you genuinely love the woman. Ironic that your legal jiu-jitsu leverages off the marital status granted Nong by Elders' foul plan, no? She is, after all, *absolutely* his widow in Amazia, with all legal rights." Khon paused. "But may I humbly offer some advice?"

What was on Khon's mind? "Gladly."

"My experience is that, under Amazia common law, the best way forward is to always strongly assert *your own interpretation* of how things are. Make firm pronouncements and just take action. Exercise Nong's authority and claims to property, money, whatever.'

That sounded like great advice, from someone who knew.

"I have always found in Amazia that nobody will ever really stop what you are doing. So don't wait for confirmations or concurrence. No, your attitude and self-assurance provide a total license to proceed. And for this Kingdom, that can be either a curse or a blessing. In your case, it is surely the latter."

"Move fast and, only if necessary, apologize later?"

"Something like that. Khun Lew, your fiancée has the wherewithal to become an historic benefactor for the entire Kingdom. She can achieve miracles for the people."

CHAPTER THIRTY
Summons to the Royal Palace

Eighteen months later, Lew and Nong received an unexpected summons to the royal district to visit the crown prince. Although a visit to the palace was a thrilling first for both, it was also an unwelcome interruption to their critical work rebuilding Inner Amazia.

In front of the palace, they were met by a soldier glistening in polished silver, his shield, armor, and decorative bangles flashing with every move. The huge sword at his side appeared capable of slicing a man in two. He silently ushered them past two fierce guards at the entryway, their lances canted out and at the ready, and into a large formal waiting room.

"Please sit," he said with a thick accent, perhaps his only English, gesturing at a row of polished wooden chairs. Lew glided a hand across a cool, smooth surface. Stained a luxurious deep wood tone, it looked carved from a single slice of tree trunk. Golden silk cushions, stuffed thick with down, rendered them luxurious.

Smiling and holding Nong's hand, Lew studied the embroidered tapestries covering the walls, fine works of art hand-stitched against blue, green or purple backgrounds, with Amaza captions below. They reminded Lew of sumptuous, giant comic books—ornate versions in silk and depicting fables or legends from Amazia history or folklore, complete with dragons, flying carpets, and talking tiger lords. A particularly grand piece displayed the Kingdom's mythical founding a thousand years ago, by the dynasty that still ruled.

The tapestries delighted him, but Lew's nerves were still on edge. And the regal formality of the palace only heightened the mystery behind their summons.

His cell phone suddenly went off and the *Star Wars* theme ringtone filled the waiting room. Network coverage was superb in the palace. The guard shot Lew a chilly stare and Nong just raised a palm to her face, sighing. Not a particularly good time for that.

Over the past year, cell phone service had marginally improved in the Kingdom, at least there in the capital city, all thanks to the ambitious young crown prince—the same progressive, outward-looking heir apparent who commanded them to visit. Informed chatter insisted it was only a matter of time before his father, the current King, succumbed to a lingering illness. The exact nature was kept hidden from the masses.

Lew checked his screen and smiled. *Sal.* He thumbed the green button, put his mouth right to the phone and tried to speak quietly.

"Salvatore! Hey, buddy, great to hear from you but as usual, your timing stinks. This is a real bad time. Can't talk. Actually, I'm in the royal palace."

"Whoa, cool beans! Waiting to see the Big Guy?"

"Nah, the *Little* Big Guy, I suppose. His son. But King-to-be. So I gotta go."

"Okay, but just gimme a sec. Incredible news today."

"Thirty seconds. Shoot."

"Remember those remaining monster lawsuits? The ones where a single bad judgment could kill us?"

"Yeah, though I tend to not think about them much, anymore. My life has moved on. But still, what . . .?"

"Well brace yourself. We got an awful judgment today."

Lew's heart fell.

"As in, *awful* fucking great! The Supreme Court has denied certiorari. That means they won't touch the case we already won on appeal, the one that joined all four of the remaining lawsuits."

"Get outta here! Don't play with me, Sal."

"No joke, dude. It's all over."

Warmth spread over Lew as he grinned wide. "Did the court cite a rationale?"

"Sure. Same as some lower courts already ruled. First, the plaintiffs never proved that angry terrestrial spirits actually exist. So second, our company naturally can't be guilty of damage allegedly caused by *fictional* entities. American jurisprudence has ruled: *No spooks, no case.*"

Lew closed his eyes and sighed, all of this delicious irony not lost on him. Deliverance felt wonderful.

But that ruling? No spooks, no case? He again pictured the Wedding Poltergeist. Try telling Elders and his men that terrestrial spirits didn't exist. Or any of the thousands of Amaza with spirit houses on their properties, for whom they critically mattered. Or millions more in Asia.

Despite the victory, he immediately decided it would be the right thing, to *fairly* compensate those last few litigants, anyway. But anonymously. Later.

"So now, you can go have fun with your new bestie, the prince." Sal clicked off.

Lew glanced over at Nong but she only returned a scowl after his ringtone violation upset palace decorum, along with the whooping and laughing with Sal. He winked back at her.

Nong dazzled in a magnificent outfit, one he'd never seen before. It incorporated multiple layers of shimmering silk and cascades of creamy pastel, topped off by an intricate headpiece—a golden diadem with two dangling rubies. All Nong had said in brief explanation was that the outfit was from her mother and 'very significant.'

So that was how one dressed when visiting royalty? But how did normal citizens even learn such a palace dress code, much less afford attire like that? Seemed over the top, especially the golden headpiece with rubies.

Nong slid a cool hand atop his, breaking his train of thought.

"Husband," she trilled, "just now, was that Khun Sal, your giant noisy brother from the fertile land of New Jersey?" For more than a year, Lew had been regaling Nong with colorful stories of his misadventures with Sal, from college on through business wars. Both looked forward to Sal's first visit, soon.

Her command of English was leaping forward by the day, dramatically outpacing Lew's progress in the Amaza tongue. Her accent was unique and attractive, breathy but clipped, and very feminine.

Early in their marriage, both had agreed to only speak in the other's language. So even for a *farang*, Lew was relatively strong in the Amaza language, correctly forming all its exotic sounds. But when he spoke it, his voice sounded so different, like it belonged to someone else. Also, many English words had no Amaza equivalents, so his speech had a strange, stilted quality. Weird but engaging.

"*Yes, dearest wife, soul of my life.*" He concentrated on hitting the right Amaza tones. "*Body-less voice from sky was huge brother with large mouth from distant land of New Jersey.*"

The doors on the far wall abruptly flew open, ending their conversation. The guards ushered the couple into the cavernous throne room.

The breathtaking royal chamber was cool as a cathedral and filled with echoes. Its shape blended a rectangle with an oval, with long walls that bulged outward at the center. Clusters of courtesans, royals, supplicants, and politicians lined the side walls, milling about beneath blue stained glass windows that let in shafts of light.

An extravagant golden throne perched atop an elevated platform at the far wall, draped by purple curtains. A petite young man sat on the throne. He wore a long golden cape with feathers and sequins—clearly, the prince—and barked out commands. Tan and plump, he wore round spectacles and his mouth flickered with gold when he spoke. Under a purple velvet cap with golden brocade, his dark hair was slicked down with oil, every hair perfectly in place.

The guards flanking Lew and Nong scowled and marched them to the middle of the room before stopping, crossing their lances and spitting out a few words.

Lew caught the local word for *down*. Already briefed on the protocol, he dropped to his knees and sprawled forward until his chest lay flat on the cold stone floor, arms splayed out like a kid playing airplane.

"*Your Majesty!*" he cried out in his best Amaza dialect, nose wedged against the chilly marble floor. "*Lewis Nathaniel Clarke from America wishes you long life!*" Gruff instructions barked by the guards let Lew know to rise.

As Nong began the same process, a shrill command from the throne stopped her at mid-drop. The crown prince then shuffled down the podium steps and casually strolled toward them, waving his scepter like a fancy flyswatter. The masses of courtiers, nobles, and guards all genuflected as he passed.

Lew understood that as the prince neared, he was to again pay obeisance by dropping to a knee. So he did. But when Nong started following suit, the prince again stopped her.

Lew caught her eye with a confused look. What was going on? She just shrugged.

Lew smiled at the prince but the young royal only returned a stern look and motioned them to follow him. He led them to a far corner of the room where they exited through a small door.

Now what?

All this unsettled Lew, who still didn't even yet know why they'd been summoned. The little potentate sure seemed arrogant and harsh, even unfriendly. And was that some kind of anti-Western bias, how he'd been repeatedly forced to humiliate himself, down to the floor, while Nong was excused?

Lew already regretted wasting time on this trip. There was plenty back in Biti that needed his urgent attention. And he'd felt none the poorer, for not having previously met Amazia's rulers. But a royal summons was not to be ignored. He could only hope this would soon be over.

They entered a small kitchen area and the heavy wooden door

swung shut behind them, leaving all guards and courtesans in the throne room.

An instant transformation washed over the young ruler as a brilliant smile split his chubby face. He beamed, melting away all that prior chill, a full set of golden teeth gleaming.

"Ah good, finally! This is so much better! Hello my dear friends, and welcome to our palace." He spoke perfect English. The prince gave Nong a polite peck on the cheek and patted Lew warmly on the shoulder.

Lew was stunned.

"Now that we are alone, we can dispense with all that royal rigmarole. Have a friendlier visit! First, let me express how wicked good it was of you both to accept my invitation!"

Wicked good? Now where did that come from? This whole morning had been strange, but the prince's sudden one hundred eighty degree demeanor shift was now making it *uber*-weird.

"Khun Lew, are you aware how famous you've suddenly become across our Kingdom? This past year, I've received nearly daily reports of your wonderful work up around Biti. We are all so grateful."

Lew had been briefed to speak only in the Amaza tongue, until otherwise ordered. Well drilled, he now started to slavishly follow format and language conventions. *"Oh Limitless and Eternal Majesty, your humble servant thanks —"*

"Oh my goodness no, no, no. Stop, please!" The prince laughed. "Let's immediately drop all the formality for now, all that *Majesty* gobbledygook! At least here, in this little chamber, please do just call me *Rodney*. Okay?"

Lew nodded, rather numb with shock.

"And please speak English. How I treasure a chance to finally use mine again! So few opportunities. It's been quite the little while."

Lew finally understood. This Rodney fellow was the *actual* man, being honest and true, whereas the stern royal in the throne room was the figurehead required for public consumption.

"Great," said Lew, smiling. "English it is. And my wife is also already quite fluent. But I'm surprised—is Rodney your real name?"

The prince chuckled. "Oh no, actually it's *Rajaratneethongkan*."

Lew grinned at the tongue-twister. "I see. Good idea to stick with *Prince Rodney*." Lew relaxed, already immensely liking the young man.

Animated, the prince rambled on, his hands flying.

"You see, out there in court, I am the living symbol of our Kingdom and must project an utterly royal air. So beyond this room, remember: you must always address me as *Your Majesty*. You understand, *chai mai*? Yes no?" The prince grinned again, his teeth glittering. "Ah, such fun. Wonderful! Speaking English reminds me of my many years in your country. I did my MBA at Harvard."

Ah, so that explained the US accent. "Harvard? Way cool. We're fellow alums." They reminisced a bit, discussing professors and school rooming arrangements, but determined their years in Cambridge didn't cross.

"And how are my Red Sox doing?" His eyes danced. "See how I said *Sawx?* Haha. And my mighty Patriots!" The prince feigned a shiver and grabbing himself, as if to warm up. "Many great Sundays spent up at Foxborough. But for a tropical fellow like me, bloody cold as hell." The prince grinned.

"But Khun Lew, we are perhaps both being a bit rude." He turned and grasped Nong's hand. She still appeared cowed by such proximity and intimacy with Amazia's next king, the equivalent of a human god.

"My dear Khun Nong! Oh my good, sweet, loyal subject! How wonderful it is to finally make your acquaintance. Words fail me. My treasury confirms that you are now, by far, the wealthiest person in our Kingdom! But don't worry, we won't tax *all* your wealth away." He laughed. "Especially since you are also Amazia's greatest patroness. Our most generous, charitable benefactor."

Nong blushed a deep crimson and wai'ed her thanks. "Your Dynastic Majesty, it is nothing."

"Nonsense, most beloved subject. Perhaps, living so far upcountry, you remain unaware of your burgeoning national reputation? Truly, you are the most famous and loved person in all the land. The royal family is jealous, haha. Every day, my other subjects grow more envious of the citizens residing in Inner Amazia, where you conduct your brilliant work."

Nong's blush deepened further.

"At the rate Biti is progressing, it will soon give Ruangbang a run for its money," the prince said, shaking his head in happy disbelief. "So much wealth creation and development, in just over a year. How are you achieving all that?"

Nong bowed her head. "I am just your humble subject, Majesty."

"Please, it's *Rodney*. Remember?"

"Yes, Prince Rodney, my apology. But all my heart and wealth are solely devoted to benefitting our people." She took Lew's hand. "And of all my resources, this man's genius is key. My husband is the brain and it is also his energy driving everything."

The prince turned back toward Lew, smiling.

"She is delightfully humble, dear friend, but I know she speaks truth. I keep hearing the same thing about you, Khun Lew, everywhere. Some kind of American business wizard helping solve problems in rural Amazia. Quite odd, no?"

"Not really, Prince Rodney. I owe a debt to your Kingdom that I can never fully repay. Amazia renewed my soul and gave me a brilliant new existence, along with my eternal soul mate. Whatever benefit I ever deliver for Amazia, it will never be enough. I am just humbled by my chance to help."

"Good," the prince said with an odd smile.

"But really, I don't deserve so much credit. We're not inventing anything, just borrowing successful ideas from elsewhere and transplanting them here. Quickly."

Rodney tsk-tsked. "You're too modest, Khun Lew."

Lew felt increasingly at ease with the amiable prince. "After the death of Nong's first husband —"

"A true scoundrel!" The prince shook his head. "Thank the Buddha he's gone. An utter scourge on our Kingdom."

Lew nodded. "Yes. But once Nong inherited Elders' estate, we explored straightforward ways to quickly redistribute that wealth back to the people to stimulate the economy."

"Such as?"

"We immediately formed a new company to own Biti's largest employer, the sawmill and factory. Then a stock ownership program distributed the equity to the thousands of workers, allowing them to share in the benefits, as well as be paid fair and generous wages."

"An excellent solution!" Prince Rodney smiled.

"Also, Nong immediately forgave all that oppressive debt Elders used to enslave families and swallow businesses across Inner Amazia. All those small businesses reverted to their original owners."

The prince bridged his fingers in thought. "Giving away her wealth, like a saint."

"We found other ways to spur the local economy, like starting agricultural co-ops and some simple infrastructure projects. Better roads and even a modest hydroelectric dam."

"Good job!" The prince smiled.

"But so much more remains to be done," Lew said. "Our region is isolated and needs better communication and transport links with the rest of the Kingdom. Still no cell phone network up there." Lew shrugged. "Anyway, we have many dreams."

"Yes, I know! Believe me, Khun Lew, I know." The prince jiggled nervously in his chair, his face bright and eyes dancing. "Which is why I summoned you both today."

Prince Rodney began to pour three glasses of fruit juice and Nong, by habit, moved to take over. The young royal waved her off. This private side, Prince Rodney's humility, delighted Lew. But even more impressive was his energy and honest dedication to his people. No way to fake that.

"Actually, Khun Lew, I have the same dreams, but on a national scale. For *all* my people." His voice rose with excitement. "A vision that has preoccupied me since my return home from the West."

He leaned closer.

"Now this next bit is kept quiet, to not disturb our people, but my elderly father, the King, is already incapacitated after several strokes and heart problems. His strength is waning and the end seems near. Only a matter of time."

The prince's face crinkled in genuine sorrow and he brushed away a small tear.

"During this interim period, though still only crown prince, I am quietly organizing ambitious plans to fully move our nation into the modern era."

"A tricky balance to strike," Lew said. "Out of respect, you cannot yet act. You love and honor your father, but must also love your people and prepare to be the next king."

The crown prince took off his velvet cap and placed it on the table.

"Let me be frank. I desperately need your help, Khun Lew, a partnership to meet the challenge of modernizing Amazia. That role seems remarkably suited to your talents. And at the same time, Khun Nong and I will ensure our precious traditional culture is not lost."

Lew did a double-take, weighing Rodney's words. Did the prince really just invite him to become co-CEO for a modernization drive for the entire Kingdom? Lew *had* planned to remain here, all along, but in a simpler life with his bride, albeit meeting the relatively limited challenge of updating the Biti area.

Prince Rodney took a sip of juice and charged ahead. "Together, I am certain we are up to this challenge. Did I mention? Before Harvard, I obtained my undergrad degree in civil engineering at Purdue. So I have a sound foundation to oversee plans for bridges, roads, and the like. But as for the rest, that's where you come in."

Lew tried to look noncommittal but couldn't stifle a smile. "Like what, Rodney?"

"So much! Modernization of our entire financial system.

Nationwide phone coverage. Commissioning of broadcasting entities. We need a thriving new market economy to unleash wealth for all our people. It goes on and on. Plus we must eventually develop a modern political system. You know, with parties and elections."

That last part caught Lew by surprise.

The prince saw that and winked. "Why the odd look? Don't our people need to govern *themselves*? True monarchs are a relic of the past. I'd have no problem being the last Amaza king. If our dynasty is ultimately reduced to a ceremonial figurehead, that would be fine, meaning I succeeded in my goals."

All this was fire-hosing at Lew. Too much, way too fast.

While trying to process the prince's remarkable proposition, he basked in a delicious, irresistibly warm notion that he was precisely where the Fates had always intended. Right there in Amazia. Had it all been preordained? It certainly felt like destiny, living now with his true soul mate and dedicating themselves to improving the world there.

Everything seemed to have fallen into place. All problems in his life, present or past, seemed resolved, or at least in hand. He opted to follow the sage advice he often heard there and resolved to not think about it, too much.

But something still bothered him.

A small matter, yes, but still . . .

"Sire—"

"Rodney!"

"Oops, sorry! But may I be so forward, Rodney, to ask a personal question?"

"For my dearest friend and new partner? Of course." The prince grinned back.

"I am uncomfortable to even bring this up but, well, it just seemed odd."

"What?"

"Before, when you made me lie on the floor in front of all those people. Prostrating myself."

The prince coughed, perhaps a little uncomfortable. "Sorry. An old custom we follow, at least for now. Nothing personal. And maybe someday we can eliminate that. But everyone must symbolically humble themselves before the all-powerful crown. I represent the Kingdom."

Lew's eyes narrowed. That missed his point. "Yes. But what I meant was why didn't Nong have to lie on the floor, also? Only me, the *farang*."

"What . . .?" The prince looked momentarily confused, but then his eyes opened wide in surprise, signaling sudden understanding. He turned toward Nong, chuckling. "Oh my goodness! Is it possible that he doesn't know?" His voice trailed off and he blushed.

She bit her lower lip and shook her head.

"Oh my," muttered the prince. "Well done, Rodney, you silly fool." He looked at Lew. "Dear friend, it appears I have made a major boo-boo. One not even a crown prince is allowed. I apologize, Lew." He shrugged and added, mysteriously, "You didn't know."

Lew was totally befuddled. *Now* what strange local custom had he missed? "Heh . . . didn't know *what*?"

The prince glanced over at Nong, who almost imperceptibly nodded consent.

"We have, as you have seen, many important cultural traditions here in Amazia. Like the wai or that prostration homage before royalty. Also, say, like those gemstones dangling from your wife's tiara. Rubies, two of them, in fact. Did you notice? Nice, aren't they?"

Lew shrugged, smiling politely. "Well, her whole outfit today is *uber*-cool and pretty sexy. And yes, I did notice the gems. Nice touch, but maybe a little over the top? Even for the richest woman in Amazia."

"I see. So you understood *none* of it. You see, Khun Lew," the prince raised a finger, making a point, "once I spotted those gemstones, everything changed."

"But I don't—"

"Because in Amazia, *pregnant* women are never required to

384

prostrate themselves. Ever. It's unhealthy! So we make that exception. Only."

Pregnant?

Lew was struck mute and felt woozy, like the blood was draining from his head. The prince's strong hands landed in a heartbeat to support him.

"Whoa, dear fellow, you're looking a bit green!" The young royal pulled a cord and a servant appeared with a glass of ice water. Lew sipped it.

"And especially," the young royal continued, "prostrating would never be allowed for a mother-to-be with *two* lovely gemstones, signifying twins on the way!"

Twins!

Lew plunged through a cascade of emotions. En route to a wondrous future and melting with love, he wrapped his arms around his bride and whispered, in his best Amazian: *"Most beloved wife, why did you not share such miraculous news?"*

Nong looked sheepish and replied in English. "I am sorry, sweet husband. But the doctor only just confirmed our situation this morning. So, as custom dictates, I rushed to find my mother's diadem and added the two gems, one for each child. I planned to tell you all this in a special, private way, right after our visit to the palace. But Prince Rodney ruined the surprise. In some ways, he seems even noisier than your giant friend from New Jersey."

Lew hugged her tight and whispered, "Yes, dearest wife, my very soul. This Prince Rodney has a noisy mouth, but I really do like and trust him. We will all be excellent partners."

He held Nong close and kissed her. Then, gazing into her eyes, he saw eternity.

<<<>>>

A Note to the Reader:

Thank you for reading my novel. I do hope you enjoyed Lew Clarke's unlikely journey to a better version of himself.

My only goal in writing this story was to create a pleasurable reading experience for you. So, if you liked PACIFIC ODYSSEY, please consider writing a review (Amazon, Goodreads, etc.) to guide other readers to this work. It is much appreciated.

Thank you so much!

Best regards,

Chet Nairene

Don't miss this other bestselling exotic travel adventure from the pen of Chet Nairene...

Pacific Dash

From Asia Vagabond to Casino King

When his family heads to Hong Kong in 1968 for a job transfer, teenager Dash Bonaventure thinks it's just a temporary detour in his life. But thus begins decades that see him wandering the back roads, beaches, vice dens and casinos of Asia, all in search for truth and adventure. Amazingly good fun!

**Available in paperback and eBook
from Amazon and other leading booksellers.**

Printed in Great Britain
by Amazon